GRIMM REALITY
or
The Marvellous Adventures of Doctor Know-All

SIMON BUCHER-JONES & KELLY HALE

BBC BOOKS

Published by BBC Worldwide Ltd
Woodlands, 80 Wood Lane
London W12 0TT

First published 2001
Copyright © Simon Bucher-Jones & Kelly Hale 2001
The moral right of the authors has been asserted

Original series broadcast on the BBC
Format © BBC 1963
Doctor Who and TARDIS are trademarks of the BBC

ISBN 0 563 53841 4
Imaging by Black Sheep, copyright © BBC 2001

Printed and bound in Great Britain by Mackays of
Chatham
Cover printed by Belmont Press Ltd, Northampton

Dedications

To my daughter Morgan, who in her identity of 'Superlady' has defeated more 'Daddy Monsters From the Swamp', than any other superhero. With thanks to: Kelly Hale, obviously and most heartily. Watch her, kiddies: she can write. To everyone who's helped or suggested something I've ignored. With acknowledgements to – spot them if you can – the worlds of Grimm, Tolkein, Baum, ER Eddison and Richmal Crompton, not necessarily in that order.

– SBJ

For Jackie, petting bumblebees in heaven

Thanks to my mother and family for always being there even when I wasn't 'all there', and to Simon, my son, who has lived with a writer all his life, poor thing. Hello to my man in Stari Grad, Sheahan for listening. Thanks to Bob's Harem for happily embracing whatever I'm working on and helping to make it better, and to the advisory committee – pussycat boy Paul Dale Smith, 'No Pyjamas' Henry Potts, and the Yanks – God bless America – Jonathan Dennis and Ian McIntire. Also Mark Rushford and Amsel Zivkovich for the cheering. And to Women Writing Who workshop (do it again!). But mostly, thanks to the Impeccable One.

– Kelly Hale

The tales within are all original in as much as these sorts of tales can be, with the exception of 'The Master-Maid', borrowed in part from a Scandinavian folk tale of the same name.

Curiously, almost languidly, Anji turned the pages of the ancient untitled book she'd found in a carved box deep in the TARDIS.

Dave had been one for pulp fiction: the smell, the faint patina of the pages. The book reminded her of him. Before, she'd always preferred new printings. Uniform editions if possible. Clean, straight spines arrayed across the shelves in neatness. Armies of knowledge. Facts. She'd always been the stiff one in the family, the daughter with improving tastes. Look where that had taken her, now.

Browsing along the corridors was half a walk spent bumping into old friends, a Penguin copy of *Three Men In a Boat* here, a pristine set of Stone's *Justice Manual* there, and half a safari into the unknown. The Doctor's heaps of books in the honeycombed cubbyholes of the TARDIS corridors might well contain the wisdom of the aeons – a lost work by Sophocles resting against *Delia Smith's Cooking Dictionary – Book Thirty Four: Xylocarp to Zwieback* – but there was no immediate prospect of laying one's hands on a particular vital bit of data. Why, for example, did the Doctor have five editions of *Life and Likings of a Lobster* all from different public libraries? All, she noted with a frown, overdue before she was even born. Not that that mattered to a time traveller, although it struck her as sloppy.

It was a conundrum that only a tall glass of lemonade with ice and a good book would unravel. She rested the book on her knee, and contemplated the woodcut that opened the text.

Prologue
The Prince Who Was Curious

The Prince rode hard through the dark corridor of the forest, the sound of his horse's hooves pounding in his head and the sound of the wolves behind him thundering in his heart. He knew much about the wolves of these woods, knew that if he slowed his pace or veered from his course they would take him down in an instant, for they were relentless hunters of the faint-hearted. But his wise old uncle had told him to stay true to his purpose, turn neither to the left nor to the right, to ride hard and fast until he was upon the moor. The wolves would give up their chase quickly once he was within sight of his goal. For across the moor was the Scarlet Hedge. And even the wolves were right to be daunted by that monstrous briar.

The advice of his uncle had been freely given. The advice of the silver fox he'd rescued from the gold and ruby cage in the chamber of his father's wife had cost him dear. For that simple act of compassion she had banished him, made of him a wanderer, forced to go his own way in the world with naught but his trusty mount, Falada, his sword and the clothes on his back. But in gratitude the fox had given this counsel: 'Even if you are offered the power of life and death, take *nothing* until True Love offers you her hand, for a Princess must be won, not given, and any other gift is no gift at all. Heed me well, O Prince, or you will be unlucky.'

The Prince's boot leather had seen much travel since he'd freed the silver fox, and his thread-of-gold cloak let in more wind than it kept out, but even so he was feeling pleased with himself. He was on the moor now, with a blue sky overhead and the great wall of thorn in sight. And somewhere within there was his Princess.

The Scarlet Hedge served, so his uncle said, to protect the Princess in her vulnerable sleep from casual interlopers, hobbledehoys, and sightseers. 'Traversing it will be no mean feat, mark my words, lad.' The Prince could see the evidence of those who had attempted it and failed, in rags and bones set out, pinned to the giant vicious barbs the way shrikes impaled flies on blackthorn. It was the blood of these men that had earned the hedge its scarlet name.

Dismounting, he laid the tip of one gloved finger against an outlying thorn and pushed slightly. It sliced into his leather gauntlet easily, and he pulled back, only just preventing it from penetrating his flesh. He could neither climb nor push his way through without being skewered like the rest.

His hand went to the pouch at his belt, to the magic gifts he had won by kindness and through good deeds and services to the many varied creatures he'd encountered on his journey. He considered whether it was time to call in the favours promised him, or to draw his sword and try to slash his way through. And, as he was considering, the heavens caught fire.

High in the eastern sky to his right, a pin-point ball of light spun and twisted lazily, casting the shadow of the hedge left and down to the edge of the moor. The ball of light was not so much falling as drifting out of the cloudless blue of the sky.

The Prince had never seen so odd a thing as this levenbolt. The sword at his side was wrought from star iron, plucked from the heavens by the fairy Belesia and forged by her magick. She had gifted the sword to his father, who had, in turn, bequeathed it to him. Maybe this lightning ball was a similar prize he could mark for later glory, after the Princess was his. Up and down was neither left nor right, so did his uncle's warning still apply?

The fire hit the ground with a sound like a newly forged sword being quenched in ox's blood. A thick hissing and spitting sound like no other the Prince knew, although he was curious about many things, the arcanum of swordsmithing among them.

Shielding his eyes with his raised gauntlets, the Prince drew near the place where it had fallen. Around it the earth had splashed up like ripples in a pond that had frozen in a pattern of ridges. At the centre of the ripples, he could see a dark shape made indistinct by the now fading light.

A sweet smell filled the air. Was it lavender, vanilla, a nostrum or a herb? He couldn't tell. He had expected the earth to stink of burning from the falling fire, but instead his senses were overwhelmed with the tang of a thousand fragrances, each curiously individual and unmixed.

The shape was clearer now, a carved wooden box. A box of the same black wood as the thorn hedge, a tracery of blood-red spirals contouring its surface. He tried to follow the pattern. A spiral. No, a double spiral. Or perhaps an illusion, like the two faces and the goblet that a juggler had once shown him. Maybe it was more than one shape as the perfume was more than one scent.

Open me.

The voice in his head was her sweet voice as he had heard her sing years before.

He had been a page at her father's court, educated in the traditions of chivalry, before returning to his own country. He had never forgotten her high child's voice. When he had heard that the sleep curse had stilled it he'd wept and sworn to free her.

You will see her free, if only you will open me.

He could see now, a catch, a dull metal clasp on the side of the box. Unadorned, practical, it lacked the artistry of the bold design. It was purposeful. It demanded he open it.

The words of his counsellors came back to him; but there was something compelling in the way the light licked at the box's outline.

Only if you open me will you have your heart's desires.

The clasp was old and brittle to the touch. Opening it would be easy. Easier by far than winning his way past the scarlet hedge. It smacked of dishonour somehow; and yet wasn't every injunction to be either obeyed or broken? Sometimes the heroes of lore won because they questioned.

Almost unbidden, and yet without the least sensation of surprise, he felt his hands opening the box, as if it were, after all, inevitable.

And then his heart's desires came true. All of them. At once.

He kissed the Princess, and she woke / and he touched her and she woke / and he merely set foot in her chamber and she woke as the dust stirred / and her eyes were blue / hazel / black as sloes. And her first words were 'Oh, my Prince' / and her first words were 'You came for me' / and her first words were 'Do you remember the song I sang when you were a page in my father's keep?' / and the wedding came swiftly / and the wedding came after three strange tasks / and the wedding came that Christmas / and there was no high wedding for they lived together in a hut in the woods and were wed by God alone. And they had a son / a daughter / twin sons. And / And / And…

And the Prince lay in the earth, his hand on the open box, his eyes glazed and his breath faint and regular, and he saw everything and nothing. And the blackthorn retained its dominion.

It was half a day later before the old woman gathering firewood from the sloughed-off, oldest thorn branches of the hedge found the Prince lying there, petals and dust blown on to his upturned, staring eyes.

She tapped the body sharply with her blackthorn walking stick, and grunted under her breath when the Prince didn't move. His royal status was obvious enough from his clothes, his unsoiled stockings and his sword. She drew it from his belt and made a few trial passes, left-handed, gay as a child. The heavy star iron moved lightly, familiarly, in her old arthritic grasp.

She saw the box at the Prince's right hand. It was a grey shape – dust draped over a skeleton of fine bone. A spider box, all webs and promises. She kicked it away with her pointed leather shoe, and it burst sickly. It was too much to hope that that would be an end of it; that one life alone had been eaten.

It was all starting again and there was no defence against it, not in all the world.

Chapter One
The Cunning Forest

William Brok was a space miner. No different from any of the licensed or the freelance exotic-matter specialists who had gone out into space on the coat tails of the second wave of colonisation. Now that he had less than three hours to live, it was that realisation – that he had achieved nothing that hadn't been accomplished by a dozen or more of his peers – that really weighed on him.

His old ship, *Esmerelda's Dream,* had betrayed him at the last, the heart of its fusion drive burning out trying to match the velocity of a nondescript asteroid in the deep velvet night of the Hen's Tooth Nebula. He had gambled that the mass of the passing planetesimal would have captured a layer of exotic matter from the Nebula, coating the miniature world like pearls forming round grit. Actually he had had only a brief glimpse of a dark and rocky *ordinary* surface before his ship had died. No q-balls full of squarks, no strange matter, not even a splotch of space-born long-chain molecules, or the cold remains of Hydrogen-3. No profit. Big loss.

The fusion engine was at the other end of the ship, a hundred metres away from the conical armoured living space. Not far enough in the case of an accident but a psychologically important separation from what in effect was a captive sun. It wasn't radioactive but it might as well have been – the drives were sold as sealed units. You bought and then you bought again when the time on the warranty came up. People who risked shipping with fusion motors out of warranty tended to vanish. William's had run out a month ago. He had been, so he'd told himself, on the verge of a big find, a haul of antihydrogen maybe or the mother lode: a quantum white hole. The readings from the other side of the nebula almost proved it. If only he hadn't looked for verification first, spent the last working moments of his poor little ship hoping to find traces on that damned rock, just because its course brought it in from extra-nebula space. He might at least have got to see that rarest of cosmic events before dying. Instead it lay, possibly, a mere few light years distant on the other side of the nebula from Earth.

Now he had two hours and forty-five minutes of life left. With his drive down, the oxygen plant wasn't making new air. He had a space suit; he could reach the drive in ten minutes. Improvise a cutting torch; get the casing open in, what, another fifteen? Leaving him two whole comfortable hours and a few, few minutes to figure out how to restart the drive. The suit's own air maker might spin that out, but even as he started to get his suit on he knew it was a fool's attempt.

Maybe he ought to be praying instead.

However, he set out for the fusion engine without getting down on his knees, and so, really, he had no business being the recipient of a miracle.

The *Bonaventure* broached the nebula like a swimmer learning the breaststroke for the first time. Fields of antigravitons pushed nebula matter away and out of its path, setting up a sparkling display of burning light. Human-Captain Christina Morgenstern thought of them as wings. Her abanak colleagues agreed the comparison was apt even though the only flying creature on their home world was a rather ratty-looking bat with an incontinent habit of relieving itself over their broad hippopotamus-like heads. As for the insectoid vuim, they only grumbled about not seeing the need for metaphors and got back to the engine room.

'You see it, Captain?'

Christina's eyes squinted against the reflection on the screen, which caught them briefly, hazel and wide, before a fresh layer of antireflectant rolled in, plating the screen. 'Just, Mr Vondra. What do you make of it?'

'A smallish human craft, Christina-Captain. Becalmed, I suppose we might say.'

'Interesting. Can we get a message laser on line? How soon before we pass them, and how much energy would it take to intercept?'

A vuim moved smoothly to answer from an adjacent console, its insect-like carapace clattering slightly. 'One of our port array lasers will be online in two minutes. We will pass in just over five if we do not match velocities. Braking in three minutes would be risky but not impossible. The ship is moving at approximately nine point five kilometres per second, suggestive of an attempt to match delta vee with the asteroid moving away at two hundred and sixty degrees. The ship itself is dark, cooling in the infrared. It may be a derelict. There's still some heat radiation from the discharge vanes at the rear of the drive – Captain! I have a spacesuit-sized heat source near the rear of the ship, possibly a survivor.'

Christina hesitated. A life in the void. Maybe a human life if the ship's design was any indication. Yet stopping to investigate would waste energy and even risk their own ship. And another body would be a drain on ship's resources. A drain on their profit margins.

She sighed. 'Take us to a match, Mr Vondra'.

At worst it would cost them time and air. And maybe the little mining ship or its spacesuited figure could pay their way somehow. She liked miners. They were hardened men. Romantic. Independent. Alone. Gullible.

On the other side of the nebula, on a little planet so like Earth as to make Fitz feel, briefly, that it might be Earth – *again*, the Doctor

10

took a huge lungful of air as if he could breathe in the world. 'Marvellous,' he pronounced. Overhead a rooklike bird cawed in response.

Fitz shaded his eyes, watching the black shape streak across the blue sky for a moment before glancing back at the TARDIS nestled among a dry and dusty group of spindly trees. Maybe, while the chameleon circuit didn't actually work, it still managed to look somehow subtly not out of place – as if the police might be expected to have a public call box in every minor woodland. That this fabulous ship, gateway to time and space, cast a familiar spell over its faded blue woodwork still amazed him. It never looked like anything else but it didn't stand out, either – just an ancient artefact in an old spinney caught in the early shadows of a chilly afternoon. Overhead the sun was just a shade past the zenith.

The hill they had landed on was tufted with clumps of coarse grass and sloped gently down towards a broad expanse of shimmering green. He could make out the grey-brown haze of a forest several miles away, and to his right a smear, a glistening thread that might be a river.

He turned his gaze to the Doctor again, who was wearing an expression that had become something of a defining fixture. Puzzlement. That look of half recognition, half distress, as if he'd been here before but could not, would *never*, be sure.

'Marvellous,' the Doctor repeated with vigorous emphasis. He caught Fitz's eye and grinned. 'Bracing, isn't it?'

Fitz nodded, clenching his teeth and wrapping his arms around himself against a sudden gush of icy air.

'You know,' Anji said a trifle smugly from within the folds of her heavy black coat, 'there are instruments in the TARDIS that happily offer information on the climate conditions outside.'

Fitz looked down at his grey flannel shirt, black jeans and scruffy boots. He'd been asleep when they'd landed and had dressed in a hurry, prompted by the Doctor's enthusiastic announcement: 'We've landed somewhere!' It was the same announcement he made nearly every time, same surprise and excitement. It was starting to get on Fitz's nerves – again.

Between Anji's tailored elegance and Fitz's thrown-on drab stood the Doctor, whose only concession to the weather was probably not a concession at all – a long coat with a cape attached and a split up the back, the kind of coat you saw cowpokes wearing in films where there was a lot of dust blowing around Texas. The reddish brown colour was only a shade darker than he imagined the dust of Texas would be. It wasn't buttoned of course and beneath it the Doctor's white shirt ballooned out as the wind gusted through it.

By the Doctor's movements it was clear they were in for a brisk march, and, although this might serve to warm Fitz up, the steely colour of the clouds rolling in made him think otherwise. 'Hold up a second,' he called. 'I need an overcoat.'

He turned back to the copse where the TARDIS was parked and found himself blinking at a forest – a *big* forest – stretching away in a curve over the hill and possibly for ever beyond it, trees so close together he could barely glimpse the faint illusion of the ship within.

From behind him Anji whispered, 'Oh my God.' The Doctor whistled softly, a long slow note that was muted and swallowed up by the sudden and ominous vegetation. He gulped loud enough for them to hear it. Then said, 'Interesting.' Both his companions whirled on him, stunned.

'Interesting!'

'Where the hell did it –'

'How could it –'

The Doctor was already examining one of the trees, his hand stroking the thick bark. His other hand waved impatiently at them and they both clamped their mouths shut as he bent down to look at the roots.

'Is it real?' Anji ventured after a tense moment.

'Seems to be.'

Fitz moved closer. He could see that the roots were deep in the soil. There were patches of weaker moss and grass in the deep shadows and where the earth was pulled in by the rapacity of the trees, but not much of that. No sign of upheaval. Not that hundreds of trees could have thrust out of the ground in a few seconds while their backs were turned – and with no vestige of noise whatsoever. The trees were so closely packed together they'd need a chainsaw to cut their way through to the ship.

The Doctor seemed determined to try, however, and was even now attempting to squeeze himself between two of the closest trees. A smear of moss darkened the collar of his coat. His foot slipped and he skimmed his nose on the bark. He exhaled, trying to make himself smaller, and then thrust his hand through the crevice, followed by the rest of his arm, and finally jammed his shoulder into the narrow space between the oaks.

'This is – this is really quite – quite a tight – Ow!' He drew back, tearing his sleeve and scraping away flakes of bark in his haste. He shook his hand, now scratched and bloodied, and blew on a cut that had pricked his middle finger. A droplet of startling red flew off and sat like a holly berry on a fern frond. 'Brambles,' he explained before putting the finger in his mouth and sucking on it for a moment. His eyes wandered over other possible options.

'I'll sidle around. It can't be this dense everywhere.'

Anji came over to Fitz. 'A forest springs up out of nowhere and he thinks he can just slide through it.'

'We've been in tighter holes than this and got back out again,' he blustered.

Anji wrapped her bright-red scarf tighter about her throat and gave his shoulder a reassuring pat. 'You're the one without a coat.' Fitz shivered again, not merely from the cold this time. The imposing primordial trees were sucking the heat right out of him. It was the sort of forest that reminded him of tiny children leaving foolish breadcrumb trails for the crows to gobble up. Crows very much like those now wheeling above his head. Struck by a

13

sudden panic, he spun back towards the open downs, reassured by the sight of the unaltered expanse. That was when he saw the flapping paper fastened to a birch tree standing all alone beyond the forest, straight as a lamp post, with one branch pointing downward over the rolling grassland.

'Come on,' he shouted to Anji. 'I spy civilisation, language, papermaking, hot soup!'

'So, William, m'dear, it seems your instruments were right.' Christina ran her manicured nail down, tracing a line on a bubble screen. 'The exotic-miner's eldorado: nothing so common as a wormhole that gives access only to a pitiful, single real-world exit point. What we've got here is a quantum white hole, a –' her lips pursed over the words, – 'Naked singularity. A point of intersection with any conceivable locus in any conceivable universe.'

William nodded, a hint of loss in his posture, shoulders slumping in the Trinary Corp coveralls ship's stores had dug out for him. 'I could have retired on that. Got a whale ranch on Titan; helped boss the oceanoforming.'

'You know we had to claim salvage, Bill. I'm glad we were able to help you out, but we have shareholders of three cultures waiting for dividends. Have you thought any more about signing up with us? We could do with an exoticist.' She drummed her fingers on the white-hole graphic, making the screen flow and resize. 'This exceeds our hopes, already.'

'Oh yeah?' Brok said. *Understatement of the century.* He leaned closer. 'And what did *you* hope for, Captain?'

'Who? Me? Personally?' The question surprised her. As if her hopes could be different from her wants. Her first thought was the obvious answer. All of it. The whole enchilada, naturally. Same as you, Billy boy. But instead, she thumbed the screen to 'display' and let the holograms answer for her.

The quantum white hole was in close orbit round the planet. If it could be called an orbit when its peculiar antigravitational

14

physics meant it was pushed towards the planet by every other body in the universe, and repelled by the planet in an exact balance. So far the ship's sensors had traced six bursts of energy from it and tracked them down. Anything could come from a white hole. Anything. Matter, antimatter, information, future technologies, the flotsam and jetsam of a billion billion universes. White holes had no causality.

'I want *that*. I didn't hope for it.'

'Well, I did!'

'No. *You went after it*. You wanted its –' she felt for a word – 'gifts. We all do. The abanak contingent work as one big happy hippo family and they want their family to prosper. The vuim, well, their problem's been on half the newscasts in the galaxy. They need funds badly: genetic medicine isn't cheap. But you and me and my human crew? We just *want*. That's part of what we are. Isn't it, Bill?'

The text on the paper was printed in thick black type, maybe hand-printed, on what Fitz took to be vellum – not that he'd ever seen vellum, but it was an odd, stiff and heavy paper with a certain lustre to it, and if that and the content didn't cry out for vellum then he wasn't a Famous Traveller.

Coming back into sight, the Doctor waved to them and they waited while he took his time striding over. His boots were thick with black mud and a bird seemed to have mistaken his shoulder for a traveller's convenience.

'It's a big forest,' he said. Anji stared at him, a snide retort dancing on the tip of her tongue, but instead she simply gestured to the notice fastened to the birch without the use of nails, staples or sticky tape.

Fitz had rallied his insouciance in the face of shivering wonder and began to read aloud in a mixture of cockney town crier and Donald Pleasance.

'Whosoever may, by dint of powers magickal –' he stuttered over the 'k' in 'magickal', unsure whether it required extra emphasis – 'or divers arts, be they alchemic, subtle or the blessing of true love, rescue from and otherwise revoke the dread curse of sleep which for forty nights and days out of each forty-one afflicts the Princess Ebonyblack, may by royal decree of her father claim her hand in marriage and one half of the rights, lands, duties, suzerainty and demesnes within the gift of her loving father. Full details of the pleasances and prospects, theretofore, may be obtained from the Castle Notary in accordance with the common practice. Lockets containing a portrait of the Princess are available on request and payment of a thaler to show purity of intent; monies returnable on completion of the quest or return of the miniature.'

A moment of solemn silence followed, before Anji emitted a burst of laughter. 'This is just ridiculous!' The crows acknowledged her assessment with raucous angry squawks.

Although the Doctor smiled, he didn't seem to share her reasons for amusement. 'Why? Kings worry about their daughters as much as anyone else. People offer everything they have for family sometimes.'

'Well, if half a kingdom gets given away every time there's a crisis, in a dozen generations every farmhouse is a castle, every farmer a king. It doesn't make any kind of sense.'

'As opposed to the Acme Instant Forest?' Fitz commented.

'No. I mean, who's left to till the fields? How could they feed themselves?'

The Doctor seated himself on a tree stump, flapping his coat tails out of the way of a brown and red ledge fungus. '"When Adam delved and Eve span who then was a gentleman?" Maybe when everyone's a king or queen they draw lots and merge the kingdoms all over again. Maybe it isn't that simple.'

'Obviously it isn't simple,' Anji muttered, glancing at the forest behind them. 'It's an interesting place, I'll give it that.'

'It's an interesting *cold* place,' Fitz said through chattering teeth.

The Doctor slapped his thighs, a precursor to activity, though the rest of his body didn't follow through by standing up. 'We need the services of a woodcutter. I don't suppose we *could* be in Texas?' he asked hopefully. His companions blinked incomprehensibly at him for a moment. Then Anji chuckled. 'It doesn't look like a chainsaw massacre kind of world, Doctor.'

Fitz gulped and was very glad of that.

'No,' the Doctor said. 'Just as well. I prefer a good solid axe.' He shot a look at the forest, hoping it had heard his couched threat and sunk back into the ground. It hadn't. He blew out a noisy sigh, got to his feet again and went to the birch tree. Plucking the vellum from the bark, he turned it over. The other side was blank, but when he'd turned it back again there were new and different words on the page. This time he read them aloud.

'"Goblin Market, outwith the walls. Come one, come all. Pax Emptor." I wonder which walls they mean.'

Fitz looked at the single pointing branch. 'Signpost?'

As the three travellers set off down the slope – one anticipating the wonders and delights suggested by a Goblin Market, one determined to find a speedy resolution to the forest problem and one hoping mostly for hot soup at the journey's end – something was stirring in the trees high above the TARDIS. The thick trunk of an oak began to bulge and strain outwards with a brittle creaking, forming a gall of timber. This wooden sac grew rapidly, showering the TARDIS's sloping roof with flecks of bark. When it reached the diameter of a Santa's sack it stopped growing. A glistening oozing liquid flowed out between the cracks, and then, with a final *snap!*, it broke open.

Something hairy, lean and brown pulled itself out of the pod. Something that, where it wasn't hair, was wrinkled like an old, old man. It dropped like an ape on to the blue box beneath it. A brief impromptu jig commenced as it felt the thrum of the alien device beneath its feet, and then, with a grunt, it slipped to all fours.

Matted hair fell across the beacon on the box's roof as it laid its head down and listened.

Chapter Two
The Goblin Market

Outside his cubical William Brok could hear, or imagined he could hear, the ant-scuttling of the vuim. He'd have to get used to that. Have to get used to being called Bill, to seeing people, to stepping out of people's way. Get used to air that didn't smell exclusively of him.

He'd been reading up on the vuim on his bedside screen. Serious folk, weird time sense, one of the few races to consider Wagner a composer of quick, hummable, stick-in-the-mind ditties. A typical vuim popular hit lasted upwards of eight hours. Good traders apparently. Maybe patience counted. The abanaks he'd traded with himself. Good people, not just good traders. Trustworthy. Probably ran the *Bonaventure*'s public relations. They had the looks for it. No one could mistrust a friendly pink hippopota-person.

His own kind weren't so easy for him to unfairly pigeonhole.

The quarters he'd been allocated were smaller than the living space on his ship had been. Because that had served for every need, it had needed to be a certain size. Some miners had gone mad through under-estimating how much space they needed; but with the rest of the *Bonaventure* available – command levels, and planning decks with their swept-back consoles, meeting rooms for negotiations, and wide empty storage bays for goods acquisition – the trade ship's designers had obviously cut sleeping space to the minimum.

Something banged hard on the wall of his cubbyhole. Ratta-tat-tat; then a splatter of impacts. Reaching up and grabbing the guide-rails he pulled himself down and out of the bed, hitting the door control – in the designer approved space-saving manner – with his right boot-heel. Like a typical miner he slept clothed and with his boots on.

In the corridor a vuim was convulsing.

It was clearly in physical distress, having a seizure or something, but he had no idea how to stop a vuim swallowing its tongue or whether they had a single air-passage that a tongue might block. He settled for shouting, 'Crewman in distress!'

The vuim resembled insects; and insects breathed through spiracles on their sides; but while he remembered that, he hadn't a clue how to recognise a spiracle. Still calling for help, he placed a hand on its chest and tried to feel for rising and falling lungs. Its greeny-grey skin was slightly cool and seemed stretched over plates or overlapping scales beneath. Somewhere its body was making a rasping sound. He stopped shouting to listen for it.

Two abanaks, chortling and hooting to each other, came around the bend at the end of the corridor and broke into a run, their little hippopotamus legs pounding. They ran like a joke, but they covered the ground.

From the bank of the stream Fitz and Anji watched the Doctor wade into the icy water, trousers rolled up to the knees, trying yet again to catch the floating hat with his piece of flotsam.

'Give it up,' Fitz called, 'you're making my toes curl just watching you.' Not just my toes either, he thought – it was brass-monkey time now. The Doctor had lent him his 'duster' but, as the name implied, it was only designed to keep out dust.

'It's just an old hat,' Anji agreed. 'I've never been convinced by the theory that you can tell everything about the owner from their headgear.'

'Aha,' the Doctor shouted, brandishing a bedraggled straw hat on the end of his stick. 'Now, what does this tell us?' Anji shook her head slightly. Fitz grinned in spite of himself. Flipping the hat into his other hand and dropping the stick, the Doctor stared at the soggy mass looking for the vast secrets it contained. He stuck a hand inside and stretched his fingers out to fill the space. 'Average human cranial capacity.'

'They wrote in English,' Anji reminded him with an exasperated sigh.

'Yes,' the Doctor conceded. 'Vanishing and self-writing English. I'm anxious to meet them: they could have a career in advertising.'

'Or as high flyers in the City,' Fitz added.

'Ha ha,' Anji said.

'What I mean,' the Doctor continued, 'is what if we only thought we were reading English?'

'Here,' an elderly voice interrupted, 'what are you doing with my hat, young man?'

An old lady, frail in a woollen shawl, was regarding them from the far bank.

'Returning it of course!' the Doctor shouted, and began to wade across the stream towards her.

She gave him a look that the Doctor had heard described in 1940s Lancashire as 'like a smell of gas.'

'Maybe you'll do,' she said.

He waded closer and looked up at her on the high red soil of the bank. Her hands seemed too young for her face, smooth lady's hands.

'Do for what?' he asked.

'You've got a strong back, anyone can see that, and you don't mind a bit of wet. Come here. You shall carry me over to the other bank.'

The Doctor considered and gave her his cheekiest grin. 'What's the magic word?'

As she gazed down at him, her eyes were deep hollows in the wrinkles of her face. The finger that crooked at him, demanding he come closer still, now looked ancient, hard, not fragile bone at all but part of a claw draped in skin. Suddenly the Doctor felt very strongly that he might be pushing things. Maybe he didn't want to know the magic word after all, not yet.

'All right, grandam.' He tossed her the hat, which she put, still dripping, upon her head. Then he turned and edged backwards towards the bank, bending to accommodate her. On the opposite bank he could see Anji and Fitz watching him, so he waved, and felt happy again. For some reason he kept thinking of Sinbad the sailor, or was it St Christopher?

A pair of bony knees dug into his ribs and her weight hit him. Surprisingly, his knees buckled slightly.

'Come on then, young man. Do you think I have all day to wait for lazy younger sons and slugabeds?'

One step. Goodness me, thought the Doctor, she really is quite heavy.

An arm hooked itself under his chin. He knew that move. Twist your bone like a blade into the soft part of the windpipe. Another step. His chin pressed down, grinding into the arm, trying to pin it against his chest so as to stop it cutting off his air. Another step. Too slow apparently, for at that moment he felt the blow of a stick on what Fitz would no doubt insist on referring to as his arse. For some reason it didn't seem appropriate for the Doctor to refer to his arse as his arse. Why was that he wondered, and then realised he was choking. The stick came down again. Same place, more force. 'Arrrs,' he said, reaching up with his left arm to take the old woman's triceps between his finger and thumb. He pinched *hard*. The stick fell, but the arm she had at his throat merely moved in tighter as she spurred him on with her sharp little heels. He seemed to be able to ignore the pressure on his neck simply by not breathing – which was slightly scary, but possibly not as scary as the old lady.

One more step. The bank was near now, but he could barely drag his legs through the water. His feet sank into the mud, broken roots and stones prodded his soles. The silt swirled up around his ankles. *If she kicks me one more time I'll drop her face first –*

Suddenly he found himself toppling face first into some suspiciously foul-smelling weeds. The Crone (as the Doctor had dubbed her, deciding that was surely the technical term) hopped over his head and on to the bank with a crackling laugh.

Anji, he couldn't help but notice, was laughing as well. Fitz helped him up wearing the hollow-cheeked expression of someone trying very hard not to laugh.

'Well,' the Crone said, 'that wasn't very gracious. You've got my skirts all wet. I can see you'll need to learn some manners. How we do things round here.'

Anji stepped in, ever the smooth negotiator. 'Perhaps you might share a bit of your wisdom, then. Where would we enquire after the services of a woodcutter, say?'

'If you've wood to chop, you should talk to the Giants,' the old woman replied, 'Good day.' And with that she was off.

Anji threw up her hands. 'Giants. Wonderful.'

Fitz nudged the Doctor. 'Why should you speak to the Giants if you need wood cut?'

The Doctor sighed, busy trying to brush the mud off his trousers with clumps of grass. 'I have no idea, Fitz. Why should you speak to Giants if you need wood cut?'

'Hey, hey.' Anji said, 'Time-out. Fitz: if this is a lead-up to a joke about enormous choppers I really am not in the mood right now'.

'Would I do that? Would I?'

'Yes. And don't.'

'You've ruined the punch line anyway.'

The Doctor looked puzzled, 'Yes, they would need large bikes, what of it?'

Anji groaned. 'If the Chuckle Brothers are through now, I think you'd both better have a look.' She pointed at a track through the heather. 'She went that way, in the direction of our pointing branch.'

Fitz shaded his eyes. The old woman was a single distant figure in an empty landscape. 'How did she get so far ahead?'

'Maybe she's got seven-league boots,' the Doctor suggested. He resisted rubbing the painful areas where she had used those boots on him, and concentrated on putting on his own socks and boots without having to sit down to do it.

'One thing's sure,' Anji said, 'we won't get warm or back into the TARDIS speculating about it.' She clapped her hands like the activities director of a nursery school. 'Come on boys, we're wasting daylight.' Then she was through the brambles, marching resolutely, following the path of the crone.

'Can't she see we're manly men?' Fitz grumbled.

'Muscles and everything,' the Doctor said. 'When did she get so bossy?'

Anji turned, and seeing they were still standing right where she'd left them, put her hands on her hips and glared. They scrambled to catch up with her.

'We're establishing picket satellites around the hole. It's expensive – they'll need to be in powered orbits, and probably armed – but worth it.'

Worth it, damn straight, Brok thought. The hole was a powerful antigraviton source. Valuable for that alone. Priceless even, but a bugger to orbit.

'The company will get a frigate out here once we log this,' Christina added, 'but until then we'll need to sit tight.'

'I could take a message back through the nebula,' Brok suggested, 'log your claim for you. Of course I'd need my ship fixed.'

'Of course you would,' Christina said. She hooked her platinum tresses behind an ear and smiled indulgently at him. Brok wondered idly if the ice-blonde colour was real, knowing even as he wondered that it likely was. Hazel eyes locked on to his. 'I think you'd probably do it, too. All fair and legal, but it wouldn't be my money to gamble with, would it? What if I was wrong and you scooted off to another company and the next thing through the nebula was an army? We're armed, but not enough to protect something as important as this. On the other hand we can't just leave it here. Oh, it's a puzzler.'

'You've already decided what to do.' He realised he was beginning to be able to read her, subtle as her expressions could be. It was a strange feeling after so long a time alone. To feel like he knew what another person was thinking. And a woman at that. An attractive woman.

'Yes. We're going down to the planet to get those signal sources.' If she'd noticed his sudden discomfort, she made no note of it. 'When we have those stowed away, we can risk the trip outside the nebula to punch a signal home. That way we'll have first claim in hard evidence. Chances are the objects alone will show us a profit on the whole cruise. Six glowing balls of maybes and might-bes. Six cures for cancer or the vuim's little problem. Six new technologies. Six elements from six alien periodic tables.'

'As long as it isn't six mad,' Brok muttered. The human captain looked mildly dismayed, as if she were considering the possibility. Then she laughed.

'I'm beginning to like you, Bill.'

'It's William.'

Two hours later, the Doctor, Anji and Fitz reached the market. It might once have been outside some walls, but, if so, the word was now merely conventional for other quite impressive walls of lacquered wood and iron that had grown up around it again. Once through the gate, the stalls and cloth-hung lean-tos rose, step upon step, until they filled the horizon, and over them through the crush of the place, a few slender towers pierced the sky. White thin towers. High German architecture, the Doctor said, but it reminded Anji of Disney. There was a blurring to the towers, a black haze wrapped around them, but at this distance and through the air that trembled with the cooking fire's smoke, and the banners flapping in the breeze, not even the Doctor's eyesight was good enough to make out what it was.

Anji could guess. 'Wall of thorns,' she said simply. 'There's a sleeping princess. There's the castle. We've read the proclamation. It'll be a wall of thorns.'

'Sleeping sickness,' the Doctor mused. 'There was an epidemic of it after the Great War. Then there's catatonia.' His voice wasn't raised above a conversational level but it still seemed to cut through the brook-babble of the crowds.

'Nah,' a stallholder bellowed, 'wicked fairy, wasn't it? Took umbrage at a misplaced invite.' Her stall was full of blue and white porcelain. Anji had seen pieces like it go for a fortune on *The Antiques Roadshow.*

'I heard it was the fish course,' her flower-selling neighbour whispered behind her hand, as if it were a guilty secret. 'Got a bone wedged behind her plate. Not as if she had her own teeth, I hear.' Her stall was full of tulips.

'You mean those yellow fangs ain't real? Swizz, I call it. I remember in fairy Belesia's time –'

Fitz leaned in towards Anji. 'You know where she got the teeth, don't you?'

'Are you about to say "The National Elf Service" Fitz? Because if you are I will cheerfully sell you to the ogre with five ears over there.'

Fitz looked. 'Hasn't he only got two... oh! Ears in a bun. Oh my.'

The older stallholder sniffed. 'The day he sells real ears I'm a changeling. They'll be mock. Cut off a vegetable lamb.'

'Ladies,' the Doctor said with a bow, 'I wonder if you could tell me whom I would see about a stall.'

'Finding one, you mean?' the tulip seller asked. 'What do you want to buy?'

'No no no no,' the Doctor beamed, 'establishing one.'

Anji and Fitz exchanged a worried glance.

'Well now,' the tulip woman said, 'the Castellan is nominally in charge, but if you aren't too fussy, there's always a few stalls begging by the cattle pens and the compost. It's the smell, you see. Folk give up and move on.'

'Christina Human-Captain here.' Her voice echoed round the ship's corridors. 'I've got the initial reports from the robot probes. There are farmers down there, probably human. We've got methane showing in quantities I'd put down to herd animals. I'll be seeking a team to go down and try to locate the material ejected from the white hole. I respectfully suggest the team consist of human and abanak only. We might be dealing with humans cut off from the earlier colonisations and the abanak are less –' She stopped herself from saying 'less buglike and scary' and suavely shifted into the more diplomatic, 'The abanak have more experience with first-contact situations. If the Vuim-Captain agrees, the vuim can handle the on-ship backup.'

'Vuim-Captain speaking.' The voice was brisk. 'The probes suggest several continents outside the spread of, ah, humanity. I suggest the vuim land a mining laboratory on one of these continents and do a standard assay. It will give us potential trade goods for interaction with the natives later, and perhaps another route to profit.'

'Sounds good to me,' the Abanak-Captain's voice chimed in.

'Me too,' Christina said.

There was a pause, then the Vuim-Captain said, 'I regret to inform the crew that the vuim taken ill earlier today has died. I wish to commend the actions of our guest Mr Brok and the abanak crewmembers, Heskarit, and Caten, who did their best to assist him. I will forward their names to his hive to be honoured when circumstances permit.' He signed off.

'Christ,' Brok whispered as he took in Christina's calm face. 'He died. Just like that.'

'It's a recessive genetic disease, undetectable until near the end.

Humans can't catch it, neither can the abanak. We're mammals, they're insects, and their biology isn't DNA based.'

'I don't care that I can't catch it!' Brok shouted.

Christina hardened her voice. 'I appreciate your sympathy for the vuim, Bill – William – but the best hope for them is to work. To travel, to seek, to learn. Maybe there's a cure. They hope so. Do you know how competent and how proud they are usually? Do you think they ship out with alien species like us for the educational experience? They know a ship crewed by them alone might never come back. A trade tour's too long for them to risk. That's partly why we've got three chains of command. You won't hear them talk about it. So I don't either.'

'It's still horrible.'

'Yes. But this find might just be their best hope for the future of their race.'

'I can't believe you're doing this!' Anji said, watching the Doctor take his pick of the least offensive stall. She circled around and gave her forehead an exasperated rub as Fitz helped the Doctor tip what looked like a roll of discoloured loo carpet off the stall. She was even more surprised by the Doctor's insistence that Fitz rescue a long paper banner from atop the middens. Something nuzzled her ankle, and she half tripped on, half sidestepped a border collie trying to snuffle its way nearer her crotch. 'No. Get away. Bad dog,' she said, then hurried to her point. 'It must be three in the afternoon by now, and it took us, what, over two hours getting here from the TARDIS? By the time we've found someone to help us and got back there it'll be too late to – Oh.' Her brain caught up and stopped her tongue. To her annoyance, the dog decided her little dance away from its persistent nose was an invitation to play and leapt up, planting both paws on her chest. 'Get down!'

'Exactly,' the Doctor replied. He had found a tiny brush from somewhere and was making fine, almost Japanese strokes of black

28

across the paper. Luckily most of the stains were on the back. 'So if we're going to be staying here overnight, and freeing the TARDIS tomorrow, based on the need to cut down at least ten trees, then we need to find somewhere to stay, and to get *that* we need to have a grasp of the local coinage and mores.'

'How is – *down* – how are you going to – knock it off, mutt!' She turned her face from the big black tongue and shoved the beast hard. It immediately leapt up again, nearly toppling her backwards.

'*Robert!*' a woman screeched. The dog was grabbed by the collar and jerked, with a strangled yelp, off Anji. 'Foul beast!' the woman cried. 'Up to your tricks again, are you? I turn my back for five minutes –' She began to beat the dog mercilessly with a piece of knotted rope. The animal yelped louder and scuttled around in a circle still held by the scruff in the woman's other fist.

'Stop it,' Fitz cried, trying to get between the woman and the dog. 'Stop it! Ow!' The clout came down on his shoulder and he dodged another blow.

As her arm drew back, the Doctor caught it. 'Stop this, right now.' The force of his grip caused her to drop the rope. He kept his fingers locked tight around her forearm, but she was too worked up to feel it. He shook her a little. 'Enough. That's enough. The animal's done nothing to warrant this behaviour.'

'Really,' Anji said breathless with shock, 'nothing happened. He was only being playful –'

The woman turned a sudden, suspicious gaze at Anji. 'Oh, being playful, was he? I suppose the two of you have plans to meet up for more fun and games tonight? Leave off!' she cried at the Doctor, trying to shake loose from his grasp. Which proved not too difficult as her statement had caused his grip to loosen considerably.

'Now, Bella,' came a soothing voice from behind them. It was the fellow who'd been shovelling dung from a cart on to a mountain of it – not so very far away from them, unfortunately. He

29

thrust his shovel into the mass and strolled towards them, wiping his hands on the front of his smock. 'These folks have only just arrived. Don't believe the girl knew Robbie at all from what I seen.'

The woman released her hold on the dog and gave it a hard kick for good measure. 'Back to the sheep, Robert.' The collie took a few slinking steps keeping his tail tucked well between his legs. He gave a fearful glance over his shoulder before spotting a path through the crowd and racing away. Bella tucked in the wisps that had escaped her kerchief in an effort to recover her dignity, but the colour was still high in her cheeks as she gave Anji a menacing glower.

'Robert won't be leaving the house this night or any other to meet up with the likes of you, miss.'

Anji gave a startled laugh. 'What?'

'We've got two children, you know. Another on the way. None of you tarts care a whit about that, do you?'

With that, she spun on her heel and marched off after Robert the dog. The three of them stared after her before Fitz ventured a tentative, 'Did she say what I thought she said?'

'You mustn't mind Bella,' the dung-spreader said. 'Poor woman had some trouble meeting her final task to break the spell upon Robert. Mind you, she's got herself a fine sheepdog by day, but as a husband he tends to stray when night comes. Some folks'll tell you it's his way of punishing her for failing, but... well, let's just say I knew Robbie *before* he was cursed.' He gave the Doctor and Fitz a sly wink, then strolled back to the rubbish heap, tossed his shovel into the now empty cart and went off to gather more, presumably.

They all took a few moments to fully absorb the information. Then both the Doctor and Fitz burst into laughter.

'It isn't funny,' Anji said trying not to laugh. She let out a horrified, 'Eeewww! He was sniffing me!'

'He ain't nothing but a hound dog,' Fitz spluttered. He rubbed his shoulder, ruefully. 'Hound lady packs quite a wallop, though.'

The Doctor, still chuckling, took up the paintbrush again, his hand steady as ever despite his amusement as he put a few final touches to his sign. 'Animal-grooms, princesses in towers – I love this place! You and Anji have a shufty round, and I'll see if I can earn us enough for room and board. There!'

He tacked the banner across the ramshackle stall, using two silver cravat pins. The sign read, DOCTOR KNOW-ALL. ADVISER, AND HELPER; DONOR IN EXTREMIS.

Fitz humphed. 'You don't think it's a trifle immodest? What's this donor business, you going to yank out your kidneys or what?'

'A donor, Fitz, in a traditional fairy tale is a character who supplies, or *donates to*, the hero or heroine the means they will require to overcome their antagonist.'

'And this extremis,' Anji asked. 'Is it yours or theirs?'

'Oh, theirs, but I'm sure I'll be able to help.'

The Doctor took in Anji's and Fitz's expressions and smiled sheepishly, 'Well, it's worth a try. I have a fair grasp of herbal medicine, you know.'

'Really?' Fitz asked.

'Mostly camomile tea and sympathy, but it works wonders – What?' The expressions on his friends' faces had gone from wary to worried. 'Oh come on, there's no need to be concerned about me. You two have a scout about. We'll meet back here in a couple of hours and compare notes.' The Doctor made shooing motions with his hands and then took some white cards out of his pocket. He pushed one of the cards through a nail that protruded wonkily from the stall. THE DOCTOR IS IN, it read.

Chapter Three
The Black Coach

Anji watched as Fitz fondled the jumpers heaped on the plank that served as a display counter. The colours were garish and entirely inappropriate for a man in her opinion – purples, pinks and greens that seemed impossible in nature and almost hurt just to look at. She wondered whether the cold was affecting his eyes.

'That particular shade is from a dye recipe given me by elves,' the woman boasted. Anji shrugged. The vendor was wasting her sales pitch. They didn't have any local tender. And might not have any for some time to come if they were relying on Doctor Know-All. Still, in a market like this, trades or bargains for services probably worked just as well. Surely there was a woodcutter's guild or something. Even if she had to barter for just an axe, without the burly man to swing it, she'd simply take Fitz and the Doctor in hand, march them right back to that forest, and put them to work. She was perfectly comfortable cracking the whip when her team needed motivation. Besides, technically, Fitz and the Doctor had bigger muscles, and they didn't mind breaking their nails. Well, not as much, anyway. Actually, Fitz was kind of whiney about it, but too bad.

She turned in a slow circle, surveying the wooden buildings that bracketed the market itself, searching for a sign that would indicate an occupation or type of business. She didn't know what she hoped to find – probably not Axes R Us or Tree Fellows, For All Your Forestry Needs. Surely the people here hung out shingles announcing their trades to the public? But the only thing she recognised was the whimsically gruesome name of a tavern: the

Singing Bone, and mostly because of the staggering, noisy drunks going in and coming out. A tavern, however, was a good place to network. She began to work her way through the crowd –

'Philtres, potions, spells,' a voice hissed too close to her ear. Someone grabbed her arm. She tried to jerk from the grasp, but it tightened painfully. She spun round, prepared to voice her outrage, but nothing, not even a woman married to her sheepdog, could have prepared her for this face in her face – a countenance that demanded the epithets 'ugly', 'old' and 'witch'. Long, crooked nose, long cleft chin, big hairy moles sprouting from both like daddy longlegs. Matted hair poked out in tufts from beneath a dirty red kerchief. The tattered shawl looked as if it had been distressed by overzealous volunteers in a community theatre costume shop, and was draped over a dowager's hump possibly built by the same. The witch's bony fingers were still pressed into the flesh of her upper arm and she squelched the urge to laugh, sensing it would only sound hysterical. Simultaneously she fought the more pressing urge to run screaming in childlike terror to the Doctor.

'Golden apples to test a lover's heart.'

'No,' Anji said, drawing painfully from the woman's grasp. 'No thank you.'

'Surely I have something in my basket to tempt a fine lady of the likes of you.' The witch's eyes were like jet marbles sitting in sockets surrounded by a thousand wrinkles. Glowing with the sort of evil health that could only come from a regular diet of fat Hansels and Gretels, she waved the basket under Anji's nose. 'Magic laces for the bodice – guaranteed to make your shape pleasing to any man you fancy.'

'Not interested.'

'Oh, poor dear,' the witch said. 'You haven't any money, have you?' She smiled sympathetically and, as expected, what teeth she had left were crooked, yellowed and slightly pointed. They evidently *grew* yellow and pointed, as Anji could see no evidence of dental caries, decay or even filing. And the mention of money rubbed Anji in just the wrong way. She hated having to rely on the Doctor for a little cash in her pocket. If she had a Platinum card with her she'd feel much better able to refuse this horrid woman's goods with dignity. 'You've nothing I want,' she said.

'I must have something,' the woman muttered, rummaging around in the basket. 'Ah, here it is. Just the thing for a fine lady like yourself.' As the witch pulled out an object wrapped in dusty blue velvet, Anji swore she could hear a hum in the air like a distant chorus of angels singing 'Aaahhh…'

'What is it?' she asked, and could have bitten off her own tongue. She might as well have had a sign around her neck that said SUCKER.

'A wishing box,' the woman said.

Yeah, right, Anji thought. Why haven't you wished yourself up a new face, then?

But, even as she thought it, her eyes were drawn to the careful unwrapping of the box. Fashioned like a little treasure chest, it fitted cunningly in the witch's hands. In the twilight, the inlaid colours glittered richly, set deep into the swirling, spiralling carving in the wood. The very contours of the box seemed to shift dreamily as Anji gazed at it. There was an aura about it, like a bottle of expensive champagne nestled in a bucket of ice on a candlelit table in a posh restaurant – the champagne of celebration after one has got engaged, or won a prize, or closed the deal of the century. It was the aura of future possibilities that all looked good.

With effort she pulled her eyes away. 'Doesn't matter,' she said. 'You were right, I haven't any money.'

'A trade, then.'

Anji licked her lips and then mentally slapped herself for it. Damn. She was usually more vigilant about body language and knew perfectly well what unconscious lip licking meant in others. Avarice. Desire. Vulnerability. The moment to press an advantage. She darted a glance to see if the woman made note of the slip. Still smiling affably, the witch shook the box a little as if she was calling a cat for kibble, though there was nothing inside to rattle around. Wishes didn't rattle, apparently.

Common sense told her it was just a pretty box, but the world told a different story. This place worked on principles far removed from common sense. Anji had seen that with her own eyes. Perhaps it was exactly what the witch claimed: a wishing box. And a wishing box might be more effective on this world than any axe.

The colours of the box seemed even brighter as the shadows grew longer. 'What sort of trade would you accept?'

'What have you got?'

'At the moment, I've only the clothes on my back. But if the box works the way you claim then I'll be able to get you pretty much anything you want.'

The witch gave her a knowing look. 'A lick and promise won't do me much good when night comes and I've nowhere to rest me bones.'

'Why don't you use it to wish for yourself, then?'

'Ha, who ever heard of a wish doing a witch any good? Don't want to end up in an oven. But you're a good girl, I can see that. Providing you don't wish down the moon, you'll do well.'

'So,' Anji pounced, 'If you haven't wished how do you know this doodad even grants wishes? What's my guarantee?'

The witch was becoming frustrated. 'It's a wishing box. Tell that by looking at it. Never mind,' she said, throwing the velvet scrap around the box again. 'You aren't as clever as I took you for.'

As soon as the box was covered, Anji felt a wave of anxiety wash over her, a primal anxiety like that of a Neanderthal watching a total eclipse of the sun. 'I'll trade you my coat,' she said, the words tumbling out rapidly in spite of her. 'It's merino wool, fully lined in silk. Look, it has welt pockets and leather buttons –'

The witch shook her head. 'It's a lovely coat, dearie, but not to my liking.'

'I'll throw in the scarf.'

'I've a better idea. You seem a good, strong girl. Perhaps you'd be willing to trade your services?'

Anji's hidden-clause detector kicked in. 'What sort of services would I be required to perform?'

'Oh goodness, dear child, nothing immoral. I know of six young sisters – sweet, motherless children they are, practically helpless now that they are alone in the world – in need of an extra pair of hands around their cottage. They asked would I enquire after an honest, hard-working young woman –'

'A servant?' Anji squeaked. She hadn't spent all that time getting an MBA to be a housemaid. No, she reminded herself, you spent all that time getting an MBA only to find worlds where economics really were voodoo, and where time really was money. Of course they had servants here. That only stood to reason. Did they have serfs? Slaves? Her mind went wandering into familiar realms of goods and services, and class-structure-based economies.

'Like one of the family,' the witch continued. 'You shall tell them bedtime stories, tuck them in at night, mend their little stockings…'

'Um… mending… yes, well, I'm not much of a hand at mending.'

'I'm certain there's other tasks. They need a guiding hand, the household's in such disarray, so disorganised…'

Ah. Well, that was different. Anji'd watched *House Doctor, Changing Rooms* and *Ground Force* religiously. She reckoned she could sort anyone's problems out if they'd only listen to reason. And that box really was giving off buy-me vibes. 'How long?' she asked coolly. 'I haven't got a lot of time to spare. Possibly I could do a couple of hours' consultancy.'

'A day. See, it says so here.' The witch produced a parchment from her cloak. Anji noticed it was the same material as the proclamation.

'Services for one day, PS,' Anji read. 'PS? What's on the other side, then?'

'Oh, we sign there, make it all binding.'

'OK. Here's my counteroffer. One day, or until client satisfaction is given, which ever is shorter.'

The words on the parchment changed as she spoke, retaining the prompt to turn the page, but recording her changes. Self-recording contracts. What she wouldn't have given for that in her job back home. She was confident her organisational skills would have the household sorted out in an hour or so, and even if it took the rest of the day, they were going to have to stay somewhere, as it would be getting dark soon. She'd get Fitz to tell the Doctor what she was doing. *You're rationalising*, she told herself *This is just like those five coats you bought when you got your first job.* But the style had been so flattering and if she'd bought just the one in black then she wouldn't be able to wear it with her browns, and how could she not get the loden green as well, and the one in leather and –

She caught her lower lip between her teeth, weighing potential gains and losses, and then said, 'Deal. Provided the wording of this thing stays put now.'

'Oh, what you've seen is what you get, my dear,' the witch said, turning the parchment over to show her the back where her name 'Anji' and what looked like an occult symbol appeared. She guessed that was the witch's mark. Probably functionally illiterate. If you could trust your contracts to record exactly, you wouldn't need to know how to read them. No, that couldn't be right. What if somebody went behind your back and changed the terms? Maybe you just went to a specialist or maybe they locked once you'd agreed –

'Deal's made,' the witch said.

The box was in Anji's hands now and she pressed it close feeling it nestle into her, a tiny heartbeat in the region of her solar plexus. How did the contract know my name, she thought suddenly. I'm sure I never said it.

'Ahahahahaha,' the witch laughed.

Oh shit, that's not a good sign.

'PS, my dear, a standard contractual term. One day *per sister*. Heh, heh, heh.'

'What? What? Oh no, no, back-up –'

As a team of horses galloped towards them, the witch hurled an ancient term of abuse that made Anji cringe in horror. 'Tourist!' Two strong arms grabbed her, knocking the breath out of her body, as she was pulled through the window of the speeding black coach.

The trader scout ship dropped from the underbelly of the *Bonaventure* leaving its two counterparts nestling like a cluster of grapes. Behind the scouts other larger drop ships rested. One, a factory/assessor module, was being powered up by the Vuim-Captain, its lights picking out the girders and supports around it.

In the forward compartment of the scout, Christina was quietly seething. The other officers were tiptoeing about so as not to set her off. Tento, a middle-aged portly abanak of maybe twenty-six long summers (his people still tended to spend the winters asleep if possible, although certain professions remained active these days, particularly nuclear technicians, spaceport staff and tour guides), nudged Alex Volpe, a thin, bearded human, and whispered, 'What's soured Madam, then?'

'Couldn't get that gruff space miner beau of hers to come planetside,' Alex said out of the side of his mouth as they hit the upper atmosphere.

The Doctor was doing a roaring trade. A brisk showman's patter, a few nerve-pressure points and quasi-chiropractic manipulations of bad backs had set him up with the murmuring approval of the crowd. Still, even he had to wonder: were the questions he was being asked getting stranger as the shadows lengthened?

How do you fix a toad's broken leg?

He was tempted to ask if there had been a car accident, but he didn't. It would have been a joke only he understood and where was the fun in that?

He made a set of splints from some tongue depressors he found in a pocket, and wrote out a list of herbs with carefully calculated dosages. He wasn't that surprised when all the herbs turned out to be known, even one he'd made up on the spot, but he couldn't quite decide what that meant. There was no technology in sight yet, but there was finely woven cloth on people's backs in a mishmash of styles from the farmer's smock and trews, to doublets and hose, stiff pleated skirts shaped like bells, slashed sleeves, dagged sleeves, tall pointed hats or kerchiefs, wide-brimmed hats or turbans, justaucorps and spurs, all mixed up and seemingly drawn from an illustrator's fancy. He half expected to see a woman with marcelled waves in her hair wearing a Hollywood version of Louis IV court dress. The people had good teeth and healthy complexions, and only a little dirt under their fingernails. They seemed a long step up from the medieval stereotype of subsistence farmers.

What temperature should a mouse-child be?

He remembered an answer from reading *Stuart Little* and kept his fingers crossed that the author hadn't made it up. A line from the book – where the mouse is born to a human, not adopted by one – made him smile inwardly as he remembered it. 'Very few American women are having mice nowadays.'

How soon can you pack up your stall?

Now that was a stumper. He looked up into the eyes of two burly guardsmen. Studded leather jerkins, weapons like Roman short swords – thankfully still in scabbards. 'A couple of minutes?' he hazarded, turning on a beaming smile. 'Just need to leave a note for my, ah, nursing staff.'

'No notes, Castellan's orders – the King wants you. Now!'

Odd how quickly sick people can make themselves scarce the Doctor thought. He could have sworn there were thirty waiting. He reached out and shook the nearest guard's hand. 'Have you ever considered a career in medicine? You obviously have the knack.'

'Shut up, and move.'

* * *

The vuim moved around methodically, regularly, efficiently. There was none of the gossip that passed between the human and abanak crew. The vuim had a word for such time wasting. It meant the meaningless clatter of wheels on cobbles and dated back a long time. Back to when they hadn't been in such a hurry. They were individuals, and, even though humans preferred to think of them as having some kind of insect hive mentality, it wasn't true: they just had a lot in common, and no desire to talk overmuch. Fear will do that to a species.

Vuim-Captain shared Christina's desire to attend the action in person, so he was on the factory ship. Timtangle, the Abanak-Captain, had the watch on board the *Bonaventure* and neither human nor vuim wanted him to abandon it.

'Disengaging,' the pilot voice said. The Vuim-Captain was careful not to let his irritation show. The human-manufactured voice of the machine pilot was something he had to tolerate like so much else – a necessary compromise. He stood in the prow and looked out on the planet below. The *Bonaventure* was orbiting geostationary, moving with the planet's surface and keeping above the uninhabited continents. The scout manned by Christina-Captain and her team would have to fly halfway around the world to find a landing point, but the factory could just drop. He felt a twinge of curiosity, perhaps a little excitement, though he kept the smell of it close. It wouldn't do to elicit unwarranted hope in the others. But the secret hope he could not allow to die still wondered whether this world would hold a cure.

Fitz wanted to bury his face in the wool. Roll around in it, crawl beneath the piles of warm fuzzies and curl up in a nest of thick stripes of deep, deep red, and dark blue. Rich umbers flecked with orange and gold like autumn leaves. The colours sang to him about the joys of toasty toes and sleeping in on January mornings under a mountain of blankets.

He'd never encountered this level of desire in connection with clothing, at least not in connection with putting it on! Being bloody cold could do that to a fellow.

The Doctor had taken back his coat when he'd opened shop. He said it made him look more professional. Fitz had merely shaken his head and let the matter go. Apparently Doctor Show-Off and Doctor Know-All were closely related.

He pushed his icy hands between a stack of browns and greens. The stallkeeper eyed him suspiciously over her clacking needles. She'd already gone through her spiel twice. 'Are you going to stand there all day, then?' she asked. 'You're blocking the light.'

He pulled his hands out quickly. 'Sorry. No. Sorry.'

It had been warmer where the Doctor was, being so conveniently close to a huge pile of shit. It was a sad testimony to his current circumstance that Fitz found himself longing to hug it. Definitely time to call it a day. He looked around to tell Anji he was headed back, but couldn't spot her anywhere.

The crowds were thinning. People were starting to roll up and close down for the evening. He walked a little way, stretching his neck, searching for the pattern of black hair, red scarf, black coat over the heads of humans and assorted 'others'. He found himself apologising to a pig after he'd tripped over it and it told him to 'watch where you put those big feet, oaf!' He barely avoided the fist of what he assumed was a troll arguing with another troll. But of Anji he saw no sign. She'd stood out considerably when they were walking around. The looks he got were the same sort he got whenever he shopped too long without buying, watchful gazes on guard for theft. But the looks at her had been all intrigue and interest. In Anji's time, an Asian woman in London didn't stand out so much. But here the human populace were mostly fair-skinned, though there were plenty of ogres and dwarves about that weren't.

Ogres and trolls and dwarves, oh my. How easily he'd accepted the fact of them. He was used to interacting with all sorts of alien species by now. But even accustomed as he was, he usually experienced a brief, dizzying rush as his mind scrambled to make sense of something that didn't smell, feel, look, taste or sound like an Earth thing. He'd become really good at making the adjustment travelling with the Doctor, but there was always an adjustment to be made. And he hadn't noticed making an adjustment to the presence of ogres, trolls and dwarves. Which was strange. Perhaps it meant he was past the need. That he'd become like the Doctor, a true Universal Man at home where ever he found himself. He liked that idea.

Colder than ever but feeling right at home, he veered left between the stalls, expecting to find not Anji, but a tavern. He had to: this was his current home in the universe and he was thirsty. Instead he found a structure of black wood, alone in a patch of scorched earth. For a moment he stood blinking at it, unable to disconnect his expectations from the evidence. But it wasn't until the creaking drew his eyes up to the deformed feet swinging to and fro over his head, with long black nails apparently still growing (or so his imagination informed him) that he realised it was a gallows and leapt back with a strangled cry. There was a sign stuck atop the hanging tree. It read STEPMOTHER.

Right. Oh God.

Fitz spun on his heel. He wanted out. Back to the Doctor. Back to the TARDIS. Instead he went smack into a troll with a ladder.

'Watch it.'

'Yes, er, sorry.' Panic fought curiosity and for a moment curiosity won.

Fitz watched as the troll rested its ladder against the gallows, swarmed up it and drew a knife. The troll began to slice and sing. At which point Fitz ran. Earnestly and with great conviction, the troll's cheery song dogging his heels as he did so.

'A witches' thighbone I will cut, and whittle me a whistle. I'll blow a song o'er hill and dale through bracken, kelv and thistle. A merry love note I will make to lure my sweetheart deep. And underneath my father's bridge a trysting we will keep.'

Running flat out now. No time to look for Anji or a tavern. No time to look –

A desperate yelp stopped the motion of his feet. He'd reached a main thoroughfare and in an instant saw both the old beggar in ragged furs struggling to get out of a rut in the road, and the swaying black carriage careening towards him. The man was yelling, crying out, but the foaming demon-eyed horses pulling the carriage seemed to trample all sounds beneath their thunder. Fitz knew in that frozen second that the old man wouldn't make it.

He ran towards the road, shouting, arms waving to warn the coach away, but realised too late there was no driver up top.

The next thing he was conscious of was the horses' hooves crashing past just inches from his left ear, and then the brush and whirr of a studded wheel grazing the back of his head as he rolled away from it. The old man was now beneath him on the opposite side of the road, smelling of wet dog. When Fitz got to his feet again he was shaking so badly that he would have thrown up – if he'd had anything in his stomach. But then, suddenly, men were clapping him on the back and women were telling him how brave he was. He supposed it had been brave, but he had no conscious memory of the act, only disjointed flashes of running, grabbing and rolling. Though it was true that he'd been brave on a number of occasions in his travels with the Doctor, both consciously and unconsciously, usually there weren't a lot of people around to see it.

The others helped the old beggar to his feet, brushed him down and handed him his cane. That was when Fitz had his first chance to really look at the man.

He was slender and stooped, with a ring of white hair framing a natural tonsure of liver-spotted scalp. His eyes were grey and remarkably clear for someone who'd seemed frail and helpless only moments ago. And, most remarkable of all, he was wearing the battered hide of a big, grey wolf. The huge forepaws were looped together over the man's chest and the head dangled sordidly between the man's shoulder blades, its mouth open in a frozen growl – with most of the teeth still intact.

'Somebody ought to do something about those black coaches,' a woman clucked. 'They shouldn't be allowed until after dark. My goodness, there are children still running about this time of day.'

Fitz glanced around anxiously as if the coach would make another sudden, terrifying appearance.

'Oh, it's long gone, son. They only come when a bargain of indenture is made.'

'You all right now, Uncle?' someone else asked the old man.

'Aye. Thanks to this brave lad here.'

Fitz felt himself puffing up and managed to beat it firmly down again. No point in feeling too cocky. That always backfired. 'It was my honour, sir,' he said in what he hoped was a genuinely humble manner. He was too shivery for vainglory.

'Ah,' said Uncle with a strange grin. He patted Fitz on the arm. 'This one knows his stuff.'

'That's sure, Uncle', 'He looks a fine fellow' and 'He's got what it takes, that's for certain' came the responses from the bystanders.

The old man was still looking at Fitz. He had a gleam in his eye that Fitz wasn't sure he liked the looks of.

'I want to give you something as reward.'

'Oh, no, that isn't necessary,' Fitz demurred. *Let it be money, please God, let it be money, just enough to buy a –*

The old man removed his wolf-hide cloak and handed it to Fitz. 'May it serve you long and well.'

It was appalling, but as the cold bit again into his bones, Fitz found himself reaching out for it in much the same way as he'd heard a drowning man would clutch at a straw.

As the factory ship dropped out of the cloud cover, the infrared sensors went wild.

'Instrument malfunction,' the irritating human voice blared.

'Unable to acquire safe-landing zone lock.'

The Captain indicated to a vuim of his own klatch that he would be accorded the responsibility of a manual landing. He set another to examine the instrumentation. The vuim moved to the manual controls, letting its long arms intertwine with the muscle-reading devices. They were another human inconvenience; the vuim, practical as ever, had let their muscles be reached via tiny holes drilled in their exoskeletons. It had been cheaper than building a second set of controls.

The vuim at the sensors reported before they were within ten thousand feet of the ground. He could find nothing wrong with the input. It was the computers themselves rejecting as impossible the picture the sensors presented.

'In what,' the Captain asked, 'lies the impossibility?'

At that moment, the vuim accorded the honour of the landing saw the impossibility and flinched. The controls cybernetically locked to his muscle movements threw the ship sideways, sending the pilot flying and staggering the Captain for a moment.

Under them the world was unravelling, landscape pulling away as if the hills and forests were fleeing. Under them, the bones of the world were becoming visible: a dry, desiccated, browny grey expanse, walled round by a tidal wave of retreating green.

Vuim-Captain watched, intrigued, reminded of the one and only time he had, for politeness's sake, sat through the human activity known as the end-of-mission show. The human's engineer performed her 'pulling the tablecloth from under expensive fragile relics trick'. Assuming the trick had worked as promised, Vuim-Captain thought it would have looked very like what his eyes were seeing, and what the machines confirmed was happening below.

Trees and grass moving as a unit, hills like amoebas melting away before them. Vuim-Captain imagined the world speaking and its words were disdain and ostracism. It was repulsed by them. You may land on rock, it seemed to say. You may land on cold unyielding stone, but the fruits here are not for you A typically human injunction from the scrubby hydroponics display gardens of a dozen space docks occurred to him: Keep Off the Grass!

He would not stand for it. 'Land us within the verdant area at flight speed.'

'Sir, we are already moving at nearly supersonic speeds!'

'We have safety devices to protect us from impacts.'

'I do not understand how the ground can alter so fast, but if we try to go faster and land we'd... splash.'

'The impact devices would fail?'

'They'd keep the lander intact, but we'd be plated over the inside.'

'Take us up. I have another idea.'

Somehow the vuim pilot didn't look reassured.

The Doctor's nose was itching, which was hardy surprising, pushed hard as it was by the pressure of four muscular arms against the surface of the glass coffin. He really shouldn't have indulged his curiosity about the lock. He tried to squint through the diffracting glass, but it was like looking through layered water and, besides, his nose was hurting now and he was getting angry. Why couldn't people just ask nicely? It wasn't as if he didn't *like* to help. Of course that was one of those irregular verbs, I *help*, he *meddles*, they *conquer and destroy.* Some people didn't want help. Others wanted it too badly. Others wanted to give it whether the recipients wanted it or not.

He wiggled his fingers up under his body and started to push. Against the full strength of the two guards he managed to lever his nose away from the pane with a soft adhesive sound. They fell back reaching for their short swords. The Doctor raised his hands to the level of his ears in a conciliatory, unarmed and harmless gesture.

'Yes, I think that does count as a closer look, thank you. But what I meant was could we open the casket?'

'No one is to lay hands on the Princess,' said the taller guard, the one with the straw-coloured hair hanging lankly out of the back of his helmet, and probably – the Doctor thought – an incipient bald patch under it. 'That's right,' the shorter added. 'It'd be disrespectful.'

The Doctor sighed. 'I didn't mean any disrespect. It's just that diagnosis at a distance is always risky.' From this distance he could almost make out features swimming beneath the surface of the glass, dark hair framing an oval shape, a smudged line of brows perhaps, another smear of red. He imagined that the Princess Ebonyblack was smiling at his predicament. He smiled back. 'I'd say this had all the hallmarks of PASS.'

'PASS?'

'Poisoned Apple Somnolence Syndrome.' The Doctor darted back out of range of the sword just as it was brandished through the place where the tip of his nose had been. 'Actually, pass means I've no idea. People come up here to check, though, don't they?' He spotted what looked like an alcove with a curtain drawn across it.

The smaller guard followed his gaze and spat noisily into the dust before nodding. 'They used to put a servant up here in case she woke up and needed anything. But the union started demanding hazard pay so the King stopped doing it. Just doctors come up here now, through the passages. With their black bags and their herbs and their leeches. Princes come from the other side.'

The Doctor looked at the high narrow window and the black nails of the thorn. 'They must be very brave.'

'They don't have no option. The hedge is growing now the Princess is asleep again. In another couple of hours it'll have thrust through these walkways and passages filling everything but the Princess's chamber. Then it'll be another forty days before she stirs.'

'Interesting,' the Doctor mused. 'The time awake, is it at all related to the phases of the moo–?'

'Then there's the beast,' the other guard said, talking before the Doctor had finished his question and showing no sign of even hearing it. 'Of course some people say it only eats the thorn, but then no one's actually seen it and come back.'

'The beast?' The Doctor felt things were looking up a bit.

'Dragon,' the fair-haired guard suggested.

'Ogre, I heard. One of the wild sort,' the other said.

The Doctor made a shushing noise and paused expectantly.

'Oi, Sawbones, what's the matter?'

'Oh nothing, I was just waiting for the howl, that's all.'

'The howl?'

'Well surely it must howl! And, dramatically, I thought it might oblige us with a show of its presence.'

The taller guard, who was still only just up to the Doctor's shoulder, got him by the ear and pulled him down to eye-contact point. 'When the King discovers that Doctor bloody Know-All can't cure his daughter, you'll be lucky if you ain't hanging on the thorn to meet the beast personal.'

Chapter Four
The Face in the Glass

The factory lander impacted the greenery at crash speed. Straight down, with all the power off, save the computer that had triggered the safety field on for an instant at the point of impact.

They'd wasted a great deal of time attempting to swoop and dive at the green land, but it had dodged every effort. Perhaps it was unfounded, paranoid, but an insistent inner voice told Vuim-Captain that the moment the lander settled on bare rock the soil and vegetation would rise up and bury them under a crushing blanket of green.

They'd retreated to the edge of space and slyly attempted to sneak down in a spiral pattern, a dozen risky darting attempts as the night over the continent had rolled on towards dawn. Finally, the Captain lost patience and reverted to his first plan – the crash dive. Now, it seemed he had gambled and won. The crew were bruised and battered but no one had ruptured a shell, or died suddenly from shock-induced acceleration of the disease they all potentially carried within themselves. The pilot's estimate had been pessimistic. It was a common failing among the vuim.

He pressed the door controls, and the lights came on as the computer started to power up the non-emergency functions. The light that came in from outside was pearly, only one step up from dark. On the planet's other side, where the *Bonaventure*'s human traders had gone to make contact with the locals, it would be early evening, but here morning was just brightening.

He motioned that a team should follow. The gangway looked like black iron in a trick of the early light and the sound of his metal-shod feet striking it echoed eerily. The still visible moon was larger than the biggest of the three that circled his home, and maybe two-thirds the size of the monstrous planetoid that orbited Earth. It was no wonder humans linked their moon to madness. Just seeing Earth's bloated moon was enough to imagine it falling.

The trees the factory lander had fallen through were pushed out and down like the flattened patterns of a bomb. The vuim had fought wars once, back before their medical needs had quietly absorbed their economy's ability to fund such extravagances. Vuim-Captain had killed – years ago. Now he even felt sympathy for trees.

Even if they weren't really trees at all. He could see that by the mixture of faint dawn light and the outspilling radiance from the ship. These tree-shaped things were moving away, gradually, slowly, their surfaces rippling and tugging – none of the swift apocalyptic motion of the land that he had seen from the sky, but some form of group activity nevertheless. *This is the same sort of earth-insect mind humans believe we have*, Vuim-Captain thought. Or perhaps what he observed was merely instinct. Could a thing evolve that lived by mimicking everything? There were creatures that looked like a leaf or a shard of crystal on his world. Some hid themselves through fear, others to lure prey. As he watched the vegetation crawl away like wounded animals, Vuim-Captain imagined entire continents closing up like hinge-leafed plants, the parasite-filled cities on their surfaces crushed within into nutritious gloop. Or some kind of vast continent eater, happily devouring the bare rock of the cosmos, being repulsed by a thin mimetic layer of pseudo-life plating the silicon mind beneath. Though scientifically intriguing, neither thought was reassuring when you were standing in the midst of the speculation.

The activity was slower now, though. Perhaps the creature needed the sun, or maybe dropping a hundred tonnes of metal on it had effectively stunned it. All the more reason to establish its nature now, while he had the chance. That was what science was for. If you trusted it, it took away the bad dreams of fantasy, and replaced them with the bad light of day. The light of day could be conquered.

He shouted back into the lander, 'Establish a holding field. I want to sever all contact between a portion of this stuff and the rest. Then – we're going to experiment.'

If it could make trees, make hills, paint the slow meanders and ox-bow lakes of streams, maybe it could make anything. Maybe it and not the cosmic debris from the white hole would be the treasure trove of this trade mission. His people's treasure trove.

Christina felt the mud ooze between her toes and hence deduced the rupture of her extremely expensive hand-tooled 100-per-cent-guaranteed waterproof boots. The guarantee issuer was thirty-five light years away, but if he had seen into her mind at that moment, he'd have started packing then and there.

The others were no better off. Alex in particular was frantic with fear. Tento took things more stolidly, but even he moved at near panic speed as the scout ship sank rapidly into the mire, lurching as another bubble of stinking mud burst under it.

'Just the survival gear, the detectors and the radios!' Christina shouted, seeing Alex trying to fit a whole scout's worth of contingency equipment into his backpack.

The ship trembled again, up to the hip joints of its landing gear and showing no sign of stopping its heavy descent. Christina grabbed Alex and pushed him out of the hatch. Tento, chest-deep in the stuff, let the humans clamber over him to firmer ground before dragging himself out. The abanak were strong critters.

'Shit,' Christina said, as they lay on the grass by the side of the marsh, watching their three tonnes of scout blowing bubbles of air as it sank

Tento waded back to the scout and managed to close the hatch before more of the peculiarly fecund mud could seep inside.

Sealed, the whole thing went under, only a couple of yards from where she and Alex lay gasping air tainted with the putrid penetrating smell of the marsh. Christina could hear Alex swearing to himself in a breathy whiny voice, damning the sensors that had detected solid ground to hell and back. Christina knew how he felt. It wasn't possible to have lost the scout ship in a muddy puddle, but it happened.

She sat up and brushed her hair back, feeling the horrible tension in her muscles crying out for a scream. She didn't. 'Alex, get on the radio and alert the ship. No more landings till we know what just happened. Check that Vuim-Captain and the factory lander are OK. If they're in trouble we may want to cut our losses.'

'Well, we can't afford to lose a scout ship!' Alex said, his hands shaking as he fiddled with the radio. His tense, high voice held the promise of crippling hysteria – the sort you had to slap. 'You know how much those things cost? How much that's going to cut into our shares?'

'The scout's sealed for space. We may be able to dig it out with ship's equipment later when it's safe to land another force.' She got to her feet. 'Let's try to make the most of our situation. Do what we came here to do –'

'How?' Alex shouted. 'All the wampum and shiny baubles are in the scout!'

Christina nodded at Tento. 'We've got Mr Smooth Talker. And I've got my winning ways. Come on, Alex. Let's go see if we can turn a profit here.'

'Oh God, oh God,' he said, shaking the radio. 'I can't get through. There's no signal. Oh God!'

Tento snatched it from him and began to manipulate the controls with his chubby pink digits, showing more finesse and somehow less patience with the instrument, while Christina loomed over his shoulder. But after a few moments he concurred with Alex.

'Perhaps there is something in this area blocking the signal,' he suggested. He gave both of them the trademark abanak smile, Buddha-like and yet outrageously toothy. The smile that made his people such valuable trade associates. There was nothing quite as good at clinching a bargain with humans as a big, grinning, friendly, cartoon hippopotamus. The abanak were an ad man's dream.

'You think that's it?' Alex asked, grasping at the hope.

'Must be,' Christina said. She gave the still twitching Alex her best 'relax, Christina's in charge' smile, the one reserved for lovers and underlings. 'Look. Whatever happens, at least we can make sure our pick-up is from dry ground.'

With a last 'hup, hup, huzzah', the crowd melted away but for the four brawny lads who had hoisted Fitz atop their shoulders. Where had they sprung up from? He couldn't remember seeing them in the crowd, and they were half a head at least taller then the average shopkeeper. For that matter he couldn't remember putting the wolf cloak on, but there it was, horrible mangy thing. Warm, though.

The old man waved to him as he was borne away, a little gradual wave like the ones the royal family gave, a salute from a person who was always waving and who had pared the act down to a few indicative motions. Weren't people in folk tales always being rewarded by kings in disguise? Rewarded, or horribly punished. He thought of the hanged woman. The sound of the knife cutting through her dead flesh, the jerk of the legs, and the creak of the rope –

OK. Get a grip, Fitz. This was a raw society; there was a death penalty. But the Stepmother graffito nagged at him. Was it a crime to be a stepmother? Of course they were always *bad* in stories but even so…

The young men bent their knees and lowered him in front of… a pub! This was more like it. It was a wattle-and-daub building with muddy plaster covering the wood between the thick beams that made its skeleton, the sort of pub that Victorians would paint black and white, and that in Fitz's own time would have been called 'Ye Olde Coaching Inn' and filled with knock-off real ales. This pub had a sign as well: THE SINGING BONE. There was no picture, just the words in a lettering that screamed Gothic. An image of the troll on the ladder seeking his gruesome prize, singing his cheerful song, hit Fitz again. He hoped this wasn't some kind of troll pub. But no, his sense of humour asserted, that'd probably be called The Bridge Club.

Making as gracious a farewell to the carriers as he could – he half expected them to demand a drink, and he still hadn't any money – he pushed the door of the pub inward. He knew Anji and the Doctor would be waiting for him with pursed lips and sarcasm but he was cold and shaken, and by all that was holy he was going to get a drink if he had to recount half *The Lord of The Rings* or as many *Goon Show* jokes as he could recast in a medieval setting. He heard a clink and looked down. There on the threshold was a shiny copper coin. He slid the toe of his shoe over it, and held the door open for two men smelling wonderfully sour from drink just on their way out. Then he bent down casually as if to tie his shoe (even though it wasn't the tying sort), neatly palmed the coin and walked into the pub with money to spend.

Inside the light was thick and amber. And there were swords on the wall. Not rusted, ploughshare beaten things belonging to someone's grandfather, but bright shiny swords freshly hammered and crying out to be taken down.

In a flurry of fists and sloshing drinks someone at the bar shouted, 'That's a stepmothering lie! I'll break your stepmothering face, you toad kisser!'

Ah. Fitz grinned. *Well, I'll be a son of a stepmother.* Wrapped in the odorous warmth of the wolf hide, he stepped up to the bar. There was nothing quite like the sound of a coin slapped on to a countertop.

'A pint, if you please.'

'Pint o' what?'

'Ale?'

'If that's what you want, mate.'

Fitz pushed the coin towards the man with a fingertip. Having no idea what it was worth he added, 'And soup?'

The man flicked a glance at the coin. 'Got mutton stew.'

'Bread?'

'Well, o' course bread! How else you gonna sop if off the platter?'

He shoved a mug across the counter and Fitz caught it, the ale sloshing a little over his hand. 'Madel!' the landlord bellowed. 'Fella out here wants some stew!'

And, lo, there was stew! It appeared in an entirely normal fashion, on a dull-coloured plate plonked unceremoniously by the landlord on to the bar top. But the bounty it represented to Fitz – and all from one copper coin – made its appearance almost miraculous. Brown and thick and greasy, with lumps of things that might be meat and might not, but if the stew tasted the way it smelled he'd be very happy. Half a loaf of bread sat on top, already soaking up the gravy. Unbelievably, there was change from his coin: three smaller copper pieces. He left the change on the bar and carried his food and drink to the end of a long plank table in front of the stone hearth. The logs burned with a mellow crackle, but even though it was the warmest place to sit, there weren't many people taking advantage of it. Maybe the smoke would become irritating in time, but Fitz needed the heat too much to care. Two young men dressed in plush fabrics sat at the opposite end arguing in terse, quiet voices over some maps and what looked like a locket.

As soon as Fitz sat down his mind began the automatic check list of necessary pretences required when in the presence of women. Other than the woman who'd dished up the stew and a hump-backed ugly old witch, there weren't any. Registering the all-clear, he took four gulps of the ale, delivered a satisfied 'ah', and after a moment's consideration, wiped his mouth on his shirtsleeve. The wolf's hide looked far too accustomed to such treatment, but there was no way his mouth was coming anywhere near it. He picked up the wooden spoon in one hand and a hunk of bread in the other and started shovelling the stew into his mouth. It was salty, but that was to be expected. Public house fare, after all. He tipped the mug, eyeing the level of remaining ale for rationing purposes. Three bites, then a swallow, three more bites, a couple of gulps, then the rest of the bread, then –

'*Murder-ed –*'

Fitz jumped, tipping most of his precious ale on to the table.

'*Murder-ed, oh murder-ed. My brother, he hath killed me dead.*'

The voice was a high-pitched, singsong whisper that raised the hair at the back of his neck. It sounded as if the speaker was standing right behind him, but he was afraid to turn around. None of the other patrons seemed to have heard the voice. The two princely sorts at the other end of the table saw him looking at them, and nodded stiffly before continuing their discussion. Almost everyone else was deep in cups and conversation. Obviously, he was hearing things. He gazed at the stew. Maybe it contained strange herbs that affected him because he had a different metabolism from everyone else here. He could almost see the table starting to melt –

'*MURDERED! SLAIN!*'

This time the screech made everyone jump. The proprietor muttered a curse, came out from behind the counter and headed straight for Fitz.

'We're in for foul weather,' he commented.

'Snow, you reckon?' someone asked.

'Too cold for snow,' another offered.

'*A LAMB TO THE SLAUGHTER!*'

Another man chuckled. 'He was never a lamb.'

The barman grabbed the poker from the hearth, and crawled up on the table. 'Excuse me, sir, I've just got to…'

Fitz remained seated – mostly because his clenched cheeks were glued to the bench. But he ventured a glance up. Lodged crossways between the rafters was a long dark shape blackened from smoke, full of cracks and holes.

'*MURDERED FOR OUR FATHER'S GOLD –*' the thing wailed.

'Shut up,' the barman grunted. He prodded it with the poker until it shifted a little. 'Singing bone my fat arse. I wish it *would* sing for a change. There. That ought to do it – my goodness, sir, you're as white as a sheet. You all right there?'

Fitz gulped. 'That's – that's a very big bone.'

'Well, in fact, Tobb wasn't all that big as giants go. Runt o' the litter.'

'His brother really killed him?'

'Aye. Years ago. The brother stays away 'cuz o' the bone, see? And it only gets loud when the weather turns bad, like I said.' He climbed down from the table, but kept the poker in hand in case the bone needed another knock.

'There's other things'll make it sing, Caspar,' one of the regulars ventured. 'Old Uncle says he saw fire fall out of the sky two days ago. And there's a new forest sprung up west of the river.'

'Forests come and go. Everyone knows that –'

From her stool in a dim corner the witch began to cackle. Several men cringed, as if her laughter were shrivelling their man-parts.

'Everyone knows. Everyone knows. Bones don't sing when a forest grows.'

'What are you on about, witch?' the barman asked irritably.

'New forest for new creatures. None too bright these creatures, either.'

All eyes turned to Fitz. There was a moment of uncertainty, suspicion, then –

'Nothing new about a fool youngest son on a quest.'

'Not him. A lady. Brown as a nut, sloe-eyed, dressed in fine cloth, though no fashion you've ever seen. High and mighty and thinkin' herself cleverer'n me. Made a bargain with the black coach, she did.' The witch cackled again. 'Easiest gold I ever made.'

Oh God. Anji!

Fitz leapt up, sending the wooden bench clattering to the floor. 'What?' He'd lost Anji! 'Where did it take her?'

'What'll you give me for saying?'

'How about I don't break your –'

'Mind your words, son,' the barman said quietly, his fingers digging hard into Fitz's shoulder, 'else you end your days trying to convince pretty girls to kiss a toad's lips. Believe me there's plenty of princes get squashed beneath the wheels of an ox cart long before that ever happens. And you're no prince under that wolf skin. Not yet.'

Fitz looked at the witch. Her black eyes glittered in gleeful anticipation. He knew against all reason that if a forest could grow in an instant and a woman be married to a dog by day and a man by night, then he could easily be made a toad or worse. That would certainly be of no help to anyone, least of all Anji, probably terrified and on her way to God knew where, for God knew what.

'I don't have any money left,' he admitted frankly. He'd left the change for a tip and the small sum would probably only insult her Witch-ness anyway.

'You and your lady friend are in the same boat, then. Give me your cloak and I'll tell you.'

He heard the collective indrawn breaths of the men in the pub. Their eyes slid away from him as if under some compulsion not to aid him in this apparently important decision.

He met her gaze and forced a smile to his lips. 'I'll take my chances with the cloak, thanks just the same.'

The barman patted him on the back. 'Good lad.'

Which was very little comfort when the Bone screamed 'MURDER-ED!' as he grabbed the bread from his plate on his way out the door.

* * *

'Doctor Know-All!'

The King was shaking the Doctor's hand with despairing enthusiasm, and gazing at his face like a puppy, albeit a puppy with round glasses and a crown. 'A great comfort to know a man of your renown is on the case. I really cannot govern without the Princess's sage counsel, you know. She has the common touch, beloved by all.' He dug a would-be matey elbow into the Doctor's ribs. 'I've never had the knack, really. Thought it would be a bit more like tailoring, what with joining different pieces of the kingdom together and making them fit nicely. But there are some cloths that don't work together without you wax your thread or bind the seams. That's my dear Ebonyblack.'

'The wax on your thread?'

'Well…' the King said, less certain of the metaphor given the Doctor's curious rephrasing, 'she certainly, er, binds the seams of conflicts and the like. She's beloved by all, as I've said. And now that you've seen her, I hope, no, I *trust,* you have good news for me.'

The Doctor had perked up a bit at the welcome, which didn't seem to reconcile with the guard's hands-on approach, though how he'd got renown in so short a time troubled him. Still, he thought it best to choose his next words carefully. He didn't want to give the wrong impression, or meet the beast. Well, not yet anyway, not without a bit more research.

'I'm not sure I can do anything for your daughter –'

Behind the humble sincerity of the glasses, the King's eyes suddenly flashed red. The Doctor blinked. Surely a trick of the light like the red-eye in every photo he'd taken between 1970 and 1990. It was a very convincing trick, however – 'without a more detailed account of the circumstances surrounding her condition,' he finished smoothly.

'Of course. You will find a full account in the tower of the former Court Magician.'

'The, ah, former Magician?'

'Oh yes. Horrible scrawny man. I never liked the cut of his jib, you know, even if he claimed to have studied at Sighs. He couldn't cure her so I had to… mmm… let him go. That was just before I made these leather trousers. Tanned the skin myself.' He stroked the leather over one chubby thigh, admiring his handiwork, compelling the Doctor to look more closely at the grain and texture. The little King grinned. 'I know you'll do better than he, within the next three days in fact, before the thorn has grown back fully. Why, your title alone assures me that my darling girl will be up and about in no time.'

On the *Bonaventure*'s bridge, superfluous to the crew's busy rushing, and yet unable to be uninvolved in it, William Brok cursed himself for refusing Christina's invitation to join the scouting party. Not that he could have made a difference on the surface of the planet – he'd spent scarcely six months on the surface of one in the past twenty years – but he was a good pilot and might have brought the little scout down safely. Instead, it may have crashed. It was impossible to know. All the remote telemetry could tell them was that the scout's radio beacon had gone dead – despite being a locked black-box unit designed to send a standard shifting-frequency signal! After it had been silenced there had been nothing from Christina or her crew, although they should have had portable communicators able to punch a signal up to the *Bonaventure*.

There had been plenty of reports from Vuim-Captain and the lander team. But William hadn't decided yet whether they made sense. If a human crew had reported the things the vuim had, he'd have assumed they'd rigged a still in the oxygen catalysis pipes and got roaring drunk. But the vuim had a stick-in-the-mud reputation these days, so the abanak insisted, and Christina's scouting party wasn't answering calls to contradict them. *She* hadn't radioed in a cock-and-bull story about landing on a planet that seemed repulsed by their presence, but that was only because *she* hadn't radioed in. What if they'd tried the vuim's trick and failed? William wondered. Scouts were far less solid than factory landers. They could have shattered the scout on the planet's rocks. He was surprised how much the idea hurt him. He hadn't known her long. And he was thinking of her in the past tense.

Timtangle seemed quite willing to let the situation lie for a few days. Giving his hippo head a dour shake he said, 'If they are dead, we cannot help. If they need help, we cannot find them to give it if they're unable to pinpoint their location. We must school ourselves to waiting. We have the picket satellites to establish, the nebula to guard. If another ship blunders through we must dart out to send off our claims willy-nilly and then rush back. We dare not land more people without more information, and we do not have enough crew to search a whole world without it.'

William knew he was right, but it didn't make him feel any better. He wondered what was going through the minds of Christina's party right now.

He only hoped it wasn't a scavenger.

Fitz squinted at the card, trying to read it by the light of faint stars that were only just poking their way through the leaden clouds in the night sky. There was precious little other light to read by.

'Out to lunch,' the card said. Fitz cursed as he tore it up, and then scowled at this own pettiness. He saw the other cards lying to one side. They read THE DOCTOR IS IN, and CLOSED FOR THE DAY.

There was no one around that Fitz could ask about where the Doctor had actually gone and he was certain old Know-All's departure had something to do with his having found trouble – or being the cause of it.

He slid down until he was sitting with his back against the rickety clapboards of the stall. The wolf's head drew up over his own, a grim snaggle-toothed hood that plunged both vision and mind further into darkness.

What the hell was he going to do now?

He heard the soft squelch of horse hooves in the mud, but didn't look up until someone said, 'There he is.'

Even through shadows of his hood, their finery sparkled. It was the two rich young men from the pub. 'You, boy. A word if you please.'

Boy? He was at least ten years older than either of them and in no mood to be lorded over by poncy little twerps in velvet knickers.

'You *really* don't want me to come over there right now.'

There was a whispered dialogue between them. Then, 'We've a proposition for you.'

'Yeah? Well, make it fast. I'm trying to think here.'

One of them jerked on his reins, and his mount danced sideways with a snort of pain and protest. 'Come on, then, Gilfred, I told you he was too dull to be of use –'

Fitz got slowly to his feet. He felt very tall and powerful all of a sudden. Gilfred's horse shied back nervously. 'Do you have something useful to say? Because if not, bugger off.'

'I am Prince Gilfred and this is my brother Prince Ansel. We journey to the Castle of Sighs and are in need someone to lead our pack animal, carry the lantern, cook for us, that sort of thing.'

'And you're telling me because…?'

'You want to find out where a black coach has taken someone. Such questions often find answers at the Castle of Sighs. It will be hard travel, but we can pay.'

Fitz gazed at them through the eerie half-cage of the wolf's teeth. Something about these two raised the hackles at the back of his neck; they were always whispering together like conspirators. But as he scratched his neck he realised the feeling might only be the result of vermin living in the cloak, and no doubt they had private matters to discuss sometimes, as any brothers might. 'How long will this journey take?'

'Two days,' Ansel said.

'But we must leave tonight if we wish to stay ahead of the

weather,' Gilfred added.

Now that he'd had a moment to consider, the proposition seemed like his best option. Without the Doctor, and with no way to find him, it was best he took action to find Anji himself.

He glanced back at the stall and the tattered sign flapping in a cold breeze. *Doctor Bloody Know-All.* 'All right,' he said. 'I just need to leave a note for my friend.' Unfortunately there was not enough paint left on the tiny brush to finish his note, and he hadn't noticed it in time to compose a good three-word message. Fitz could only hope the Doctor would read volumes in 'Gone to find...'

The room to which the guards showed the Doctor was five-sided and stood at the top of a tower – one of several on the market side of the castle. One wall had a door to the stairwell and the others a window each. From those windows he could see, in order of rotation, sky and, below, outhouse roofs; more sky and part of a buttress running down with thrusting spikes of thorn – making it the Princess's tower; a wall of stone, an apparently brand-new construction scant inches away and blocking the view of pretty much anything but down – *really* far down; and, lastly, the market – mostly packed up now as dusk fell.

Luckily, the shutters opened inwards, so he opted for the window with the new building close to it, trying to get his arm around between the window and the wall. Yes, just about. He could feel that the mortar between the stones was still damp. If he could pry out some stones and get into another tower, hook this shutter fixed behind him with a bit of wire and leave the other windows tightly shuttered, he'd give a first-class magic impression when the guards couldn't find him. His shoulder, however, refused to co-operate, being broader than the gap, and, anyway, if the guards couldn't find him the King might have a nice new weskit made out of their hides instead of his. He'd have to think of something else.

He turned his attention to the inside of the room. A long thin bed occupied one whole length of wall, the sheets nicely new and tucked in hard at the corners. He made a mental note to tip any maids who might be passing. A wooden table along the next wall was cut so that a diagonal insert accommodated the end of the bed. It was as untidy as the bed was neat. Something bothered him about the haphazard pile of thuribles, alembics, astrolabes, yarrow stalks and mismatched tarot cards – what maid would have left such a mess on the table and the bed so spic and span unless she was under instructions to do so? He pushed it all on to the bed. Under the mess was a curved crystal surface set into the wood. The Doctor gave it a half-hearted tap, and actually jumped a little when it rang with a fine bell-like tone. 'Well, well, well, what have we here?' He grinned. 'Now whatever would a court magician be doing with a glass table like this?'

'He would be watching the world and those moving about in it,' the glass (or maybe the table) said (the Doctor hadn't been able to make a distinction aurally). He'd never been much for table talk, or séances and table-rapping for that matter, not since those nice ladies had shown him how they'd made the noise by dislocating their toes, but he'd have to be mad to chat with furniture. Willingly surrendering a little sanity to the exhilaration of discovery, he pulled a wooden chair across the floor and, steepling his fingers, leaned over the table, a look of rapt contemplation on his face. Light from deep in the crystal lit his face from below, making his brows beetling and solemn – at least he hoped it did. No point dealing with spirits if you couldn't look like a sorcerer.

'Is there anyone in there?' he intoned, unclasping his hands to do a quick set of hopefully impressive gestures.

'Yes, of course there is. Don't be such a fool.' The voice was louder now, and a distinctly irascible note had crept into it. 'I am the spirit of the crystal globe. I see all! I recount all!'

The Doctor looked into the depths, reminded of his attempt to see the Princess through the glass coffin. The face in this glass was much less pleasant and he was grateful for the distortion rather than regretful. The face was green and warty, with tiny tufts of hair sprouting out at random points. The points being mostly warts. The exceptions being, the Doctor hoped, ears. 'What can you recount for me?' he asked.

'Anything! Everything! That is, anything upon this world or above it. Ask me not of spheres mortals should not plumb.'

The Doctor gave the face a hard stare. Real spirit or not, this sort of instant limitation smacked of confidence-trickery. 'Above it, then. Show me something interesting. Show me a sight!'

'Nothing easier.' The face in the glass looked smug. Above it a picture began to form. Six lights fell from the heavens, burning and scorching their way across the sky. 'These fell upon the world not so long back, but one fell before these six, alone and curse-bearing.' The picture shifted to a scarlet-robed young warrior – a prince, the Doctor decided – borne upon a bier. A man with a long white beard leaned over the body and shook his head. As the image focused in the Doctor could see that the Prince's lips were moving. It was a difficult bit of lip-reading but the Doctor thought the Prince was running over again and again the colour of his wife's eyes. Unless she was related to Argos, the thousand-eyed watcher set by Hera to protect nymphs from Jove, the Doctor doubted that the Prince had it quite right. Or maybe he was remembering differently, seeing differently.

'How many eyes did his wife have?' he asked the glass.

'He didn't have a wife,' the smug frog snorted. 'They found him raving in the meadows beyond the thorn. He dreamed, and dreams, that he rescued Princess Ebonyblack; but cannot agree how or where they live, nor see the folk around him though he cries out for them, or greets them one moment then mourns their deaths the next.'

The Doctor bit the back of a finger nervously. He felt this ought to mean something, something dangerous. 'Is he the only one? You said there were seven fire falls?'

'Oh yes, great danger I'd warrant,' the glass spirit said unctuously. 'Pity you're cooped up here, nice young doctor like you, lots of good you could be doing out there. Princess ain't going nowheres, and you've only got three days at that.'

'Yes, yes. I know, and usually the horse talks but what if it doesn't? I don't want to be some monarch's knitting pattern.' The Doctor looked slyly into the glass. 'I can't help but feel you're dying to suggest something. This *is* a sales pitch, isn't it?'

'Oh, Doctor Know-All, one showman to another, I only want my freedom. This glass is too cramped. Break it and I will convey us both from this place. I've been here since I was a tiny sprite. I'd like to see the world.'

The Doctor smiled. The power of advertising was evidently strong here. That was why the King was so certain he could help – they were taking him at his own estimation. And what was wrong with that? After all, if *he* wasn't certain he'd be all right, who would be? He started to look around for something heavy, continuing the conversation over his shoulder. 'Do you promise not to pull me straight down to hell, like some nasty long-leggedy beast?' he asked, tossing a lead model of a gryphon from hand to hand.

'Sprite's honour!' the thing in the glass said.

'Hmm.'

Now *that* looked promising. He raised a large rune-covered black sword over his head. 'Ready?'

'No, no, no!' the thing squeaked. 'Not that one. Use a blunt instrument for Belesia's sake! I'll have glass in my hair for weeks if you smash it to flinders.'

'How about this?' The Doctor waved a stout walking staff, the head of which had been carved into a grinning gargoyle.

'Fine, will you get on with it?'

The Doctor drew back the stick and brought it down hard on the crystal.

From the shattering hail of glass, an evil chuckling arose, and a whiff of sulphur and brimstone suffused the room.

The Doctor looked at the tiny hairy figure with a mixture of surprise and amusement.

'Sorry about that,' the creature muttered. 'You try spending seven long years in an item of domestic furniture with delusions of prophesy and see how smelly you get. I know I could have taken fish in the flood, but I just can't bear scales.' He coughed again, and his cough sounded exactly like an evil snigger.

'You aren't a spirit?'

'Yus, spot on, that Know-All. I'm a gnome right strictly sub-lunar. Know any maidens turned bottles crying aloud for corks, then I'm your man, squire.' He twisted round, beard bristling. 'Did you hear that?'

'I didn't hear anything.'

'Thought I heard a cat. The Duke of Sighs used to hunt gnomes with a pack of trained cats. That's how I ended up here.'

'Hiding?'

'No. Caught. Not paid me gnomage you see, avoiding the gnoll tax. Duke's out for his due, the bastard.'

The Doctor wondered if 'bastard' was a purely technical term. He decided not to ask. Instead he rubbed his hands. 'So whisk us away, then!' He sat on the bed like a small boy waiting for a conjurer to do a trick.

The gnome belched. 'Give us a chance. I've been in a glass for nine years in the form of a green-faced pollywog. I've got to get me breath back. In fact I think I'll do it in the morning. I hope you don't snore.' And he hopped into the far corner of the bed and proceeded to hog the blanket.

'Hang on,' the Doctor said, 'didn't you say seven years just now?'

Chapter Five
How the Sisters Got Their First Wish

Anji was riding a choo-choo train through a magical forest at Disneyland. It was a guided tour of some kind, en route to Sleeping Beauty's castle. She'd never been to Disneyland before and she wanted to get off the train and visit the shops. She could have easily jumped off because the little train was moving so slowly, but no one was allowed to leave. She could reach out and touch the trees as the train passed. They felt real. They felt *too* real, which for some reason meant that they weren't. Above the arching branches she could see the spires of the castle, glowing in that rosy-hued way typical of Disney. But there was something crawling on the spires, veins of smoky black, twisting up and around. Every so often a glint of starlight sparked off a needle of jet, and she realised suddenly she could see in the dark, and shuddered. The towers kept stretching themselves upward, higher and higher, as if trying to escape a relentless fungus, until they were so high she couldn't see the tops any more. And the closer the train got to the towers the thicker and darker the forest seemed to get. The strange gangrenous growth that was strangling the towers was moving through the forest as well, swallowing up the dark light that only she could see by. She looked around at the other tourists, but they didn't seem to notice anything amiss. She called out to the driver. 'Stop the train! We'll never make it through!' The driver turned around. It was the Doctor. He touched the peak of his cap and smiled. 'It's a thorny problem, miss,' he said. 'But I'm afraid the only way *out* is *through*.'

She awoke to the same claustrophobic darkness that had lured her to sleep. Not that she'd wanted to sleep. After she'd been pulled inside, still clutching the box to her chest, sleep had sort of hit her over the head. Now this sudden sightless consciousness brought her heart leaping to her throat. Were the invisible arms that had dragged her through the window attached to a creature sitting right beside her in the Stygian black of the coach? Was it waiting for her to wake up so it could do something horrible? She listened with the stone silence of a child for the scritch of monster claws beneath the bed, the wishing box held beneath her chin like an old quilt. An image of the Doctor from her dream smiled at her again, telling her the only way out was through. Well, screw that! She wanted out now. She wanted him to save her, not be smug and say cryptic wise things in dreams. Her mind hammered out a mantra of *I hate you I hate you I hate you*, while the child within tried to squeak out 'Daddy' loud enough to be heard, though not loud enough for the monster to realise she was awake and aware.

But, unlike a child, she knew this mess was entirely her own making. Much as she tried to convince herself she'd only wanted the wishing box to help them get back to the TARDIS, it was a lie and she couldn't escape that any more than she could escape –

Oh. The coach had stopped moving. Adult common sense began to reassert itself. She started groping about, tentatively at first, then punching blindly at whatever might be in there with her. But after a few moments of hitting the sides, the ceiling, the seat next to her, in front, and behind, she soon realised she was quite alone. Outside a lark began to sing. The door opened with a pneumatic hiss on to the cool grey of morning. Anji rubbed her eyes against the sudden light and then nearly fell on her face in her scramble to get out. A whip cracked, the horses leapt forward and in seconds the black coach was a smudge on the horizon. She picked herself up and found herself standing in a yard of pebbles and dew-speckled grass. A round stone well stood to her right, a patch of cabbages to her left. In front of her, ordered rows of tulips, their petals blood red, edged the cottage like stiff pleats on a petticoat ruffle.

When the witch had said 'cottage' Anji had assumed something more along the lines of the little house Snow White had happily and slavishly tended for the seven dwarves. This was more the sprawling country estate of landed gentry sporting a quaint cottage façade.

Worse, she discovered that her expensive woollen overcoat and perfectly tailored trousers had been replaced with a skirt, a shapeless blouse and a very dirty apron. And much, much worse, her fingers were now clenched around a plain wooden box with dented corners, bent hinges and a rusted lock.

Before she'd quite got her head around that, six sets of shutters were thrown open from the second-storey windows. From each window a face looked out. They were not the faces of innocent little girls, but the faces of big girls with attitudes.

The children had found the little cottage in the clearing and were nibbling the icing on the windowsill when the pink hippopotamus came out of the woods. 'Little children, little children, come away from the cottage! There is a great and mysterious power within and I fear for your lives.'

Though the children were very hungry, they did as he bade them, for he seemed to have their best interests at heart. He showed them his scrying glass and said, 'This marvel has guided me here. I must take the magick it shows me back to my people who cannot prosper without it.' So kindly did he seem that the children could not help but ask, 'Please, Hippopotamus, sir, when you have done that, will you show us the way home, for this forest is so dark and we have lost our way, and our father must certainly be worried by now.' He patted them on their fair heads with his funny three-fingered hand and said, 'You are dear little children, and I will help you if I can.' Then he opened the door of the cottage and went inside. Just then the door slammed tight behind him and the cottage seemed to lick its lips. They heard a terrible cry from within and the smell of cake changed to the smell of roast pig. A man who was friend to the hippopotamus and who had been hiding, howled in terror and ran away. The frightened children ran after him, calling, 'Please, sir, can you not show us the way home?' But the man vanished into the trees and the children could not find him though they searched high and low.

'Morning,' the gnome shouted. 'I took the liberty of relocating us in your sleep. Thought you'd find that less disturbing what with the Crystal Labyrinth and the Fifty-Five-Fold Abyss and all that malarkey. Weird angles looking at you funny and never being able to see a jelly without shuddering.'

The Doctor sat up on a grassy bank. He looked around, and broke into a giant smile. 'I know a bank where the wild thyme grows.' He nodded at the gnome. 'Thank you. I was wondering if you could do it. I was expecting to be carried down a sheer wall in my sleep by means of a rope made out of bedclothes.'

The gnome looked affronted. 'Just 'cause I'm not a bloody sprite.'

'No, really, I can't help feeling I shouldn't believe in you at all. You're unexplained, you see, and I'd hate to think you were inexplicable.'

'Oh, but I am. My old mum had this dictionary. I'm "Inexplicable Blessing Wottlewort" – and if you fancy laughing I'm also a bantam-weight boxer!'

'That's the same weight as a chicken, isn't it?' the Doctor asked absently. He was feeling quite light-headed. He ought to be looking for Anji and Fitz, and he ought to be looking into those lights from the sky. But really the sky looked blue enough to be safe.

'Don't move.'

The voice was brittle, strained, nervous. The gun jiggled in a slack-handed grip, but the trigger finger looked tight. The Doctor felt he'd know a gun if it was pointed at him a mile away behind a lead screen, but even so he couldn't remember if this sort had a stun setting. Its owner looked as if he'd been stunned himself, though. He was a tall, gangly man in space-wear with a dark beard that made his chin look like the tip of a knife. Standard-issue fatigues with a belt and a backpack – might be military, might be commercial. Might be from four or five different centuries allowing for ups and downs in technology and backwater worlds.

'My name is Alex Volpe,' he snarled. 'You're going to get me away from this mad world.'

Fitz walked behind the Princes on their fine mounts, leading the sorry, sway-backed little donkey by a rope. And no wonder it was sway-backed. These guys didn't know the meaning of travelling light.

He'd listened to their conversations the previous night with interest, and today with a yawning boredom. The clomping rhythm of the animals' hooves and the self-concerned exchange of dialogue between the two Princes lulled him into a numb half-conscious state. He was aware, for instance, that somewhere at the end of his legs were two blistered feet, burning with the cold and shuffling leadenly along the path that was supposed to be a short cut that would connect them up with the main road within a few miles of the Castle of Sighs. Above the close branches of the trees he could see that the sky had become a dull, soft grey.

He'd learned, however, that the brothers were headed to this Castle of Sighs in order to find a method to break the spell on the Sleeping Princess. He'd seen her portrait in the locket they carried. She looked sweet and pretty, even if the proportions of her face were a little skewed by the hasty rendering. One of the Princes fully intended to claim the reward of her hand in marriage, and once they got to the castle the competition between them would be in full swing and gloves would be coming off. Ansel had a hard edge and hot temper that even his annoyingly sunlit, perfectly windblown, artfully tousled locks could not disguise. Fitz knew many women found that sort of thing appealing. Drawn to the looks, the implied danger, they would be charmed, wooed easily, used ruthlessly and dropped as casually as Ansel had dropped a half-eaten, mealy apple at the side of the road. And no doubt, if he won the prize, the Princess would become one of those sad little queens who spent their days awaiting (or perhaps dreading) the infrequent attentions of their philandering husbands. Gilfred was harder to read. Sporting a ruby earring and beat-poet goatee that Fitz might, once upon a time, have secretly envied, Gilfred was outwardly friendly, almost gracious, but his words and gestures revealed almost nothing of his character. Fitz suspected that while Ansel would perform the derring-do, Gilfred would somehow manage to reap the rewards.

At the moment he couldn't care less of course. It was merely an exercise to occupy his mind and keep him from thinking about his feet, about the return of gnawing hunger, his need to urinate and about how much he didn't want to duck into the forest to do it. This forest, though apparently well travelled and certainly not sprung up from nowhere, made him feel as if they were being watched constantly. He had enough trouble using the gents' facilities at Victoria station. He decided to bite the bullet a while longer and eat the crust of bread he had left from his unfinished meal at the pub – which was akin to the same thing.

As he was digging around for his feast, the Princes rounded a bend in the path and disappeared from view. He realised this only when he heard the sounds of a mild altercation from up ahead. He urged the donkey into motion and hurried as fast as the animal would let him to see what was going on.

An old woman – no, the very same old woman that the Doctor had carried over the stream – was sitting on a rock at the edge of a much smaller stream, pleading with the two men on horses. She looked weak now, her skin as grey as her hair, and he could see her breath puffing out as it rattled from her sunken chest.

'Surely you've something you can share with a starving old granny?'

'I'm afraid we've nothing left, my good woman,' Gilfred said.

Fitz's mouth dropped open. There was a leather pack full of dried meat and fruit on the donkey he led. He'd fully intended to pilfer a little of it later if they hadn't offered any to him the next time they stopped to rest the animals.

Ansel growled impatiently, digging his spurs into his horse's sides. He trotted off, barely acknowledging the woman. Gilfred reached into the pouch on his belt and tossed a tiny copper coin at her feet. 'I'm terribly sorry, but we're in a bit of a hurry. Fitz!' Startled, Fitz drew his hand from the food pack. Gilfred's eyes were dark with an unspoken threat. 'We must put on speed now. There's a storm coming and it's best if we were out of the woods before it hits.' Then he too spurred his horse and followed his brother down the path, turning his back on both the old woman and a shocked and seething Fitz.

What utter bastards! Defiantly he thrust his hand into the leather bag again and then, with a start of panic, felt around its empty insides. Dear God, they were right. There wasn't anything left! He looked at the woman, apologetically. She bent down to pick up the coin with stiff fingers, and sat turning it back and forth, thoughtfully resigned to her fate. There was no way she'd make it to anywhere she could spend the coin in her weakened condition. He looked at the bread in his other hand and then handed it to her.

'I'm really sorry. This is all I have.'

She gazed up at him and smiled. 'Bless you, sir. It'll do.'

'Fitz!' came Gilfred's cry from ahead. He winced.

'Sorry, sorry. I have to go. You should try to find shelter soon.'

'You as well. There is a storm coming. Watch your back, child. Watch your back.'

With that warning in his head, the snow began to swirl around him in fat, lazy flakes as he hurried to catch up with the brothers.

'It was the oven,' Alex said. 'It smelled of cake. Marzipan, you know, and that heavy icing they use for wedding cakes – at least, at first. Tento thought he'd tracked the energy signature into the cottage but there was just this vast pot-bellied stove in there. I – I saw it through the window. And it – it *licked* him inside it, this – this – this great big tongue the colour of lead. And he *burned* – and he was screaming that awful way people will, you know, that way – then I couldn't smell cake any more –'

For a moment he was silent, reliving the horror he'd seen, his eyes jiggling back and forth in their sockets. Then he fixed the Doctor with a look of cold despair.

'We're from a ship, you know, a starship. Trading between the worlds, but I've lost our captain in the woods, and something's going to eat Mr Tento when he's quite, quite done. So you see you have to help me. You just appeared from nowhere, so you must have technology. Technology or something. I can't stay here. Please, don't make me hurt you.'

The Doctor moved closer towards him, motioning the gnome to move away to the side. Inexplicable needed no further bidding but threw himself into a gorse bush with a muffled yelp.

'Give me the gun,' the Doctor said, keeping his voice even. 'I know you don't want to hurt anyone. And no one wants to hurt you, not here, not now. I'm looking to understand this world and to free my own ship. If you choose to put down the gun I promise I'll help you get back to your trading vessel. You'll be free there. Safe there.' He had been moving nearer and now his hand came to rest on the side of the gun. It felt feverish, as if the metal had a disease. Volpe had probably been blasting at shadows before their appearance on the bank.

'Let me help you,' the Doctor said, 'as a favour to me. I like to help. I get the feeling this is a world that enforces bargains. I've given you my word, my promise.' He fished in his pocket with the hand that wasn't on the gun, putting his fingers on the first thing he found. It was the TARDIS key, but he couldn't afford to hesitate: his man was near madness, he needed to be drawn back, he needed human contact, he needed trust.

'I'll give you a third thing. This is the key to my craft. Without it I'm as trapped here as you are. With it, and your help, we can be free. Help me find my friends and learn what drives this world and then I'll take you home.'

'He will, you know, he's done right by me, the lad has,' Inexplicable shouted from inside the gorse bush.

Volpe let go of the gun. There were tears in his eyes.

The Doctor slipped the weapon into his pocket and decided to drop it down the next well they came to. He gave the TARDIS key to Volpe. 'Look after it, we'll need it.'

The first wish came true like this. Marlo, the big-boned one, had been drinking soup, which aside from the horrors of cleaning, hauling, polishing and washing up, was an aural torment in a class by itself. Anji, hands red-raw from lye soap, had heard her say, 'I'm so tired of soup.' Hardly Ibsen of course, but Anji felt something like a static charge up the back of her neck, raising the little hairs there. Like a thunderstorm coming.

'All these vegetables,' Marlo droned on. 'Who in the world would want to eat a swede?'

Anji had been a little wistful that Fitz wasn't there to treat that as a straight line. At least it would have distracted her from the electric buzz that was building up a charge at the base of her skull. She wondered if this was what an epileptic might feel just before a seizure.

Then Marlo had said, 'Oh, I wish we had beef!' And the feeling had burst out and through her, so that she had to clutch the edges of the sideboard while her whole body shuddered with it, and she had sensed a dull red glow from the dresser in her room above the kitchen where the box lay neglected.

And the soup had *changed*. Anji watched as it writhed in the bowl, broken down and recombined in a way that should have made the girl eating it want to throw up.

It hadn't. In fact, Marlo hadn't even noticed. But she reacted sharply enough to the spoonful, hurling the bowl against the wall, and shouting, 'Beef broth, again! I'd die for vegetable soup. Ai, get out to the vegetable patch and dig up some swedes.'

All the sisters called her Ai. It saved them the trouble of remembering her name. She had taken to calling herself Cinderanji, but only half in jest.

So that was how she came up with the plan. It was a desperate one, but she'd tried leaving, only to find the doors and windows locking and bolting themselves as she reached for them. And when she'd turned around, nearly in tears from fear and frustration, there was the sisters' ogre retainer standing right behind her wearing an expression beneath his overhanging mono-brow that was part threat and part moony-eyed leer. Later, she'd been sent out to fetch firewood, but decided to run like hell instead. After an exhausting hour she discovered that she'd been circling the house at a distance of about four hundred yards and was unable to physically get any farther. The most horrible part of her failed attempts was that, meal time or not, she would always find a dozen or more pans to scrub waiting for her in the kitchen.

But the wish thing niggled. The witch had sold her a wishing box. She was presently a servant. Perhaps she could only currently grant wishes for her mistresses. How ironically galling that would be!

So maybe she was surrendering to magical thinking and turning a set of coincidences into a key, but she was going to leave even if she had to wish her way out.

Or get someone else to do it for her.

Thus passed Anji's first day in the house of the Sisters.

That night Alex, the strange Doctor and the weird little gnome huddled in the woods and told stories to help keep themselves alert in the cold hours. The Doctor told the story of the Tar Baby and Brer Rabbit, which Inex found hilarious. The gnome was still giggling in his sleep now, as the fire's last embers died.

Alex saw what the Doctor was doing of course. Tossing stories into the night like bait, trying to get a hold on the composition of the colony and its history, looking for traces of folklore preserved over the generations that might show who or what the humans had been who had come out this far. It must have been frustrating for him when all his tales had seemed new to the gnome, although to give him his due he'd hidden it well.

Everything had fallen silent now, as Inex dozed deeper, a silence that felt to Alex like the pause before a gunfight or a dismissal without references. He hadn't told a story, and something made him interpret the Doctor's silent presence as being a living question: why?

'I like action stories,' he said, bluntly. 'But I don't pretend I could tell them.' It was a stretch to say 'like'. He preferred plug-in pleasures when he could get them, but he suspected that the Doctor's preference might be for the outlandish or the childish. Monsters or Tar Babies. 'If I wanted to read about people,' he went on, 'I'd be a pretty sad puppy. I don't have to read about people. I've been one all my life. I want tales of things I can never have and places I will never go, and tastes too sharp or rare for me.'

'Oh, I feel the same,' the Doctor said and grinned a grin that was sadder at the edges than Alex expected, almost making him think the man was not so bad after all. But it was obvious how he was pandering to the infantile side of the gnome. Playing the father figure here, and the sad brother there.

'That's why I like stories of hearth and home, and the fireside at night,' the Doctor continued wistfully. 'And comedies where the only things wrong can be fixed by everyone thinking Bertie Wooster is a fool for half a chapter. And romances where people say "la, sirrah" and carry fans. And adventures where no one is maimed or tortured, or beaten because they *can* be. Worlds of wonder, Alex. Look around you.'

Then he turned and lay down by the fire and seemingly went straight to sleep, leaving Alex alone, awake and somehow colder. Alex picked up a stone, a heavy one, but after a while he put it down again and, eventually, he slept.

When he woke he was surprised to find he still had the key, and he realised he had been expecting the Doctor to steal it back.

In the darkness at the core of the forest, the snow fell sullen and silent, no longer stirred by wind that chafed the bones of bare branches and rattled firs so that they shook like giant fists.

Now these *were* old woods. Fitz couldn't believe in any magick putting them up in an instant. This forest had gravitas, solidity, immanence. All his most distant ancestors were gathering to warn him that this was a *bad place* and it felt like they were doing it just behind the trees.

Gilfred rubbed his hands together, and blew a thin stream of condensing water vapour out of his mouth. 'We'll never get through these thickets in the dark,' he said, addressing his words to Ansel alone. 'You and Wolfskin are the handiest, maybe you could rustle up a shelter?' Ansel, who might have resented his appointment as intermediary if he hadn't enjoyed the direct thrill of bossing other people about in person, turned to bark an instruction. Fitz adjusted the packs on the donkey and pretended not to hear.

The brothers had been getting steadily less pleasant and more autocratic since they had left the old woman by the stream. He'd considered striking off alone as soon as they were out of the forest. But the light snowfall had quickly churned itself up into a real storm, with winds blowing needles of ice against exposed flesh and making it hard to see where they were going. By the time night fell they couldn't get the lantern to stay lit for more than a few minutes. Now he was too cold and hungry to make the break. His discovery that there really was no food in the packs had led to accusations that he'd somehow managed to eat it all while the brothers' backs were turned. Fitz suspected they knew this was not only impossible, but that there was another reason for the empty packs. But they were all too weary to fight about it any more. He wondered if he could eat snow and get water that way but he thought it might freeze his stomach solid if he tried it.

Ansel started a rambling story about how farmers built shelters, heavy on the 'we could' but meaning 'Fitz will' nevertheless.

Still ignoring Ansel, Fitz saw, faintly and vaguely at first, a light shining through the gloom. 'There's something over there,' he shouted. The Princes had made it quite clear that Fitz ought to say 'my lords' after an exclamation like that. But he was not so overjoyed by a light that he felt it necessary to pander to them.

Briars and brambles cutting both legs and flanks, they led their animals, tiptoeing and light-hoofing their way towards the light.

A wooden hut squatted on bare patch of ground already thick with snow. There was a cheerful light spilling out from under the door, and a smell of meaty soup from within.

Ansel handed the reins of his horse to Fitz and began to circle the hut, sniffing loudly. Fitz failed to suppress a laugh.

Prince Gilfred glared at him. 'Don't you know any woodcraft?'

'No,' Fitz admitted – not any likely to be applicable here. 'What's he doing?'

'Cake,' Gilfred said decisively. 'Witches make huts and houses from it and lie in wait for small children and other mammals. They stick up pretty pictures with flour and water, and the whole thing exudes this smell, like an endless bakery. Right up until the crunch.' He giggled, as if he'd said something funny.

Fitz really wanted to think that he was being lied to. Yeah, let's see how much crap the wolfskin boy will take. But Gilfred seemed completely in earnest even if he did find the whole trapping-little-children-for-food idea amusing.

Ansel bounded back to them. 'Smells like real food to me.'

'No, wait, wait,' Fitz said. 'Look at this thing. It's not made out of the same wood, is it? The grain's all knotty and the colour's this honey-yellow tint.'

'The same wood as what?' and 'So it's rather fetchingly appointed, so?' Ansel and Gilfred said at same time.

'So, why bring all this *other* wood to the middle of a different kind of wood and build a hut out of it? How do you know it's safe just because it doesn't smell of cake? Maybe the bigger ones don't eat children, eh, have you thought of that?'

Prince Gilfred looked at his brother and shook his head. 'Wolfskin can sleep out in the leaves if he wishes, my dear brother. But we shall see what hospitality will be accorded to princes questing bravely.'

Fitz watched them enter and swore under his breath. The hut was certainly not big enough to hold the three of them, the horses and donkey. Selfish idiots. Maybe he wasn't skilled in their weird woodcraft, but if they'd been willing to listen just maybe their combined body heat and that of the animals could have kept them all alive outside. The temperature was dropping by the minute and he doubted their mounts would last the night without shelter. The horses were just things to them. Just moving things that people of their sort rode at a whim, and handed the reins of to someone else when they got tired of the exercise. A couple of days on the road had brought him to the surprising realisation that he really got on with horses and donkeys. He couldn't bear to think of them out here, their life slowly ebbing with the falling heat. He considered running into the hut, dragging the Princes out by their fancy collars and forcing them to huddle together in the shelter of the closest trees – well, maybe not the trees; all the trees looked resentful in the eerie light of the falling snow – but he couldn't leave the animals out here to die.

He could barely feel his fingers as he grasped hold of the three leads. Maybe if he tried to keep awake, tried to keep their circulation going, rubbing them or something… but he wouldn't be able to do that all night. In a moment his tears would be freezing on his cheeks.

Then he saw a glitter of lights moving low through the thickets. Not the warm light of the hut, but a silvery bouncing of Tinkerbells that resolved themselves into a distinguishable, astounding multitude. At the level of his knees the wee folk surrounded him. Tiny lanterns born aloft on sticks gave off heat, and for that alone Fitz felt something in him lighten and break open. They set the lanterns round the animals, somehow managing to exclude him from the circle of warmth and light. One of the lantern-bearers came forward, a little grey man in a red cap, his eyes pools of silver like his lantern's light. 'These will preserve your good horseflesh living. Thus our debt is paid.'

Fitz was sure they'd mistaken him for someone else but dared not call attention to it lest they withdraw their favours

'Do not seek us again, enchanted though you be, for you reek of men.' The creatures turned as one and started back into the forest.

Enchanted?

'Wait,' he cried, 'what debt, what enchantment? What, er, who are you?'

The little man swivelled his head around like an owl and glared at Fitz with his liquid silver eyes. 'Who spoke to you, man-thing? Interloper. Dreamer of what is,' the little man spat. 'Not all loves you. We owed you no debt.'

First they did. Then they didn't. OK. Fine. At least the animals would survive the night. He guessed he'd be sleeping in the hut after all. He shot a glance at it. Oh, and didn't it look friendly, now? When he turned back to thank them, the little men were gone and, to be honest, Fitz was glad. They were creepy little buggers. He went to the hut and banged hard on the door. 'Little pi-' he began but decided that under the circumstances the joke might not be a joke at all. Stuck up and spoiled as the two Princes were, they knew things, things that seemed stupid and yet might get a person killed by not knowing them. The hut, for all its strange appearance, at least had a warm fire inside. Maybe it *was* a way station for weary travellers and questing princes. In the morning he'd tell them about the little men. Or perhaps not, but first he was going to get some food if they hadn't scoffed it all. And then some sleep.

The door of the hut opened easily and closed tight as a drum behind him. Although the snoring Princes had clearly – from the bones on the floor and the dribbled gravy on their velvet – managed to make quite a meal of it, there was still a lot in the big black cooking pot that stood on a heap of glowing coals in the hut's centre. Vaguely he wondered why there wasn't any smoke, but then realised that wasn't a bad thing really. Scrabbling up some bearskins from a heap in the far corner, Fitz wrapped them around himself and began to eat some of the stew straight from the pot. It felt cool on the hand but hot in the belly. It tasted like nothing he'd ever had before, but was tasty nonetheless.

He didn't exactly fall asleep. It simply happened between one mouthful and the next.

Chapter Six
The Wishing Game

Alex huddled in the corner of the roadside inn and shivered. He hadn't got much sleep. His survival gear seemed flimsy and shoddy next to the thick cloth, velvet and fur-trimmed clothing of the natives. Travel hadn't helped. The Doctor had got him a wraparound cloak in return for taking a stone out of the hoof of a tinker's mare. The inside of the cloak was rough and unlined, and hadn't exactly kept him snug through the night.

'Thank you, Doctor,' he'd said anyway, but he was getting sick of saying it. He hated that. Being beholden, being babied through a new world by someone who always looked you straight in the eye. Someone who couldn't, or more likely wouldn't, say exactly who he was or where he was from, but who balanced his alienness with an ability to fit into a society like a hand into a tailored glove. That ease said things to Alex. It said industrial espionage or worse. It said special training. It said covert agenda. It said that the Doctor wasn't to be trusted.

Perhaps they hadn't found the white hole first. Christina would just love that. He'd already compromised mission security by sharing his tracker with the Doctor. He'd panicked. He could see that now. Let himself be bought with a worthless old key.

Groaning, he straightened and took in the surroundings he'd been too tired to survey the previous night. The inn was the first civilisation they had come to, and he reckoned that the signal wasn't far away now, maybe down the lane or over the next hill. He'd got a couple of other signals, too, further away in this direction, but the nearer energy was drowning them out.

He gave the tracker a half-hearted couple of adjustments, trying to get a precise fix, and gave up when it read as being four hundred metres up. He had no sooner put it down than the Doctor clanged a tankard of brown stuff in front of him. 'Breakfast's on its way. I hope you can stomach ale. The landlord wasn't keen to feed anyone who'd drink water. I think it's against his profit margin. Of course on some planets he'd just sell it at three times the price of the beer.'

'Thank you, Doctor,' Alex said, imagining his lips pulled back into a snarl.

'Where's Inexplicable?' the Doctor asked, wiping a brown foamy moustache off his upper lip and plonking his drink down. 'This tankard's pewter,' he said at a tangent.

'Down the hall abluting. Oh, really,' Alex answered. He was getting used to the Doctor's habit of running two separate conversations or more at once. He didn't like it, but he was getting used to it. 'The signal tracker thinks the item is that way but four hundred feet up. It must be on the fritz. We'd have seen anything that high and close on the horizon.' He took a swig of the beer and gagged. It tasted like he imagined boot polish dissolved in water might.

The Doctor had abandoned pewter as a topic and now had his head half out of the window. A hot embarrassed flush crept up past Alex's threadbare cloak. This had always happened to him at college. He'd end up stuck with the nutter. The harmless old lady you nod to in the lift who's got it in for Aldebarans because they send all their money to Aldebaran banks. The man with the theory that shows space travel is all faked on DisneyMoon, and doesn't even see *that* as a contradiction. The horribly embarrassing relatives who come out only at Christmas or Yom Kippur or Zero-Rad Day. Last night the Doctor had been chatting with a band of fishermen trying to dredge the moon out of a narrow lake. And why hadn't he felt that sinking dreadful disgust that any intelligent being should feel at such stupidity? Or had he been sniggering inside? Alex didn't know, but he did know that every eye in the pub would fasten on the Doctor's bottom in a moment and he'd have to try to grin. 'Get back in here,' he hissed. 'What are you doing.'

'Looking at the clouds,' the Doctor said. 'Did you ever do that as a child? I think I did. I remember narrow-bladed grasses like a fakir's bed, and white shapes in an orange-yellow sky. I remember seeing castles. Castles much like that one.'

Suddenly oblivious to the thought of what the inn's patrons might make of his actions, Volpe craned round to see what cloud shape the Doctor had fixated on. Then he too saw the castle. Tall, thin, built upwards. A giant's castle.

'It's in there. The energy source, it's in there.'

'Good,' the Doctor said, pulling himself back inside the inn. 'We can go there after we've eaten. I ordered fish. It's supposed to be good for the brain and I think I might need it.'

Inside Alex's breast pocket the Doctor's key rubbed at him as he slumped back into his seat. It worried him. What kind of spaceship opens with a bronze bit of metal? Only one faked on DisneyMoon. Maybe it was a... charm. The little alien that called itself a gnome had told him about charms in its endless yadda-yadda. Charms for binding. Charms for blinding. Charms for catching. Charms for snatching. Illusion charms. Maybe the Doctor was only making him see the castle. Maybe he'd given him the key to trap him. It could have a microtransmitter in it. One thing was certain: it hadn't been done out of pure good trust.

On the second day of her period of indenture, Anji decided to set to work with what she'd named 'the Wishing Game'. It was Sunday, and the house was filled with damp half-dried washing and everyone's temper was frayed. Just the background for what she had in mind.

'Oh, I do so long for Saturday,' she said. 'Isn't it nice when the house is all washed down and gleaming, and the washing's on the line?' She considered whistling a little song but decided she'd die first. *Come on, Jermaine, pick up the cues.*

Anji had chosen Jermaine as the target because the stiff-backed sister, harridan-in-waiting though she might be, at least seemed to have a sense of humour, albeit one verging on the macabre.

Jermaine yawned. 'I suppose you'd like us to wish it was Saturday too, silly girl. You'd wish your life away if we let you, dreaming of dark-skinned suitors and Prince Handsome-but-dim.'

Not my life, Anji thought, just my damn contract.

'I wish it was Saturday too,' Latoya said unexpectedly from the chimney corner. 'It's market day on Saturday. I could get a piece of cherry-coloured twist to set off my ivory sleeved gown.'

'That old thing,' Jermaine sniffed. 'We'll all need new before long.'

While they had been talking, Anji had felt the power building up behind her eyes. Suddenly the sun had skittered across the sky, and a night-black shroud had fallen. Seven times the day jumped at Latoya's wish. Her heart came up into her throat. Between the start and end of her gulp, a week passed.

'Oh, I'm hungry, Ai,' Latoya moaned. 'Fetch me a slice of that pie, quickly girl.'

'Cut me one too and stop lollygagging,' Jermaine snapped.

Anji wiped her hands carefully on her apron. She was anticipating trouble when she left: at least she could give them their pie. Maybe they'd choke on it when she waved the contract under their faces.

The pie was seething with maggots. It had been left out of the cold room a week.

She bit back a giggle. Served them right. That was when the broom fell on her shoulder, the bristles bearing her down towards the ground.

'Look at this mess, sisters,' Marlo hissed, swinging the broom up again. 'This idle lump-in-the-bed has left our food to spoil. If I'd known when first she came how lazy she would be –'

No. Oh no. Anji sensed what was coming and put out a hand to ward it off.

'I wish I had another week of her services so she'd come to know what hard work is, and that it can not be avoided in this world.'

No! In Anji's pocket, a week added itself to her contract.

After that, she nearly abandoned her wishing game, but the desire to cheat the sisters overcame her. Next she tried tempting them to wish for a huge castle to live in instead of the dilapidated house. Surely if they were wealthy and surrounded by servants, she would be able to wait out her remaining week feigning idiocy below stairs, or cataloguing the library. Unfortunately, the wished-for castle didn't come with servants, and it was an evil two days of hard work scrubbing grey stone before she could get a sister to wish for somewhere 'cosy'. *One more try*, she vowed that night on her narrow cot. Three times was the charm, so they said. Maybe it was that kind of world. The next day she did everything wrong. She let the parsley sink in the butter, she spilled the milk and burst into tears in the pantry, she hooked a stool out from under the thinnest sister and let her fall on her bony rump. It took slightly more effort, actually, to get so many things wrong as it would have to do them right, but she persevered. She knew what she was aiming for: 'I wish we'd never taken on a servant.' Get a sister to wish that and surely she'd be free.

Unfortunately, they wished she'd never been born and she had to spend a day, a most uncomfortable day, as a kind of poltergeist-Anji, able to fetch and carry, able to do her contractual work, but without the means to speak or rest or carry on her human life. That scared her. Then Michaela wished that Anji would sing to her, and the necessity of having a voice seemed to bring the rest back with it. She sang the chorus to 'Stupid Girl' by Garbage, which Michaela thought was hilarious, believing Anji was singing a telling song about herself – which, she supposed with a sigh, she was.

She found she had begun to dread random wishes, and added

apparent sullenness to the faults the sisters saw in her, for fear of prompting some desperate change for the worse.

Christina pushed her way through the cornfield. Her tracker still showed a source of white-hole energy in this direction, and she was determined to find it. It wasn't quite a sane hope, but she'd decided that if she could find at least one of the fragments, the luck of the mission would turn. So far it was disastrous. She'd started out boldly leading them up from the marshy land into the edges of a wood. She'd been careful to skirt the trees, keeping them at the edge, but then she'd noticed that both Alex's complaints and Tento's harsh breathing had fallen silent. Turning, she'd discovered she was completely alone. That was how long ago? She wasn't even sure how long she'd been travelling by herself. The hours blended into each other and were counted only in blisters, and the occasional breaks for sleep and survival rations when her body demanded. Sometimes she thought it was only two days, but once, almost delirious, she had imagined it had been a week, or even two. Time had lost its meaning in the alien landscape, in the corn. She was so far out of the loop as to render the idea of a 'loop' meaningless. The only sound out of her comlink had been a long ululation of static.

She tried to tell herself that she wasn't worried in the long term, that anything she could detect with the malfunctioning equipment she had to hand would have to show up from the *Bonaventure*. If necessary she'd park her arse atop the signal source and wait for the other captains' greed to send reinforcements. It would be professionally embarrassing but not fatal. But she wasn't kidding herself very well. She was cold, hungry and alone, and the corn was getting taller. Each new row was a few stalks' length higher, as if different varieties had been planted, with the larger in her chosen direction. Soon they would reach over her head.

A feeling that she was on the verge of being lost, and not in the purely accurate and mundane sense in which she was already, but in some far more dangerous and profound sense, started to trickle up her spine. She had a gun, so she drew it and felt the weight as a reassurance – assuming it worked better than the sensor or the comlink. She set it to a wide-cutting beam, intending to slice down a few rows of corn, to make her own crop-circle mark.

Then she heard something clearing its throat, politely, but loudly. It sounded like a big throat, and the corn rustled.

A face like an Egyptian cat's, but twice the size of a horse's and covered in downy blue fur, pushed its way through two rows of corn to her left. Eyes, yellow and slitted, blinked at her. A paw at the end of a greyish blue forearm, its claws scarlet as if painted, flexed within reach. In the corn-coloured haze surrounding the main shape of it, she could make out a great feline body topped with wings.

'Hello, mortal,' it said. 'How are your riddles?'

Christina gulped. 'Fair,' she said, not knowing if having good riddles was a good thing or a bad to this mythical monstrosity. Sphinx. This sphinx. She remembered they liked riddles and ate people. *This is an alien, an unknown alien.* But her mind said sphinx and her spine crawled.

'Hh,' the Sphinx said, 'I'd stay away from the wodewose, then: his are *hard*'. And it hunched its shoulder back into the corn, and started to move away.

'What's a wodewose?' she shouted, thinking she might as well have an answer to a question for a question answered.

'The wildman of the woods. You're heading for one, where the corn ends. It's riddles he has in his strange box, new riddles never seen on this world, and I am sore bested. Be grateful that I have lost my appetite in defeat.'

Christina was. Very. The heavy weight of the blaster didn't seem nearly as reassuring as it had a minute ago. Still, the new riddle box sounded like it might be something unusual. More unusual than a sphinx, maybe? I wonder what form the energy has taken, she wondered. Might it look like a box?

Alex Volpe pushed past Inexplicable into the pub's lavatory, and shut the door behind him. The indoor plumbing was less basic than he had feared, and, he noted, came in a variety of sizes from, what? Pixy up to, maybe, ogre? Up to quite an impressive volume, anyway. He selected a human-sized toilet whose flushing mechanism (a bucket) was full of water. The water was fed to the buckets by narrow arch-supported channels as if tiny Roman imps had set out to provide plumbing by aqueduct. He wasn't inclined to rule that out, not on this mad world. He'd just take care of business. He took the key from his pocket and threw it into the bowl. Then he washed it down. The water in the bucket helped. That was that, then. Beholden to no one, not obligated, not marked with the Doctor's key, he'd taken the first step to getting his spoils back to the *Bonaventure*. He felt free again.

Until, ten minutes later, he started to eat the fish the Doctor had ordered for breakfast.

'Report?' Vuim-Captain looked at the green-grey face of his subordinate on the screen. He had ordered that all experimentation should take place in a dedicated compartment and be observed from outside. The vuim had learned medical and scientific caution. It had taken a full day to set up, and there had been a strange unrelated problem with the atomic clocks that the scientists did not yet understand, but which they assured him would not hinder the work. Now, however, they were ready to begin. He had told Timtangle a little of what they had found, but he would master it fully before deciding how it should be shared.

'We have a portion of the substance of the world's surface in a force-box Vuim-Captain. I am about to subject it to mild stimulation.'

'Are the room locks secure?'

'Yes, and as I say it's in a force box. As I move the tools the field will follow the contours of the instruments. It will be the force field itself that cuts and prods.'

'Good, we should take no risks. It has properties of life. It moves, it adopts camouflage. It may be able to anticipate our intentions. It *must* have detected our approach. I suppose we do not yet know how?'

'Light-sensitive organs on the upper fold surfaces? The ship's shadow might have triggered ancestral memories of hunting fliers.'

Vuim-Captain hissed. 'It is too big. It reacted when we were too high. Besides, what predators would hunt landscapes? We have too much speculation. Cut me some fact.'

The Doctor performed the Heimlich manoeuvre with considerable finesse. Alex's ribs felt like they'd nearly cracked, but the chunk of fish had been successfully ejected. Around their table the rhythms of hubbub had paused briefly as a glint of metal caught the light in the gobbet of white meat.

'Treasure,' the gnome squealed and pulled the fish on Alex's plate apart with his bare hands. The Doctor meanwhile had placed a careful finger on the table and gently pushed the key he had given Alex out of the coughed-up fragment in which it had been embedded.

'Hmm,' the Doctor said. He gave Alex a look that cried out to be delivered over the top of a pair of glasses, before going on to tell Inexplicable, in a self-congratulatory way, that he'd taken a life-saving course during his years as a corporate troubleshooter in the mid-eighties. Alex nursed his aching sides and tried to wring some advantage from the Doctor's passing personal slip. He hadn't reckoned the man was that old. If he'd been running around the stellar companies in the 2780s, he had to be at least a hundred, maybe a hundred and ten. While it wasn't impossible, it implied wealth. The sort of wealth needed to buy top-of-the-range, age-defying genetic treatments, to get the skin-honers and tissue-replacement patches from the white market, not the black. Alex had seen his own father eaten away by a rogue age treatment. His father had been a big man once, and not a vain one. He'd got the treatment to keep him looking young in a young person's job market, to make it possible for him to keep selling his waning skills ahead of the competition. Instead he'd ended up in a life-support 'biot-suit, until he'd finally dissolved into a mass of twisty blue-grey DNA strands, writhing at the core of a crystal cylinder. Young DNA, though, the coroner had said.

The Doctor was rapping the key on the table. Absent-minded-like, but the sound set Alex's teeth on edge. I'm waiting, young man, it said. What is your explanation for this outrage?

'Hey, Inex,' Alex said, 'can you go and ask them where they catch their fish?' The gnome nodded, and as he left for the bar, Alex turned to look at the Doctor. He wanted to say, 'Yeah, I threw your stupid key away old man, I'm on to your game, walking through the world all sweetness and light, taking stones out of hooves and teaching farmers how to store butter longer. You don't get to be a hundred and ten without an angle. You don't earn your bread by being all things to all men. You don't travel to the edges of human space and lock your ship with an antique key. You don't fool me.' Instead he said, 'I've got a hole in my pocket. I guess if they've a river out back, and their toilets wash into it, and they fish it down stream…' He faded out. It wasn't very likely. The key was heavy, brass or some other alloy. It should have lain on the bed of a stream until the buffing of the stones and the water washed it smooth.

'Maybe,' the Doctor said, 'maybe it's a *magic* key.' And he winked. Alex felt sick. Damn him. Damn his whimsicality and his brown leather walking boots that never seemed to get unpolished, and his hail-fellow-well-met bonhomie. I'll see you done down, Doctor, he thought. Maybe I'll even hurt myself to do it. You walk among us, but you aren't one of us. You aren't slaving for your living, you aren't beholden to a boss. You don't desire what we desire, or need what we need. You're less real than that bloody gnome, and you'll never know how much you're hated for it.

'Can I have it back?' he asked, and smiled his 'virtuous corporate vampire' smile.

'If you want it.'

The Doctor put the key on the table and pushed it over with one finger like a man putting a new stake into a poker game.

'They get the fish from the mountains,' Inexplicable said, cutting into the atmosphere between the two men as if he had no notion of it. 'There are freshwater lakes up there, glacier-melt waters. The fish in them grow big and fine. Two families catch them and pack them in glacier ice and send them down to the low countries by mule train. The King of the next-door country apparently has them delivered straight to his castle, they're so prized. So!' He paused portentously. 'I got a free round of ale to recompense us for our shock.' The barmaid behind him started to offload the tankards from her tray.

'Excuse me, er, miss?' Alex asked. 'That batch of fish – when did it come in?'

'Oh, it's perfectly fresh, sir. It came in yesterday.'

Chapter Seven
The Hut, or What Was Next For the Pot

In the morning, the forest was full of birds. Starlings, sparrows and robins, all mobbing and squawking. The cores of the elf lanterns – long glowing silver worms – vanished down a thousand avian throats, and the twists of silver frost that formed the husks melted away into the grass and the rootlets of the trees.

In the hut, Fitz woke first, cramped and cold. He felt as stiff as if he'd slept for a fortnight. There was a red subdued glow from under the pot, but precious little heat. The Princes were mumbling and each was trying to hog the complex mat of bearskins that they had spread over themselves. Someone chuckled. It wasn't one of the sleeping Princes.

'Heh, heh, heh. You've tasted my hospitality, now you must pay for shelter and for stew.' The voice came from nowhere and everywhere, and the tiny wooden hut seemed to have developed a cavernous echo. Fitz shook Gilfred and Ansel. 'Wake up, wake up. We've got a problem.'

'Three stayed the night, one must stay to feed the pot. I'll take the last person to leave. It will be quick.'

Fitz's stomach heaved. Did that bit about feeding the pot mean what he thought it might? Bloody hell, he'd eaten some of that stuff. 'WAKE UP!' he shouted, and dragged the tattered bearskins off the Princes.

'Some people draw lots,' the voice said confidently. *'There are bones of various sizes in the ash of the fire. No hurry. If you could vacate by ten of the clock, it will give time for things to simmer before the next guests. The windows are tightly*

shuttered by the way, and the floor and walls are sound.' Ansel was scrambling on the floor for his weapon. *'If you break anything in here with those swords I'll have to take two, one extra as payment for damages.'*

Ansel raised his sword anyway, wild-eyed and spinning about, prepared to have a go at the walls anyway, but Gilfred restrained him. 'Maybe it means it,' he began and whispering another word that Fitz didn't quite catch before continuing. 'We must think, and think hard. Fitz, lad, I know we've not been the best of travelling companions. We were raised to view anyone outside the royal family as servants, you see, and it takes a horrible thing like this to shake the grip of childhood loose. I hope you'll shake our hands before we part, whichever way this goes.'

'We're parting?' Fitz asked, seeing how this was going. 'Parting as in me, as one person, parting from you as two people? I count that as very gentlemanly, letting me go about my business like that and settling it between you like true noble lords.' He grabbed his pack and started scuffing the wolf cloak towards him along the floor. He'd begun to think of it as lucky, although given his current situation he couldn't imagine why.

'What I meant, Fitz,' Prince Gilfred said, hand resting lightly on his sword, 'is that since my brother and I are both trained swordsmen we should leave the hut and confront its owner. It's probably just a scabby little goblin that scavenged some witch magick and is trying to get into the hut business. A show of steel will see it off. You can see that makes sense, can't you?'

I can see you're using my name you bastard, Fitz thought. *Softly softly*.

'Suppose the best swordsman goes out with me, I could run off, and while the goblin's chasing me, you could attack it from behind, or I could lead it round into an ambush.'

'I had hoped you'd agree, Fitz,' Gilfred said, 'it would have made this much quicker. Now we'll have to –'

Fitz flinched. This was where he was going to end up trussed for the beast's pot roast.

'– draw lots. Ansel, see if you can gather up some things of different lengths. I'm loath to use bones, it could well be disrespectful.'

They left the inn just after two in the afternoon by the sundial in the garden. The Doctor had stared at it for several minutes, until the gnome had nudged him and asked what the matter was.

For once the Doctor had looked less than ebullient, lost, diminished even. His face was grey, shadowed, and somehow pained. 'Occasionally, in the last hundred years or so, I've been taken this way,' he said, gasping. 'There's no help for it, no organic cause, not that I know. It'll pass.' He darted a look between Inex and Alex. 'When we meet my friends I'd appreciate it if you'd keep this to yourselves. They worry so.'

He managed a wan smile, and urged them on.

Alex was still trying to work out whether the key thing could have been a trick, and decided to ignore the Doctor's sickness, taking it as a planned distraction. How could the key thing have been worked? If the Doctor had paid the innkeeper the night before to slip a copy of the key into his meal – he might after all have any number of copies of the key – then the whole thing was explained. Except he'd have to have known in advance that Alex was planning to throw his precious key away. Was that impossible? He might be one of those creepy psycho-strategists, dropping a hint here, making an arch comment there, until suddenly a trade federation is in ruins and a commissioner in hiding. Or he might have had that awful gnome watching him in the toilets, maybe even creeping underneath where the waste pipes ran to fish the real key out again as it was washed into the stream. He might have handed it up to a kitchen maid. And then he pulled the fish apart like that so that it couldn't be examined for the slit in the belly by which the key was put in. Yes, the gnome could have done it, but Alex sensed the Doctor's mind at work in the planning. Maybe Tento's death had been the result of that mind, too. The Doctor and his seeming gnome had been very conveniently to hand at the end of the trail through the forest that Alex had pelted down in his panic. Maybe the thing in the cottage had been a robot, its form masked with holograms and pinpoint release hallucinogens. Maybe he was walking with murderers.

Walking with murderers to see Giants.

Fitz held the short bone. It had come to bones finally, as he had known it would. And to the short one. He was fairly sure they had fixed it somehow, an old boys' trick for getting some lower-class, barely tolerated playfellow into some scrape. But he couldn't prove it, and they had the swords. If they threatened him, he'd just about decided to grab a sword and score it along the wall so one of the Princes would be on the dinner list too.

On the other hand, they hadn't used force, and they had abided by the draw, and he hadn't seen them cheat. It was possible they did intend to fight the beast. It was even possible that they might be right about the threat itself being small. He clutched at his wolf cloak like a boy with a teddy bear. What would the Doctor do? Well he knew that, and wouldn't it look great on a gravestone: HE DID WHAT THE DOCTOR WOULD HAVE DONE?

'Get going,' he said.

Prince Ansel smirked, but Gilfred looked Fitz in the eyes and nodded slightly as if at least according him some respect.

'Now, quickly, before I change my mind.'

And they were quick.

'*So, it's the youngest and the most tender,*' the voice said. '*I can't complain about that.*'

'But I'm not the youngest,' he cried, with a sudden rush of hope. It was all a case of mistaken identity. The voice wanted the youngest and surely he was the oldest of the three –

Outside the sound of horses galloping away confirmed that the wise do not put their trust in princes, and also rendered his age a moot point. Under Fitz's feet the wood of the floor began to convulse, and the pot spread wider, bending down and forming a mouth with wide iron lips. *'Come to me morssseling,'* it lisped. *'I want to kissss you'.*

It wasn't any beast from outside, or any scheming witch with a pointed nose and warts – it was the hut itself. He'd slept in the stomach of a predator and eaten the offcuts of its last meal. He felt a disgust that went beyond terror. He was tainted. What could he do but die? *'That's right, my little love. You ate of me, now let me eat you.'* A steely grey tongue thrust out of the cooking pot, and licked around the rim.

Fitz took a step towards it. His legs moved without his command. He was getting ready to die when a whiskery voice sounded at his ear. 'I can get you out of this if you trust me.'

It was his cloak, the wired articulated jaws moving, its eyes, which he'd assumed were glass, rolling in their sockets. Overloaded with horrors, his legs gave way, staggering him backwards against the door, which miraculously gave slightly. 'It demanded only one,' the wolf whispered, 'the last to leave. Back out slowly and let me fall from your shoulders inside the hut as you close the door.'

Numb, Fitz followed the cloak's instructions. The door felt wet and fungoid under his hand, but it opened and he let the cloak fall from his shoulders.

Outside there were no birds now, and no horses either. His donkey brayed in terror, its lead wrapped and tangled round a holly tree. In a moment's clarity as he pitched forward into the dirt, Fitz vowed that the Princes would answer for their lies.

From inside the hut there was a sound of rending, and then the half-cough, half-rattle of something large trying to get a hair out of its throat. The door shot open and the wolf cloak shot out, rolled up and covered with a thin grey ichor, a torn and ragged furball.

'Caaark, wolf-hair,' the hut spluttered, *'Oh well that's the way*

the bone breaks; you win some, you lose some.' Fitz heard bolts slamming home, and he realised the hut was locking itself, fastening shutters hard, sealing the door. Soon there was nothing to distinguish it from any abandoned dwelling. There was no way to strike at its interior even if he'd had anything he could use to harm it. He kicked it, and didn't even leave a mark, though his soul cried out to destroy it, to cut it down, to burn it out. Finally, he settled for using a branch from one of the trees to write the word UNSAFE in the earth before the door. It felt like a failure, but at least he was alive.

After Fitz and his donkey were out of sight, the hut put out its tongue and licked the letters away.

Vuim-Captain heard the scream through the open screen channel, and from the echo in the lab ship's guts a moment later.

The technician was dead; a spike of solid material (bone? white metal?) had projected out of the force box and into his eye. His plated skull was broken open at the back. The material in the box couldn't break the field, the technician had been right in that, but instead had bent it *around* the spike. When Vuim-Captain lifted the body up and off the bayonet, the blood flowed off the frictionless surface of the field.

Force boxes were supposed to be one-way. It must have taken incredible strength to drive the field back into the technician.

Reflex, the Captain mused, or intentional aggression? He moved around the technician's body, keeping it between him and the material with its single shining spear. There was a metal scalpel on the floor. It was new, shiny, the same colour as the spike.

Could it be the same?

Duplication of matter?

Through a field of force?

The next vuim to study the material, Cathenar, recorded his experiments as he proceeded. The death of his predecessor suggested that the planet material could react quickly and lethally, so instead of putting it in a force field, the vuim had lined the inside of the room with dense-matter shielding. The planet material was loose on a tray, and Cathenar was in a force field, and under that he wore a deep-space survival suit. He lost a certain amount of his native insect-quick dexterity, but gained a marginally better sense of safety.

He gestured gracelessly at the laser aimed at the substance on the tray. 'This is the unit we use to flash spectrographic samples off asteroids. It is rated capable of boiling a small sea.' This was stretching the truth a little. Even the Scarlet Sea on Vuima, a mere 438,000 cubic metres of lukewarm saline solution, would have changed temperature by only about twenty degrees under the bombardment, but Cathenar felt a little hyperbole was good for his nerves. 'The material has been under constant observation by ship's sensors, and we believe we have detected a quantum flicker at the molecular level. The matter is literally pulling in new molecules to replace those destroyed by the attack. We can only suggest that it is a living transmat, and that it can detect and draw on similarly organised atomic structures over some considerable range. If this is the case it is impossible to destroy so much as a single compound of this… stuff, so long as there exists elsewhere, maybe anywhere on the whole world, another compound that it can seize to repair itself with.'

Behind him the laser shone on, powerful, wordless, and unable to concede its uselessness. He wished he did not share its futility.

Elsewhere, torn apart and drawn upon, a crystal tower seemingly a millennium old shattered, releasing a foul black nameless thing that howled once and died. Elsewhere a duckling laid a swan's egg. Elsewhere the beards of three dwarfs turned white in an instant. Elsewhere rocks shattered, and rare gems flickered and dissolved.

* * *

The Doctor's malaise faded quickly as he walked, and by the time the castle began to grow clearer his mind was far too full of wonder to worry about it, or to do more than keep a mental pair of fingers crossed for Fitz and Anji's welfare.

He was going to see Giants! Giants that would be at least a hundred feet tall if the proportions of the castle looming ahead were indicative, and if they were that tall their legs would have to be like tree trunks, or their own weight would –

No no no! That wouldn't do at all. He could think of nineteen separate reasons why there couldn't be Giants, from primitive folk memories of acromegaly or thyroid hypertropism through to the inverse square law; but he had to admit that he'd seen a gnome in a magic glass, and been magically removed from his castle room. Assuming that he hadn't been carried down while he was asleep, and he *was* willing to set aside the suspicious bruise on his knee as merely circumstantial. He remembered that Alex had claimed to see them appear, but then the man was so nervous and fidgety that his testimony wasn't sufficient proof. Evidence for a miracle based on someone's word always supposes that their lying or being mistaken is more miraculous than a lapse in the laws of nature. Giants, on the other hand, would be large-scale direct evidence.

He wanted to believe, but he had a lot of experience to put aside: in the last hundred years, nine times out of ten the banshee had been a thing from Antares 5, the foo fighters bemused alien jellyfish, and the ghost usually a teenager in a sheet. Even when he hadn't got a full explanation for things he'd always felt there ought to be one.

In a way he'd be pleased to find indivisible Giants.

He wanted Giants that couldn't be reduced to men on stilts, or aliens from a low-gravity world in cyber-braces. He wanted Giants that rumbled the world with their ultimate bone-shaking largeness, Giants that couldn't be explained away.

* * *

In the top floor of his tower the Giant rested his chin on his great broad right hand, the colour of a swathe of hairy oatmeal, and looked at the box his servants had brought to him, before he'd sent all but one from the castle.

A small thing to bring so much disruption. The sooner the boxes were gone and far away the better. Carefully he placed a cloth of gold over it.

Chapter Eight
The Duke of Sighs

Long, long ago in a far-off kingdom there lived the Duke of Sighs, so called because all that looked upon him could not help but sigh at his beauty, his brilliance and his gracious manner.

One day the Duke set out hunting. He wished for no company, being weary of the constant exhalations of the Lords and Ladies that followed him about the Court. 'Oh,' he mused to himself, 'what a burden it is to bear, this uncommon handsomeness of mine. Truly I could stand it were it not for my rapier wit and devilishly interesting character. One or two of the three might be supportable, but all three! Lackaday, it is too much! How shall I ever find a bride worthy of me?'

It was in this hopeless mood that he had set out alone in the forest to find surcease in the hunting of the merry doe, though his heart was not in it. He wished only that there existed a woman as beautiful as he was handsome, as charming as he was witty and as unique as he was interesting. If ever I find such a woman I will marry her on the spot, he thought. No sooner had he thought this than he spotted a white hind drinking from a stream. The hind was so beautiful that even though he'd drawn the bow he could not release the arrow. The hind saw this and spoke to him. 'Good Duke of Sighs, for the kindness you have shown in sparing my life I will grant a boon, for I am no ordinary hind, as you can see. Here in the stream I guard a treasure that will show you the very thing you seek.' He approached the stream and there in the water beneath the white hind's hooves was a cask made of silver and mother of pearl. 'In your kingdom there are two ladies like no others of this world,' the hind said. 'One wears the beauty of the night beneath her rags and the other the beauty of the day. This cask will guide you to them, but be warned – it is not an easy choice. For day and night are only pieces of a greater puzzle. Solve the puzzle and you will find the woman worthy of so great a lord as you.' The Duke thanked her for her advice. The hind bowed her graceful head and bounded into forest. When the Duke retrieved the cask from the water, he found to his amazement that it was instantly dry. He opened it and saw the hind had spoke true, for there within were the images of two ladies, each beautiful but like night and day. He hid the cask in the folds of his cloak and returned to the Castle of Sighs determined to find the ladies and take one to be his bride.*

The proclamation arrived just as Anji had run outside to empty the contents of her stomach into a patch of weeds. All the girls were screaming and she'd thought at first it was because of the dead thing on the kitchen table. But after she'd splashed a little icy water on her face she realised they were all somewhere in the front of the house and were reacting to something else entirely. Their voices were full of excitement, not revulsion. Soon enough their excitement acquired the usual shift in tone and she heard scuffling, threats and naturally the one-syllable bellows of 'Ai!' as they pushed and shoved each other to get to her first.

The ogre was in the kitchen whistling and choosing herbs from the dried bunches suspended from the rafters.

'Ai! Oh, there you are,' Jacqueletta said as Anji came back inside. 'We've received an invitation to a ball at the Castle of Sighs –' More ear-piercing squeals. 'Will you all shut up! The Duke is seeking a wife and – Oh! What is that thing doing on the table?'

The ogre took a big pot from a hook above the oven. 'Ai's gonna cook it for me.'

'I bloody well am not!' Anji said.

'She can't!' Titonia blubbered. 'Tell Stupid she can't.'

Michaela pinched her. 'Cry-baby.' Titonia howled.

'Shut up!' Jacqueletta shouted. She poked at the fat little elf. Its head lolled sideways, little chunks of greenish viscera protruding from the back of its broken neck. 'She won't have time to cook it, Stupid. She has to make us new gowns for the ball.'

'What?' Anji gulped. ' I don't know how to –'

'Why can't she cook it for me first?'

'The ball is tomorrow night. She'll have to get started right away. Oh, stop moping, Stupid, eat it raw like you always do.'

Anji felt the bile rising to her throat as the ogre grabbed the elf by the ankles and stomped out of the back door muttering under his breath. 'Look,' she said, trying to ignore the little green shoe left on the table. 'There's no way I can make six –'

'I wonder what they're wearing at court these days,' Jermaine pondered.

'I want mine the colour of a moonbeam,' Marlo said.

'A sunset,' Latoya declared. 'That orangey, pinky, purply bit just after the red.'

'I want mine that shade of green,' Titonia sniffed, pointing at a patch of grass, 'that blade there, not those others.'

'Remember that gypsy pot-mender from last summer?' Michaela asked. 'He had the ruby earring and it was so pretty against his brown skin –'

'Wasn't pretty after Stupid bit his ear off –'

'Hello! Are you listening? I can't do it!'

All the girls turned to her.

'But you must,' Jacqueletta said. 'We have to be the most beautiful girls there.'

Anji stared at them. Without a serious attitude adjustment there was no dress in the world that could make these horrible, mean-spirited, self-absorbed young women beautiful. She snorted. 'Look. I tried my hand at spin-doctoring for a paper in political science once, but –'

'Spin-doctoring?' Jacqueletta said, her brows rising in glee. 'That solves the problem of where to get the fabric on such short notice. Stupid! Stupid! Come here!'

The ogre appeared at the door. He had a leg in one hand and spoke through his chewing. 'What?'

'Take Ai up to the north attic where the flax is stored. Let's see. If she spins all day and weaves all night – we'll each need about twelve yards – that leaves her the rest of tomorrow to transform the linen into quality goods and then sew the gowns. Yes. That should work out.'

'No it won't!' Anji cried. 'Haven't you silly cows noticed I can barely thread a needle?'

'You can't cook either, but that hasn't stopped you.' Jacqueletta gestured at Stupid in the doorway. He tossed the elf's leg behind him into the yard and shuffled in sullenly.

'Why don't you just wish for the damned dresses?'

'Don't be such goose. What good would that do?'

Stupid grabbed her by one arm and with a move that was part pro wrestler, part fireman rescue, hoisted her up and over his shoulder. She tried to scream in fury but all the air was knocked out of her. In one hand he locked her wrists together. Her rump and legs dangled over his shoulder. The image of a deer carried on a hunter's back struck her, instantly followed by Stupid's tusk-like teeth tearing off bits from the elf's leg. She moaned in dread and panic, and desperately grunted out the words as he started to carry her up the back stairs. 'Make a wish. Titonia, come on, say I wish –'

'I wish.'

'I wish I had –'

'I wish I had new shoes.'

Anji growled as the energy shot through her.

Suddenly Titonia was holding a pair of silk-embroidered pumps. 'I hate these shoes,' she said. 'They're so last year.'

* * *

The Doctor looked at the wrought-iron monstrosity. It had to weigh at least two hundred pounds, and it looked like someone's attempt to build a lethal metal vaulting horse. It reminded him of those trick photographs on *Ask the Family*. Ah ha, he'd got it.

'Boot-scraper,' he said triumphantly.

'Are we really sure this is wise?' Alex asked, dabbing at his brow with a linen napkin that the Doctor felt sure had been stolen from the inn. The five steps up to the door had winded him. No wonder, each was about nine feet high.

'Do you think we ought to knock?' Inexplicable grinned, gesturing up at a black metal lump maybe fifty feet up the neck-straining expanse of the great oak door. 'Oh yes, I think so,' the Doctor said. 'It'll give you a chance to show off some magic. You just fly up and knock now, go on.'

'Doctor!' Alex yelled. 'We are not going to wake the crukking Giant. We are going to get in, take the white-hole debris and get out. It doesn't even belong to him, it just fell here.'

'He's got a point,' Inexplicable said. 'It's in the nature of things, stealing from Giants. I don't think there's a law against it, not technically. Just ask King Jack III.'

'Have you got your fingers crossed?' the Doctor asked curiously, as if stumbling on an unaccustomed example of a quaint folkway.

'Yess,' the gnome said reluctantly, 'wards off the little folk.'

'You're worried about the little folk,' Alex moaned. 'Now I've heard everything. We're about to go into the Giant's castle and the gnome is worried about the little people. What about the Big People, you snivelling puddle of spit?'

'Now now,' the Doctor admonished, 'if you're that keen to be surreptitious, yelling your head off at Inexplicable here is hardly going to increase our chances. Besides, its uncalled for, infantile and plain rude. I think you owe him an apology.'

'Apologise to that thing!'

'Apologise or go your own way. But if you want my help to get your fallen wonder from the Giant – and I think you're right that it should be in safe hands – then you'll conduct yourself with a bit more decorum.'

'That's right, Doc,' Inex said, 'you tell the lanky piece of piss. If he thinks I'm small he'd better hope he never meets the real wee folk. They'd have his ears for tents, they would.'

'Are you quite finished?'

'Sorry,' Alex mumbled, and Inex responded with a half-hearted ''S all right.'

'You do realise that while you were bickering the door has swung open by itself. Remarkably quietly for what must be composed of thousands of pieces of oak. I'd have expected more weather distortion. Come on, then.' And the Doctor was off inside before Alex or Inex could react.

'Where did you find him?' Alex hissed to the gnome.

'Oh, he found me. His kind always do.'

Wolfskin had not gone very far when he heard a great commotion from the forest ahead: a terrible howling and snarling. Because of the magical wolf cloak, he was able to move swiftly and with great stealth towards the sounds. In a clearing in the trees, he saw Prince Ansel and Prince Gilfred beset by a pack of wolves. Both had swords drawn and stood back to back, desperately slashing out at first this wolf, then that one. A great grey wolf directed the attack and Wolfskin found that he could understand the speech of the wolves and so knew what they were planning.

'Eats Her Tail and Copper Paws, you will draw the attack of the metal fangs. White Ear, Moon Cub and Howls Alone, you circle behind. We will take the bay mare first. Its death cries will unnerve them and they will fall beneath our teeth and claws easily –'

'No!' Wolfskin cried, leaping out from his hiding place in the thickets. 'Do not kill them. I beg you!'

Each pair of wolf eyes, twenty in all, turned to him. Their low growls rumbled across the ground. The grey wolf that was leader showed his fangs. 'Do you claim this meat for yourself, brother-stranger?'

'Would you eat the flesh of your own kind, King of Wolves?'

'Nay, brother, I would not, but these men are not your kin or your kind.'

The big wolf moved closer. 'You wear the scents of man and wolf and sorcery. But you smell of many other things I cannot understand.'

'I have travelled far through many lands.'

'You have farther still to go I sense.' Then the King of Wolves looked over his great shoulder at the two Princes still surrounded by the pack. 'It is true that good men taste better than wicked ones. So be it. I will spare the lives of these two for the sake of he that was their brother, and ours, whose skin you wear as a cloak. But we will have the horses. We are many and hungry and have dens of little ones to feed.'

Wolfskin thanked the beast and called to the two Princes, 'Your lives have been spared, but the horses are forfeit.'

'We shall not leave our mounts!' Prince Ansel cried and, with that, he thrust through the breast of the nearest wolf. A great howl went up from the pack as Prince Gilfred sprang upon his horse and pulled Ansel up behind him and the two men galloped away through the forest. The bay mare started after them, but in a blink the wolves were upon her and she fell under the gnashing of their teeth and ripping of their claws.

The great grey wolf was in a cold rage. 'We have lost our sister and meat for our larder. You must now give us your beast of burden.'

Wolfskin bowed his head, accepting the price in shame and sorrow.

'But heed my warning, brother-stranger,' the wolf said. 'Those two are cunning and will betray you as they betrayed their own flesh and blood.'

* * *

'Tell me something I don't know,' Fitz muttered as he hoisted the packs over his shoulder. He tried very hard to screen out the sounds of his little donkey as it died, but he didn't run from it and he didn't bother trying not to cry as he trudged wearily on, following the trail of his betrayers.

A mile or two ahead of him, the two Princes slowed the foaming horse to a walk, and cast anxious glances over their shoulders.

'The sly little sorcerer,' Ansel spat. 'Did you hear him growling and whining at them? Likely he set them upon us as revenge for leaving him to feed the Pot.'

'Perhaps,' Gilfred mused. 'We must rid ourselves of him and soon.'

'We'll wait for him along the trail. I shall gut him like a fish with pleasure.'

'No. Let us make haste to the castle that we might arrive before him. Leave the rest to me. His murderous intentions will be rewarded in kind.'

From the second that they stepped into the black marble hall, the weight of all the masonry, pile upon pile of it, pressed down upon them and drove out any tiny vestige of good humour, leaving room for fear. Alex shivered. Outside, the sun – summer in winter for a brief uncomfortable moment – had been baking their backs through their clothes as they had scrambled up the Giant's steps, but now his halls plunged them into a darkness lit only by guttering candles. Candles the size of an albino blacksmith's arms in the cups of great candelabra as distant as the moon.

'Cosy,' Inexplicable muttered. Even the gnome, who Alex thought surely would have become immune to the crushing of the spirit in the face of the vast, seemed cowed and fearful. He looked less like a spirit or a mythical creature now, and more like an old man – bones shortened by age, back bent and twisted under the weight of the Giant's house. Alex could feel his own resolve crumpling. Maybe they should run. Leave now. Get out before the dreadful great dense bulk of the giant began to come down the grey stairs in the distant end of the hall. In his imagination he saw not an oversized man, but a mass of bloated white tissue tufted with hair. A huge, domed, cancerous shoulder forcing its way past the stair post so that the arm unfolding out from under it – liquid, unformed, gargantuan and boneless – could reach down and scoop them all up in one mechanical shovel-sized hand.

The Doctor nudged Alex and he jumped. 'Do you know "Colonel Bogey"?' And before Alex could stop him, he began to whistle. It was quite a jaunty little tune, the mere idea of it setting Alex's teeth on edge. The supreme irritation he felt at the Doctor's stupidity made him focus intently on the man's fool face.

'You'll wake the Giant!' he whispered, managing to put his whole larynx behind it. If the Galactic Olympics had power whispering as a sport he'd have been representing Earth.

'Oh, I doubt it,' the Doctor said. 'I've been thinking about the relative size of the eardrum and resonant frequencies. You see, if the Giant is big enough to live comfortably in a hall this tall –' he waved his hands about – 'then his ears are going to be maybe fifty times the size of ours. So that tiny little bone under there –' he poked a finger just behind Alex's ear – 'is going to be bigger and mass more, and need more energy to move it. I think Giants may be pretty deaf to most human-sized sounds.' He grinned. 'Haven't you ever wanted to be a mouse in the wainscoting? We ought to sing a song about mice. There's a song about one in a windmill Miranda liked.'

'He's cracked,' Inexplicable whispered. He took the Doctor's sleeve in his hands, as if to stop him from wandering off and hurting himself. 'Look, Mr Know-All, there are Giants and Giants, ain't there. There's yer human Giants, like people, only bigger, and there's yer hideous monstrous Formorian buggers with one great staring eye and fifty tiny ears. So, please, please for once in yer noble adventurous logomantically reasoning life, let's just go and do the deed and get away. We don't need to talk about it. We just get the wibble-stone or starfall or what ever it is and scarper.'

'That's *Doctor* Know-All,' the Doctor began, only to be interrupted by Alex.

'Wibble-stone?'

'Oh I suppose you're the great orator now are you?' Inexplicable snapped. 'It just came out. I can't be calling it "anisotropically aligned quantonium" for the whole burglary. We can't steal something if we haven't got a proper name for it.

'It's the scientifically correct name,' Alex growled.

'It's the babblings of a clockwork-figurine maker whose been sniffing too much mercury. It's clockbabble!'

The Doctor cleared his throat. 'There now, I expect we feel much better for that, don't we? Come on, you two. We can't let this place make us feel devoid of significance. We can agree to differ for now. Alex, you may have to expand your view of science before we're done. Inexplicable, you may have to accept that some things can be set, tied down, recorded, and described, and that some people like it that way. Just because something is explainable doesn't make it less marvellous. Now, let's find that wibble-stone.'

It was as he finished speaking that they heard the sound from the vast stone staircase that stood at the far end of the hall. The sound of rats.

In the screen's blue-lit square window, Cathenar gestured proudly around himself, his bulky suit splashed with dappled light from the reflecting surfaces. Following his gestures, the robot hover cameras tilted downwards. On the floor of the sealed room, apart from the bare oval patch of floor on which the scientist crouched, the protoplasmic material had created a miniature landscape. In one place a stream of more liquid material bubbled up out of a rocky basin composed of a denser variant of the same stuff. Across the tiny hills, florets of mock lichen, grey and mauve and feather-fine, sprouted from ground that was as alive as they were, or as inanimate. The vuim experimenter felt sure he had seen tiny motile forms detach themselves from the mass and move around independently before being reabsorbed. It was marvellous. He said as much.

On his screen, in the orange ordinary light, Vuim-Captain scowled.

'I accept the detail is marvellous,' he said patiently, 'but accomplished as it is, what practical benefit does it have?'

'It is pushing its mimicry to a point hitherto unseen, Captain,' Scientist Cathenar said, hurt at the tone the Captain was taking.

'No. No, it is not. This toy is nothing. Remember, it mimicked *everything* we saw when we were trying to land. This rough approximation – this model gardening – is an irrelevance. It is simple by comparison, utterly simple. Do not be distracted. If it can make trees, it can make complex molecules, chlorophyll, and xenophyll. It can repair and replenish itself. I am not interested in how well it makes toys. I want to know if it can be made to make specific things. Has it mimicked any of the test packages yet?'

'Well it ate them, but as yet, no, no it hasn't.'

'Not even the language-memory modules?'

'Yes, something of a long shot, sir, I always thought. It did seem to take longer over them, but that might have been the steel casings.'

'Just study, and determine worth. Refrain from venting your sarcasm. A thing that can *make* a tree is fantastic enough if it is working from an example, a pattern of complex instructions ingested and reprocessed. I cannot believe that this *creature* is making things up out of nowhere. We must be able to determine how it gathers data, and hence provide it with the data we prefer. We must be able to use it.'

'What if it doesn't mimic? What if it just evolves?'

'Pardon me?'

'What if it doesn't need patterns? We don't know how long it took to produce the landscape we found outside. Maybe it's been millennia, just a slow adaptation to conditions.'

'And in this random evolution, I suppose it simply happened to evolve so close an approximation to the plants and geography that reflects perfectly the hills and streams of Earth, the planet of the species to colonise it?'

'*If* Christina Human-Captain was correct in her assumption that this world was human-settled – the mother ship still reports no contact with her scout vessel.'

'I take it as proven by the landscape outside. I have walked on Earth, Cathenar, seen the heather blow on the hills of Scotland when we met with that chemical company about their synthetic medicines. These hills are the same. Even the air tests the same. The plants breathe out carbon dioxide in the right quantity, the minerals react just so.'

'But the minerals are natural, at least, surely?'

'Are they? It formed a blade of steel from somewhere, each molecule pulled from elsewhere by forces we can hardly duplicate in our most advanced machines, still less apply with this fanatical, organic precision. We can trust nothing on this world, plant, animal or rock, until we know how to make them *be* for us – Cathenar?'

'Apologies, Captain, this suit is beginning to wear me down. Feels like I've been wearing it for a month.'

As the scientist spoke, Vuim-Captain suddenly noticed that his attention had been drawn elsewhere. Fixed downwards into the room's tiny rolling hills.

'Captain!'

The cameras zoomed to follow the biologist's gaze.

On the tiny hillside, the hill had grown a scale replica of their lander.

* * *

When the ogre heard the girl weeping his heart was filled with pity, for she had never treated him unkindly, though he was frightful to look upon. He opened the attic door a crack and saw her slumped over the spinning wheel. The room was filled to the rafters with bundles of flax. Her great dark eyes overflowed with tears as she looked up at him and he thought his heart would break.

'Kill me and be done with it,' said she, 'for I know full well the task those wicked girls have set me is impossible and I would rather die at your hand now, in dark of night, than wait for morning's light to shine upon my hopeless state.'

And she was so lovely with her doe-brown skin and her hair as black as coal that he knew he could no more kill her than he could take a knife to his own heart. He came into the room and knelt before her.

'Oh, my dearest Ai, I know that I am but an ugly ogre whose countenance you fear, but I have grown to love you more than life itself and I would do anything in my power to ease the burden of this task. I wish with all my heart there was someone who could do such a thing as this.'

And with a loud crack, an old woman appeared out of thin air. She was hideously deformed: one foot huge and flattened from treading, her lower lip enlarged and drooping from licking thread, and a thumb broadened out of shape from twisting it. 'What you wish I can easily accomplish,' said she, and she shooed the troubled girl from the spinning wheel and sat upon the stool.

'Granny!' the ogre cried in delight. 'What are you doing here?'

The old woman patted him on his pocked cheek. 'Bricklebrit, my dear boy, I've come to help, just as you wished.'

She looked at the stunned Anji and winked.

The rats were the size of lean and hungry dogs, all bone and

116

muscle, and they came down the stairs in a pack. Their screeching howl was like the shattering of glass.

The Doctor swept the gnome up on his shoulder and ran for the wall. 'Come on! The edging on the panelling might just give definition of shapes to a giant, but if we wedge our backs against one side and brace our feet with the other –'

'We're going to climb the wall panelling?' Alex panted.

'Unless you want to fight the rats,' the Doctor said simply, giving Alex a push up the wall. 'Go! This is their territory and they outnumber us.'

Alex felt the rough wood splinter against his back and managed to work himself a couple of feet higher. He was starting to feel disorientated. He knew that he was still himself, still five foot nine inches tall, still positioned advantageously between the myriad smaller animals and the few beasts larger than man. He knew that it was everything around him that was monstrous, distorted and unreal, but he felt he was being squeezed into nothingness, into nonentity. Below him, the Doctor, now also climbing, kicked at a rat scrambling over a pile of its fellows. They're making a pyramid, Alex realised, a rat pyramid. They're going to learn to climb. How big were their brain cases? As big as a dog's? Bigger? How well could they think?

'Keep going,' the Doctor called. 'I've got Inex and we're right behind you. Take it gradually, rest if you need to. You can't fall while I'm here.'

But you could fall, Doctor, and where would that leave me?

As if answering Alex's thought, the Doctor said, 'At the top of the wall there are tapestries rolled up. Probably let down to cover the walls in deep winter. We can make our way along the top of them and get to the stairs that way. We won't have to touch the ground.'

Inex was blue with fear, clutching the Doctor's shoulder with a death grip. 'Rats,' he mumbled.

* * *

The Giant stirred on his bed, and sniffed the air. 'A gnome's heart,' his heavy voice pounded, 'pumping fear. A man's heart, slower than the gnome's but still fast for the man-cattle's kind.' A great lolling tongue flopped out of his massive mouth, and a hint, no more than two or three pints, of drool spilled out. The tongue drew back. He sniffed again. 'Two hearts in a new beast. Smells of man-cattle... and other. Two hearts beating in a new kind of chest, in a new juice.'

He raised himself, and the bed creaked.

Vicious spikes of sunlight were trying to penetrate Anji's shuttered eyes. The mattress felt unusually uncomfortable and there was a hard lump under her back, but even so she didn't want to open her eyes just yet. Didn't want to face the regimen of morning run, shower, dress and work. Not today. Wait. Oh, hell. Didn't she have something scheduled for today, some important entry in her daily planner? Something about a party for some CEO from the Castle of Sighs?

No. That wasn't it at all. She groaned, realising she was lying on the uneven floor of an attic with the full light of day screaming at her to 'wake up, for God's sake! The day's half gone!'

Last night she'd been forced to close her eyes when the blur of impossible motion in the room had overwhelmed her. But even with her eyes squeezed shut she could still hear the whine and hum of a thousand spindles spinning and the hot sigh of the flax coming up from the bundles on the floor and down from the stacks in rafters, twisting round and round into continuous loops of colour and light where there should have been only a soft beige sheen. And the loops were fed into looms where the patterns emerged so rapidly that it was like watching one of those time-elapsed films of flowers blooming. In the centre sat the ogre's grandmother with her strange deformities and strangely familiar face, smiling only with her eyes, a bodhisattva of the spinning wheel keeping it all in motion. The sounds became a kind of white noise: the flap of the treadle, the whirr of the flywheel, the clatter of looms like London traffic, a constant thrum that numbed her to sleep in Bricklebrit's lap.

Oh dear. She'd have to deal with that at some point, but not now. Not yet. Just a few more minutes of not looking, not seeing, not knowing.

Perhaps last night had been a dream caused by emotional trauma and the sounds of crickets and frogs outside. And if that was dream, then perhaps the sisters, the cottage, the witch and the wishing box were part of a dream, and in fact all her travels with the Doctor were part of one long dream and maybe she'd open her eyes and happily find herself in hospital coming out of a coma, and maybe Da–

'Ai! Ai! Open the door.'

This dream royally sucked. Anji sat up with a moan. Her right side was numb and began to tingle painfully as the blood started circulating again.

'What's she doing in there?' 'She's pushed something against the door.' 'Who will draw our baths?' 'It's nearly three o'clock. I need to dress my hair –' 'Ai! Open this door right now or I'll have Stupid break it down! Ai!'

She rubbed her eyes.

The attic was bare save for the spinning wheel, the loom, and the six gowns folded neatly on the floor. And beside her lay the plain little wishing box, which had apparently been the pea beneath her mattress.

'This should be easier,' the Doctor said, as the gasping Alex recovered, his legs dangling over the side of the curtain rod. Luckily the Giant appeared to have no interest in pelmets or frills. The tops of the tapestries were merely wrapped around the iron rods that supported them, iron rods thick enough with the heavy fabric to make a walkway for the three travellers.

The fabric was soft underfoot and the iron solid, but they were still a long way up with no safety net, and they moved cautiously towards the stairs. How they would cross the gap between the rod end and the banister the Doctor hadn't yet decided, but he was confident he'd think of something.

Somewhere in the tower above them a great echoing crash resounded.

The Giant stuck a meaty fist under his bed and felt about. His hand thumped heavily on the wooden boards. A clattering pile of bones was swept out as he sought a pair of great black shoes shod with iron. The rest of his clothing seemed little more than a vast patchwork cloth, and he grunted as he fastened it about him like a toga, bare hairy flesh showing through where the cloth was worn.

He shambled to the window, and pulled back the finely woven tapestry depicting the death of tiny men hunted by great grey hounds. In the light, the patchwork of his clothes seemed to distress him and he pulled at part of it that was coming away. The blue patch, a human's long coat gutted and sewn together with the others that made up his outfit, ripped in his hand and he brushed it off on to the floor. Maybe the blood-bearers below would have good cloth on their backs. It was time his patchwork was mended.

Chapter Nine
The Golden Acorns of the Wood

'I've only one glove,' Michaela said, holding up one glittering ruby mitt.

'Well, you know,' Anji said breathlessly on her way out of one sister's room to answer the bellows of another, 'all the fashionable ladies only wear one glove so when a gentlemen goes to kiss her hand he doesn't get his moustache caught in the bead work.'

Michaela giggled. 'Ooh. Do you think the Duke will kiss my hand?'

'I don't think he'll have much choice.'

Michaela's one glove was only a little problem compared with the glorious fabrications Anji had been forced to use to explain the others. The gowns were all in the specified hues but had all the style of sacks with holes for heads and arms. Yet the girls hadn't noticed at all. They'd squealed with delight over the rich patterns and shimmering silks. It was after they'd tried them on that the trouble began.

'The boning is awfully stiff and chafing,' Jermaine gasped. It was indeed. She looked like she was wearing an iron maiden over cloth of gold. She'd have trouble dancing. Even breathing too deeply seemed a risky enterprise. Anji stuck the diamond-studded combs into Jermaine's coiffure and said, 'Men adore anything with a lock and key. Just don't let the Duke find the key too early or you'll lose your mysterious allure.'

'There's a key?' Jermaine called but Anji was on to the next one.

Titonia looked like she was covered in snot the exact shade of her specified blade of grass. Her weeping did not add much to the effect. Anji told her that the wet look was very daring and could only be carried off by sylphs and, of course, sylph-like girls such as Titonia.

The fashionable explanation for Marlo's moonbeam dress nearly didn't work. The 'men prefer a woman with good broad hips' didn't begin to justify the sagging full-moon-sized bustle at the rear. Marlo was going to be a hard sell and Anji was grateful for the interruption of the pounding on the front door so she could devise a strategy.

Christina was not the kind of person who succumbed to futility and hopelessness. She had, up until this moment, believed that futility and hopelessness were the chemical by-products of a lazy mind. So, to find herself where she was now, with her bottom planted in a pile of damp, decaying leaves, weeping in hopelessness at the futility of it all, was humiliating to say the least. She'd long ceased worrying about meeting the wildman of the woods and had actually been longing for a confrontation, if only to break the monotony of wandering in circles following the elusive siren of the white-hole energy from her tracker. The feeling that now racked her body was cold despair. She could not possibly go on. She was lost and she was going to die and no one cared and nobody loved her and she was all alone and if only she'd taken that scruffy William to bed when she'd had the opportunity and why hadn't she changed her will so her mother wouldn't be able to contest it and would the company find a way to absorb her shares of the profits, the bastards, and how long did it take to die of hopelessness and futility anyway? Oh hell, it'll probably take forever, unless a bear ate her first. She remembered her Trinary Company business class guru intoning nasally, 'Sometimes you eat the bear, sometimes the bear eats you.' She'd been eating the bear every day for quite some time now, so it was bound to happen eventually. It was so unfair. Fame and fortune within reach and here she was defeated by a landscape. She railed loudly at the injustice of it all, startling a group of sparrows from the branches above her head. She didn't notice the small bird that settled on a tree stump nearby until it spoke to her.

Why a sparrow speaking should make her faint and not a sphinx in a cornfield was a question Christina Morgenstern would never be able to answer.

'What?'

The footman took a step back at the brown-skinned serving girl's curt greeting. 'I bring a message for the marriageable ladies of the household from the Duke of Sighs.'

From upstairs the demanding screeches from the marriageable ladies of the household made him wince. He had delivered the first proclamation and did not envy the servants of this household.

'I'll see that they get it,' she said reaching for it.

The hand that offered the scroll pulled it back.

'You have a look uncommon strange for these parts,' the footman said. 'Whence your people?'

'Whence?' she laughed, tugging the parchment from his tense fingers. 'Let's see… a galaxy far, far away? Excuse me.' She started to close the door on his foot.

'And were you a princess in Galaxy Far-faraway?'

'Well, I had a woman come in to clean my flat every Tuesday.' She sighed, her luminous dark eyes thoughtful for a moment. 'She hoovered the carpet in a pattern just like those Japanese gardeners rake gravel, you know? Very Zen. It was wonderful. I never really appreciated it. So, yes, I guess I was a princess. Bye, bye now.' And she closed the door in his face.

Despite the girl's lack of courtesy (or perhaps because of it), the footman felt a wave of elation. Her curious manner of speech and form bespoke a woman of a very different world. His lord, the Duke, had courted many women, from the blue-skinned Queen of the Pavonines to Uwila the owl-girl. But those women were born to this world, made up of its parts and part of its dreams. This dusky princess from Galaxy Far-faraway with her talk of 'hoovering' and 'gravel gardening' was surely the Duke's sought-after bride, the one he was so desperate to find that he'd cancelled the great ball and thus dashed the hopes of every young lady throughout the land.

As the footman climbed into the carriage he heard a horrible screeching from the upstairs chambers. He could only pray the ladies of the house didn't kill the bride before the Duke of Sighs returned to claim her.

Rain was falling, tiny drops on to her face. She licked a drop from her lips, and blinked away the drops from her eyelashes.

'Thank goodness,' said a chirpy little voice. 'Lor miss, ye give us quite a scare, faintin' dead away all ladylike, and no mistake.'

Christina groaned, realising that such an authentically chirpy voice could only mean one thing – the sparrow *was* talking to her. She rolled her head back and saw the sparrow hopping to and fro on the tree stump. It dipped its wing in a hollow in the stump and flicked dirty cold water on to her face.

'So very pale, she is,' it said, and splashed about in the water again for another shower.

'Knock it off!' she sputtered as the drops flew.

'We only wish to help, miss.'

'I only see one of you.'

'I speak for all.'

'Yes. You *speak*. That's very interesting.'

'Not so interesting. We are everywhere. We hear everything. The wodewose has terrible hard riddles in his wood. Riddles he cannot answer. Riddles within riddles, boxes within boxes. Can you help us?'

She sat up with a grim laugh. 'Help you, how? I can't even get out of this forest.'

'Anyone may enter his forest, but only the wodewose knows the way out. You must bargain with him. If we help you, will you help us when we have need?'

She shrugged. 'If I can, sure.'

'He comes! He comes!' cried the sparrow and it took flight suddenly, alighting on first this branch, then another before diving down to land on her shoulder. The little claws walking back and forth made her shiver. 'Three riddles he will pose. Three answers you must give thus: a needle, a diamond, nothing. Remember.'

'A needle, a diamond, nothing,' she replied, caught up in the tension of the moment.

It shot up into the branches above her head with a final cry, 'Remember your promise!'

Anxious moments became a full minute of dread. She could feel the forest opening and closing as if the branches were so many doors in a vast house. A rush of silence preceded its master through the corridors of trees. All things that made noise fell silent as it moved through, even the wind, then sounded again when it passed. She could hear it moving closer, faster, an inevitable, inescapable force of nature, like an avalanche. And yet, being human, she came up to a crouch and tried to run away from it, sprinting for a dark patch through the ferns, only to find herself brought up short, spinning away and scuttling back in a panic when she realised the dark patch in the ferns was a face. A face that seemed to consist of a pair of glowing eyes embedded in fur above a slack, wet, open mouth – a horror broken by a sudden grin, sharp teeth that turned the creature, momentarily, into a man.

'Another riddle,' the face croaked. 'Want answers now.' The ferns parted, or rather the creature moved them aside. Beyond was a group of trees, hunched and leaning with their branches hanging over a tall blue box in the centre of them. The grouping reminded her of worried relatives gathered round the cradle of some colicky infant stubbornly refusing their remedies. The trees seemed completely at a loss at this noisome presence, and this made them angry. She felt the anger in their twisted shapes, in the dry sick grey bark of them.

The wildman of the woods bounded over to the box, granting her a view of his naked, very hairy backside. He ducked in and out of the close trees, circling the box and sniffing it, before loping back to her. Thankfully, his beard was practically an apron and covered the parts she wasn't really keen on seeing. He was older than dirt and, indeed, seemed to be made mostly of dirt, with the hair and wrinkles merely adding textural interest. But when his eyes focused on her she caught her breath. They were the green of every leaf and there was a world behind them. She felt the coarseness of his palm like tree bark as he took her hand and led her closer to the box, to within arm's length of it. A branch stirred and she could see a beacon or lamp on top of it, and as he guided her around she saw the door and the legend on one of its panels, and she stood dumbfounded for a moment before the absurdity struck her. She couldn't help it. She laughed. Her finger inched toward the blue painted wood and tingled as it approached it – tingly wood, in a living wood –

She snatched her hand back suddenly, feeling a prick of pain like from a splinter. There was a watery bead of blood on her finger and a smear of blood on the panel. But she couldn't see any splinters in the wood. Maybe the box had thorns. Tiny blue thorns.

'What is?' the wodewose asked, pointing at the box.

'Well, I know what the words say, but I really have no idea.'

The trees around it straightened suddenly and she took a startled step back, then forward again, trapped between two kinds of strange.

'Know. Know this. What is?'

'I don't know! An emergency beacon of some kind, I suppose. Have you gone inside? There are probably instruments inside.'

He shook his head, sending twigs and clumps of mud flying. 'No! No! No! Come with skyfallings. You come too. Skyfallings.'

Skyfallings? Oh Jeez. Skyfallings! She patted her pockets for the tracking device. Gone! She must have dropped it –

The wildman's arm shot out and she squeaked like a frightened little girl before seeing the tracker in his outstretched hand. She reached for it uncertainly, wiped the residual grime from its surface before activating it. White-hole energy could take any form, she supposed, though why this particular one she couldn't fathom. But the blue police box didn't read as white-hole energy. She shook her head. 'I really don't know…'

The wodewose plopped himself down before the box like some yogi on a mountaintop, suddenly composed and businesslike. The changed manner of his speech so startled her that for a moment his words didn't register.

'What you seek, though close by, cannot be found within my domain.'

'The skyfallings?'

He nodded. 'Three riddles have I. Answer true and you are free to seek what you desire above all.' He made a motion too fast for eyes to follow, a bit of legerdemain that produced three golden acorns in his outstretched palm. 'One for each answer.'

'What are they for?'

'Moments of great need.'

Whatever, Christina thought. 'Ask away.'

'Open I wait always, never blinking. Through me, all clothes are made, without winking.'

'A needle,' she said. Too quickly. His eyes narrowed.

'Someone has told you the answer.'

'Oh, come on,' she bluffed. 'That was an easy one.'

'They get harder,' he said, smiling. 'Deep I lie, until I rise. A star from the oldest pressed flower.'

This time she was careful to appear to be thinking hard. 'Hmmm, let me see. Is it – no, no, can't be that. Maybe… oh, I know. A diamond?'

The wildman threw back his head and howled. The forest reacted with a deafening clatter of wings, squeaks, chitters, roars and angry caws. Somewhere, far distant, his howl was picked up and echoed back by many others. She shuddered. Wolves. His fist closed around the acorns and he pointed one long filthy finger at her.

'Someone has been telling!'

'No! Please. I can't have all the answers. You're too clever by far.'

He drew back and looked at her askance, smug expression on his brown deeply furrowed face. 'Here's one. What's bigger on the inside than on the outside?'

The third answer the sparrow had given was 'nothing'. But that answer didn't seem to suit the question. She wanted to try something cheesy and sentimental like 'a mother's love' but the sparrow said the third answer was nothing. What if that hadn't been the answer at all, but merely the sparrow's parting shot.

'Sorry, wildman's a comin'. Never mind. That's a big Nothing, honey.' She stared at the police box, gnawing a thumbnail and thinking furiously. Hmm. What was bigger on the inside than on the outside? She swallowed, hard.

'Um… nothing?'

The wodewose leapt to his feet with a cry of triumph and did a mad jig. He snorted and cackled and pointed at her. 'Ha! I tricked you.' His beard apron whirled around him as he danced. She squeezed her eyes shut as his voice took on a singsong quality, reciting the other riddle. The one with the answer, 'nothing'.

'Wiser than God. Worse than the Devil. The Rich do not possess me. The Poor cannot be rid of me. If you eat me you *die*!'

'Bugger,' she hissed. 'Damn. Damn. Damn.'

Just as suddenly as he'd begun, the dance ended and he scrambled up the blue box and perched on its roof, elbows resting on his drawn-up knees, chin cupped in his hands, looking pensive, almost despondent. A hollow victory it seemed.

'What is?' he sighed. 'Not yours. Not skyfallings. What is?'

Using his distraction, Christina began to edge back through the tufts of ferns. But his eyes caught her and she couldn't move or look away. In their fire she seemed for a moment to see other, more normal, more weary eyes. He opened his hand and the acorns dropped at her feet. Just like that. She knew without asking that he was giving them to her despite everything. Slowly she bent to retrieve them. Her mind tried to insist the acorns themselves were useless, but accepting them was politic. She gazed at him on his perch, long beard hanging between his legs and brushing the side of the police box. He looked sad and deeply puzzled.

'Go,' he said.

She turned, pushed through the fern fronds, walked maybe fifty metres, found the trees thinning, found a path paved with pebbles, found an orchard with pears and apples, found a yard with geese and chickens beside a cottage with a round stone well, and at the well was a brown-skinned woman dipping out water from a bucket and offering the dipper to a man standing next to a white horse. The man had a plume in his hat.

Chapter Ten
The Giant's Treasure Chest

Alex stuck his head up above the level of the ceiling and gazed at the first floor of the castle. The broad stairway had presented them with a banister that, in itself was a causeway, but as they climbed it had narrowed and grown confined. Finally it had offered a route to the upper storeys that, while spacious for, say, a cavalry troop – with horses – was still a tight squeeze for anyone of the gargantuan dimensions implied by the hall. So maybe Alex should have guessed what he was going to see, but he didn't and the shock nearly drove him down a step, back to the Doctor and his familiar spirit.

'I don't. It's. I can't.'

He'd been expecting the same as the floor below: scenery that dwarfed them by maybe fifty times, that turned them to mice. A landscape that ate up their efforts, making the crossing of a room a route march over enemy territory. But the first floor of the Giant's castle was worse than the ground, not because it was larger, more dwarfing of the three thieves, but because everything was nearer their scale. It was as if by climbing upwards through the tower they were growing larger, becoming acclimatised or habituated to it. All through the hall Alex had been marshalling his courage. He had told himself over and over that if there could be such things as Giants then there was a way to make it all right. Horrible but all right. You just had to think of them as something known and commonplace, dangerous like a reactor leak or a meteor. A giant (with a small 'g') might eat you, but so might a cougar or a lion if one ever got out of its cage, and if its ancestors hadn't been altered to go into allergic shock at the taste of man. Thought of like that, a giant was a real danger like any wild animal. It had certain characteristics. It could be faced. It could be prepared for. Even if a giant were a hundred feet tall, that would be a fact. But a Giant with a capital 'G'; a Giant that was a hundred feet tall on the ground floor of its house, and only twenty feet tall on the first? How could that be prepared for? On the second floor it might be two hundred feet and on the third? Maybe on the third it would be vast, beyond any comprehension of size.

His heart was pounding now, and his breath was coming in gasps of awful fear. The Doctor's hand fell on his shoulder not, thank God, as a surprise – a surprise would have made him wet himself – but as an expected bit of human understanding. The bastard. He just couldn't let anyone suffer, could he? He had to make himself felt. As if his stupid key was the key to the human heart.

'What do you make of that, then?' he asked, waiting for the Doctor to undergo the same kind of vertiginous moment of unreality that he had experienced.

The Doctor looked round carefully. 'This floor must be split into more conventional rooms. This antechamber leads off through nine doors. We've no way of knowing which leads up.'

'Up,' Alex croaked.

'Your detector put the source at four hundred feet, remember.'

'We. We can't go up.' Alex was sweating. He must see it, mustn't he? Must see what the floor implied. 'We don't know what's up there.'

Above them, inevitably, footsteps echoed.

'Sounds smaller,' Inex said, joining them.

'It's smaller generally here,' the Doctor said, as if he'd only just noticed. He turned and went down a step. 'Still big!' he shouted, and came back with a look on his face that Alex would have taken for pure glee, if it weren't for the fact that no one in their right mind could find this fun.

'How to blend cosiness and grandeur? It can't just be that

downstairs is painted in cold colours, can it?' The Doctor grinned. 'Or do Giants go in for ostentatious cyclopean architecture? Are we to suppose that the ground floor was simply a, "I'm bigger than you are, Jack, laddy, and no mistake" fashion statement? If so it *must* be Freudian.'

Alex felt a moment's relief. 'Do you really think that might be it?' He could see how that would work. It was power building in stone. Stage setting and he fell for it. The 'Giant' was probably a midget with a good team of designers.

'Leave it out, Doc, you old tease,' Inex said. 'Can't you see the lad's nigh boneless with fear? Of course the buggers don't build for show. They're always cramped and always short of space and half their temper and nastiness comes from never being able to get away from the walls. You haven't seen two people rub along together through life till you've met Giants, and that's a fact. Claustrophobic beasts.'

'So,' the Doctor prompted gently, 'as our expert, would you like to explain why the floor below is designed to accommodate a "Big" Giant, and this floor only built to house a "Medium" one? I could see a growing Giant being forced upwards into floors with fewer rooms like a hermit crab seeking a larger shell, but to begin big and shrink?'

Overhead, somewhere, metal clattered.

The Giant came down to the second floor, banging his metal boots on the stairs. On the way his patchwork became too heavy and oppressive and he sloughed it off instinctively as a snake sheds its skin. On the middle step his feet slipped out of the oversized shoes, and he slung them over his back, holding the laces like ropes. He did not think about why, but made his way, shoeless and naked, to the treasure room, grabbing at sheepskins hung there to dry as he entered. It was to this place that the intruders would come. They were below already, moving and scuttling. They would come here seeking his harp that wept diamonds when its strings were plucked, or the clockwork orchestra with its twenty-nine articulated figures so lifelike that he had bitten the head off the thirtieth in a moment of intra-musical hunger.

Or the box in its cloak-of-gold wrapping.

If they should take it…

If they were brave enough, hardy enough, strong enough…

If they spirited it far away…

He rubbed his hands together convulsively. Broad, hairy and horse-choking in size, his knuckles cracked like thunder.

'I'm sorry I really don't see what the fuss is,' the gnome was grumbling.

'Inex,' the Doctor said. 'You said Giants are of different kinds. Some like men, and some Formorian. I recognise that name from Erse and Celtic mythology. So, Giants as a race come in different sizes, yes?'

'Different sizes, different skin colours, different numbers of heads, different opinions about calcium-bread, yes.'

'But does a particular Giant come in different sizes?'

'Well not at the same time.'

'Let me try.' Alex leaned towards the gnome in a friendly way, and before the Doctor realised what he was about, he had seized Wottlewort's nose between his finger and thumb and squeezed. 'Can they bloody change size or not, you squirt?'

Inex glared at him, 'Ebryfing ch'nges size, you lummoiks. The world moves and we move with it, what else should happen? Giants are the size they need to be.'

The Doctor slapped Alex's hand, and he left go with a yelp. The blow hadn't been hard but the unexpectedness of it stung more than the impact.

'I don't approve of torture, Mr Volpe.'

'Torture! A bit of a tweak?'

'And if he hadn't answered where would you stop? If it had

been a matter of life and death where would you stop? I think, under everything, you could be a good man, Alex. Start now.'

'Oh, and you've never threatened anyone, even to save a life, I suppose?'

'Maybe. But if I did it was with their own weapons, and even then…'

He paused and seemed to be looking away or inside or at some oblique angle to the rest of them. 'I think I threatened a man with his pet rat once. He'd been spreading the plague and I needed his antidote to cure a dear friend of mine. At least I think it was a rat, but I remember it danced to a penny whistle. Only to save a life, and only the threat. Still…' He shook his head as if to dislodge the memory. 'Come on, the Giant's moving about and we have to find where he's put this starfall of yours.'

'Did you ever see a film called *King Kong*?' the Doctor asked Alex as they moved through a series of rooms that, while large, were still on the scale of humanity, or at least monarchy. 'May have been a bit before your time.'

Inexplicable glanced up from his examination of a dozen tall jars stoppered with wax. 'What's a film?'

'This is going to be one of those discussions where the people have absolutely nothing in common, isn't it?' the Doctor said dryly. 'Think of it as puppet theatre with a nigh unlimited budget. The point is the filmmakers advertised Kong, this giant ape that was the film's beast, as being fifty feet tall, stressing the spectacular. Then they needed the creature to interact with Fay Wray, who was playing the beauty, so they actually scaled their Giant Ape model so it looked eighteen feet high so it could hold her in its hand, and have her large enough to see.' He shushed Alex who looked ready to interrupt. 'Then, they found that when it had to climb the… er… castle at the end, it didn't seem big enough, so they made it look twenty-four feet high.'

'So?' Alex managed. 'That was drama, storytelling. Not reality.'

'Yes, and interestingly, most of the filmgoers of the time didn't notice. I certainly didn't. Now what if this is drama too? The Giant is the size it needs to be. I only wonder why we were able to notice.'

Dressed in sheepskins fastened about his waist with strips of human skin that he'd tanned and hardened into leather, the Giant sniffed the air. He had a couch in the midst of his treasures where he liked to lie and dream of molten gold poured into thieves' mouths. Spitting and burning. Sprawled on this couch he intended to wait until the creatures came close, and then, snip, snap – he would take them in his great hands and move them until they broke.

He closed his eyes. Across the treasure room floor, on its plinth of onyx, the weeping harp – stirred by the breeze of the Giant's flatulent breath – shed a few half-hearted industrial diamonds, and flaking pieces of carborundum, before falling quiet.

Softly at first, and then rising through man, carthorse and elephant in its volume, the Giant began to snore.

They came into a long gallery lined with pictures, row after row of heavy, thick, oil-painted portraits. All of the same great head, majestic, beetle-browed, glowering, the clothing painted on almost at random by finishers with lesser degrees of skill.

'It's too quiet,' the Doctor said. 'If this were a wood I'd be asking if you could hear anything, and you'd say no, and I'd say no, not even the birds. Where are all those rats now? Or silverfish.' He shuddered. 'Creepy things, silverfish. I once had a phobia about them, but Freud wouldn't tell me what I'd said under hypnosis.'

Alex glared. 'I don't think you know what planet you're on half the time.'

'A good point,' the Doctor conceded. 'What planet *are* we on?'

'Ah, er, well, I don't know if it has an official designation. We charted it as WHO one because of the white –' He mentally kicked himself. He'd been careful not to spell out in so many words the nature of the energies he was seeking, and his talk of quantonium, a rare but far more frequently found substance than the inner energies of a white hole, had been, as the ghastly gnome had put it, mere clockbabble. Still, the Doctor seemed to be listening harder to the wood panelling than Alex's words, so maybe, just maybe, the slip had gone unnoticed.

The Doctor jammed his head harder against the dark wood. 'Snoring. I can hear snoring.'

A moment later they all could, and a moment after that they had hands over their ears.

'Ah, that's the ticket,' Inex shouted approvingly. 'Get 'em while they're asleep.'

'I think you're right about that part of the plan,' the Doctor agreed, 'but –' and he gave Alex a hard look – 'we're going to take the starfall and nothing else. We are not thieves. We are removing a dangerous power that shouldn't be here. I hope that's clear.'

The snores led them – or led the Doctor, who led them – up a further flight of stairs to a floor slightly smaller than the one they had just negotiated. The ceiling was low, maybe fourteen feet from the ground, and Alex had adapted so completely to the even greater heights and vistas of the earlier floors that he found himself crouching as they moved.

The snore was worse this close. It was half rasping bass and half a subsonic rumble through the floor and the walls and the air.

'I'm reminded of the "fat wild woman's teeth",' the Doctor said cryptically. 'It's coming from in there.' He pointed ominously to a door. 'I think this must be the place for taking off shoes and administering the oath of silence.' He didn't stop to field any demands for clarity from his two companions, but carefully pushed the door ajar.

'Yes. That's a Giant all right,' he said, and shut the door again. He addressed his companions over his shoulder, his eyes fixed on the centre of the door. 'Alex get your white-hole sniffer ready. Inex, we're going to fan out and have a look round, but remember: no oh-it-slipped-into-my-pocket-honest-guvnor nonsense.'

Behind the Doctor's line of sight, Inex hastily started emptying his pockets, but whether it was because of the Doctor's injunction or be cause he anticipated better pickings in the room than he'd had on the previous floor, Alex wasn't sure.

But when they entered the room, he saw that if Inex had been motivated by greed, then avarice had not led him false. The rooms on the first floor had their trinkets and their bibelots, their discarded swords and suits of armour split distressingly like, and probably for the same purpose as, lobster shells, but this great circular room had all the debris from below and more, piled into mountainous heaps of dazzling largesse. Glittering gold and sparkling jewels of every hue spilled out of tumbled chests and boxes. Luxurious pelts, spotted, striped and black and white, were stacked twenty high. Clockwork curios and musical instruments lay strewn about like discarded toys.

The Doctor grinned, and held a finger to his lips, before speaking entirely normally. 'Quickly, Alex, what does your scanner say? Is it in here?' Alex scowled, but given the bloody snoring there was little chance anything else could be heard. Indeed he was surprised he could make out the Doctor's voice. He decided to answer in kind, at ordinary volume, and let the Doctor lose his words in the oceanic mutter and roar of the thing whose stomach rose like a domed summit over the golden foothills. 'I think so. The readings are muffled. Gold's quite a heavy metal. It might be interfering with the signal. I don't think the designers expected it to have to work through opulence.'

The Doctor nodded, although he couldn't have heard, and they fanned out around the room in a kind of golden daze. Even the Doctor seemed transfixed, though Alex got the impression it was the volume and intricacies of the pieces rather than their raw worth that held him.

* * *

The Giant had been listening to the little hearts beating away on the other side of the heaps of gold for a while now. When the very littlest one came close he would eat him. There was no other use for such small fry. But the middle-sized ones were often good with needle and thread or had in them a rousing song or a story or two. He liked songs and stories, and his coat was in such tatters that it shamed him to be seen in it. If they could stitch or sing he could restrain his appetite for a time.

Oh, they were slow, though, slow beasts and cautious. Maybe if he opened one eye.

Alex sidled around the room, back to the wall. He knew at one level of his mind that he was reacting oddly. No benefit he might get from locating the energy would make this risk a viable one, and the raw gold and gleaming gemstones around should mean nothing to him. One poor deal ago, he'd walked the desolate shores of Albraxiz, where the hydrochloric acid sea gently moulded the sapphire beaches into smooth gems the size of medicine balls, and all he'd valued there had been his sun shade, and the sealed bathing suit that kept him from getting splashed. There were worlds where people shook better-quality gemstones than these out of their boots with a hobbling curse. There were worlds where zinc was worth more than silver, and arsenic worth more than platinum. It shouldn't matter to him that he was surrounded with thick, yellow, buttery-lit gold. But it was making his mouth water as if he could live on it, not by trading, but by pressing it to his lips and tearing off a chunk.

But the Giant! he tried to tell himself. The Giant is just over there. He's only pretending to be asleep. Even that didn't break the spell, although he was able to muster enough self-interest to head for the far wall, to try to put as much distance as possible between him and the beast. Currently the Giant's head was turned away from Alex, which was how he liked it.

'Doctor, he's awake,' Inex cried from his perch atop the heap of gold cartwheel-sized coins. Oh great, now the gnome's observant, Alex thought, as Inex scrambled back over the top and went skiing down sending gold showering to either side.

The Giant's massive hand impacted just behind Inex, scooping up the top of the mound and lifting a spilling heap of gold into the air that sent Inex flying. On the other side of the room, Alex's sensor started beeping fit to burst. He grabbed hold of something wrapped in a golden cloth, and thrust the sensor in his belt. The Doctor was shouting for the Giant to 'calm down' and 'pick on someone your own size'. He was managing to avoid the monster's attempts to get hold of him by – Alex couldn't tell exactly if it was a formal martial art – seeming to be in two places at once and having far more arms and legs than you might expect. But Alex knew it was only a matter of time before someone said hello to Mr Gullet, and he was decidedly of the opinion that it wasn't going to be him.

He started to edge out of a castle window, his treasure clutched to his breast. Did he feel regretful at leaving the Doctor and his brat there to be eaten? No, he firmly answered himself, making his way along the window's ledge to the next room – a trip made easier by the fact that the ledge was a good seven feet wide. The Doctor's kindly façade and pretence of virtue sickened him. And as for that animal he'd befriended, well, the fact that they were going to be Giant chow before long only made the acquisition of the white-hole object more toothsome.

Through the next window, a round one, it was a simple sprint to the passageway. Running, and beginning to feel his breath catch at the back of his throat, Alex felt the shape of the object in his hands like a boy feeling a present before opening it. It felt like a hard box with carving or scroll work. He guessed the Giant had stuck the energy source into a Giant-sized snuffbox, or a gewgaw-holder. The first thing he needed to do was get out of the castle, find somewhere quiet and get it open. Oddly, he wasn't afraid of the rats. He knew somehow they would scatter and flee from the Alex who held aloft this fabulous treasure.

* * *

The Giant flicked Inex up into the air, and threw his head back, mouth gaping open, intending that the falling gnome would drop - plop - down his throat like a tiny piece of fruit, or a... the Doctor searched for the right word even as he flung himself at the monster's ankle. Like a Tic Tac, he thought as he bounced off the thick hairy tree trunk that was the creature's leg. We're little sweets to him.

Maybe it was the impact, however small, maybe it was luck, but the gnome came down spinning, at an angle, and landed a full body blow to the Giant's nose. Wottlewort was small, even next to the Doctor. To the Giant, briefly rendered cross-eyed by the need to focus on this painful speck of food, he was almost invisible, yet he seemed to have magicked up some extra mass from somewhere, because the Giant's nose spread most satisfactorily over his face. He roared, and the noise shook the chamber.

The Doctor by this time was climbing up the Giant's leg, and trying to convince himself that everything happening was somehow fitting in the same room they'd entered. This floor had been smaller, but now the limits of the treasure hall were becoming vague grey blurs in the distance, and the height of the creature that had been able to lie in the centre of it was becoming impossible to fathom.

'Inex, hang on,' he shouted. 'Don't let him get you. I'll think of something!'

The Giant got the little flea between his finger and thumb.

'So, shall I squeeze?' he rumbled. 'What good are you, too small to taste, too tough to digest, thief and companion of thieves!'

'Oh, throw me out of the window, if you please, Mr Giant,' Inex shouted, defiantly. 'Boil me in bitumen and roll me in porcupine quills. Behead me and display my brains on cocktail sticks, and grateful I'll be. But don't send me back to the vile durance of my just and extremely well-deserved punishment.'

'What's that?' the Giant rasped. 'On the lam, are you, wart?

Bothering good and true citizens with your criminal recidivist ways. By my harp's hard tears, I will not see the good law flouted!'

And while the Doctor was out of sight, busy with the crucial climbing problem of the groin, the Giant dealt with the gnome just as he deserved.

'Ah, ha! Another sand flea!' A hand the size of two mattresses closed around the Doctor and plucked him from his precarious grip midway up the Giant's sheepskins. 'I was hoping some of you would be worth domesticating, but you're all too puny. Look at you, spindle-shanks and bone.' He turned the Doctor to and fro, holding him tight with only his forefinger and thumb. 'Eating you would break my aching teeth, but what good are you living?'

The Doctor now hung level with the Giant's open mouth. He had hoped things here worked to a pattern that wasn't fully visible to him yet, and that in that pattern, even being eaten might not be absolutely irreversible. But he could see the sleeve of Inex's tunic stuck in the Giant's gums like a piece of spinach, and a stick of bone, ulna maybe, lodged between the back molars, and all in all it didn't look promising. Still, if Inex survived yet, in the belly of the beast, or elsewhere, he needed to be alive and uneaten to help him.

'I can sing the periodic table to the tune of "The Modern Major General" –' he cried in a voice that sounded squeaky and desperate even to his own ears. The breath from the cavernous maw was all blood and decay, a stench that blew his hair back, squeezed his eyes shut and made him gag with every huff.

Eaten! He was about to be eaten! Not chased and hunted and given half a chance. No. Crunched, chewed and swallowed in one gulp. And, of course, the unpleasant digestive process that followed. Best to be thoroughly chewed first. To be swallowed whole and then digested, stomach acids slowly corroding his flesh –

'I can set bones, dress wounds and tell amusing stories about people from other lands. I know several long narrative poems, including one complex enough to be considered a life form!' His body kicked and struggled as the Giant upended him, then turned him round again, trying to decide whether to bite the head off first or the feet or just stick the whole of him in his mouth. The massive tongue rolled out for an experimental taste and his boot soles back-pedalled furiously against the slippery pink hills and valleys. He was close to having a Fay Wray moment. A womanly scream would not go amiss here. Perhaps if he flashed a tantalising, distracting bit of skin, or bared his torso –

'I can cook omelettes if you've got fresh eggs. Nuns taught me how to do trapunto.'

The tongue drew back. One huge eye squinted down suspiciously. 'That some kind of stitching?'

'Yes!' the Doctor cried. 'The abbess did the most intricate patterns on white silk, scenes from the lives of saints. I'm not that good of course, but I can do you a fair climbing ivy.'

The Giant considered for a moment, before a dismissive snort sent a hurricane of spittle over the small morsel he held between thumb and forefinger. Then he opened his mouth wider and popped the Doctor in.

The Doctor stiffened and spread-eagled his limbs, trying to keep the jaw from closing, trying to prompt a gag reflex. If he could head-butt the uvula then just maybe – but he dared not move for fear he'd slide down the back of the throat like an oyster. 'Aacck,' the Giant intoned trying to bring his back teeth together. The Doctor's hand slipped and then his foot slipped and the heel of his boot thrust against a swollen mass.

The Giant howled in pain, a roar and exhalation that sent the Doctor flying from the dank pit of the mouth and into the stack of furs on the massive oak table across the room. He rolled and tumbled, quite unable to stop his momentum, and went over the edge of the table, only managing to grasp the edge with his fingertips at the moment before he would have plummeted to the floor. He elbowed his way over the top again. The Giant was holding his jaw and whimpering, a waterfall of drool pouring from his mouth.

The Doctor's ears were ringing and he had to shout just to hear himself and so managed to be heard over the Giant's sobs of pain. 'I could take care of that abscess for you. And remove that pig you seemed to have lodged back there. And there's a wonderful thing called flossing you should try.' He made a dramatic bow. 'Doctor Know-All at your service.'

Chapter Eleven
The Master-Maid

In the morning the giant had to go out and pasture his goats, and as he was leaving the house he told his new servant that he must mend his stockings while he was away. 'And after that,' the giant said, 'you need not do any more work today, for you have come to a kind master, and your stories amuse me. But what I have set you to do must be done well and thoroughly, and you must on no account go into any of the rooms that lead from the west of the one in which you slept last night. If you do I will take your life.'

'Well to be sure, he is an easy master,' said the tailor-for-today as he walked up and down the room humming and singing to himself, for he thought there would be plenty of time to mend a pair of stockings. 'But it would be amusing to steal a glance at the other rooms as well, for there must be something that he is afraid of my seeing as I am not allowed to enter them.' So he went into the first room. A cauldron was hanging from the walls; it was boiling, but the servant could see no fire under it. I wonder what is inside it, he thought and dipped a piece of thread in, and the thread became just as if it were made of copper. That's a nice kind of soup. If anyone were to taste that his throat would be gilded.

Then he went into the next chamber. There, too, a cauldron was hanging from the wall, bubbling and boiling, but there was no fire under this either. 'I will just try what this is like, too,' said the tailor, thrusting another piece of thread into it, and it came out silvered over. 'Such costly soup is not to be seen in all the palaces of the world. But everything depends on how it tastes.' And then he went into the third room. There, too, was a cauldron hanging from the wall, boiling, exactly the same as in the other two rooms. The tailor took pleasure in trying this also, so he dipped a piece of thread in, and it came out so brightly gilded that he declared, 'Some talk about going from bad to worse, but this is better and better. If he boils gold here, what can he boil in there?' He was determined to see and went through the door to the fourth room. In it was a cauldron much larger than the other three, but this hung over a huge fire in the centre of a great stone hearth, and on a bench someone was seated who was like a king's daughter dressed as a serving girl.

'Oh! In heaven's name what are you doing here?' said she who sat upon the bench.

'I took the place of servant, tailor, dentist and doctor here two days ago,' he explained.

'Days you say? No manservant has lasted more than one day in service to my master,' said she. 'He is a cruel giant with a terrible temper.'

'True, he will not let me leave the castle, but he has not been unkind. I have only to mend his stockings today and I shall be done.'

'Yes, but how will you be able to do that?' she asked. 'If you darn them as other people do, ten new holes will start for every stitch you take. This cauldron boils for you. I am to cook you when you fail.'

'He intends to eat me still? After all I have done for him?'

'It is his nature,' said the girl sadly. 'But I will teach you how to mend his stockings; you must use his silver toothpick for a needle and his hair that you will find on his pillow for the thread.'

'Yes, I will attend to that,' said the man, and stayed sitting where he was the whole day talking with the girl, whose name was Janet. She told him that she was the seventh daughter of a

145

'We must cross the Bay of Moons,' she said. 'To the Castle of Sighs.'

He stopped pacing suddenly and spun about with a look so wild and strange that it took her breath away. As much as she desired to draw her eyes from that gaze she found she could not and a hot blush rose from her bosom to her hairline. It was not because he was handsome or kind that she blushed, for most men looked at a girl, taking in her attributes and judging them fair or otherwise. Some men looked past or through. His gaze looked at her from the inside out, saw everything and judged nothing. It was merely the way he looked at the world; she could have been *anything* for all that the look meant at that moment. She knew then that no matter how good and noble his intentions, no matter what instructions she gave and how sincerely he promised, he would betray her.

'Sighs,' he mused, 'yes, the tailor king mentioned that place.'

'It is the court of the Fairy Belesia,' she whispered. 'All questions find answers there.'

'Then that is where we must go. Now. Tonight.' He took her hand and pulled her to her feet. He smiled the smile that had first enchanted her. A gentle 'trust me' smile. And she found herself trusting again. She did not return the smile, however, but looked him in the eyes and matched him for fervour. 'What you will shall be done, Doctor. But you must promise to do exactly as I say or my charms against the Giant will be all for nothing.'

'I will. I promise.'

She knew he would try. She also knew he would fail.

When Fitz saw the spires of the castle – just the tip-tops cresting the hill – he sighed and nearly wept from sheer relief. It was impossible not to: the sight of it made his heart so light and full at the same time. He'd been bone-weary and numb with despair this last stretch of the journey, though he kept telling himself the reasons for it were stupid. He'd been in far worse

Of course now things were different. He was working his way through the household services. Dentist, tailor, hypnotherapist! Who knew what dreams that might bring?

'So, was your mother always so strict?' the Doctor asked.

'Oh aye, Albert this, Albert that. Albert can you build us a causeway, Albert can you sink this fleet – but me ask for something, and then it was all "we'll see" and that. She had to have control, you know.'

The Giant lay back on his couch among the gold, and part of his great mind drifted back to the earlier stages of his life. Doctor Know-All did have a dab hand with a needle, a soothing healing touch with a tooth, and a soft and calming voice. He was starting to be glad he hadn't eaten the man after all. It was easy to drift away to the sound of his stories and comments and questions.

Lulled, he hardly knew what memories and incidents were being recalled.

The Doctor looked at the hypnotised Giant, and kept his voice even, warm and devoid of anything abrupt or too eager. 'Really?' he said. 'Not even a little oak tree? I'm sorry to hear it. I don't see why your mother wouldn't let you grow one on blotting paper if Mrs Gorgafat's eldest did. And you found the thing that the young man stole in a crater you say? Hmm, and how did that make you feel when you looked at it?'

'It reminded me of that oak tree, somewhat, like it might grow yet, grow beyond any neat squared paper. Somewhat, it scared us. No, threatened. Held a dark promise.'

The voice wasn't the Giant's. Or at least, the Doctor thought, it was *more* than the Giant's voice alone. 'It threatened us. They threatened us. Then we began to hurt.'

'Oh, my poor teeth!' That was the Giant again.

Teeth, the Doctor mused, yes, those teeth. That strange damage – some had circular holes cut straight through them, and others

147

had geometric slices cut out at the edges. It didn't look like natural damage at all; in fact those teeth were remarkably clean in comparison. Apart from the abscess which would probably go down after the Doctor had finished growing enough amoxyicillin for a five-day course, he'd really only needed a good scaling and sandpapering.

'You still have your treasure,' the Doctor said, trying to reach that wider voice again. 'That box couldn't have been worth much.'

'A nuisance. Gone and good riddance.'

The Doctor couldn't tell which voice was speaking now. He leaned closer to the Giant's ear. 'Tell me more about the box. What's inside it?'

'Webs and promises. A terrible gift for Dreamers of What Is.'

'Go on,' he prompted in his best psychiatrist's voice.

But the Giant, comfortable despite the faint fading twinges from his teeth, muttered, 'I am going to eat you soon,' and slipped into proper sleep.

Leaning back against the cushions, the Doctor crossed his arms and frowned. Webs and promises, terrible gifts – that didn't sound good. Where there were webs there were usually spiders lurking about.

He'd once read that the mind was a web of autonomous systems mindlessly instilling the illusion of an operator. The human soul was supposedly an illusion, a faked ghost in an otherwise deterministic machine driven by the necessities of causation. While he didn't agree with Hume or the reductionists he did fear that they might be right. Right by their own logic, mindlessly of course, right only for evolutionary reasons. Brains that think like *this* survive, brains that think like *that* do not. When a fly treads on a web its fate is predetermined, predicted and conveyed by the messages running down to the spider waiting at the centre. To escape it would have to be able to break a chain made, not of sticky secretions, but of cause and effect; the very causation that made this happen rather than that. This and that, he repeated to himself, liking the sounds of the words. This and that, kiss and cat. This *and* that. Oh my. Boxes full of this *and* that. What happens when every thread leads to a different spider? What happens when everything is suddenly possible right now, all at once, at the same time?

There were things yet to learn here in the castle, but instinct told him he hadn't the leisure of time to coax it from the Giant. He thought of Janet, the Master-maid, big brown eyes, black curls and rosy cheeks. Humble, wise beyond her years, all in all a classic representation of a type whose antecedents he was only now beginning to fit into a pattern. Yet she was certainly human, or so perfect a model that he could sense the cells in her body decaying as she moved inexorably towards her eventual death – hopefully of old age. But if he was right in what he was beginning to suspect, everything human on this peculiar world was in danger. In danger at least of madness, and, perhaps, of things worse.

'I think we should make good our escape now. Tonight.'

Janet looked at the man who had come in answer to her most fervent prayers. What he was suggesting frankly shocked her. 'But you have not yet served your seven days, my lord –'

'Please don't call me that! I am no one's lord. I don't have time for bowing and scraping, and I'm afraid I can't wait any longer. There is a danger here, far greater than whatever should befall me if I don't follow the traditional form in these matters. I have friends out there somewhere. We must leave tonight.' The firelight from the huge stone hearth cast his pacing form in undulating shadows over the flagstones and she thought for a moment she saw the shadows of seven other very different men as he moved from one side of the room to the other. She could not help but feel that the agitation and urgency projected by these many shadows boded ill.

'But where to go?' he mused. 'Where to start?'

'We must cross the Bay of Moons,' she said. 'To the Castle of Sighs.'

He stopped pacing suddenly and spun about with a look so wild and strange that it took her breath away. As much as she desired to draw her eyes from that gaze she found she could not and a hot blush rose from her bosom to her hairline. It was not because he was handsome or kind that she blushed, for most men looked at a girl, taking in her attributes and judging them fair or otherwise. Some men looked past or through. His gaze looked at her from the inside out, saw everything and judged nothing. It was merely the way he looked at the world; she could have been *anything* for all that the look meant at that moment. She knew then that no matter how good and noble his intentions, no matter what instructions she gave and how sincerely he promised, he would betray her.

'Sighs,' he mused, 'yes, the tailor king mentioned that place.'

'It is the court of the Fairy Belesia,' she whispered. 'All questions find answers there.'

'Then that is where we must go. Now. Tonight.' He took her hand and pulled her to her feet. He smiled the smile that had first enchanted her. A gentle 'trust me' smile. And she found herself trusting again. She did not return the smile, however, but looked him in the eyes and matched him for fervour. 'What you will shall be done, Doctor. But you must promise to do exactly as I say or my charms against the Giant will be all for nothing.'

'I will. I promise.'

She knew he would try. She also knew he would fail.

When Fitz saw the spires of the castle – just the tip-tops cresting the hill – he sighed and nearly wept from sheer relief. It was impossible not to: the sight of it made his heart so light and full at the same time. He'd been bone-weary and numb with despair this last stretch of the journey, though he kept telling himself the reasons for it were stupid. He'd been in far worse situations after all, and the donkey was only a donkey – an old, sway-backed donkey not long for the world that had never known anything but burdens and a stick across its back its whole miserable life. But the donkey had been good company in a way the wolf cloak, for all its magic, was not. The only animated things about the mangy hide now were the fleas. He'd already worked out that the cloak was probably under a spell, but he wasn't sure if it was merely an object with magical properties or a real wolf that had been cursed. For a while he'd even entertained thoughts of breaking the spell by befriending it. He thanked it for its assistance, asked it questions about itself, told it about his friend the Doctor and all the places he'd seen in his travels and how he worried about Anji and how much he hated Ansel and Gilfred. But after a while it was too much effort and he couldn't stand the sound of his own voice, the strained sincerity and the brittle edge of his own laughter at his own jokes. He was utterly alone, betrayed and friendless, on a journey that seemed futile. He couldn't imagine why his feet kept moving, yet had no compelling reason to stop them. So when he saw the spires he knew by his response he'd reached his destination at last. And as he trudged up the long incline of the hill, bringing more of the castle into view, he felt the burden on his heart lighten with each step. When he reached the top he sat down and took in the view of farmlands, orchards and the town built into terraced hillsides that overlooked a sea. The Castle of Sighs was like a centrepiece on a table, arranged so that its beauty could be appreciated, but never interfered with by conversation or passing the butter. Fitz sat on the hilltop by the side of the road for a long time. Coaches and pony carts, carriages and knights in armour riding huge horses also in armour – all these passed him, making their way in some haste towards the castle. Finally, a tinker stopped and asked if he wanted a lift. Fitz hopped up on the wagon's wheel and sat beside the man. 'As I've had a good deed done by me,' the man said, 'I'm obliged to pass it on to the next fellow.'

So, as the late-afternoon sun bathed the castle walls in rose-gold and even the shadows seemed to sigh in contentment, Fitz travelled the road that would lead him to the castle gates and, somehow he knew, to Anji and the Doctor.

'I must marry none but the loveliest, the most noble and the most exotic of women,' the tall man said. He struck a pose in his white velvet and satin knickerbockers, in his lovingly oiled leather riding boots, and stiff, scarlet, military-cut coat with massive yellow rope frogging. He looked like a toy soldier, but the sword at his side was real enough, and besides that he had servants, and men-at-arms, and a castle stocked no doubt with dungeons, and the instrumentalities by which complex differences of opinion had been so often settled in history. So bearing all that in mind Anji didn't laugh in his face. Instead she darted a curious glance at the woman huddled to her left.

Anji's first impression of her when she'd stumbled into the yard had been a jumble of 'white' 'blonde' and 'dressed all wrong' before they'd both been swept on to horses by the Duke's henchmen. Her fellow 'prisoner of lurve' was only a blurred presence in the corner of her eye on that harried ride to the castle. Now that she'd had a chance to really look at the woman, she was struck by how cool she seemed with it all. And even dragged, as the woman evidently had been, backwards through several large hedges, her opposite number was pretty gorgeous. Not that Anji could see what men went for in that creamy-skinned, pale-blonde, long-legged, pouty type. It wasn't as if any of them had a chance in hell with that sort.

'I am the Duke of Sighs,' the man said. 'Prince-Under-The-Throne of Eorn's Dale. Grand Chancellor of the Five Favoured Isles. By the Grace of She Who Watches, I hold power here.' He moved towards them, his feet twinkling in a dainty step down the marble stairs.

'The Sun-maiden, with her hair like the corn rising from

summer's heart.' The Duke bowed to the blonde. 'And the Moon-maid, dusky and desirable.' He bowed to Anji. 'Both born, so my oracle tells, of other places, other climes. Taught by strange teachers, amused by different toys, enchanted by other tales, fed on divers sweetmeats and the Unusual Fruits of the Outland Paradises. Oh, how delicious is the choice fate has bestowed upon me! My oracle has shown me wed, but will not show me she whom I have honoured above all women else. It shows me only fragments, and I will have wholes!'

The fair-haired woman audibly suppressed a snigger, and Anji, thinking about it, couldn't help but join in.

The Duke scowled, and his weak but handsome face seemed no longer weak, but also no longer handsome. He clicked his fingers, and one of the black suits of armour – giving no sign of a man inside it – clattered over the floor to the crowd of courtiers and silk-clad ladies who were waiting nervously along the walls. A delegation, Anji guessed, here to protest the cancellation of the Grand Ball.

'I would not harm one spot on your skins, my ladies,' the Duke said, 'but my will here is not to be defied.' He gestured at a dumpy woman in obviously handed-down finery, standing at a point in the crowd where ostentation faded into desperation. 'I appoint her your joint maid. Officer, where the mistress offends the maid must pay. Do your duty.'

The black-armoured thing backhanded the whimpering woman across the face. A fine mist of blood boiled off the dark gauntlet and she wheeled back, only to be caught by the arm before she hit the floor as the guard raised his hand again, awaiting the signal to administer another blow.

'No!' Anji screamed. 'Stop it! You can't do that.'

'Can I not?' the Duke said, as if momentarily, honestly surprised. Apparently no one had ever told him that he couldn't. 'Oh ho, my Moon-maid, you would command me I have no doubt. Ah, if only you two were not so differently beautiful. How shall I choose between Noon and Midnight?'

'Perhaps a test, my lord Duke,' the blonde woman suggested winningly. 'Let us compete in some way to win your hand.'

Anji shot a look at her, her mouth open to protest, before realising what was going on. She looked at her competition with new interest. The woman was feigning enthusiasm with the best of them, yet Anji could see a faint stiffness to her body, and there was a light fey disdain in her voice that showed she wasn't any more impressed with the himbo than Anji herself. Like Anji, she wore a gown of dazzling beauty, exactly like hers in fact, only she seemed to look better in it. And again, like Anji, she showed signs of bruising from the way the black armoured guards must have thrust her into it.

'A test, ho-ha!' the Duke cried. 'Oh yes. But there shall be three tests: a test of beauty, a test of grace and a test of wit, for my one true love must surpass all other women in those qualities if she is not to dull me with her dim light and thus eclipse my own radiance. Guards, take them and their maid to quarters, and let them prepare. Feed them pomegranates to perfume the skin, and let them be bathed in rare oils.'

'And let them have medicine for their maid,' the fair haired woman chimed in, 'for otherwise she might bleed on our silks, and skimp on our manicures.' Anji really thought the Duke was going to twig that one – there was genuine loathing in the Sun-Goddess's voice. But evidently his ego was so large that sarcasm merely bounced off. He nodded and waved that the guards should comply.

'I'm Christina,' the blonde woman said, talking more to the maid than to Anji. She was trying to get the woman to stop crying long enough so they could bind her torn cheek where the iron fist had cut across her face. Anji dabbed at the wound with some green ointment from the basket of herbs and powders the guard had presented them. There was, she supposed, a fifty-fifty chance she was attempting to mend damaged flesh with hair gel, but the smell reminded her of a zinc-based medicine her mother used to use, so she went with that.

'I'm Anji. What's your name?'

'Rozered,' the injured woman said.

The Ill Luck and What Came After

Now there was once a woman who had ill luck aplenty. First her horse kicked the milking pail, so the cow's milk was lost; then the cow trampled the wheat, so that the grain was lost. Then the dirt in the grain choked the sow, so the pig was lost. Then the Duke decreed there should be no ball, so her daughters cried and cried. And that wasn't right. Everyone knew there ought to be a ball when the unmarried heir to a land came of age, so that true love could shine out of every girl's face whether common or noble. And besides, it didn't follow from the horse's kick at all, so it couldn't be real bad luck. So she came to the castle to speak to the Duke, or, better still, to Her, blessings be upon her. But the Duke set his men-at-arms upon the poor woman and bound her to serve two outland wenches, and for the life of her she couldn't see how that bad luck worked either, for the horse and the cow and the grain and the pig all followed in nature's way, just as the good luck to come would. Bad upon bad for a time, then good upon good to those that learned how to endure. The face of the world turns, the high brought low, the humble raised. But where was aught natural in this ill luck that proceeded from the wilfulness of the Duke and his disdain of all good custom?

'Well I think I see where the pig fits in,' Anji said, covering the unlucky woman's wound with a square of muslin. 'He's giving the orders.'

'I see why you might think that, miss,' Rozered said. 'The Duke is a little vain perhaps, but he must be humbled and tempered in the fires of true love. Suffer for the sake of his love and be restored to her after great hardships. And pardon me for saying so, miss, but I don't see how that can happen if he's only two to choose from.'

Considering her injuries, Anji thought her too forgiving by half. She bit back a sharp response, knowing the woman needed calm, not anger.

At least the ointment seemed to be helping. Some of the smaller cuts were already healing and the puffiness had gone down considerably in just a few short minutes. Anji, in the absence of pockets, stuffed the little tin into the long sleeves of her dress in case it proved useful later.

Despite the medicine's efficacy, the rough bench wasn't much of a hospital bed and the quarters were obviously a guardroom, not a guest apartment. They'd have to get out of here. 'We need to find a way out,' she mused aloud. Then, embarrassed at having stated the obvious, she offered, 'I don't think either of us are inclined to keep our opinions to ourselves and we can't let her take beatings for us.'

Christina grinned. 'I'm hazarding a guess that you aren't from around these parts.'

'No,' Anji said, 'I'm… well… I'm a traveller.'

'A space traveller?'

'Well, yes.' It was explanation enough for the time being.

'Me too!' Christina offered Anji her hand. 'The way I see it we've got to work together. Old leather and lace in there is dreaming up his tests and I for one have no intention of winning, especially if any of them have to do with how well we perform in the sack or the kitchen – but hey, looks like you've got the kitchen stuff down at least.' Anji withdrew her hand, painfully aware of the dry, cracked skin and torn cuticles, wishing she'd rubbed a little of the medicine on her hands before responding to the friendly gesture. Christina made a darting 'just joking' motion with her head that reminded Anji so much of a snake that she wondered if the woman wasn't part of this world after all. 'Honest,' Christina continued, 'I don't want to see either of us screwed over, or screwed, as the case may be. We space chicks have got to stick together, right? Dump the chump somehow.'

'Maybe…' Anji started, then stopped, wondering if she shouldn't keep back the box and its odd other-directed wishes, keep it secret. Part of her wanted to, even though she wasn't sure why. But surely this had to be her time to use it. She'd done her chores for a full week; two in fact after her cheating had backfired. The fact that it had felt like cheating suggested that even the Duke might be bound by his own agreed tests. Maybe she could wish their way through them. Of course the box was back in the cottage, but there was at least a chance that it was ownership and not proximity that mattered. She looked Christina in the eye, willing her to believe. 'I've got a wishing box.'

A cure for cancer. A billion billion trade units in anti-matter held in a magnetic bond. An idea waiting to be taken into a brain that would change society as much as hyperdrive, as much as computers, as much as agriculture. Something never seen before that made every woman willing at the press of a button. Alex didn't know what was in the box, but he knew, he just knew, that it was better than his dreams of wealth, of power, of endless indulgences in rooms, minimalist and beautiful. He'd always wanted to afford taste.

He felt in his pocket for something to prise open the box, and found the Doctor's damn key. It was flat and metal, but he couldn't bear the sight of it. He put the box down on a flat stone, and stood for a moment weighing the key in his hand. Not heavy enough. He dug into the soft earth around the stone. It was dirt mixed with red clay, damp and thick. He packed it round the key until he had a hard ball the size of a fist. He clenched it in his hands until he left bone-shaped channels in the clay and all the liquid was a stain on his fingers. Then he threw it. Hard and far.

There, now. That was better. Damn the man. Damn him for being so utterly betrayable.

Turning back to the box on its little hollow rock, he saw that it was in fact slightly ajar, a soft light seeping around the metal rim of its lid. Hadn't the stone been flat a moment ago? He looked again. The box was on a rock, that much was certain, but the stone was strange. It was flat / and hollow / and curved upwards in a gentle dome. And the box was shut / half open / open. And his hands reaching for it were stained red / yellow / brown with mud / and were clean / and were missing a finger / but he couldn't tell which.

He managed to shut / open the lid so he couldn't / could see inside. He screamed / was struck dumb. In this state something came to him. It was big and horrible and, worse, he knew it was dead. He'd seen it pulled into the oven. He'd smelled it burning. 'You're dead,' he said as if his old friend Tento might not know. 'You're dead but you shouldn't take this box. It's worse than death. I'm dead too, except I'm not. I can feel the acid in the Giant's stomach from eating me, from the many Alexes that were eaten. Some of me died in the crash, and some of me in that fire oven. You mustn't take this box.' Fleeing the dead, he got up and ran.

'A what?'

'Um… a wishing box. I know how it sounds, but –'

'No, no, that's great. Can you wish us out of here?'

'So far it hasn't granted any for me, just the damn sisters. Anyway, it's back at the cottage.'

'Really? Hmm,' Christina said. Now *that* was interesting. A fellow outsider to this world just happens to have a 'wishing box' that just happens to be at the cottage where her locator just happened to pinpoint the energy source from the white hole right before that idiot Duke had both of them carted away.

The train of her gown swept the floor, turning dust bunnies

into Tasmanian devils as she went to check the door for the tenth time. 'Still here?' she said to the black-armoured guard. 'We haven't had our perfumed-oil baths yet, you know.' The helmet turned, to look at her seemingly, but she sensed no animating flesh beneath the grilled mask, and found herself stepping back from it. Her heel caught in the hem of the dress and she kicked it out of her way with a growl as she turned back to her fellow prisoners. The dress was so damned heavy, and the boning was a bitch. She smiled at Anji, who was obviously feeling the effects on her ribcage as well. 'I suggest we figure out a way to fetch your little box back here so I can wish us the hell out of here.'

'While you're at it,' Anji said, 'maybe you could wish the Duke a case of painfully large haemorrhoids so his head won't fit up there quite so comfortably any more.' She grinned wickedly and her joke seemed to remove all traces of strain from her face. Christina felt a twinge of competitive panic, quite unexpected, and foolish really. So what if Anji was pretty? So what if she looked better in the gown? It wasn't as if Christina wanted to win this stupid contest or anything. But not winning – *trying not to win* – went entirely against her nature. She suspected it was the same for her counterpart.

The wishing box was important. She could sense it in her acquisitive soul.

'Perhaps we can send our maid on an errand. Perhaps to fetch your treasured pot of pinks?'

'And then he changed himself into a great silver wolf and commanded the pack to attack us,' Gilfred told the watchmen at the gate. 'We barely escaped with our lives, thanks to my brother's skill with a blade.'

Ansel mimed his thrust into the wolf's breast, and smiled grimly. 'But alas, one of our horses fell to the wolf pack.'

'Leave it to us, my lords,' said one of the watchmen. 'He shall find himself in chains and binding spells ere he pass these walls.'

159

Gilfred gave the man a 'brothers in arms' pat on the shoulder. 'Good. Good. You shall know him by the wolfskin he wears about his shoulders. And use caution, my friends. Though he looks like a beggar, he is cunning. The sooner he is in the dungeon awaiting execution, the better it will be for all honest men.' He slipped the man a coin. 'Send word to us when you have him in custody.'

The watchman nodded. So the brothers went to claim the hospitality that was their due as noblemen. Good food, hot water, clean clothes and servants to lay it all out for them.

So the Master-maid took a knife and cut her little finger and dropped three drops of blood upon a wooden stool; then took the knife and cut the doctor's little finger and dropped three drops of his blood into the cauldron, and then she put old rags, and shoe soles, and bones, and all sorts of rubbish into the cauldron. She filled a chest with a lump of salt, and a water flask which was hanging by the door, and she also took with her a dried-up leaf with the edges curled; and then she and the doctor went away with all the speed they could, and when they had gone a little way they came to the sea.

'But I see no boat,' said the doctor in some distress.

'Not to worry,' replied the Master-maid, and took out the leaf with edges curled. She placed it upon the foam that lapped at their feet and said, 'Little leaf, little leaf, become a boat that we may sail across the sea.'

And as she spoke, the leaf became a boat. They pushed it from the shore, got aboard and picked up the oars and began to row.

Now when the giant had been asleep a good long time, he began to stretch himself and feel a little hungry. He thought he could smell the doctor cooking in the pot.

'Will it soon boil?' said he.

'It is just beginning,' said the tiny tiny voice of the first drop of blood on the stool.

So the giant lay down to sleep again and slept for a while.

Then he began to move about a little again. 'Will it soon be ready now?' he called, but he did not look up any more than he had done the first time.

'Half done!' said the small small voice of the second drop of blood, and the giant believed it was the Master-maid again and went back to sleep. When he had slept for many hours he began to move and stretch himself. 'Is it not done yet?' said he.

'It is quite ready,' said the soft soft voice of the third drop of blood. The giant sat up and rubbed his eyes, but he could not see who it was had spoken to him. He called for the Master-maid, but there was no one to give an answer.

Ah well, she has just stolen out for a little, thought the giant, and he took a spoon and went off to the cauldron to have a taste; but there was nothing in it but shoe soles and rags and such as that, all boiled up together with just a hint of blood. Then he understood what had happened, and fell into such a rage that he hardly knew what he was doing. Away he went after the Master-maid and Doctor-Know-All so fast that the wind whistled behind him. It was not long before he came to the water, but he could not get over that. He did not like getting his feet wet or having sand between his toes. 'Well, I will soon find a cure for that: I have only to call my river-sucker,' said the giant and he did call him. So his river-sucker came with its thousand mouths and lay down, and drank one, two, three draughts, and with that all the water in the sea fell so low that the giant saw the Master-maid and the doctor out on the sea in their boat.

'Now you must throw out the lump of salt,' said the Master-maid, and the doctor did so, and it grew up into such a great high mountain that the giant could not come over it, and the river-sucker could not drink any more water.

'Well, well, I will soon find a cure for that,' said the giant, so he called to his hill-borer to come and bore through the mountain so that the river-sucker might be able to drink again.

But just as the hole was made and the river-sucker was beginning to drink, the Master-maid told the doctor to throw one or two drops out of the flask, and when he did this the sea became instantly full of water again, drowning the hill-borer and filling the sea with so much salt that the river-sucker protested to the giant that were he to drink it he would surely die. While the giant and river-sucker were arguing, the Master-maid and the doctor reached the land. He proposed they go straightway to the Castle of Sighs, but she said, 'The giant will not be so easily forestalled. You go ahead of me. I can hold him off with my spells a little while more. But when you get there you must not even give yourself time to greet anyone. Go straightway to Belesia's stable. There you will find her fairy steeds. You need only tell them where you want to go and they will bring you fast as the wind back to me. Please do not fail in this, for if you do not follow my instructions you will soon forget I ever existed, I foresee it.'

'How could I forget you exist?' the doctor laughed. Then his face grew troubled. 'Ah, and how can you know how much I have forgotten already? Very well. I will do as you ask. I will not fail you.'

But when he got to the castle, there was such a commotion going on that he was hardly noticed. For it seemed the Duke of Sighs was about to choose a bride.

Chapter Twelve
Tests of True Love

'Now, ladies,' the Duke said. 'This is the test of beauty.'

Anji gritted her teeth, dreading some corseted version of bathing suits and high heels, the most ludicrous costume combination devised by man. She fervently hoped not, because she hadn't waxed the bikini area in quite some time – since she was fifteen in fact. She glanced obliquely at Christina, who was managing somehow to look down her nose at the Duke and at the same time bestow upon him an ingratiating smile. She played her part well, Anji had to give her that. Annoyingly, perfectly well, with her upswept hair and jewelled comb and all that cleavage. Christina's gown was the colour of peach sorbet, all glittering ice crystals with tantalising glimpses of soft colour. Anji was in bridesmaid's turquoise. It wasn't fair –

Wait. What was she thinking? She didn't want to win this contest anyway.

'Both of you are delightful to my eyes,' the Duke continued, 'and so I cannot choose between you –'

She adjusted the puffs and pleats on the dress and rejoiced in its frumpery.

'– nor will my oracle decide the matter. Therefore I have appointed an impartial and disinterested judge.'

He nodded at the circling crowd around the edges of the throne room, and from its depths, from the wall-hugging river of people, a man stepped forth. He was very tall and thin and dressed all in black. Funeral clothes, Anji thought, with a high starched collar and a formal tie, items a century at least later in design than the clothes of the people around him – stiff cut and painful to wear for long, made more uncomfortable by the great, thick band of iron across his chest.

'This is Iron Johann, whose heart broke into pieces when his wife died, and who can smell no flower, and see no beauty. He is the justice here. Each of you will strive to please him and the one who can win from him a smile or the touch of a hand will be the more beautiful.'

Anji saw Christina grimace. She managed to wipe her face blank before the chortling Duke noticed, but Anji felt her whole body clench. This was far worse than bathing suits and high heels she'd imagined. This was abusive, cruel. That poor man. The Duke was laughing at his grief with the same solipsistic disregard he gave to Anji's and Christina's feelings. Only this man had truly suffered. Though his face showed little trace of emotion, Anji knew somehow that the iron band was the only thing holding him together.

'And if we don't?' she asked. It wasn't at all what they'd planned in the robing rooms, but she felt she'd be untrue to herself if she didn't ask.

'Nothing,' the Duke said. 'Nothing will happen, not to you. Of course your maid is another matter. My Iron Guards need the touch of flesh to replace what they no longer possess. The oracle taught me how to awaken them. They are *my* magic, not Hers, and when they must be fed it is the brave sacrifice of my people to feed them.'

Christina and Anji exchanged glances. If Rozered was carrying out their instructions there might be a chance, but they couldn't afford to have her absence discovered.

'Oh, one more point,' the Duke continued: 'Johann is quite blind. You will have to speak to him of your beauty, or find some other way to impress it upon him.'

Fitz had been whistling that song, the one in *The Wizard of Oz* that came after the poppies but before the horse of a different colour, when Dorothy and her pals see the Emerald City for the first time. He could never quite make out the words whenever he watched it, but he remembered they seemed happy words, full of promise, and the tune was cheerful, so he whistled as he stood waiting with hundreds of others to pass beyond the castle gates. So slow-moving was the queue that he also had time to remember that most of *The Wizard of Oz* had terrified him when he was a kid – those flying monkeys pounding the stuffing out of Scarecrow – eesh! Though for a brief period when he was seven he entertained the notion of growing up to be a flying monkey, mostly because they didn't take crap from anybody.

'Excuse me. Sir?'

Fitz assumed the query was for someone else until the tap on his shoulder insisted. 'Sir?'

A young woman was smiling at him. A pretty one with black hair, big brown eyes and a red-lipped smile that promised many things he'd barely thought about over the past few miserable days.

'Yes?' he gulped, smiling back so hard his face hurt.

'Would you mind if my little sisters and I went in before you?'

'Well, actually…' He did mind. It had taken an hour to get as close as he was.

'Oh please. I beg you, as a well-travelled gentleman. My sisters are not accustomed to long journeys. They're exhausted, poor darlings, and I'm at my wits' end trying to keep them entertained.'

He thought the 'well-travelled gentleman' business was a subtle dig. He knew he looked like hell and surely she was mocking him, but her smile was accompanied this time by a gentle squeeze of his arm. She wasn't afraid to touch him, even with the wolf's glass eyes no doubt glaring at her as its head dangled between his shoulder blades. He was exhausted himself and so hungry he felt hollow in his bones. But she had these dimples and a rather impressive pair blossoming over the top of her charming and tightly laced bodice and she did say little sisters and he supposed children should by rights go first. He sighed, though it sounded very like a groan, and nodded. 'All righ–'

The words had scarcely left his mouth when she opened hers and bellowed, 'Girls! He said yes! Stupid! Bring the cart!'

Fitz tensed, thinking she'd just called him stupid – which was certainly how he felt when he found himself behind an ox cart, a surly ogre, and six girls jostling, arguing, whining and bitching at each other. Six far from little girls. Especially the one called Marlo.

Christina stepped towards Johann. She could see the Asian woman dithering, and she was damned if she wasn't going to go out fighting. While they had agreed to spin things out long enough to keep the contests even so that Rozered would have time to hurry to the cottage and retrieve Anji's wishing box, she wasn't about to lose this round. It was a best-of-three competition. She could afford to walk this, lose the second – hell, she'd break wind if necessary – and hopefully by the time they had to cook up a draw on the third, the maid would be back. Even if the box would still only grant wishes for the sisters as Anji had said, she also figured they were on their way here like the social-climbing *parvenues* they were and it was a stone-cold cert that at least one of them, or, better, two, would wish that they were in the competitor's shoes sometime during the course of the contests.

She wasn't sure exactly when the desire to be judged the more beautiful had hit her. Maybe she was missing the easy power she'd felt with William Brok back on the *Bonaventure*, that thrum of desire she'd evoked in him with the tiniest of gestures. Of course Billy boy hadn't been around a woman in ages so she hadn't had to strain herself or anything. Or maybe it was the way Anji wore her 'sunlight-on-a-summer-sea' dress with dignity while she was lumbered with a giant knobbly coral comb out of a child's first dressing-up box, and a gown that looked the colour of thrown-up oranges. Still, that appeared not too much of a hindrance. The judge was blind, and she was betting the warmth and smell of a woman were all the beauty left to him – and the sound, of course. She was up for whispering sweet nothings. It was only business after all.

Anji watched sourly as Christina slunk over to Iron Johann, making the crowd go ooh at her measured, stealthy stride, moving as if she were about to begin a languid shedding of clothes. Naturally, the Duke was lapping it up, and she hoped Christina wouldn't go any more over the top, mostly because there was no way she could possibly match it. Dammit. What was she trying to pull here? They were supposed to come out in a draw, and the woman was looking too good! Glossy-magazine good. It couldn't affect Johann, although Anji's heart ached for him, but if the Duke fixated on Christina, he might forget the contests entirely and stick with *force majeure*. They needed it to stay even. To stay acceptable at least. She supposed it was Christina's risk in a sense, but Anji had the feeling that, macabre and sick as the Duke's games were shaping up to be, he would still abide by the inherent rules she'd sensed and observed. But how long before he decided to change the rules? Could he? By refusing to host the ball, by his use of the iron guards that had the crowd alternating between crawly obedience and raw panic, it was clear he was pulling away from his society more and more. He hadn't broken away entirely yet. If he did – she didn't want to complete the thought but it came unbidden anyway – if he ceased to care about the way 'things-were-done', then she and Christina were powerless to do anything about it. He could get his iron guards to hold them down and do whatever he wanted. And who would dare to interfere? It was such a short step from tyrant to sociopath.

I wish the Doctor were here, she thought, then shook her head like an etch-a-sketch. She didn't like that squiggly picture. Not a good idea to rely on the Doctor for salvation. She'd begun to forgive him for some things, and in other matters she likened his behaviour to that of an *idiot savant*. 'Special' in the way that Parsifal was special. If he rescued her from this predicament it would be the same way he got her into it, by accident, and not by riding in on a white charger.

I wish the Duke would turn into a toad, she thought instead, hard, just in case.

The ivy under Rozered's feet crackled, and the window ledge on which she was supporting herself by one elbow creaked ominously. With her other hand she inserted a bread knife from the kitchen at Sighs into the crack between shutters and tried to lift the latch to the servants' room over the kitchen. With a jiggle and a shove the rusty hook gave way. She ducked her head as the shutter swung out, nearly losing her toehold in the process. Arm hooked over the sill, feet scrambling in the ivy, she managed to pull herself up and over the ledge. *I'm too old for this sort of thing,* she mused, pausing a moment to catch her breath and slow the pounding of her heart. Then she peered into the darkened room.

On a dresser under the eaves the box glowed a dull bronze.

Christina had her head thrown back, dancing close enough to Johann to brush against him with her hip, her hands, and – at least once, Anji was sure – her breasts. The man stood rigid, his breathing shallow, showing commendable self-control or else simply restricted in movement by the spell of the iron band. Anji was barely breathing herself, but inside she was crawling with embarrassment. She hated the Duke at that moment, and she didn't often actually hate. Mild dislike was about the worst even the seediest would-be groper at office parties had caused before now. This hate was like her own iron band being tightened around her head, an emotion that made her physically ill, and a good part of it was directed not at the Duke but Christina. Prancing about like that. Loving it, seemingly, like that. Being – oh

God, was that it? Being the neighbour's perfect daughter? The one your parents held up as an example of how a daughter ought to behave, who never ever gave *her* parents grief. The one who played with you until another better little girl came along with a Barbie's Dream House, who stole lipstick from Woolworth's and slipped it in *your* pocket, who shagged the boy you fancied at the first nightclub you went to. The one who taught you to tense up at the wrong moments and insist on looking at the horse of pleasure's teeth before you'd take a gift. The one who got you so wound up with being the 'right' daughter doing the 'right' things that it had taken you three months to get round to introducing Dave to your mother. The one you wouldn't let Dave meet, *ever.*

Anji hoped it was somehow the Duke making her feel this way, or the magic of the castle, or a rule of the world, something. Because seeing Christina in her sparkling gown, seeing her *dance* – Anji very much wanted to be the good one with the dark centre. She wanted to win.

Christina silently cursed her clumsiness. Erotic was fine, on a bed, in private – well private-ish anyway, she thought, remembering that time after the first tripartite ship agreement got signed in Earth orbit – but how could she be remotely sexy when the hideous puke-coloured train on this nightmare of a dress kept tripping her up?

She'd got close enough to whisper a few times, but found herself saying, 'I'm really sorry' instead of the sweet nothings she'd planned. Her hand, and she hated that it did, brushed against the iron ring around the thin man's chest. The metal was cold as ice and a dark blue. 'I don't want to do this to you,' she murmured, 'but the Duke is threatening me. Us. I wish there was another way. I really do.'

In the silk pouch hidden beneath her dress, one of the wodewose's golden acorns turned black.

* * *

Having confiscated a bushel of suspiciously golden apples from the sisters, the guards were still bristling from the vitriol hurled at them by seemingly sweet young girls when Fitz passed through the gates. He'd just smiled at one of them in commiseration, and the fellow had started to smile wearily back, when suddenly there was a cry of 'It's him! The Wolfskin!' A sword was drawn. 'Halt, sorcerer!

A spiked club appeared. 'Not another step or you die where you stand.'

'Your wolf powers will avail you nothing in the Castle of Sighs.' A set of chains with manacles rattled in shaking hands as a voice intoned some incantation.

'Son of a stepmother,' Fitz howled, 'those toad-kissing bastards have done it to me again!'

'Johann?'

The voice was soft, tenuous, yet seemed to reverberate from the high marbled ceilings, the crystal pillars and even the heads of the crowds – a breathy sound but everywhere at once. Christina stopped mid-sinuous and shuddered. It was like what she imagined the first sound uttered by God would be, all wonder and command. Perhaps a little confused by the hoopla it was evoking in the crowd.

Johann gasped, but the breath could not get past the iron band, and so he made little 'ah, ah' noises in his throat. Blind eyes began to wiggle back and forth, but saw nothing.

'Johann? Love?' The voice was dissolving from that infinite intimacy into something smaller, more present. A woman's voice.

'Stop it!' the man hissed, stabbing the air with his hands to push Christina away. But she was nowhere near. She'd stepped back and back until she'd backed herself straight into Anji. Spinning about, she looked at her comrade, her competition, with a panicked, questioning gaze. But Anji just shook her head, obviously at a loss. Then the crowd gasped as one.

If it weren't for the glow, the golden aura of light that surrounded her, the woman who walked out of the Nothing and on to the rose-marbled floor would have looked like any hausfrau returning from market. She was dressed in brown, with a blue apron, a rusty-coloured shawl and a white cap on her greying hair. Her cheeks were rosy and so was her nose, but her eyes were much bluer than eyes had a right to be.

Johann wheeled about at the sound of her steps, the iron band tightening with every ragged breath he tried to take. 'Who's there?'

The woman's stride resounded, more certainty with each step, and the glow about her faded the closer she came to him. 'Johann, you fool,' she chided gently, 'you've got your sash knotted again.' And with that, she reached out and pulled the iron band from his body as if it were a ribbon on a baby's bonnet. It fluttered to the floor, nothing more than a ragged strip of black silk. He took a deep breath. A sound came out.

'Greta?'

'Who else?' He flinched when she touched his cheek. 'Oh course it's me, fool husband. Open your eyes.'

And then Iron Johann found that he was no longer blind, but could look upon his good wife who was alive again. He wept for joy, and all the people cheered. But the Duke of Sighs, who the people had begun to call the Duke of Toads in secret, looked upon the happiness of his man with displeasure.

'Judge, my justice, judge,' he commanded, 'you are not employed here to weep, whether from joy or grief, but to be disinterested Fate itself. The maid of the sun has danced, the maid of the moon stood apart in splendour. You can see them both now, so judge.'

But Johann shook his head. 'You may vent your spleen on me, oh Duke of Wind, but how can I judge between the stars when the sun is shining.' And he took his wife's hand, and to a music

*that sounded from the air, and the motion of the feet of the
crowd, and even the grinding of the Duke's teeth in his wrath,
they danced from the court, and away over the hills to their
own home, and their own life, and their own story.*

'A draw,' Anji shouted. 'He couldn't judge between us, and you
appointed him. That makes it final.' Surprisingly the court seemed
to agree and there was a murmuring of voices in her favour. Anji
thought she caught the words 'good form', but she wasn't certain.

The Duke's face was almost purple with anger, and for a
second, wisps of flame, blue and sharp, flickered around his
nostrils. Then he laughed, grudgingly, as if he found humour an
inconvenience, and then began to clap his hands.

The court, when they realised the Duke's intent, picked up the
ovation and clapped too, until the golden rafters rang to the
sound. The Duke motioned, and the sound ended. Only one burly
farmer misclapped and left an echo, and out of the corner of her
eye Anji saw the iron guards fall on him and drag him away.

'The test of grace,' the Duke intoned.

Servants dressed in livery of silver and sea-green, rather bilious
to Anji's taste, ran out with stepladders and piles of musty books.
'The prize of grace will go to the maid who can walk unaided
supporting straight and true the largest pile of books,' the Duke
explained.

Right, Anji thought, and the vicious humiliating aspect of this is?
The piranha pit? The evil mind-sapping books? The neck strain?
She essayed a wink at Christina. Rozered had to be on her way
back by now. They could get through it.

'And for every book that is dropped, a servant will be whipped,
and for every book that is not carried a child will be branded with
a coin bearing my likeness, minted for the occasion.'

Anji and Christina looked at the heap of books. There were at
least a thousand.

* * *

Fitz had the cell all to himself. In fact, he wouldn't have been at all surprised to learn he had the entire dungeon to himself. But he'd got bread and beer out of the deal. And oddly enough the bread wasn't stale and mouldy, but a crusty dark loaf that he softened in the beer and munched on with a curious sense of detachment about his predicament. They hadn't taken the wolf cloak from him as he'd feared they would. Why he'd feared it he had no idea. The dirty piece of hide had caused him no end of trouble, but it was like a second skin now. He couldn't imagine life in a dungeon without it. Of course, life promised to be short. They were going to hang him, or possibly burn him at the stake, sometime tomorrow. No one could agree on the proper method of execution for his brand of evil sorcery. Probably be a big turn-out for it, though. Family picnics, parties and stands selling sausages. That would be nice –

He tensed suddenly. Noises. The jangle of metal, the groan of iron doors, footsteps, two men, one heavy, one light-footed. Odours. The warder's greasy diet and also another's – a cloying scent of fear – sweat, perfume and oiled leather.

Gilfred! Gilfred was coming with the warder. To talk to him? To gloat? Why? Fitz carefully placed the bowl of beer on the stone floor and got ready.

When the cell door opened he was sitting on his haunches, with the wolf's head drawn over his own. His back pressed lightly against the damp wall, and his hands dangled between his knees so that he appeared to be in repose, resigned to his fate perhaps. His lips curled back in a snarl when he saw the Prince, fopped-out, fresh as a freaking daisy, but he turned it into a cool smile.

'Hello Fitz.'

'Oh, hey, how ya doin', Gil? Fancy meeting you here and all that.'

'I've come to relieve you of your cloak.'

This was not what Fitz was expecting. 'What?'

'I've taken it upon myself to rid the populace of the danger it presents. If such a powerful talisman should fall into the wrong hands, as clearly it has done with yours… Well, we can't have that, can we? The Duke has granted me the honour of disposing of it. So hand it over like a good simpleton.'

'Hmm. Let me think. No.'

The warder grinned. Gilfred drew his sword from the scabbard. 'Oh. Good. Over your dead body it is, then.'

The wolf's teeth grinned. 'How about over yours?'

And Wolfskin sprang at the two men with such fury that they fell back through the door and then he was upon them.

The dead thing didn't take the box / did / didn't. Alex couldn't tell, he only knew the feelings didn't stop, the feelings kept on and on, so no matter where he fled, the box was with him. He was inside it or it was inside him or he was the box now and there was nothing wonderful in him. Perhaps he'd lost the dead thing in the worlds of himself. He was a skein of bone and flesh in the guts of a monster. He was a broken body in the deep mire. He was a splatter of grease on a witch's griddle. He was a man with a key in his pocket that opened a box and saw nothing and cursed his luck and kicked the box down a hillside.

The key. If he could find the key. The Doctor's key. Something about it, something that was a defence. Maybe it was fixed more solidly in one reality, maybe it was magic. Alex didn't care. Agonisingly, moving with limbs broken / scorched / torn away / unharmed, he began to crawl in the direction he thought he remembered throwing the ball of red clay.

Anji was up to twenty-five books and her head hurt. OK, astronauts took what, five, ten gees, so if the men running up and down the ladders carrying and placing the books were good at balancing they might get six or seven times her weight on her head before she passed out. Her plan was this. Take a step. One step. The books have been carried. So the servants get a whipping. Anyone still serving at this castle with Mr Psycho on the throne had to be a certified masochist –

Or too bone-scared to flee.

Fine. Her conscience wasn't shutting up about that. But the servants weren't children: they had some sort of choice to be there. She'd risk them, but she wasn't going to give the Duke an excuse to hurt a child. Not one. She wondered how much five hundred books weighed. They were hefty. Maybe three or four pounds a book. Her neck was going to snap like a twig.

A servant ran up the ladder with a set of encyclopaedias.

The Doctor slid through the people massed at the courtyard gates, his ears snatching at gossip, the murmurs and rumours and rumblings of the world. He gathered that a ball had been cancelled, and that the Duke had either chosen his bride inappropriately, or was in the process of choosing her in an odd way. But as he slipped past the harried watchmen and through the courtyard proper he heard hushed whispers of a more disturbing nature: 'iron guards' and 'evil oracles' and the plaintive, 'Where is our Lady? What has become of Belesia?' There was something amiss at the Court of Sighs, but discovering what would have to wait. As he'd promised, he spoke to no one, met no questioning gaze with questions of his own. Instead, he followed his nose to the stables.

Jacqueletta removed the golden apple from her pocket. She'd plucked it from the bushel before they'd reached the gates, thinking she might have to use it on the gentleman in the elegant silver-wolf mantle. She hadn't of course. He'd been simplicity to charm without it. She tossed the apple lightly in her hand, feeling its weight, its satiny skin, wondering how best to make use of it.

Being sensible, Jacqueletta knew she herself had little chance of turning the Duke's head, golden apple or no golden apple. At twenty-four, she was past prime for the likes of noblemen, but she hoped with her guidance one of her sisters would catch his eye. Then they would all live happily ever after in the manner to which they would like to become accustomed. She had no lofty aspirations for true love, at least, not until she saw the man approaching the stables.

Her heart stuttered in her breast.

He wore a riding-coat of claret velvet, and his doeskin breeches fitted, she noted with a little gasp and hot blush, with nary a wrinkle. His boots were up to the thigh!

The apple left her hand and rolled across the yard.

Christina grunted under the strain. Why they hadn't just said no, she couldn't fathom. Refuse to play, force him to see the real pain he was inflicting, refuse to accept any responsibility for his twisted contest. But she felt with a little mental shiver that her reasoning was that of her old world, star-logic, and that in this place the only way was to beat it on its own terms.

Her head was pressed down into her shoulders now by the weight, and she could see Anji was the same. Five hundred books a piece. It ought to have been impossible, and yet it wasn't. They were at the limits of their endurance, had been since about the fiftieth book, and yet each one, while it bore down harder, didn't seem to carry with it quite the weight of its foundations. If every book weighed just that much less than its predecessor, it might explain it. Christina imagined the last few tomes as being so light that they would pull her and Anji up into the sky. She was losing it. Everything sounded like thunder, and the walls were turning red.

The Duke clapped again, but this time the audience refused to follow his lead – and just as well, Christina thought through the red haze. A breath of wind from their hands would have this lot down.

There. That was the last one. Without thinking she took a step forward, and started to fall.

I wish there was a way to save the servants and the children and not get squashed, she thought. And in her pocket the second acorn turned black.

And, seeing Christina move, Anji took a step.

And she started to fall in slow motion, each book following an independent arc.

And the air strobed around them, white and silver, as they fell.

And the Duke screamed. 'There is magic here! Who dares bring magic to my gracious choice of bride?'

And between Anji and Christina, its weight carried by the volume at the keystone with only a featherweight still resting on the kneeling women's heads, a perfect arc of books hung like a promise, something strange and wonderful.

And the Duke ran towards them drawing his sword.

Impossibly, an iron guard moved between him and them. The Duke, looking inside its empty helmet, looking through the portcullis of its face, dropped his sword with a tinny clatter and a tiny huff of petulant breath.

'The third contest will not be so easy,' he shouted. 'Beauty is in the eye of the beholder, and grace may be counterfeit, but either wit is there or it is not; and I, and I alone will judge, and I will not award a draw.'

Something bumped against the Doctor's shoe. He looked down. A delicious golden apple gleamed warmly in the light from the lanterns. The Doctor reached down and picked it up.

Chapter Thirteen
The Contest of Wit
(or, The Apple and the Doctor)

'The third contest will be one of poetry,' the Duke said, pacing back and forth in front of his canopied throne, rich golden drapes forming the backdrop to his rapid feverish movements. 'Poetry with the most sublime of meanings must come from my wife's lips. All must hear her and be charmed.'

More guards marched into the hall now, two full phalanxes moving like drilling cutlery, clattering like black-enamelled beetles. They carried pikes tipped with obsidian. It was obvious to everyone that the Duke intended to have his way.

William Brok pounded on Timtangle's door. He'd been promised a high-level access pass when he'd agreed to join up as a specialist but the little gem at his cuff wasn't opening anything these days. Of course it was midnight by the ship's clock and maybe the abanak was asleep, but William knew he wasn't anywhere else obvious.

Just as William was about to nurse his bruised hands and go back to the bridge in case the captain had shown up there, a sour-faced heavy-eyed Timtangle, skin mottled mauve with annoyance, stuck his head around the opening door. 'Do you know what time –' he began, but he didn't finish the word because William hit him, open-handed, to the left side of his face just over the ear, and then landed another to the jaw muscles. William had been reading up on the abanak.

Timtangle fell back into the room, and William lunged in after him.

The abanak was rolling on the floor in pain, and William stepped around him, and clicked the button that closed the door. When it was shut he knelt down, placing his weight on the Captain's back.

'Now we're going to get a few things straight,' he said. He rummaged in his pocket and pulled out a string of paper print-outs.

'I know paper's not recognised by the trade courts, but it's evidence to me.' He waved his hand in the air to trigger the motion-sensor lights. Then he shoved the paper in front of Timtangle's eyes. 'Do these symbols mean anything to you?'

'Computer gabble, nothing more, waste static,' the captain pleaded. 'William, you're overwrought about Christina. I know you think we could be doing more, but I can't risk the ship.'

'I read most of the comp internal display languages. I can tell the codes for a scout ship launch when I see them. Where are they going, Timtangle? You told me there were no messages from Christina, and that you weren't prepared to send any scouts after her. The Vuim-Captain's messages claim he's got the lander situation sewn up and he *doesn't* want help. So where are they going, Timtangle, and why aren't they looking for Christina?'

A flare of lasing light burned briefly across the room, and William, falling back with a hole cut cleanly, almost politely, through his leg, realised with an accompanying scream of pain, that there was one thing he hadn't thought to ask the ship's computer about the abanak. Whether or not they might be expected to be sleeping alone.

Huffing and puffing, Timtangle pulled himself upright. 'There is, I believe, a human custom in these situations.' He kicked William in the ribs, his little hoofed feet hitting hard and with precision. 'Well done, my dear.' He nodded to the abanak with the gun, who had come out of the compartment's bathing room. 'I think we can no longer allow Mr Brok here the run of the ship. He's far, far too inquisitive.'

The bastard just wants a trophy wife, Anji thought, as a nervous, nameless servant massaged her aching neck. Across the width of the audience chamber, another performed a similar office for Christina. The arch of books, unsupported by Anji or Christina now, hung in midair. Occasionally a page fell like a leaf. Anji trapped one under her foot, and got a glimpse of the black Gothic lettering. Lettering exactly like the writing on the notice at the edge of the wood. How long ago was that now? She'd been two weeks with the spiteful sisters, but some of it had passed like a dream or a speeded-up film. Then her brain caught up with her eyes and she shook off the servant's hand to scramble after the page.

> *On the etiquette of tests:*
> *What a tester says before*
> *witnesses shall be the test;*
> *nor shall he claim it is other.*
> *Words must be weighed*
> *and measured finely as*
> *Gold dust. If a man calls*
> *for the finest weaver he*
> *may be required to wed a*
> *spider. If he seeks the most*
> *beautiful of songs, he shall*
> *marry a nightingale.*

Ah. There it was. The Duke wanted sublime meaning and Anji felt an idea settle on the tip of her mind. It was possible this world helped you along if you played by its lights.

'Oh Great Duke of Sighs,' she cried. 'Tell us both what poetry you desire that we may shape our conceptions to your pleasure.'

'I must have poems with vast and subtle meanings,' he replied majestically. 'I care not what form you transfigure with your muse, rhyming or free, sonnet or epic of blank verse as you will; only raise me high on the transcendental meaning within.'

Gotcha, Anji thought. You sad poser.

And bowing she backed carefully away towards Christina.

What an apple this was!

The Doctor turned it round and round in his hands, marvelling at its perfect appley appleness, the satin warmth of its skin, the subtle shading of its golden colour from rose yellow at the top to the buttery yellow at the bottom, even the curve of the stem was perfect. A platonic apple. He put it to his nose and inhaled the fragrance of it. All in all, the most tantalising apple he'd ever held.

'Good evening, sir.'

'Good evening,' he replied absently, still absorbed with apple thoughts. Then realising what he'd done, 'Oh no! I've just –'

But what it was he'd just done or not he'd no idea. He looked at the girl, shiny black hair curling over her shoulders, skirt swishing back and forth as she scuffed her toe in the dirt. The buckle on her shoe twinkled, catching the light from the lanterns. From under dark lashes, big brown eyes darted glances, shy or flirtatious, and her teeth were pearly against the red of her lips. The features were familiar, and he felt he ought to know her, but he couldn't remember where from or why he ought to. And, as it was a feeling he knew from long experience, it made him a little melancholy but not surprised.

'And this must be Eve,' he murmured, smiling at his joke.

Her fine brows drew together, but she said nothing to contradict him. 'It's a lovely night for a ride, isn't it?'

The moon was already high overhead. 'Yes. I suppose it is.'

She shot a look at the heavy bar across the stable doors, then leaned closer into him, her shoulder brushing the sleeve of his jacket. He caught the perfume of apples again as she whispered,

'You can't steal a fairy horse, you know: they raise all manner of alarm if you try.'

'I wasn't going to steal! No no no no, far from it. I was going to... do... something else entirely. What gave you the impression I'd come to steal a horse?' With his right hand he stuffed the note that read 'IOU One Horse' deep into the recesses of a pocket. He'd figure what that was about later.

'Because,' she began, her fingers starting a slow meander from beneath his earlobe and down over his jaw, 'you are the highway robber, charlatan, fabulist, rogue and confidence trickster, Doctor Know-All. And long have I loved you –'

Her fingers had picked up considerable speed during the litany, and he caught her wrist before the fingers wandered too far a-field. 'I'm sorry. Say again?'

'Long have I loved you –'

'No, no, all that *other* business.'

Gilfred raced through the empty corridors, clutching the grip of his sword in a hand slippery with his own sweat. He could hear Fitz some distance behind him, a relentless loping rhythm that never paused or wavered in its unhurried pursuit. He knew somehow that, like a wolf, Fitz could run for ever in this fashion until that final burst of speed was needed to take down his prey. The Prince had seen the warder fall beneath Fitz, who'd seemed at that moment neither man nor wolf, a creature nonetheless passing familiar that sent a shiver of preternatural terror through him. He hadn't stayed to see the tearing of the warder's throat, nor had he pondered long that weird familiarity. No. He'd scrambled up the steps and run like a madman. He hadn't even thought to bolt the door behind him. Stupid. Stupid! And now, here in the soft pink light of the castle's corridors, he found no one about – not one servant, not one iron guard. Could *every* single person be in the great hall watching that fool of a Duke choose between a lanky white-haired bitch and a dusky little slut? And where was that idiot Ansel, who'd been so keen on slaying the sorcerer in wolf's clothing himself?

Shouting his brother's name for what seemed like the hundredth time, Gilfred took a turning and found he'd turned wrong. Very wrong. Into a narrow cul-de-sac with a single door – a door evidently bolted from the other side. He wasted no time venting his frustration on the door, but turned again, fingers wrapped tight about the grip, holding the sword before him like a brand, intending to make a stand where he was. Wolves respected steel and fire, and if Gilfred had lost some of his fire he still had the steel. He waited, not breathing, ignoring the pounding of blood in his ears, listening hard. But there was nothing to hear but the hiss of oil in the sconces, nothing but his heartbeat and the soft rattle his weapon made as his arm trembled. The depth of silence was agonising. Unable to bear it any longer, the Prince cried, 'Show yourself, sorcerer! Do you fear the bite of my steel, coward?'

'No,' Fitz said softly, stepping into the light. His features were hidden in the shadows of the wolf's head he wore as a hood. 'I have sharper teeth than you, O Prince.' A sword of star iron gleamed darkly in his hand.

For a long moment Gilfred felt paralysed, held sway under the spell of the wolf's hide the man wore like his own skin. He forced himself to look at the hand that held the sword, the dirty, ragged nails and swollen red of chilblains marking him as merely a man. Then, with a cry, he brought the sword up at the same time as Fitz raised his own aloft and they met blade to blade, swept into fury by the sound of their weapons clashing and the sparks of fire that flew off as they battled.

'Do you not recognise me, dear brother?' Wolfskin asked, as he parried a thrust from the Prince's blade and brought his own blade round again with lightning speed.

Then the wicked Prince Gilfred knew Wolfskin was his own

little brother that he and Ansel had bound and gagged and thrown to the wolves in the dark wood so long ago. He fell to his knees, pleading with the spectre. 'Have mercy, my brother! I have wronged you greatly, but I beg you spare me, for the sake of our father, who nearly died of grief when he thought you dead.'

Fitz looked down on the kneeling Prince, the desire for vengeance slipping away like the phantom swallow of hot blood he could taste at the back of his throat. It had seemed, until this moment, the most important thing in the world to taste justice. A blade thrust to the carotid artery, the perfect retribution for fratricide. But it was not his vengeance he sought at all. He was wearing a ghost about his shoulders. Not a magic talisman, not an enchanted creature, but a dead boy who'd taken up a temporary and desperate residence in a badly tanned hide.

The arm holding the sword lost its adrenaline thrill and power, and the point of the blade he'd pushed up beneath Gilfred's left ear drifted down, etching a fine line all the way to the prince's collarbone. Blood welled up around the scratch, and the sight of it startled Fitz enough to pull the blade away and shake some sense into him. Still, the weasel *had* conspired to kill his younger brother.

'You're quite a piece of work, aren't you Gilfred? You and that hopped-up brother of yours. Where is dear Ansel, by the way?'

The answer came in a two-fisted hammer blow to the back of Fitz's head.

Christina stood up, ready to jump through the hoops of Anji's plan. Look earnest. Wag her tail. Good dog, Christina. Good bitch.

Though the plan made perfect sense, it still required her to go first and make a fool of herself. She folded her hands stylistically, took a breath and began, 'Twinkle, twinkle little star –' The Duke's beneficent expression twitched. Looking like a fool was one thing, but by the time she got to 'diamond in the sky' her knees were shaking and she was sorely afraid. There were actual *flames* coming from his nostrils, and tiny crackling sparks of blue-white electricity were shooting off from the tips of his hair.

'You dare to treat me like an idiot child?' he shouted. '*Be seated!*'

A guard grabbed her by the shoulders and flung her down on to the hard stone floor. Still, Christina exalted. Part one managed, and only a few bruises. It could have been much worse. She only hoped Anji pulled her part off as well. Otherwise, they were both toast. Literally.

'And how long *exactly* have you loved me, did you say?'

Jacqueletta half skipped, half ran alongside the Doctor to keep up. 'Ages and ages. Months. Several weeks. A long time, anyway. Ever since I first saw your likeness on the posters – oh toads, there's one now!'

He stopped so suddenly that she jogged past him for a few steps. In an alcove, his portrait was being inked on a parchment tacked to the wall. As he watched, a list of various crimes were set down, some of which were rather esoteric. Consorting with 'wives after the first, and divers companions' and what in the world was barratry? Something about ship captains cheating the ship owners, he thought, but how could that apply to a highwayman? Finally, the price on his head – a considerable sum, outrageous even. Still, he looked quite dashing and dangerous when the ink was dry, French cocked hat, rapier –

'Not sure I like the lace cravat,' he said. And the lines shifted so that his likeness was no longer wearing it.

The girl gripped at his sleeve, grabbing a bit of skin with it. 'Do not tally here, Doctor! If you're caught, they'll hang you. Come. I shall hide you at the cottage. On the morrow we'll gather your purloined treasure from wherever you're hiding it and make good our escape –'

He peeled her fingers away from his arm. His eyes narrowed.

'Do you have a sister?'

'What?' The soft snick of her lashes as she blinked and blinked was like a metronome counting the beats of her thoughts. He knew by the tempo that a lie was coming. 'No,' she said, plucking imaginary threads from her skirt. Giving the fabric a final brush, she looked at him again, her lips pursed. 'What's that to you anyway? If I had a sister you fancied more than me, I'd row her out to sea, toss her in and watch her drown before I'd let you have her.'

'Uh huh. Yes. Hmm. Good thing you don't have one, then. If you'll excuse me, I should like to study this poster now.'

She put her fists on her hips and all resemblance to someone he couldn't quite remember disappeared. He knew her sort all too well, an amalgam of everything he found unpleasant in human beings. It appeared that Love, like everything else here, altered in scope and dimension rather quickly.

'I'm sure I could never give my heart to a fool who'd risk swinging from the gallows in order to linger awhile over his own likeness.'

The Doctor smiled tightly in return. 'And very wise you are.' *Go away now.*

From the twist of her lips as she left the alcove, he knew she'd soon be turning him in for the reward, a reward he was quite certain had been placed upon his head only moments before she'd said 'good evening' at the stables. He couldn't help but feel that someone was trying to tell him something and he intended to stay right where he was until he found out what.

He sat down on the stone bench, crossed his arms, then his legs, waiting for enlightenment. He waited for several seconds, then stood up again, peering at the poster, willing the lines to reveal a key he could pluck off the page. As he did so, he polished the already shiny apple on his sleeve and bit into the flesh.

* * *

Anji stood up, hoping she remembered Dave's rhyme right. His grandfather had taught it to him as a child and he'd told it to her.

> Scintillate, scintillate globule vivific;
> Fain would I fathom thy glory specific;
> Loftily posed above the capacious;
> Closely resembling a gem carbonaceous...

The Duke beamed, but the look in his eyes told her that, as she'd hoped, he'd only understood one word in three, maybe not even that. 'Ah', he cried with his hand to his breast, 'the meaning speaks to me. My choice is clear. I will have the woman whose wit brought me this revelation.'

He jumped from the throne and ran towards her, his feet pattering wetly on the floor.

But this time as he closed in, two of his own guard interposed, crossing their pikes with a clash so that they formed a barrier in front of his green face.

Anji smiled. Just as she'd hoped, 'the rules', the 'good form', had stymied his choice – since for all the long words of the parody, there was no difference in meaning between it and the children's rhyme he had scornfully rejected. But why was his face green?

And small?

And warty?

In the edges of the woods on the rain-lashed path, Rozered hugged the glowing box close to her and ran. The beast was behind her, and it was no beast she knew. Not a raggle-taggle wolf ripping the guts out of a hen house and limping off into a packless loser life. Not a great lumbering bear, hungry for little girls and a lost life. But something big in a way that was not Giant and not World.

Looking backward, she walked into it suddenly. It roared at her, alien, incomprehensible, with a mouth big enough to swallow loaves whole, great flat chomping teeth like tombstones as it reached for her with huge spatulate paws. She ducked and slipped beneath its arms, darting into the very forest she had skirted so carefully, desperate and hoping against hope that this monster would fear the traps the forest's guardian set for mortals, fear the terrible wodewose at least as much as she did. But the beast came after her, shooting arrows of lightning at her head, her back. The lightning scorched the bark of trees, burst the holly berries as she sped past, and fried pine needles to an odorous crisp –

A blood-curdling scream came out of the depths of the woods, and all the forest trembled from the wrath and indignation in that cry. Though Rozered expected the wildman to react with outrage, she had not expected it to happen so quickly. Her knees buckled from the rumbling raw thunder of the sound and she fell. The box tumbled into a pile of wet decaying leaves. She made a desperate grab for it only to see it swallowed by the earth like a calf sinking in the bog. The wodewose screamed again, louder, closer this time, and she covered her head with her hands, hoping against reason that her sightlessness rendered her invisible. She heard the forest open behind her like a shutter thrown wide in a storm. There was a startled shout, a poignant squeak of disbelief and horror before it was cut short by the sudden rending and tearing of the throat that had uttered it.

Gilfred took in Ansel's half-dressed state and mussed hair, and so didn't bother to ask where he'd been. Ansel had already scooped up the sword of star iron, and was making test passes, admiring the jewelled pommel and elegant curve of its blued hilt with a fiendish, greedy eye.

'I'll gut him with his own sword,' he said, eyeing the crumpled heap of Fitz on the floor, 'and festoon the walls with his entrails.'

'Get the cloak first.'

'I'm not touching that thing. It's filthy.'

'Don't argue. Just help me get it off of him.'

'Why?'

'So we can take it away and burn it.'

'But I can keep the sword, yes?'

'I'll thrust that stepmothering sword up your...'

But Ansel had stopped listening to his brother, his senses attuned to a sound that made the hairs on his body stand up. A howl echoed through the corridors. A howl that began somewhere far away, was picked up by others, went on for dreadful seconds and crashed over them like a tidal wave.

'It can't be,' Gilfred whispered, coming to his brother's side. The wolf cloak seemed to squirm in his hands as if anxious to be with its true brothers. He would have dropped the thing if his tense fingers had allowed. Side by side the Princes stood, stone still, listening now to the low growls, the sniffing, panting and whining of a pack on the prowl. The sword of star iron clattered to the marble floor, chipping the stone.

Princes Ansel and Gilfred ran.

'It is over.' The voice came from behind the throne. One of the golden draperies that reached up to form its overarching canopy parted, and an old woman stepped into the court. Anji recognised her as the mad grandmother who'd given the Doctor such an inexplicable amount of difficulty weeks ago. And there was something of Bricklebrit's grandmother there as well, if only in the eyes.

'What is the meaning of this?' the Duke croaked. 'You said I must have my choice, and I will have it.'

'Oh yes. Your first wish.'

'No,' he rasped, 'I was cautious. Never wished. Not bound. Made them work for me without it. My will. Yes!'

The old woman's voice was firm but sad. 'Not even one wish?'

And the hall echoed with thoughts. He wished only that there existed a woman as beautiful as he was handsome, as charming as he was witty, and as unique as he was interesting. If ever I find such a woman I will marry her on the spot, he thought.

'You deny this?'

The Duke's toad face split in a horrific gape of shock and fear. 'No, my dearest Fay, not that.'

Out of the crowd, which parted like the sea, a woman came.

Anji gasped, recognising her.

The Doctor had never tasted a better apple. Of course not many apples tasted of violets and lightning, and his head hurt. It tasted like memory, but not his.

A box opening to the happy face of a child.

A ship the size of a city ploughing across a black, burned continent, records and images from shattered memory banks falling like microscopic confetti into the receiving earth.

Bombardments of different spaces and different times.

Then his.

A crowd of people in what looked like Renaissance clothing. In this world's clothing. A memory he'd had before. Before all this, in the time-spilling engines of a great sphere. A sphere like unto the world. *Like the world.* The image was sharper now, the events closer, he suspected. Him bursting into a long hall, flinging the great oaken doors aside; running to warn, to defend, to help. To tell them something wonderful and terrible. If only he knew what.

He took another bite.

Was there a word for remembering prophecy... again?

It was an hour of hell, of all hells, before Alex found it. By then he was definitely screaming in every world in which he still had a voice.

A hairy creature was sitting in the middle of a ring of darker grass, throwing the ball of clay from one hand to another.

'Give me that,' Alex managed to shout, eventually, timing his words to the possession of a working larynx.

'Too late for you,' the creature said, 'but I can spare you pain if you will take it to its owner.' It broke the clay ball open one-handed, crushing the mass until it split, showing the metal at the core.

Alex, sweating with worms in his eye sockets, dying this time where the scavengers preferred the eyes, tried to consider for a second how he could work a better deal, tried to trade at the last. But he had no leverage and no firm place to stand. He had nothing to bargain with, and he couldn't bear the pain to go on. He was starting to long for the dead worlds rather than the dying. All his marvellous wishes reduced to a quiet grave. 'Yes,' he managed.

Even if 'spare you pain' was a euphemism for a quick death, he'd earned it.

The hairy thing took the key and pushed it between Alex's lips, suddenly and without ceremony. It tasted of grit and, for a second, a quick-setting modelling material Alec had used as a child. Then his world narrowed and grew dark.

Giants that were any size. People living the lives of old stories. Energy from elsewhere.

The images rolled on.

'The world, the world's alive!' he shouts. As in a nightmare, no one pays attention. The people move away, a crowd sated with experience already, not wishing to see another spectacle. A witch with a hideously wrinkled face and jet-black eyeballs passes by him leading a huge toad on a leather strap. 'Beautiful, as handsome,' she laughs under her breath, 'unique, heh,' as she drags the toad's choke chain tight with a *snap*.

'*It's alive.*' The Doctor howls, tearing his hair.

Anji stands there with a woman he doesn't know. Both seem tall as pillars, and graceful as statues, and their faces are beauty itself.

'Not my type,' Anji says.

'*It's alive!*' He tries again, spitting apple out. Remembering having foreseen all this once before. Re-pre-déjà-vu.

'Yes, yes, we know.' A white-haired man in a black robe, his accent vaguely Irish and kindly. 'Of course it's alive, what else would it be?'

The Doctor got his hands on the robe hem, and held on for dear life.

'Really alive! One thing. One world. One organism.'

'Yes, we *know*. We call it Albert.'

The Doctor felt himself caught in a dream he'd had once too often. Nothing for it but chorus and response now.

'The planet's called Albert?' he hears himself asking. Then, 'But that's the Giant's name.'

'Sometimes it is, yes.'

The Doctor jumped with rage. 'I don't care, you phantoms! I'm not doing this yet. You can call the planet Albert, you can call the rock Peter, and the wind Mariah, but it doesn't reduce the importance of the fact that you're living in what I hope is mutually agreed symbiosis with the biggest living thing this side of… well, I can't remember when I've seen anything bigger!'

'Have you quite finished, young man?' If the words were reproachful, the tone wasn't, yet the voice was huge and everywhere and only in his head.

A woman dressed in shimmering blue silk and purple velvet trimmed with gold and pearls stood before him now in the great hall. Her hair was crowned with gold-dusted grape leaves, and the clusters of fruit that dangled gemlike from the stems seemed to be ripening and shrivelling on the vine simultaneously. If she was beautiful it was in a way not entirely comfortable or easy to look upon. He wondered if he should be trying to see her at all, but that only made him want to look harder. In doing so he was able to see, imposed or superimposed, or underlying that, no less or no more real, the whip-cord thin, the ragged figure of the old woman who had ridden him across the stream days ago, maybe longer.

He took a deep breath. 'I've really just said and done all that, haven't I?' he asked faintly.

The Fairy Belesia nodded and touched a jewelled hand to his temple. 'Rest now. There is much to do.'

Everything went away.

The abanak team located the source of white-hole energy near a brook, not far from where Glenko had lost the human the first time, in the midst of some strange human fit. The energy seemed to be in a sort of containment unit of dull grey metal: an obvious incongruity sitting on a moss-covered rock. Snuffling around the rock was a small four-legged animal – a very stupid red animal that instead of fleeing the threat of their bulk and numbers, paced back and forth in front of the rock, whining and trembling. All their shouting and hoof stomping did nothing to drive it away. Finally, one of the team drew a weapon and took aim, whereupon the creature dashed into the woods.

If they had bothered to look they would have seen the creature watching them from the deep cover of brambles with the haunted eyes of a human looking out from a fox's face. But then they'd never seen a fox and wouldn't have known the difference.

Now that the wicked Duke was no more able to bear down his will upon the company, the servants arose and laid forth a great banquet set upon plates of lapis lazuli and polished tourmaline, and centrepieced with great sculptures cut from ice, and palaces wrought in butter.

Then Belesia ordered that the Doctor be taken and his body borne to rest on a great couch, and she called the woman Anji to attend him. 'This is my only reed,' said Belesia, 'and though he bend before the winds that blow from space he must stand stronger than my oaks or all will be lost. It is for him and you to take up these six skyfalls, these boxes of despair and ill will.

On him, mostly is this geas laid, but on you also, who chose out of greed and were redeemed by your compassion. On you falls the task, and on another.'

'Bloody hell,' Fitz said staggering into the chamber, one hand clamped to his head. 'Hack me a bit off that ice swan would you, love? I've got such a headache. Has anyone seen two complete bastards with a wolf cloak?'

Chapter Fourteen
Four White Horses

The horses the Castle of Sighs provided were white as the untrodden snow, and stood high and proud as the company entered the broad courtyard of grey marble. 'These are the finest steeds of the Castle of Sighs,' the head groom said, 'and it doubts me that the Mistress intended they should be yours for all the letter of her command. Besides, 'tis a bitter morning to be off.' A blanket of snow had fallen in the night, and lay thick all around reflecting grey marble shadows.

The Doctor flung back the blood-red war cloak that swathed this shoulders, and his hand fell on the pommel of the sword by which the Dragon Duralkin was brought low, which had been the favoured sword of the Lady Belesia's brother in the time before the great war with the Gnolls. His breath, despite the cold, created no mist in the icy air as he spoke. 'Great things are asked of us by fate, not least that we should be thwarted at every turn by petty men and little matters that touch not the robe hems of the mighty. Already dark forces are moving; the wildman of the woods is troubled and the Sphinx has fled to the ice caves of the western mountains. Now is the time of the four riders. Fear not, yeoman, for Belesia's blessing is about us.' And he mounted the greatest of the horses that moved like wind in the grass.

The others followed each to their great steed.

Tlot-tlot-tlot-tlot –

Anji felt the hooves of her horse flying like a storm over the cobble road spiralling out from the Court of Sighs. Her mount seemed to know how to adjust to her inexperience. Her saddle was inlaid with a mosaic of porphyry and the reins were of the leather of elfland –

That wasn't right. She was riding bareback, hanging on by the mane alone. Yes.

She concentrated on urging her beast to keep pace with the others. Fitz, whose trials with the donkey – which he had told them all about at length over the previous night's meal – had apparently served him as a horseman's education, was cutting a reasonable figure: back stiff, a sword of some strange metal given him by Belesia slung at his waist, a wolf cloak about his shoulders, fur curled and clean in the wind.

The Doctor and Christina rode like champions, no saddles, no jingly things (braces and bits, was it?), and no gaps between them and their horses. Just graceful organic ease. The Doctor's riding was hardly a surprise. She'd seen him ride on Hitchemus. And he was what? A hundred years old at least, maybe more if half Fitz's tales were true. He'd had time to do anything. Ranching in the West, whispering in horses' ears in rural Ireland, even winning the bloody Derby maybe. But she was finding Christina's success hard to swallow. The woman was a space trader off an episode of one of her brother's favourite shows; she'd come from a future, post-animal-use society very probably. Why was she better on a horse than Anji?

They were out on the open moor now, the forest rising up before them like a black wall.

Tlot-tlot-tlot –

Christina felt her spine grind once more and wondered what the hell she was doing. The stables had smelled awful, and these spindly beasts weren't her idea of a horse, and what bed had the Doctor got out of the wrong side of with all that 'Ho, heroes of the land arise' nonsense? She hoped he wasn't like this all the time. Anji had made him seem quite intriguing at last night's feast. She

196

dug a heel into her horse's spavined flanks, plodding along to the other's rackety cantering. Between the man who had been introduced to her as Fitz, and the Doctor himself, she was profoundly outclassed. Riding a horse for a bet once round the circumference of an old-fashioned spinning space wheel didn't equate to mastery of the things. This one didn't even seem to have a bloody off switch, and its audio-command circuit was either fused or voice-specific. The castle official who had helped her mount had told her all the commands, but they didn't do a thing for her. Her horse's hooves clattered on the golden surface of the tiled road beneath them. The blank eyes of a scarecrow watched as they rode past.

Tlot-tlot –

Fitz felt a good deal of satisfaction as the land flowed by. He'd earned this. The Queen of the Castle, Belesia, willow-slim in her sheath-like dress of silver and diamonds with her glorious mass of auburn hair framing her maiden's face, had given him his sword herself when she had charged them to gather the six boxes. The only thing he missed was the ragged old cloak the Princes had stolen. This new one – the skin of Ieten Maluneth the Skin-Shifter, he'd been told – was far more majestic, but it didn't feel nearly as alive. That ought to have been all to the good after the revelations of the previous night, but still he missed the old hide. Last night in the great banquet hall he'd told the Doctor about the cloak and what he'd learned of its origins, of the brother the Princes had murdered. Belesia had said that the world would end all treachery in time, but he was determined that the ratty wolf cloak was going to be a Fitz-heirloom if he had to prise it from the Princes' cold dead hands.

Tlot –

The Doctor felt the differing stories flow over them as they rode, the boxes from the Mad Duke's oracle in his saddlebag subtly exerting their diffracting influence on consensus reality. It wasn't really bad yet. The tone of High Fantasy was even a bit exciting and fun – a small price to pay for removing the dangerous things from the lands of men.

Acquiring the boxes had been hard enough. The Iron Guards were kept in the closed room of the oracle, suits of armour worn by Mr Nobody animated by Might-Have-Beens. The Doctor had insisted that Fitz and Anji remain outside. And he had gone in. He had retrieved them. He had. He hadn't yet.

Damn, they'd caught him again.

He fell back out of the oracle room, his fingernails torn from clawing on the iron armour, to find Anji and Fitz and a complete absence of horses.

The boxes in the room – the one the Duke had found, and the two he'd tormented out of some poor shepherds or villagers – were whispering to each other. Their language was reality. Reality hinged together like a three-sided mirror so that you could never quite see your own back.

The Doctor didn't think they were alive, not like the planet, not yet anyway, but he had the feeling that they deeply wanted to be, and that they would wait for ever if necessary, and that they would turn anyone to their ends if they could. They were trying to buy him off with closure, showing him everything ending happily with him as a hero, a rather haughty hero, riding into the sunset. They'd given him companions, even an extra one – the woman he'd seen next to Anji before he'd fainted in the hall – but they hadn't drawn them right somehow. They'd given fancy as fact, and several fancies at that.

He knew this world, as it stood, was multiform, complex, enticing, but it was poised on the precipice of incoherence and chaos. This world had a wishing economy – a land of fairy tales held together by a powerful living symbiotic skein. Here there was no 'perversity of the inanimate', here things would conspire to help the good by the light of the vast alien mind underlying it all. A wonderful thing, provided there was only one mind, and that its ideas of good were not too alien. He thought maybe they weren't. The Giant had eaten people, but not the innocent Mastermaid, and maybe – he still hoped – not Inex. The Duke hadn't turned to rape outright, but had – by Anji's account – been hemmed in by threads of tradition and culture, rendered controllable not by a Magna Carta but by the way the world turned. There was some stability here, no worse than many a world, and while there were known dangers, there were families and children, and there was no black presence brooding over their minds as if they were toys or pawns on a chessboard. The world itself was not an enemy.

Not yet. He very much feared that the 'boxes' were new rivals. Each box could fix itself into a part of the world, grow, taking in a mind here, a mind there. Each could give gifts – clumsily at first, maybe shattering a few minds, maybe killing a few communities, but eventually, inevitably, staking out their own rules until... Oz brawling with Fairyland, Middle Earth holding the coats, and Witchland slipping the hex signs into its boxing gloves. Eventually no logic left, not even this world's logic. A war of wishes. Until one of the boxes won.

The world would be scarred by war, changed by it. Even if Albert-Belesia-Wodewose ended triumphant, it might have more recourse to the Iron Guards.

There had to be a better way.

'I want to tell you a story,' he said, one foot on the threshold of the oracle room. 'I think you can understand me, after a fashion. At least I think you are quantum fields, and thought is a quantum process, and I think I'm thinking. If you could be quiet and listen, I think I could get nearer this time. That would be jolly wouldn't it?'

He stepped inside.

No change. Good. Unless they were co-operating enough to precisely delineate a firm reality, which would be very, very bad. 'Now,' he said taking the optimistic view. 'I'd like to tell you about Doctor Pangloss.'

In the blue-lit cabin surrounded by night, Vuim-Captain almost spat into the communicator, a tremendous effort of disdain for a dry throated vuim.

'No, you listen, Timtangle, I don't care if you've committed all the scout ships to some ill-thought-out venture trading among the humans. I want pick-up. I have discovered things here that will revolutionise our technologies. We will be immensely rich, and maybe for my kind it will mean even more than that. So I do not have the whim to argue. This is what you will do. If you have stupidly used all the scouts, you will launch another lander and it can pick me up. I must show you what we have. We'll need to clear the full cargo hold; you'll have to get it stripped bare. Every ounce we can pack will bring more profit than a tonne of Hydrogen-3.'

At the other end of the circuit, Timtangle evidently got a question in. Vuim-Captain clasped his green almost human hands tight together, wringing them with glee.

'We're going to sell things. Everything. Every kind of thing you can dream of, and countless things you haven't even begun to dream. Imagine a nano-factory you don't have to program that will build you, atom by atom, anything your heart desires. We're sitting on the mother lode, Timtangle. And before you get smarmy with me, you may have the high ground but I'm the only one who knows how this stuff works, so I want to see that lander moving down now.'

The Doctor shoved the boxes into his saddlebag. 'So I think I've managed to persuade them that if this is indeed the "best of all possible worlds" then there is in fact no need to alter anything and that their optimum growth plan would be to reinforce the existing reality. Besides, if there are an infinite number of like worlds to this in the local quantum bundle, then there are an infinite number in which they get their own way – whatever it is – in absolute techno-colour, so all they have to do is scan for the right one and then gleefully impose it on us.'

'So we're safe as long as they believe it's all going their way, or until they find another way of looking at things that works better for them?' Fitz said. 'I'm not sure that's our best victory ever, Doctor.'

'It's not intended to be a victory,' the Doctor admonished. He winked at Anji. 'Is it?'

'More like a stopgap, I'd say,' she ventured. 'It sounds like you've bought us some time.'

'Indeed, and I think we'll need it. Anji…' He hesitated. 'Do you think you could persuade your rival to come with us? I've got a feeling the planet expects it.'

Anji humphed, and pointed at the fourth horse. 'Behind the times, Doctor. She practically begged me for our company. Belesia told her we'd be going into danger but she –' Anji stopped suddenly. 'Doctor?' The Doctor's face had gone slack and vacant. A tremor twitched along his jaw, the only sign of life. Fitz was at his side first, Anji a moment later.

When the Doctor spoke again his voice was low and strained, all his enthusiasm drained away. 'While I was in there I remembered something, but it's only just sunk in.' His eyes blazed back alive. 'I forgot all about her just as she said I would. She may have already died.' Without another word he vaulted on to the nearest – the biggest – of the fairy horses. It sprang to a gallop and was out of the castle courtyard before Fitz, Anji or the saddle-laden Christina emerging from the farriers had time to react.

The Vuim-Captain approached the second lander. It had come down in the hinterland of his own factory, in the scorched swathe of burned and blackened ground his landing technique had wrought. Striding towards it on long legs he had carried his prize evidence, the tiny precision-engineered replica of the factory lander. Remembering the death of the scientist, he wasn't certain that the force box he carried it in was safe enough, but he had no other options.

Once aboard, carried up by a lift built into one of its landing legs, never relinquishing his hold on the box, he took his seat on the command deck, like a prince of his people in the days before their disease.

He held the box tight on his thin lap and intended to carry it on his lap all the way up to the *Bonaventure*.

He did not lay it aside to manipulate the screen controls to watch *his* factory lander lift up on its antigravity drive and begin sweeping the continent, pulling mile after mile of surface material into its great analysing holds. He knew his vuim crew would be carrying out their orders. He didn't need to see that to know it. That was his people's strength.

William Brok had a splitting headache, and a long sour pain in his guts that was worse. He'd been shoved into a sleep tube and the end bolted shut, he just about remembered the sound of it being locked before he'd curled up in a ball of sick indignation and fear for what felt like hours. Maybe he'd been out of it for a while. Something was going wrong. The abanak had taken the other two scout ships down, something Timtangle had refused point-blank to rescue Christina. They'd gone down but they hadn't come back. He'd confronted Timtangle, and ended up here.

Grimacing at the pain, he hauled his butt down the bedroll drawing up his legs so that he could get a good kick at the hatch. At least the tube's internal lights worked so he could see where to kick.

He kicked it once, twice. Then he rolled over and was sick, noisily and messily. There was blood in his vomit. That bastard thing had killed him; he'd got a perforated intestine or something, something broken inside, and he was going to die here, in a metal tube smaller than a minership's living space, with nothing to show for his life but pain and metal. He should have shorted the drive on his mining ship and died like a star, rather than end pre-buried in this tomb.

He couldn't kick. The reverberations through his bones and up into his stomach were too hard. He tried to hammer on the inside of the cylindrical sleep tube to make enough sound to get someone's attention. He knew it must fail: Timtangle would have had him put out of the crew-ways on some dusty half-lit spur. A bit of dying human cargo on the edge of the great holds. Gradually his thumping grew less, and the pain rolled over him again. Almost, like a blanket, he welcomed the darkness that came with it.

It was the light that stirred him. A vuim staring into the tube, its glittery eyes, curious and yellow. 'Mr Brok,' it hissed. 'You helped crew-vuim, friend of mine, in his illness. I help you. Come, there will be pain but I can carry you. There are medicines will help you.'

It laid strong hands on his body, and pulled. Only then, finally, did he black out.

As the great plough-shaped force fields sliced through the matter of the world, and tractor beams grabbed and stuffed, grabbed and stuffed it piece by piece into the maw of the eating machine that the vuim had made of their factory, the world screamed. As above, so below. Its pain rolled out, bearing madness.

His daughter's eyelids popped open, and then so did her mouth. She screamed and screamed and the little Tailor King tried to explain. 'I had to do it, precious. I had to! I was desperate. It was the only way to save you from this dread curse.' He bent into the glass coffin where she thrashed about, kissed her screaming mouth hard, hard, his hands pressed into the soft flesh of her face as he tried to make her shut up. His kiss seemed to calm her. The screaming stopped and she stared at him for a moment, her eyes blinking dully. Oh, but she was so beautiful, so like her mother. He stroked her body, remembering her mother's beauty and the pleasure it gave him. She moaned. Her eyes rolled back in her head. Ah, yes. She would show her gratitude to her father. Hadn't he saved her? Wasn't she his by rights now? Why shouldn't he claim his own daughter's hand in marriage?

He reached down and picked up her left hand from the ground, then the right one, unable to remember which hand tradition dictated should be claimed in marriage. Clean unsullied hands the Devil had demanded in exchange for breaking the curse. They were covered in blood now. But the Devil would understand that. Just as he would understand that one of them must be the King's by right.

'What are you doing?' the cloven-hoofed pink Devil demanded. 'Give those to me!'

The King stared at his daughter's hands, then at the axe. Then he began to scream.

Glenko hailed his captain, not bothering to hide the comlink from the humans. There was no reason to be covert about it. He and Tunteki were hardly noticed amid the confusion and hysteria in the castle's yard. He'd been as stunned as any of the humans when the mad little man had chopped off the girl's hands. The man was raving now, thinking the girl was his daughter, though reactions from the other humans indicated this wasn't so. The man was local nobility and the girl was a servant of the lowest sort if her garments were any indication. Tunteki had rushed over and tried to staunch the bleeding, but she'd gone into shock quickly. Glenko thought he was wasting his time. There was no hope for her given the primitive medical technologies available on the planet. In other circumstances he would have used this as a bargaining tool in trade. But he was no longer convinced the planet had anything useful to offer in return.

'Report,' came Timtangle's tinny voice over the radio.

'We've lost contact with Domdan. Has his team reported to you?'

'Not yet. But you've located an energy signal I take it?'

'Yes, Captain. A local minor monarch would appear to have it in his possession.' In the background the madman was babbling something about fashioning silver hands for his daughter. 'That raving you hear is his. The energy discharges have all been placed in containment fields of some kind. We don't know how, but Tunteki has a theory that it's something to do with the planet itself, like a mollusc extrudes a nacreous substance around an irritant. It seems far-fetched to me. The one we have is in the shape of a box and the one in this king's possession seems to be in a kind of box as well. It's possible we weren't the first trade contingent to arrive here.' He heard his abanak captain gasp.

'So Brok may have been playing us for fools all along, then? Of course, he's been working for someone else the whole time!'

'Possibly. Though we haven't found any hard evidence of prior contact. Still, I feel the sooner we locate the white-hole material and get off this world the better.'

'Ah, well. The Vuim-Captain would disagree with you on that point. His team have made an interesting discovery. Maybe a planetary-scale application of the white-hole energies. Maybe something we can harvest more easily.'

'I look forward to hearing about it when we return. If you hear from our other team, I'd appreciate being informed.'

'Likewise.'

They signed off, leaving Glenko to watch the human goings-on with growing unease. The female's blood continued to spread over the stones and dirt. The little king was still raving, but quietly now. Glenko shuddered.

* * *

It took only minutes for their horses to follow the Doctor's down to the shore. They saw him pacing, looking out over the expanse of water and searching the sand beneath his feet in turns. Fitz dismounted and walked over to him.

'The tide's come and gone,' the Doctor said, without looking at him. 'There's no sign of her, where she might have gone, what might have happened –' He threw his head back with a groan, half a roar of abject misery, pulling at fistfuls of hair, before plopping unceremoniously down on the sand. Head in hands, he pressed his thumbs to his eyeballs so hard Fitz thought they might pop out and go rolling into the foam lapping at his boots. After a few moments the Doctor sighed heavily and looked again out over the bright water on the bay. 'Could you let off a string of loud curses for me, Fitz?' he said softly. 'I don't have the energy to berate myself properly right now.'

'What's happened? Who's gone missing?'

'Her name is Janet. The Giant's Master-maid. She helped me escape. I promised I'd come right back for her. I promised!'

'Well,' Fitz began in an effort to be comforting and sensible, 'you couldn't. There were other things going on that were more important –'

'That doesn't matter here!' the Doctor cried. Fitz flinched, and Anji, who'd come down to see what was going on, took a startled step back at the anguish and anger in his voice. Christina hung back, not wanting to trust her mount to negotiate the rocks that led down to the beach, but the Doctor's voice had carried well enough to make her eye the scene with speculative interest. 'You need to understand something – *all* of you.' The last he shouted over his shoulder to include Christina. And he continued to speak loudly enough for her to hear every word over the lapping of the waves. 'On this world, there is no grand or noble ideal that takes precedence over a single creature. A promise made even to a tiny ant is as important to keep as an appointment with destiny. More important, possibly.'

'So,' Christina called down, 'this Janet's a tiny ant, then? It's no wonder you can't find her –'

'She's a sixteen-year-old girl who may very well be dead because of me! And I'd try to keep your flippancy under control if I were you. It's not only ants that can get stepped on, you know.'

'But what could have happened to her?' Anji asked, scanning the shoreline and the rocks above. 'I mean, maybe she got tired of waiting and went off on her own.'

'Maybe. But she was holding back a Giant that wanted to cook me and eat me when I left her here.'

'Oh. So you think…?'

'He cooked and ate her instead? Well, I see no evidence of a fire for the purpose. Of course he wasn't above a raw nibble now and again –'

'Excuse me. Don't mean to be flippant or anything,' Christina called out. Three pairs of eyes shot daggers at her. 'Is it possible she might have decided to hide, and just possibly someone or something else found her? Because there's what looks like maybe a cave over here and some things that look like footprints in front of it and some drag marks –'

The Doctor bolted to his feet.

The vuim factory lander moved back and forth across the land. The stuff of the World tried to hide, to change, to fight, but its strengths were not the vuim's strengths, nor its ways their ways. The lander's tractors and force-field tools were designed to slice through bedrock, to lay open seams of minerals and to bring in tonnes of rock and ore. They cut deep and fast.

'Robbers,' the Doctor pronounced as he mounted his horse again. Anji and Fitz automatically followed suit, and after a moment Christina did the same. The Doctor tucked a small leaf with curly edges into the bridle and added for emphasis, 'Cutthroats, thieves, pirates.' The horse began to trot with no prompting and their horses did the same. 'They must have hidden their cache in the cave intending to return for it sometime in the night. Janet took refuge there knowing the Giant wouldn't be able to fit his hand inside –' Christina refrained from rolling her eyes, taking her cue from the other two, who were listening and nodding earnestly as if his assessment of the evidence made perfect sense. 'Then, sometime later, the robbers came to retrieve their stolen goods and stumbled upon her.'

'And robbers and cutthroats being what they are,' Christina said, 'she's alive and well so long as they prefer her that way.'

There was an icy silence, then the Doctor said, 'I don't know that any of them are alive and well, robbers included. Because, you see, none of them left that cave in any normal fashion.'

'There are passages then,' Fitz said. 'We should go back –'

'No passages, I looked, believe me. They went in, but they didn't come out.'

'Well, what are you going to do?' Anji asked. 'If it's as important to keep your promise as you say –'

'I've already broken my promise. I can only hope the World will set that aside until we've completed our... mission. Then I'll accept the consequences of what I've done.'

And with that his horse broke into a run. And in concert, the others followed.

Chapter Fifteen
The Glass Tower

'Can he be saved?' the vuim asked, rubbing its almost-human-but-too-long fingers together in consternation.

'I don't know,' the human said. 'This isn't my field. He needs a doctor.'

'You are doctor.'

'Of nucleonics. This is biology.' The plump human sighed. 'All I can do basically is turn the medical unit on and hope its automatic diagnostics can work out his injuries and patch them up before Timtangle's bastards notice that the medical suite's in use.' He jabbed at some switches. 'It's all up to the machine now.'

'Thank you, Dr Sam,' the vuim said, 'even if it is not your field. My klatch owes this William, I would like him to live.'

William floated in a haze the colour of sunflowers, and felt no intrusion as the sensors, probes and samplers of the medical suite picked their way in and out of his body, mending and sewing.

It neutralised a threatening blood clot in his brain, force-cloned a length of intestine and layered it around a tear in his gut, sucked out the blood from the internal bleeding, eased a minor hernia back through the muscle wall, gel-sealed a cracked rib, and pumped him full of Non-Euphoric HealAll, the company general-purpose medicine of choice.

That was all it could do. It was still touch and go.

Timtangle met Vuim-Captain at the port from the docked lander. It was partly a courtesy, partly that he didn't want the vuim roaming the ship until he had got him firmly behind his changes, or until he had discovered that he didn't need him.

'So, what have you got for us?' he asked, looking curiously at the grey-swirling surface of the force box the Captain was cradling as if it contained his heir.

'We can talk in your quarters,' the vuim answered. 'Have you cleared the holds yet?'

'We have maximised the available space, yes,' Timtangle replied falling in behind the striding insect as he set off towards the abanak's quarters. 'But you must understand that we can not jettison other trade items until we are sure that the goods you are proposing to load outweigh their value.'

Vuim-Captain craned his long head down to the level of Timtangle's, and whispered. 'They outweigh everything.'

Hearing that, Timtangle grinned inwardly and fiercely, and thought of profit, and of splitting it two ways or not splitting it at all.

The cows in Grammer Munpher's herd went mad at noon, shaking their heads back and forth and staggering as if they'd been at the beer trough at the Singing Bone, rather than drinking from the clean stream water above the town.

Her sons had corralled the beasts in the lower meadow, but they were ornery and skittish, and Tom Munpher got kicked in the knee by one and went down like a sack of potatoes and had to be carried back by his brothers cursing fit to wake the dead.

The dust was dancing above the ground, and there was a scent like cinnamon in the air. Grammer Munpher made hex signs on the red barn with the blood of a pig and a cock pheasant, and laid up her oldest son with his leg splinted and bandaged with wintergreen and rue. The first to heal, the last to sting to buggery and teach him not to get behind an angry cow.

Still she wasn't at ease and the cows were mooing shrill and high, and the crows in the spinney past Farmer Dewloft's land were circling without landing until they fell exhausted from the sky. Black bodies on the yellow corn. Crow circles.

There was a sound under everything, like two great fists grinding together knuckle on knuckle. Gradually at first, then with an increasing rattle, the red and black branches of the briar around the Princess's Tower began to creak and groan, straining, and tearing away from their rootlets in the masonry.

Everything was shaking. In the market, plates and goblets fell and broke, and men lost their footing, and women stumbled. In the Inn of the Singing Bone, the bone-flute gave a single despairing parp, like a broken child's whistle, and sounded no more.

Like a wedding cake rising in tiers, the land broke and pushed up, the first tier taking in the town itself, and maybe forty acres of land around. Some farms, some forests, half of Grammer Munpher's lower meadow, all of Farmer Dewloft's rooky wood, rose thirty feet on a cracking piston of molten red stone. The crack sounded like the breaking of the world's bones as the earth shattered. Then it happened again, another fifty feet of rock hosting the town, and the ragged torn land still higher. The market men, the travelling traders, started to pack up now, and there was a brisk if futile trade in ropes and ladders, in climbing gear, and sovereign amulets against falling. At the edges of the new plateau, people looked down eighty vertical feet. Some managed to lower themselves down or be lowered. The Munpher family rigged a block-and-tackle arrangement from Dewloft's elms and made a good five silver coins and twenty bronze swinging travellers down, before the earth heaved itself up further and took the trees up beyond the reach of their ropes. Others still found themselves marooned on lost pieces of land, great mesas flaking off the rising sides of polished stone like naps off a flint. Toppling iceberg shards of downs, and oaks: nature tumbled and wanton.

It didn't stop. Thirty, fifty, eighty, a hundred feet. The earth groaned, birthing a tower of blood-red stone, a tower carrying towers skyward. On it people cowered, and pulled their hats down over their faces, and told their friends they'd always loved them, often in inappropriate ways.

By the end of the harrowing of the earth, of the torture of the rock itself, the Princess's Tower, half the town of the Tailor King, a dozen farms, and two dark, dark woods covered the flattened end of a thousand-foot spire of ugly red rock that oozed and spat with veins of molten fire. Before long it hardened to the consistency of red glass. Unclimbable.

Gloomily and ill at ease, the four riders picked their way across a landscape that grew stranger with every step. The further they rode, the more bizarre it became. Not here the great forests that for all their darkness, even for all their mobility and magic, still stood straight as signposts marking the glory of nature. In their place were scrubby bushes, gnarled and twisted, and things rooted in the cracked and desiccated earth that looked more animal than plant. A maze of twisted stone pillars carved with shapes that looked like Easter eggs, but which bore red-brown stains, moaned when they came too close.

And it wasn't only the landscape. In a cornfield they found complex geometric circles that on investigation ended in a pair of still red-hot dancing shoes beside a charred and smoking corpse. They'd gone to the aid of a man by the roadside, chasing away the crows that had pecked out his eyes only to have the man rail at them, saying, 'A father must feed his children!' A woman propped against a tree, ground soaked with the blood of childbirth, stared dead-eyed at the sun while a mewling bear cub, placenta still attached to umbilical cord, tried to suckle from her. Anji and Fitz wanted to rescue the cub, but after a quick examination of the woman, the Doctor had mounted his horse and urged them to do the same quickly. They were on the road again and galloping full tilt just as a huge bear came charging out of the forest. When the earth began to shake they thought the bear was gaining on them.

Then they saw the real cause. Far, far on the horizon, they watched a great shaft of earth and stone thrust up into the sky, higher and higher as the ground trembled. Their steeds danced sideways, forward and back again, a waltz of balance and fear as the tower of rock shifted the earth and pushed up higher still so that it seemed to pierce the stratosphere. After a few minutes the ground stopped rumbling and they rode on, knowing without question where they had to go.

The first river they came to after that was flowing uphill, and making a noise like a young boy crying.

They washed their faces down with water from the oddly flowing stream, and, while Fitz tended the horses and Christina stretched and moaned to no one in particular about her aching backside, Anji took the Doctor by the sleeve and led him out of earshot.

'Tell me again what we're doing, Doctor,' she demanded. 'And why.'

He gave her one of his innocent, vaguely affronted looks, but Anji'd damn well had enough and he knew it.

'We're trying to save the world,' he said, almost apologetically.

'Working to preserve this, are we? A world where people are hurt and punished and toyed with?'

'There's good and bad here,' the Doctor admitted. 'But we've been asked to save it from an alien disruption, an invasion from *outside*. Should we refuse to help because their world is sometimes harsh?'

'This is more than harsh. I don't even want to think how many people are probably dead from that planetary tantrum.' She gestured in the direction of the red glass but didn't look at it. Neither did he.

'On most planets volcanoes are oblivious to the people who've decided to grow vegetables in their shadows. It isn't personal. Neither is this.' He took hold of her shoulders gently and made her face him and a truth that they shared. 'Should I have let the Kulan conquer Earth because some people were unemployed and some were being tortured and there hadn't been a year without a war somewhere in – oh, probably the whole of human history?'

'Of course not, but that's a twisted bit of logic and a little manipulative, don't you think?'

'Fine. What do you think we should do?'

Anji rubbed her forehead. Part of her wanted to say, Let's go hack down some trees with Fitz's sword, free the TARDIS and get the hell out of here; but another part of her – and this was a new part – heard herself replying, 'Save the world, I suppose, as long as you aren't putting saving the world over saving the people on it.' He drew in a sharp breath and stared at her as if she'd just accused him of abusing his own child. Immediately, she started apologising. 'Look. I'm just upset, OK. This is all too much. It's lost all its wonder for me and now it's just... so damned ugly.'

'It's the boxes,' Fitz said, coming in on the last sentence. 'They're mucking things about, aren't they?' He glanced over at the horses by the stream, their heads turned to the distant needle that pierced the clouds. Anji suppressed a shudder. The horses were quivering and strangely calm at the same time as if anticipating some great cataclysm they would never be able to outrun.

'I'm not sure,' the Doctor said. His eyes, like those of the horses, were now fixed on the tower. His voice was a rough whisper. 'Must be at least sixty miles from here and look at it.' He drew his gaze away. 'These brutalities, these things that seem out of sync even for here, I don't think they have anything to do with the boxes. Those forces would be trying to overwrite the existing motifs of the world. What we're witnessing are warped versions of what already exists. No, there's something else at work here, something that's damaging the planet itself, hurting it. And the boxes will only stay quiet so long as their time of greatest potential hasn't come. This chaos might well be it. We may not have as long as I'd hoped. You!' The Doctor set his vivid gaze firmly on Christina. Anji and Fitz turned, startled. They'd forgotten about her and from her expression it seemed she'd been content to keep it that way. 'I think it's time we had a proper talk about who you are, where you're from, and what you're doing here.'

'William? Can you hear me?'

The sunflower colour was fading now, and William could see faces through the glass – one male human, podgy and covered with sweat, one vuim, thin, green and unreadable as ever. If he could see he figured he must be cured. Also he only ached, he didn't agonise. As the glass slid open, he coughed and spluttered into speech. 'Yes, what? Oh, thank God, I'm all right.'

'For now you are,' the vuim said. 'We are in sore straits. The abanak have put the ship on contagion alert, and declared that only their kind is immune. Human and vuim crew are confined to quarters. As far as we know, I and Dr Sam here are the only non-abanak crew not confined."

'It appears they have no problem betraying a trust so long as they can make sure that no one tells anyone else about it,' Doc Sam said. 'Anything valuable they can get on board while the rest of the crew is locked away won't appear on the manifest at any divvying up, you can count on it. We missed the round-up – we were sealed in the nucleonics lab, doing deep quark analysis of the antigraviton flux from the white hole. We came out just as the last of the contagion announcements were running. If we hadn't overheard a group of abanak laughing at the "penned-up humans" we'd probably have gone for it too.'

William groaned. 'This is all my fault. I found out something was wrong. I got worked up and confronted Timtangle about it. He probably ordered this fake alert because he thought I'd already talked to the rest of the crew.'

'It is certainly a marvellous model,' Timtangle said in a deliberately slightly bored way. Oh, he could see the potential all right: these thought-directed builders were another facet of the planet's 'wish granting', the powers the humans on the planet below attributed vaguely to the world and specifically to the 'boxes' that seemed to have formed around the energy from the white hole, but he wanted to see how much the vuim had grasped. If it proved to be hardly anything, there wouldn't be much point bargaining with the vuim.

'It is far more than a model,' Vuim-Captain stated. 'Force box. Point-magnify sections L5 though M23. Give X-ray view.' The force fields forming the box adjusted to his request, a trick no more startling than light bending on its journey past a gravity source, to show the tiny lander ship within. Timtangle leaned closer. Inside the replica ship he saw (and not by X-rays but by a technology named after them), the vuim crew about their tasks. Tiny vastly detailed simulacra.

'Before we removed this ship to show you,' Vuim-Captain continued, 'it had within it another model, and within that too a crew, and a further smaller model. The models went down as far in scale as the scanners we could rig could reveal. The smallest model was nine angstroms long. When we took this out of our real lander, the smaller ones inside it vanished.

'But, that's impossible!' Timtangle burst out. 'Absolutely impossible. That's smaller than a nanometre. Building atom by atom you couldn't get detail that fine, things would have to clump!'

'Worse than that, it was inhabited!' Vuim-Captain flexed his hands like a grimace. 'We theorise the building mechanism is not limited by the quantum structure of baryonic matter, it takes no account of Heisenberg, it doesn't stop anywhere.' His bony, inexpressive face contrived to give a sense of anguish to his words. 'Call it alien laws of physics from outside our space-time. Call it magic if you want. What matters is, it works! We guess that every part of this substance lives and communicates with the rest. At first we thought it had molecular control, then atomic. Now we know it goes on further to scales we cannot plumb with

216

science that blurs and falters at such tiny distances. What we have here is not only a tool unparalleled in history, but an absolutely new and unlooked-for discovery in physics in its own right!'

'We'll be very, very rich, my friend,' Timtangle said.

'Yes, and Christina, of course. Have your searches located her?'

'Ah, now *that* we need to talk about.'

Christina endeavoured to meet the Doctor's gaze, trotting out a repertoire of useful expressions learned through years in the adversarial arena of trade negotiations. She started with a surprised 'Whatever do you mean?' and ran the gambit of 'How dare you imply...?', 'I'm only trying to help', 'I don't have to take this abuse', 'I'm harmless really', before finally breaking down and hauling out the big guns – a look, pose and smile that said, 'I'll show you all my secrets, Doctor, if you'll show me yours.'

She could hear Anji sputtering her outrage in the background, and peripherally, the lanky fellow, Fitz, looking gob-stopped, but she didn't let it break her concentration. The Doctor stared at her for a long, long moment and then... he laughed. Right in her face.

'Is that supposed to make me go all wobbly in the knees and forget what I was asking?'

Christina pushed the sultry wave of hair that was obscuring her left eye behind her ear again. 'It was worth a shot.'

'I should think a well-travelled person like yourself would take into account the variables involved in any sexual attraction. I could have a fetish for bunny slippers, which, I note you aren't wearing.'

'Nooo,' Christina said, 'I don't think so. You haven't got a fetishistic aura, or a homosexual one, for that matter. I'm pretty good at spotting those.'

He laughed again. 'Really? Yet, you failed to notice the "not entirely human aura."'

'Oh. That explains it.'

'No. No, it doesn't.'

'Not every man finds you irresistible,' Anji said with sudden feral intensity. 'Deal with it.'

'You should talk,' Christina shot back.

'Um,' Fitz interjected.

'What the hell is that supposed to mean?'

'Oh dear,' the Doctor muttered.

'You're the one getting all cosy with him over here.'

'Hey,' Fitz tried again.

'Cosy! I should have expected you to come up with that interpretation. You with that disgusting lap dance you were doing for the Duke's test of beauty.'

'Ladies, can we please –' the Doctor began.

'What about that poetry business? Setting me up to look like a moron while you stood there being all virginal and clever in your little party frock –'

'Hello?' Fitz shouted. 'Problem. Big problem here!' He pointed. They all turned. Christina stumbled backwards and fell down hard. She barely noticed the jolt of pain. She was too busy looking at the trees. All of them. Hundreds and hundreds of trees that weren't there before.

'Oh look,' the Doctor said. 'Our forest has found us again.'

'I will not leave Christina on the planet,' Vuim-Captain stormed. 'We have an agreement. Our three races are bound to aid each other, to seek mutual profit. This –' He seemed lost for words. 'This is mutiny, Mr Timtangle.'

'Yes, *Ccklukchuvkl* of Vuim, I'm afraid it is. My people admire the humans, we really do, but this isn't an ordinary find. This isn't a one-stop pick-up on a long trade tour. This is fortune. And when fortune comes knocking it's time to decide just how much a given word is worth, don't you think? You could still be useful: your people have the lander and its prize. We could up our tents and steal away, buy worlds, and come again to get more wealth. This place could be our honey pot.' Timtangle looked oddly hopeful and slightly dejected, as if it would make him feel better to be betraying only one partner.

'I have stated my position. Do not demean yourself by suggesting that you understand honour so little that you expect me to depart from it.'

Armed abanak stood in the doorway, their hides grey and plain, unemotional, resolved. At a nod from Timtangle they escorted Vuim-Captain out.

As they left, Timtangle took the little lander out of the force-field box and held it aloft.'Vmmmmmmmm,' he said imitating the sound of labouring antigravity engines. 'Bring your riches up to me.' He realised it sounded like he was saying 'vuim' and laughed.

The clear and obvious path into the forest made everyone but the Doctor uncomfortable. Anji likened it to one of those bug traps – 'bugs go in but they don't come out'.

'Like the robber's cave,' Christina said.

'No. No. This is more like an invitation,' the Doctor told them. 'Look at how the sun sparkles through the trees and shines on the path. It's got little pebbles and everything.'

'I'm sure the path into the roach trap looks very shiny to the roach,' Fitz said.

'Actually they're attracted to the smell. Mmm. Marzipan.'

'They don't use marzipan in roach motels.'

'No, I smell marzipan. Can't you?'

'Oh god,' Christina moaned.

Fitz knew the smell of marzipan or anything yummy in a forest was not a good sign, but before he could stop him the grinning Doctor made a slightly sinister 'follow me' gesture, then plunged into the thickets beside the path. They could hear him crashing through the forest like an idiot.

'Ah ha. Oh.'

His cry of triumph died away into a note of puzzlement.

Pushing through the vegetation towards him, Anji caught a glint of familiar blue. TARDIS blue. Then another. Then another.

The two abanak weren't expecting William, a vuim and an out-of-condition human doctor to jump them as they came around the corner. Unused to violence, they went down like two fat alien skittles. Vuim-Captain bent down and took their weapons easily, one in each of his narrow hands.

'Good work, human-William, Dr Samuel, vuim of the north klatch. Tell me of happenings as we go. It is vital that we prevent my fellows docking their lander with this ship. If we can retain hold of the riches it carries we can bargain with Timtangle, gain a new compact, and force him to seek the humans lost on the surface.'

William was pointing behind him, an ashen look on his face.

The Captain turned. More abanak. A lance of white fire pierced his side, and he fell, shooting as he did so. Fire laced the air, and the smell of cooked meat made William shudder. He wasn't healed yet. He couldn't fight. He was strangling a hippo with his belt. Odd, it all seemed to be happening so slowly.

A hundred TARDISes, some obvious fakes, some mere husks dangling like pine cones from the trees. Others real, firm and humming gently. One full-sized box, ice blue, was nibbled from, its colour stained with saliva and a fragment of its corner showing human teeth marks.

'Oh dear.' The Doctor sat down on a tuft of grass and rested his head in his hands.

'Don't you know which one it is?' Fitz asked, his voice curiously strained at the edges. The Doctor's lower lip protruded and his head sank lower. Fitz sighed, feeling as if he'd just reminded a mourner that it was a funeral.

'I should, shouldn't I?' the Doctor said. 'But I don't feel anything. Maybe it's because I haven't got the key.'

Anji watched Fitz turn puce.

'You. Haven't. Got. The key? What happened to it?' Fitz asked, ending on a high whine of worry and dismay.

'I gave it to someone.'

'Who?' 'Why?' Anji and Fitz said at the same time. Christina was eyeing them as if they had all gone mad. She wandered over to one of the blue shapes. It was the same as the strange box the wodewose had shown her in that other forest, but that had been east of here, she was certain. Of course she'd seen that the trees could move. But taking things with them? It shouldn't have boggled her mind after all this time on the planet, but it did. She imagined the forests like gypsies and the blue boxes their caravans. Yet the wildman hadn't known what the blue box was at the time –

She remembered the acorns in her pocket, and pulled them out. Two of them were black and shrivelled. A tiny noise came from the black acorns and she held one to her ear. 'Plant me, my wish is done.' The other made the same plaintive sound.

She pressed them into the earth.

Wishes. And one unused. Hmmm.

She turned at the rush of motion behind her. The Doctor and Fitz were scampering around the full-sized blue boxes examining each one. Anji stood with her arms crossed over her chest wearing a look of mild irritation.

'What are they looking for?' Christina asked.

'The real one,' Anji answered.

'The real what?' Christina prompted.

'Its called a TARDIS,' Anji said. 'It looks, well, like *that* – like a, a big blue box with windows, and a roof like that and a light on top, and it takes us anywhere in time and space. At least it would if its lord and master over there hadn't forgotten the first thing about steering it in a straight line from the Earth to the moon, and if it hadn't developed a lookeelikee problem, and if he hadn't given the key away to someone he'd never met before called Alex.'

'A tallish man, gangling, pointy beard,' Christina leapt in. 'He would have been dressed like me the first time you saw me.'

Anji shrugged. 'I don't know. He tried to kill the Doctor, though, left him to be eaten by a Giant, apparently.' She cocked an eye at Christina. 'That the sort of thing your friends do?'

'He was probably scared shitless,' she said. 'We landed, and the world swallowed our scout ship. After that we got lost in a wood whose trees were like mirrors. Turn and turn again and the way vanished. He must have thought he was going to die here.'

'Well maybe we're going to join him at that,' Anji said. She straightened her jacket decisively. 'But not if I have anything to say about it.' And with that she marched over to her two companions to organise the search properly.

In the holding cell, William nursed his bruises and tried to make Vuim-Captain more comfortable. The vuim was breathing heavily now, rasping and spluttering, and he had a feeling that he'd seen this before. Perhaps it was the exertions of the fight, perhaps the shock of the Abanak-Captain's illegal seizure of the ship, but the leader of the vuim was showing the symptoms of their disease. A disease with only one swift prognosis by the time visible symptoms broke out.

'This one's got the door part open,' Fitz shouted. 'You did lock it before that forest shot up, right?' Thanks to Anji's systematic elimination of all the fakes, they'd got the number of possible TARDISes down to twenty-eight. Twenty-seven now. This one had grown with doors that opened out.

The Doctor shrugged, hopping from foot to foot in the cold. It looked for all the world like an affectation to hide his panic. 'I can't remember, of course I did, I think. It's a reflex, isn't it? You don't want to come back and find it full of red squirrels.'

Fitz had his back to the doors of the TARDIS in question. A furious squeaking and scratching erupted from inside it.

'I can't believe you gave away the TARDIS key,' Anji said for the fifth time.

The Doctor was a little tired of hearing it. He plonked himself down on a snowy boulder. 'It just seemed like the natural thing to do. I didn't expect him to run off with it; where was there for him to go? Honestly, I thought I could reach out and get it back from him at a moment's notice when he'd settled down. All right, yes, maybe I got a bit carried away with the Doctor Know-All business –'

'You think?' Anji muttered.

'Of course,' Fitz said, shaking a squirrel off his trousers, 'if we can't find the real TARDIS the question is moot anyway. There's no point blaming the Doctor – yet.'

'I have spare keys inside,' the Doctor grumped. 'And I don't know that I even need a key to get inside really. Perhaps here I only need a magic word or phrase.' He bounced up again, clearly thrilled by the idea, and proceeded to race from one blue box to another, trying phrases like 'open sesame' and 'abracadabra' and 'drizzle, drazzle, drone' on each but to no avail. The last one he kicked. 'Open up, you stepmother!'

A terrified moan from within had him jumping back. 'Hello?' He knocked tentatively. 'Is there somebody in there?'

'Help me please. The door's jammed.'

Anji rushed over. 'Rozered? Is that you in there?'

'Yes!'

'Is it bigger on the inside where you are?' the Doctor called.

There was a long moment of silence. 'Er... no, cramped and dark.'

He made a rude noise. Anji batted his arm and glared meaningfully. 'Hold on. We'll get you out.' Muttering to himself, the Doctor began searching the ground for something to batter in the door. Fitz joined him. Christina moved closer to watch the action, careful to stay on the periphery of it nonetheless. She was glad Rozered was safe, but her presence here was worrisome.

After a moment the two men found a hefty bit of wood and made short work of the door while Anji fretted that they were going to smash the woman inside if they weren't more careful.

But finally they managed to tear the splintered door panels out and pulled a bedraggled plump little woman in her forties from a disappointingly cramped space. The first thing Rozered did was to apologise for losing Anji's box.

'I'm sorry. I kept hold of it as long as I could. But then I dropped it and the earth swallowed it and then the terrible wildman came and killed the beast that had tried to steal it from me and he dragged the body away –'

'What sort of beast?' the Doctor asked.

'It were a pinkish grey colour, long round snout, big flat teeth. Wore a garment all of a piece with many pockets and it had three-fingered hands and a hammer that shot bolts of lightning from the handle –'

Christina made a squeaky little sound and when they turned she had her hand over her mouth as if she'd only burped.

'One of yours?' the Doctor asked.

'Maybe.'

He scowled at her. Then he scowled at the collection of blue boxes scattered through the glade. 'I'm trying to help you!' he shouted up at the sky, the world. A group of sparrows took flight from a fir branch above his head. 'How can I help if you block me at every turn?'

In her pocket, Christina felt the acorn buzz and jump. She clenched her fist over it. No. Not yet.

'It's like an animal that's been injured,' Fitz said. 'It knows it needs help, but won't let you near enough to do anything for it.'

The sparrows settled high in the branches above Christina and sent a light shower of snow on to her head.

No. It's the last one. I'm not going to waste it on –

Then she saw it. The small smear of blood on the panel of the box closest to her.

'This TARDIS,' Christina asked, quickly, 'bigger inside than out, you said?'

'Oddly, yes,' Fitz said.

'It's this one.'

'How can you tell?' the Doctor asked, running lightly across the intervening distance and laying his hand flat on the blue and white lettering of the panel.

'The wodewose – Rozered's wildman I suppose – he showed me it in the forest. I never forget a possible acquisition.' He looked at her askance, but said nothing. Her blood was like a scarlet letter, damning her for she didn't know what. Dear God, it was glowing like a beacon. How could he not see it?

The Doctor reached out for the door, hopefully, tentatively starting to push, but at that moment a fox yelped among the dark trees. It was a harsh broken yelp that sounded choked and muffled, and a thin shiver ran up Christina's back at the sound.

Sitting in a dejected heap of dark-green leaves, its russet fur tattered and crusted with snow, a lanky fox stared at them. It coughed again, choking, and pawed at its throat with an almost human gesture of distress.

The Doctor motioned the others back, and moved towards it with measured, quiet steps, the blue box that had seemed so important to him moments before taking a back seat to the needs of a sick animal. His hand inched forward and he touched the fox's fur with the tips of his fingers. 'Hush, now,' he said, and hooked a hand inside its jaw, stretching it to keep the animal's sharp pointed teeth apart, letting his fingers fit its gum line so it couldn't bite easily. With his other hand he felt for something caught, and in return, the fox obliged by being sick over his walking boots. In the middle of the puddle of carrion something gleamed. The Doctor picked it up, and spun around holding it high. The TARDIS key.

The fox cleared its throat noisily. 'So, I gave it you back,' it said. 'Pleased to see me?'

Christina's face went pale with shock. 'Alex?' she said.

And Fitz leaned back on the TARDIS door in mock horror, and fell in.

Chapter Sixteen
The Cabinet of Other Worlds
(or The Third Brother and What Became of Him)

Christina blinked, and something hazy swam before her eyes. There had been a transition – like stepping on to a new ninety-nine-per-cent Earthlike world for the first time, the tiniest set of changes in pressure, in gravity, in the defraction of sunlight into a different blue, adding up to a new vivid life.

They had left the fairy horses with Rozered, who'd declined the invitation to travel in the blue box. She was confident the animals would lead her from the forest with no trouble. 'They're fairy horses, aren't they?' She smiled, stroking one contentedly. 'I'll be home in no time.'

Christina almost wished she'd gone with her. She'd stepped into the black opening of the blue box and now was in a large room, and – for all the fluting column and banked controls of the room's central many-sided table – it felt like a room, not like a control deck or a laboratory. The quality of light suggested that there was a natural sun nearby, beaming through two open patio doors across fresh pine decking. But it seemed to come from indented circles set into the walls, and there was a tinny hum and snatched scent of ozone, and there was no way all this was in the same place.

'OK,' she said, and sat down pointedly on the floor. 'I'm just going to sit here until someone explains all this preferably with a nice cool glass of something.'

The three of them ignored her.

The Doctor was darting round the central table, pushing a big red button here, sliding a little lever there, the fox curled on his shoulder as he moved. The damn thing seemed to be whispering to him. Goodness only knew what secrets of the *Bonaventure*, the abanak, or the vuim it was spilling. Assuming she believed it was really Alex. The devices the Doctor was handling reminded her of the sort of activity blocks they used to test for intelligence in cold first-contact situations. Put this shape in here, move that rod, lift that bar, get a free nice feeling from a nerve inductor. It looked random and childish and it was starting to annoy her, when the central column began to rise and fall, and a noise like an obstreperous elephant started up from somewhere *below*.

'Hang on, everyone,' the Doctor said.'I've been practising these short hops.'

Fitz winced.

There was a moment's discontinuity that could have lasted a month or a microsecond.

'Or not,' the Doctor said, fanning away a thin line of white smoke rising from the console with a big black Stetson he'd grabbed from a free-standing cupboard full of hats. Christina blinked. Surely that hadn't been there before. A giant mahogany thing full of headgear, she was bound to have seen that. Right. Threatened with the prospect of space travel in a remarkably spacious wooden box with a light on top, and she was worried about hats! Her friend, well her colleague, was supposedly this reddish-brown vermin that would have been hunted on half the worlds in the Kursaal system. The planet was tearing itself to bits under them, and there was still no sign of a stinking profit to be had anywhere. So far they were down one scout ship and one disability pension for being suddenly foxy. Maybe funeral benefits too, if Tento was the monster killed by the wodewose. She wondered what had happened to the vuim on the other side of the world.

The Doctor patted her on the shoulder as he headed for the door. 'Come on,' he said 'there are things to do. Maybe we can persuade the planet to turn Alex back, if we can save it.'

Vuim-Captain whispered something harsh and leathery into William's ear. A curse? Their situation warranted it. No, the Captain was trying to draw his attention to something. A hard shape in a pocket. A small box, jury-rigged with a tiny force field – maybe an hour's more field strength left to it. William winced, partly at his injuries, which despite the medical treatment were still a constant painful reminder of his failure – though no longer life-threatening – and partly at the box. He knew only one substance dangerous enough to require transportation in a force field: antimatter. He thought of a cold hard cluster of anti-hydrogen held inside the box, away from its matter walls, by the penetration of the force field. Was the vuim so paranoid that he'd walked aboard with his own life, and that of the ship, trickling away in microvolts in his tunic?

'Not antimatter,' Vuim-Captain gasped. 'Something new, open it'. His rasping voice faded away with his consciousness.

William wondered if he could believe him. Maybe the vuim would rather they all go up in a white three-dimensional expanding sphere of unleashed atomic fire than to die slowly in a cell knowing that Timtangle would be likely to kill the rest of the vuim to keep his treachery secret. William remembered thinking something similar himself when the pain had been at its worst. Now, though, he wanted to live.

As they disembarked from the TARDIS, it was immediately clear that it had not taken them to the hoped-for destination. Oh, it had borne them up the great shaft of rock that had burst out of the planet's heart, it had taken them to the plateau in the sky, but inside the keep of the Princess Ebonyblack it had not gone.

The Doctor gave it a friendly pat anyway. 'I'm sure you did your best.'

Anji just knew he was the sort who'd give a car a pet name. Probably a girl's.

This close to the Princess's tower its perspective was lost, like being at the bottom of a sheer rock face in the mountains. The keep had lost its Disney whiteness now in the red glare from the fused glass. When she stepped away fifty, sixty yards and craned her neck back, eyes following the blood-red colour of the glassy surface as she tried to see the top, the tower started to fall. Anji hit the ground with a thud, banging her head, adding to the already nauseous flutter caused by vertigo. Fitz, tight-lipped, his hands shaking, helped her to her feet and neither of them looked up for a while after that. Christina hadn't even tried, but was sitting curled against an uprooted tree using a chunk of broken masonry for a pillow. The fox sat next to her preening its fur. She wouldn't look at the fox.

The Doctor was stamping back and forth at the base of the tower looking for a way in, but all the entrances seemed to be high up the shining glass walls, as if the only way had been through the rest of the castle when the tower was still attached. In the rubble of masonry at the base where a portion of another tower had fallen, the Doctor found something in the smashed and pulverised stone. 'Give me a hand, Fitz,' he called. Anji saw Fitz hesitate and she knew he expected to be digging out a body or two. But the Doctor's movements indicated an urgency of a different sort. Fitz joined him, tugging at the thing he was trying to rescue, pulling at the stones on top of it alternately, until it was loose enough to work free. It was a crystal sheet, maybe a looking-glass mirror, but denser and somehow deeper than its thickness appeared to the eye. The Doctor propped it up against a pile of rocks. 'Hello!' he shouted, rapping on it three times with the knuckles of his left hand. In the glass a green warty face rose to press itself against the inside.

'Hello, Doctor!' it said.

'Hello, Inex,' the Doctor answered, and he turned to give Fitz and Anji a brilliant smile. 'I'd like you to meet a gnome friend of mine. I'd hoped that the Giant's justice might have sent you back here rather than through the plumbing.'

'So let me out!'

'Can't yet, sorry. Maybe soon. I need you to be my wizard's glass.'

The thing in the glass howled and swore but the Doctor ignored it. 'I suggest we make camp before it gets dark.'

Christina's head shot up. 'We're going to camp outside? When you have a nice, spacious, well-appointed ship?'

'We need to keep looking for a way into the tower. I don't intend to stop when it gets dark. Besides, camping is fun. Sitting around the fire, toasting marshmallows, singing songs. You still haven't told me what you're doing here.'

She sighed. 'We're just traders, merchants. We found a white hole and it ejected some material that ended up here. So we came down to find it.'

'Someone else found the white hole's energies,' the fox said with Alex's voice. She flinched. 'What difference does it make? It's all gone to hell.'

The Doctor's gaze didn't waver; he didn't even blink as he scanned her features. 'Have your people taken anything else from this planet?'

'How should I know? I've been out of contact for days, weeks, maybe. I don't even know they're still out there.'

'Doctor!' the gnome's voice squealed from the glass. 'Ask me and I'll show you!'

'Yes! Excellent!' The Doctor bounded back to the crystal and sat cross-legged before it. Pulled by curiosity, Anji and Fitz followed him and stood watching over his shoulders. 'Show me what has been taken from the world.'

'You're not going to like it.' Inex said.

And he showed them Hell on the other side of the world.

* * *

There are dead worlds that have never been touched by life, worlds where lava falls a thousand feet high light the methane clouds with a vivid darting red. They can have a massive, untouched grandeur. There are planets where the impacts of a thousand asteroids have left craters, and rills, and great exposed continental shelves. They can have the expectant peace of cathedrals. No devastation wrought by nature resembles that made by intelligence. The vuim had been diligent; they had been painstaking; they had had a due regard for the likely monetary value of their harvest, and they had, aside from that, considered nothing.

They'd laid bare the bones of the world, and it was ugly. The rocks were melted from point-pressure heating where the tractor beams had scoured the surface until it broke. The things removed from that surface had clearly resisted, maybe splitting and fragmenting into competing organisms under the evolutionary thrust of the assault. The tracks the cutting beams burned into the hot, baked, black dirt spiralled and waved, patterns distorted like some ritualistic tattoo. Or the brand on a slave.

'Christina.'

The warm breath from the fox's nose moistened her hand and she pulled away quickly. She scooted a little further down the fallen log on which she was sitting. Fitz, Anji and the Doctor were hunched around the fire, discussing the mess those incompetent vuim had made of one of the south continents. They looked shaken and grim. She'd watched the pictures in the glass only long enough to realise that, brutal and careless as the vuim's methods had evidently been, it looked as if they'd got some profit out of this evil little world. She still hadn't decided what sort of spin she'd put on the matter when the Doctor turned his attention back to her.

The fox leapt up on the log and padded towards her.

'Christina,' it whispered again.

'What?' she hissed. Why wouldn't the creepy little beast leave her alone?

'I have found a way into the tower,' it said. She stiffened, holding her breath, eyes intent on her travelling companions. No doubt they could find a way in too as soon as it occurred to them to ask their preternatural database in a glass, but if she could get there first she could gain some advantage. She didn't know exactly what kind, but there had to be some way off this planet for her, some way to get in on the vuim's spoils.

The fox continued, 'If I show you the way, will you promise to return the boxes to the white hole where they can cause no further harm?'

'The boxes?' she asked, arching her eyebrows. 'What boxes?'

'The boxes in the saddlebags the Doctor brought with us from the forest. The saddlebags right there.' She looked down and to her left. Near the end of the log were worn satchels of leather, dropped with seeming carelessness only a couple of feet from where she sat.

'The energies from the white hole?' she asked the fox from the side of her mouth.

'Of course. There is one more, I think, nearby, trying to put its roots into the world.'

'How –' she started to ask. How did he know that? And how could this possibly be Alex Volpe? The Alex she knew would never sacrifice the chance for profit for some supposed greater good. This was a trick of the planet itself, trying to get her co-operation, get her to do its bidding. Return the boxes to the white hole my arse, she thought, but I'll take them *away*. Oh yes. Besides, the planet knew no astrophysics. You could no more put something back into a white hole than you could pull something out of a black one. It would be like putting the genie back into the bottle, or getting the salt out of the ocean. Alex would have known that.

'What makes you think I'll steal from these people?'

The fox gave a soft snort, Alex's derisive tone with a faint growl at the edge. 'Don't forget I know you. You think once they're in your possession you will have what Timtangle wants. He'd give you anything for them. You know that. But you mustn't let him have the boxes. You must ask for a scout ship. Ask for your friend William to pilot it. Then send the boxes back to their mother. Promise this.'

'All right,' she said, keeping her voice low. 'You lead. I'll follow in a minute.'

Anji got to her feet. 'I'll be back in a few minutes.'

'Where are you going?' Fitz asked.

She sighed. She was weary, sick at heart from the images she'd seen in the glass, but the needs of her body couldn't be denied any longer. 'None of your business,' she said mildly.

'You shouldn't go alone,' the Doctor said, starting to stand up.

'I've been "going" alone since I was about two, Doctor.'

'It's not safe for any of us to be out there by ourselves. Take Christina – Christina? Now where has she run off to?'

Fitz leapt up scanning the darkness beyond the ring of firelight.

She probably slipped away to have a nice, quiet pee, Anji thought as she took the same opportunity.

'Your friend Alex is gone too,' Fitz said. He turned around, a full circle, and, noting the other absence, put his hands on his hips with a sigh. 'Damn it, Anji.'

'You go after her,' the Doctor said. 'I'll track down our missing merchants –'

He froze suddenly, head cocked, eyes wide. Fitz heard it too and spun around just in time to see two madmen come tearing out of the darkness. They charged at him, knocking him aside. It was only when he saw the wolf cloak that he recognised the two Princes.

They were filthy, their fine clothing hanging in shreds, hair and eyes equally wild as they wrestled the scrap of fur and hide between them and flung it into the flames of the campfire. It smoked for brief second before the flames engulfed it. A choking stench brought instant tears to Fitz's eyes. The tattered Princes danced and twirled about insanely, grabbing each other, crying, 'Free at last! We're free of him!'

Anji had never been comfortable using raw nature as a traveller's convenience, considering how it was never as convenient for a woman as a man, especially when wearing leather. The trews Belesia had provided were fine for riding across the moors, or traipsing through the woods, or climbing rocks, but now the leather was proving unco-operative, mostly, she knew, because she was in a hurry and didn't want Fitz or the Doctor to come looking for her and, God forbid, *find* her. She'd spent frustrating agonising seconds loosening the lacings to get them down and even more time trying to wriggle the bloody things up over her backside again. So it shouldn't have surprised her that she was caught with her pants down. She was almost too mad to scream, but the big clammy hand over her mouth made it impossible anyway.

Fitz dashed to the fire, now raging, flames high. The smoke rolled out, filling the small clearing. Oblivious, he swam through it trying to plunge his hands into the flames to rescue the cloak but the Doctor jerked him back. 'Have you lost your mind?'

'Let me go! Let me save him!' The Doctor had to tackle him and pin him to the ground to keep him from trying it again.

'Fitz! Think, think. It's a ghost. The person is long dead. You couldn't save him anyway. Come on. Calm down now.'

Fitz lay still, the tears from the smoke all mixed up with the sorrow and rage. After a moment he shook the Doctor off and sat up, staring into the fire. Gilfred and Ansel had collapsed to the ground. Ansel was giggling. Gilfred was watching the flames, tears rolling down his cheeks as one hand plucked convulsively at scruffy clumps of grass. 'Our swords wouldn't cut it,' he said. 'No lake or river would swallow it. We buried it but it came rising to the surface as soon as we were done. We couldn't light a fire, not even to warm ourselves: the tinder wouldn't catch. But now we're free.' The flames danced in his eyes as he watched the haunted wolfskin burn. Then suddenly, he gasped. 'No.'

Within the heart of the fire a glowing shape was rising from the ashes of the wolf cloak, a pillar of white and gold too bright to look upon but impossible to look away from, and when it was the shape of a man it stepped out of the fire.

The white heat of the man shape cooled to a red glow. Ansel was hunched on the ground whimpering. He might have been praying or bowing to the glowing form – it didn't really matter. He was down, lost, dead inside his skin. Gilfred rose and stood before the phantom shape, his mouth open as if he were screaming but no sound came out. The red cooled to a rusty brown, then black. The charred crust began to flake off as the form within it trembled until the shell cracked and fell away, nothing but dust at the feet of a naked man. He was very young with golden hair and he blinked like a new-born baby.

Ansel made a scrabbling run on all fours, plunging into the thick darkness beyond the camp. Gilfred continued to stare at the figure, his body swaying, his feet nailed to the ground. Then his arm moved and there was a soft sigh of a sound. It took a moment for Fitz to figure out that that meant something. But by the time he did, Gilfred had pulled his short sword from the torn scabbard.

Fitz felt like he was moving through water, so slow, his own hand reaching for the sword at his side, the Doctor shouting 'No no no,' a mosquito's whine he brushed away with his other hand. He felt the weight of the sword in his hand, brought it up and back again as he moved between the naked man and his wicked brother. His eyes locked on to Gilfred's, saw the madness fading, the sorrow of understanding coming to the fore, and then another look – triumph as the Prince turned the battered sword on himself and thrust it beneath his breast bone. The crack of ribs, the rending of muscle and sinew, the sickening squelch of blood sliding around the blade – these sounds were clear, sharper than the thud, thud of blood pounding behind Fitz's eardrums, or his ragged breathing, or the Doctor's final sorrowful 'No' as Gilfred fell to his hands and knees forcing the sword up to the hilt. Pain twisted his mouth into a grimace for a moment, and then the pain of dying ripped even that away from him. His body twitched, huge spasms, rivulets of blood wound around the hilt of the sword, but there wasn't much. Fitz knew in some disjointed way that what had seemed to go on for ever hadn't really, for the Doctor was at the man's side in an instant trying to help him. Not that he could.

Somewhere not so far away a wolf howled. Then another. There was a cry, the desperate terror of a hunted creature caught. Growls, whines and snarls slippery with salivation pierced the night air. And other sounds Fitz didn't want to hear. But it was a pop from a log on the fire that made him jump.

The naked man – a boy really – said, 'I'm cold,' and began to shudder convulsively.

'Fitz. Fitz. Fitz.' The far away sound of the Doctor calling him.

'Yes.'

'Could you pop back to the TARDIS and fetch this fellow some warm clothes?'

'Yes.'

By the time he returned the Doctor had the boy sitting by the fire wrapped in his duster, encouraging him to drink from a mug filled with hot soup. 'This is Prince Offram,' he said. 'He's a little confused. But he remembers a grotto close by and passages beneath the old tower where he used to play with his brothers long ago.'

The Doctor confirmed the existence of the grotto with Inex. It was part of a network of caves and tunnels that the gnome said might collapse any minute. But even his odd and outré knowledge could not confirm the location of the entrance. The Doctor thought he might be impeding them out of spite or to bargain his way out of the crystal.

'Everything's shifting about in here,' Inex protested. 'It's like trying to peer through smoke! I can see through in patches but I can't tell the wind which way to blow.'

'Sorry,' the Doctor said. 'I'm sure you're doing the best you can.' The face in the crystal turned away sulking, but the Doctor didn't have time to humour him further. Offram continued to look confused, and, like someone coming out of a long coma, remembered snatches of his childhood, but hadn't connected the dead man with the brother he knew. The Doctor had thrown a blanket over the body as if that were enough, but Fitz thought they ought to bury it, or at least keep it in the TARDIS until they could.

'I don't think we're supposed to,' the Doctor murmured, as he gathered up a few supplies and picked up the saddlebags from where he'd tossed them. At Fitz's expression he inclined his chin towards the thickets where several pairs of eyes gleamed yellow in the dark. Fitz shuddered, but not out of fear.

'We're going to leave the body to the wolves?' he whispered, shocked.

The Doctor kicked dirt over the campfire. 'The world hungers for justice. Let it eat what it can.' He handed the saddlebags to Fitz.

'What about Anji and those other two?'

'We'll look for them as we go.'

The Doctor flicked on his torch and turned his back on the camp and everything in it.

'Ow, ow, ow, ow,' Bricklebrit intoned obligingly as Anji beat him with her fists. 'Stop it, Ai, you're gonna hurt your hand.'

She kicked him instead. 'Let me go!'

'Promise you won't run away?'

She started to promise then remembered the Doctor's warning

237

about promises, so she took a deep breath and counted quickly to ten. 'Look. I have to get back to my friends. They need me.'

He shook his misshapen head solemnly, his thick brow forming an accordion pleat over his flattened nose. 'Too dangerous. There's wolves on the prowl and things worse. You could get hurt.'

She'd heard the wolves behind them as he'd carried her and it seemed they'd gone a considerable distance, well away from that danger. Naturally, the thought of encountering a pack frightened her, but she said, 'That's not your concern!'

'I don't want nothing bad to happen to you, Ai. I love you.'

Great, Anji thought, *I need this right now.* 'That's really... I mean, I'm flattered and all, but well, you know what they say about love −'

'Who?'

'People. Great... various... wise people. Wise men.'

'Like Chompy the Elder?'

'Yeah, sure. Chompy the Elder would tell you that if you love someone −'

'I reckon Chompy ain't your expert wise man on the subject, Ai, on account of his being a stoat at present.'

She sighed noisily, 'Right. Not Chompy, then. But somebody wise once said that if you love someone *let her go* − if she comes back to you...'

'What if she gets lost in the forest, or eaten by a bear? Don't you see, Ai? It's for your own good. I been following you since you left Sighs. There's terrible magick at work in the world and you ain't prepared for it.'

'I *know* there's something terrible going on, Brick. That's why I have to get back to my friends. We have to get to the Princess Ebonyblack to stop it. Belesia told the Doctor.'

'A bitty little thing like you? Storm the Princess's tower? Stop the force of heaven?' He scoffed and shook his head.

'The Doctor will know what to do once we're inside. I'm sure of it.' *Almost* sure.

'Supposin' I were to help you get into the tower, what'll you give me?'

'I'm not going to play this game! I won't kiss you or sleep with you or anything else with you!'

He looked hurt by the implication. 'I'm only after a wish, Ai. You have the power to grant wishes. I saw it. At the cottage.'

She could have lied, but she said, 'I don't have that power any more, Brick.'

''Course you do, beloved. That's the gift you brung with you.'

His words and the way he said them made her feel hopeful and melancholy and undeservedly special and that was, well, just confusing. Concentrate on the facts. 'What makes you think you can get into the tower?'

'Got one of me granny's spindles. This here one spins thread out of anything. Bricks and briars. Anything.'

She turned from his certainty and tipped her head back. From this distance she could almost make out the turrets high above the plateau, wisps of clouds fluttering like the veil on a princess's pointy hat with the stars shining through. She imagined the spindle rolling and twisting, spinning spider silk from the tower walls to expose the long staircase winding up and around within. She knew what he offered was possible and the knowledge made her dizzy and breathless. Or perhaps it was vertigo, for she felt herself falling backwards, wanting the solid assurance of the ground again, but instead her body met the broad chest of Bricklebrit the ogre. His hands steadied her gently. Somewhere far away a wolf howled and left her shaking.

'Don't you fear now. Wolf can't stand the taste of ogres. They stay well clear. Now what say you? A wish for my help?'

She swallowed hard then hardened her voice.

'All right, but here are my conditions. You can't wish that I'll fall in love with you or marry you or that we're already married. You can't wish for anything involving sex.' At this he cleared his throat nervously and she knew he'd thought of it. 'And don't bother wishing I turn into an ogress because that will just annoy me. No wishes about my staying on this world, or your coming with me when I leave. And if the wishing part doesn't work you can't ask for anything else. And… well, I think that just about covers it.'

He'd been looking at the ground as she spoke and she supposed he was trying to hide the plodding mental wheels grinding to a halt. She'd been quite thorough, she thought. But when he looked up he was all grins. And that all-grins grin took up an alarming portion of his face. 'Done and done,' he said.

He'd agreed much too quickly. She ran through her checklist again. 'I said no sex, right?'

He ducked his head and nodded, then without so much as a 'by your leave' picked her up and threw her over his shoulder in the fireman's lift. She started to protest and then decided, oh screw it, better than walking. In that fashion, bargain made, Bricklebrit and Anji made their way to the tower walls.

As might have been expected, it was Offram who found a way in, not by any resurrection of his childhood sense of direction, but by putting his foot down a rabbit hole and falling into a tunnel system. The darkness of the tunnel was oppressive and the occasional trickle of dust and soil spilling down from the earth above their heads had Fitz cursing, shoulders rounded by the need to progress in a half-crouch. If Offram was uncomfortable he didn't complain much about it. He hardly spoke at all. The Doctor seemed to manage better by taking vast, extended steps and never fully straightening his legs, but Fitz tried it and it was agony.

This time Anji found the spindle's work compelling. In the soft purple of predawn, she lay on her side on a slab of masonry, elbow propped, cradling her cheek in the palm of her hand just watching as the glass unravelled and piled up in loops of dark-pink angel hair. She wondered if the people here had ever seen spun glass so fine, or spun glass at all for that matter. Perhaps they were introducing a new industry to the world's economy. She liked that idea. Bricklebrit sat on the ground leaning back against her improvised bier. He'd set the spindle to work and now all they had to do was wait for a big enough hole to form in the thick walls for them to walk through. After that it would be a hard climb. She wondered how long it would take. She knew Brick would carry her when she was tired and felt a twinge of guilt that she would be quite content to let him. The whirr of the spindle was hypnotic and she felt relaxed for the first time in days.

'So what's your wish?' she asked idly.

Brick started. He shook his heavy head. 'Not yet. Not yet, Ai.'

'Oh, come on. Tell me. Is it bigger than a bread box?'

'I can see the stairs,' he said ignoring her. He got slowly to his feet, like a big old bear. 'Won't be long now.'

Chapter Seventeen
The Beast With Three Faces

The grotto was magnificent enough to have made the bent-double, elbows-wearing progress through the caverns worth it. It seemed to underlie the cellars and the foundations of the tower, and there was a promising stone stair leading upwards, but there was also debris and the signs of habitation, slovenly habitation.

The Doctor picked up a gnawed chicken bone. 'Human teeth,' he said, 'and it's still warm.'

'I wish I was,' Fitz said, experiencing an odd impulse to drape Prince Offram over his shoulders. Even though he'd known the cloak had been an enchanted person, the fact that he'd had a naked man (albeit enchanted) on his back for most of his time on this world was grossing him out a little.

'Do you think there might be someone still here?' Offram asked sending the beam of light from the Doctor's torch zigzagging over the ceiling. He was treating it like a highly novel toy. He swept the light over the floor, zoom, zoom, zoom, spotted a cutlass and picked it up.

'Oh, yes, I think so,' the Doctor answered from behind a grey pillar. He dragged a mouldy chair with a fractured leg into view and spun it about. 'Fitz, Offram, this is Janet. Don't play with that Offram, you'll poke somebody's eye out.'

The girl tied to the chair and gagged with a strip of very dirty cloth made 'untie me' noises, and, Fitz suspected from her glare, was getting ready to kick the Doctor in the shins as soon as he untied her feet. The Doctor cut her gag with a pocket knife, and then, to Fitz's astonishment and delight, planted a kiss on her mouth.

'I forgot,' the Doctor said when he came up for air, 'I'm so sorry.'

'No time for that,' she cried. 'Run, you fools, run! Save yourselves!'

'From a few bandits?' the Doctor laughed. 'I think my gallant sword-bearing assistants here will make short shrift of any rogues and cutpurses we may encounter.'

'No,' she moaned, tugging at her remaining bounds as he sliced through the ropes, 'not them. They couldn't have their way with me because of my spells, so thought to leave me here as bait for the troll. But something else came! The Beast. It took them all, even the troll. It... snuffled,' she finished, frantic with fear.

Fitz and Offram exchanged worried glances. Nothing called the Beast could be good news.

'We'll take the stairs up,' the Doctor said, helping her to her feet. He put his arm around her and she leaned her dark head against him. 'If a beast is foraging down here, we'll stand a better chance defending ourselves from a higher position on a narrow way.' He said 'a beast' rather self-consciously as if trying to crank the wheel of terror back a notch.

It was a good plan, ruined only by the fact that at that moment the stone stairs collapsed in a shower of breaking rock dust, and the battery in the torch suddenly stopped working.

'You'd think this close to the goal I'd get a bit more co-operation,' the Doctor muttered.

From up ahead came the sound of scales dragging across a stone floor, and a faint slopping noise that might be a thin noxious slime dripping from two great fangs, and a hiss that might be a great serpent.

'Oh shit,' Fitz said.

On her hands and knees Christina parted the brambles, rapacious vines and weeds to peer into the crack in the foundation of the castle's remains. 'You have got to be kidding me,' she said to the fox as he darted into the hole then back out again, his bushy tail abristle.

'It's a tight squeeze for you, yes. But it widens further along.'

'How much further along?'

'Twenty metres or so until we get to the scullery. Then the stairs and what's left of the thorns. Come on!' He wriggled through the brambles. She saw spiders skitter away angrily and knew there would be many more. Christina looked at the improvised bag she'd made for the boxes from her soft leather tunic. She'd barely looked at the things when she'd dug them out of the saddlebag, though she'd felt their play over her hands and arms, flowing warmth like sunlight and a bracing chill like ocean spray.

She knotted the sleeves of the tunic together more firmly, took a breath and let it out, then dived through the fissure into the Promised Land.

'Did you see, it?' the Doctor asked Janet. 'It's important. If you didn't see it we stand a chance.'

'It was dark!' she shouted, catching her voice in her snapping mouth before it could echo.

'Splendid! Hand me those saddlebags, Fitz.'

Fitz passed them blindly and the Doctor snatched them as if he knew precisely where they would be. He guessed that if he could see the Doctor he'd be rolling up his sleeves and grinning. 'Stand back. This will be dangerous.' There was a pause. 'Fitz?'

'Right here.'

'Did I mention you were to guard these boxes with your life because they're horrendously powerful, and also might come in useful in very specific sort of near-fatal danger?'

'Nooo,' Fitz said, 'more along the lines of, "make yourself useful and lug these about for a bit will you?"'

'Ah.' The sound of the creature was growing louder and closer. 'It's just that I had a really clever plan, but it rather relied on having the boxes here, and I'm afraid it looks as if someone has taken them and filled the saddlebag with three similarly sized rocks.'

'You need a wishing box?' Janet asked, her footsteps darting away in the pitch black. 'The leader of the robbers had one in his spoils. He claimed it popped out of the ground in front of him when he was having a picnic with his aunt.'

Fitz managed a disbelieving grunt, although the sounds were drying his throat with fear.

'They were quite a good class of robber,' Janet conceded from over to his left. 'He thought the wishes were all used up, and threw it over here somewhere...'

The slithering grew louder still. 'Got it!' Janet's voice was firm. The box she carried was slightly luminous, its swirls and patterns moving on its surface. Fitz tried to think how many boxes that made. Safe bet that Christina and Alex had stolen the three from the saddlebags. Rozered had claimed that Anji's was sucked into the earth, so maybe this one was that same box. Four. That left two. Somewhere. It was possible Christina's fellow space thugs already had them, hence her need to complete the set. It was looking like Unethical Business Practices United 5, Doctor 1.

Janet's pretty face glowed eerily in the light of the filigree box in her hands. 'I've had some experience with Giant magick,' she said, her voice echoing strangely. 'Maybe I should do whatever it is you're going to do.'

'No, I think not,' the Doctor replied, gently prising the swirling treasure from her fingers. He held it in his left hand and pressed his right thumbnail into the crack between the lid and its base.

'But I've used magick,' she insisted. 'You wouldn't even have this box if it weren't for me.'

The energies of the box were seething. Her dark eyes fixed on it and her fingers twitched as if she would snatch it back at any moment.

'Janet,' the Doctor said softly, 'think now. You didn't even want it until it made you want it. You can feel that, can't you? It only wants to force itself upon you like the robbers would have if you hadn't been too strong for them. You must resist this even harder.'

Her nostrils flared as she hissed in a breath. She nodded and looked away.

'Hurry, Doctor,' Offram urged, waving the cutlass about. 'The Beast is nearly upon us.'

'I thought I told you to put that down,' the Doctor said. He had the lid open now and went down on one knee, placing the box on the floor. 'Fitz,' he said, his voice sounding remarkably unhurried. 'How many days elapsed on your way to the Castle of Sighs?'

Fitz thought. 'Frankly I'm buggered if I know. I can only remember about four days, maybe three, but it feels like weeks.'

'It may well have been. Remember Anji telling us at the banquet that she'd tricked one of the sisters into wishing a week had passed. The whole fabric of space and time pushed out of joint by our absent friend. And that was all from a distance, with the box shut. By Anji's account it seems the world's own magick was working to reduce her ability to disrupt by contracting her to serve. The world wants aliens – like you and me for instance – to have the boxes, to take them away, but if I'm right it doesn't want the boxes too active while they are taken.

'Now, in respect of activity, what I'm doing here is like banging in a nail with a loaded revolver, without a safety catch on, in a gunpowder store, on the *Lusitania*.' He paused. 'I was intending to end that sentence with a pithy joke but actually I think it stands as it is. I really, really, really think I should be the one to do this. I'm pretty sure I have it figured out.'

The light from the box was spilling over his face now. Rainbow light, light of other days. 'This is just something I have to do,' he said, but to whom it wasn't clear. 'We have to get past the Beast. And besides, if I didn't do this I'd always be wondering what it would have been like.'

'Doctor!' Fitz shouted aghast at this obviously specious reasoning. The Doctor's sudden wilful desire for knowledge seemed all too clearly the result of the box's influence. 'This is crazy,' he said. 'We can go around the other way somehow or –'

But it was too late.

The Doctor felt the box look at him as he looked at it. Behind him a billion billion world-lines stretched away, all the possible pasts leading functionally identical hims to this moment. Oh there were differences – there had to be – but even if he'd remembered everything he'd ever done, how little some of those differences meant. If he'd plucked a rose in that garden in Highgate in 1936 or if he'd merely picked a daisy from the grass, would it have altered him, the him here now? What if the choice, the difference, had been slighter, a quantum state in a single atom in his nose, or the colour of a hat worn by a shopkeeper on the other side of the street? In the now it all ran together, and into the future it ran on, separating again into a billion billion paths, each so small, so tiny in its difference, that a strong mind – one that wasn't dazzled or bemused by the display – could reach out and drive itself along one path in preference to the others. Madness lay in failing to choose or in trying to choose too many, in endless channel-surfing for some glorious utopia. Well he was in no danger of that. All he needed was to remove this beast; he'd take his wider chances in the realm of macro-causation, of everyday chance and risk.

So you wouldn't want your memories, then, Doctor?

You won't catch me with that old temptation.

There is a 'you' who stands where you stand who has walked the same paths but who recovers his memory in the next hour in every detail. There is one who stands where you stand who recovered it an hour ago. Or a day ago, or before you even came here. There is one who has faced every trauma arising and is healed and knows his father's face, and his mother's voice. You need not choose the future Doctor. I can also offer you the past.

Sorry, no good. I will not change the past, it is done, it is at rest, it has become the present.

Oh, hypocrite. I see you, time traveller. What do you do but change the past? Dabbler, dilettante, disturber of the long dead dust of past centuries, walker among those long deceased. Tomb raider. Necrophile. The world to you must be a charnel house.

No! I walk in my present and the world lives in it. My past is my past and I will not change it to serve myself. I will not pick a past from your sour old chocolate box. I choose only the future and I choose… carefully.

The Doctor reached forward towards a world in which the Beast was a great dragon. It would sense the wisdom of languages in the Doctor's hearts and break him, shattering his breastbone to scoop out the delicate information-meat inside. Janet, Offram and Fitz would die too, boiled in its molten breath as it breathed out its marvellous new words.

He reached for a world in which the Beast was no beast, but the human bandits, making beastlike sounds with curious instruments, playing and tormenting their captive with the threat of an imagined beast. A girl is broken by their crude games, sold to other men for more games. Fitz, Offram and the Doctor fight or bargain their way past, but further futureward it falls apart in bickering and bloodshed. He crushed that world in his fist and tossed it aside, grabbing another in which the Beast was a troll, and it sought man meat, grasping the struggling Fitz and tearing his limbs off, before dying finally to Offram's sword thrust but not before Fitz was dead. He discarded it, beginning to doubt if he could find a world in which they all could pass.

Then he saw his chance.

The Doctor snapped the box shut with a bang. 'Run. *Now*,' he shouted, and pelted forward, dragging his friends behind him. Then, for no reasonable reason, he darted back and snatched the box up again like a hot pan from the flame as an explosion of light filled the space illuminating the horrors he'd set, each upon the other.

In the central space a thing with the head of a dragon, a human, and a troll screamed, rending its own flesh, unable to agree on its actions. A living bundle of three separate realities, hands with knives cutting claws that ripped scales while spitting fire and hissing venom that burned the faces with the teeth that ripped the soft underbelly of the thing fused by the power of the box. It yowled its anger and pain after them as they fled.

They ran past old wine racks, they ran past another staircase. They stopped and turned back, realising what they had dashed past. Resonating to the Beast's evil three-toned hellish voice, the ceiling began to collapse above the stairs.

'This way!' the Doctor shouted, darting into a passage under stone steps. He pushed and guided Janet before him through the narrow tunnel while the earth rumbled above their heads, trying to pull Offram and Fitz along in his wake, feeling like a mole as rocks and choking debris fell from the roof. He and Janet were scarcely out into the open air when the exit caved in. The Doctor stumbled, rolled and was on his feet in an instant, shouting Fitz's name as the clouds of dust exploded out. Coughing, barely able to call but still trying, the Doctor and Janet began to dig furiously, tossing chunks of stone aside. The earth continued to tumble down in spurts from inside and they were forced to wait until the trembling abated afraid they'd cause another collapse. Janet was exhausted after fifteen minutes, though she kept trying. The Doctor made her stop while he searched for a branch to lever some of the bigger pieces out of the way. When he came back she was pressed close to the heap of debris that blocked the entrance, tears trailing through the dirt on her face, but she was smiling.

'They're alive! I can hear them.'

'Fitz! Fitz!' he cried.

The response was muffled but the words were clear to the Doctor. 'We're OK. There's a passage sheered up by timber and another set of stairs. We're going up. With luck we'll meet you there!'

'All right!' the Doctor shouted back, then he turned and slid down the mound of dirt until he was sitting with his back against it, knees drawn up. He put his head in his hands and wept.

The Master-maid knelt before the Doctor and put her hand upon his knee. 'Why do you weep? Your friends live still.'

'Yes, and for that, I am well and truly glad. But now I have no way into the tower and I am the only one who knows what to do once inside.'

'Have you no horse?' asked Janet.

'I've left it behind,' replied the Doctor.

She took a silver whistle from her pocket. 'Blow upon this and the horse will come within the hour even though it be on the other side of the world. After that you must ride to the top of the tower.'

'How shall this be done?' he cried. 'The walls are high and sheer and made of glass.'

'It is a fairy horse, my lord.'

And then the Doctor smiled at his foolishness, leapt to his feet and blew upon the silver whistle and soon his white steed was at his side.

Astride the white horse, the Doctor gazed at the tower, an obelisk of garnet in the first rays of the sun. He had taken his mount some distance in order to get a running start, not even sure if a running start was necessary, not sure if the horse would sprout wings or run its head into the wall or veer off at the last moment because this was *impossible* and its rider was mad. Janet sat behind him, her arms locked about his waist, just tight enough to hold on, but not tight with fear. In the saddlebag on the left he carried the three rocks. Well you never knew what *might* come in handy. In the one on the right was the scrying crystal that Janet had folded like magic origami into a neat five-sided envelope with the furious Inex protesting within to the last, and the box from the cavern.

The Doctor leaned down and whispered in the horse's

twitching ear, 'I hope to hell you know what you're doing.' Then he gave the horse a gentle nudge with his heels and it leapt forward, their bodies whipped back by its sudden burst of speed. The Doctor pulled forward again, feeling Janet move with him, and he leaned over the horse as far as he could, seeing the air and the earth rush by him, seeing the tower growing larger and larger until he could see nothing but dark red glass. And his breath caught. And he almost closed his eyes but forced them to stay open. He had to witness that moment when the impossible became possible. *If* it happened. The tower was a blur of lurid red, hissing like neon, filling his senses with the taste of blood and light, the smell of apples and death. He felt a rush of terrible wonderful lust as the wind lashed his face with his own hair and a beautiful girl hung on to him for dear life, and he was young in a way he'd never been, and his eyes were wide, wide open and he saw the impossible moment crashing over him, the tower falling, the world upended as his horse reared back and galloped up the sheer face of the glass tower, sparks of fire shooting off from its hooves and leaving molten trails of blood-red glass in their wake.

'Yippee!' the Doctor whooped. He laughed like a schoolboy all the way to the top.

Soon it would be born properly.

Christina and the fox Alex, Anji and the lovesick ogre, Fitz and his cloak-brother, the Doctor and the Master-maid – all converging. The will of the world worked for it in this respect; where there was a tower there must be as many routes to it as seekers; it was a law of nature.

Soon now. Soon this Doctor would provide all it needed.

The Fox and the Cat.

Once upon a time there was a girl who, though she had everything a girl could want – beauty, friends in high places, and a magic acorn – still wanted more and more. Now it happened that a great magician was travelling about the land and she had heard that the secret of his magic was held in three boxes he carried with him. So this wicked girl went to meet him and soon he fell under her spell. One night as he lay sleeping, she stole the boxes from under his nose and slipped away into the night. On her way she met a fox and the fox said, 'I know what you have hidden in your gown, my pretty maid. And I know of a tower where more such treasures exist.' Now the girl, though greedy, was no fool and she said, 'And what will you demand for leading me there?'

'Naught but the magic acorn you have in your pocket,' said the fox. And the girl thought, I shall promise him this, but I need not give it to him, for once I have all the power in the world for myself, what need is there to keep such a promise? So she agreed and the fox led her to the tower and up and around the winding stair until at last they had reached the door at the top.

'I will not enter this room,' the fox said, 'and so will take my payment now.'

But the girl just laughed. 'I may give it to you or I may not. But I will have all the magic treasure first and then decide what small bit of it I shall share with you, O Fox.'

'Be it on your head, girl,' he said sorrowfully. 'But I warn you, what you seek you will not find, for another has been here before you and taken it all. It will have yours as well and leave you naught but a husk in the taking.'

'What?' cried the girl. 'We shall see about that!' And she opened the door. 'Heavens! What monstrous trick is this?' she said. For it appeared her friends in high places had stormed the tower before her and even now were plundering the treasures within. But when they turned she saw they were under a spell and their friendly grins were frozen on their snouts as they marched towards her, arms reaching for the magic boxes she carried.

'Oh, would that I were more clever than a fox so as to hide me and my treasure from this danger!'

And in her pocket, the magic acorn obliged her wish and turned black.

William opened the box. Inside it a tiny figure crouched: identical to the Vuim-Captain, even exhibiting his injuries. The real Captain's voice sounded faint, matched to a shrill, almost inaudible duplication from the box, as he struggled to explain. 'The planet made a copy of the lander, an exact copy, so when I left my real lander to come here, the copy me left its lander too carrying the copy lander from its copy, and so on, down and –' He coughed, and a thin whitish fluid dripped from his chitinous mouth. 'I decided to bring it – them – with me. Maybe it will make something for you, a gun, a key, anything.'

William reached a finger into the box, 'All I've ever wanted is the freedom of open space and being beholden to no one,' he said. 'I don't know what it'll make of that.'

He touched the tiny body reverently.

Through the touch, it learned. The fragment of planet in it, brought up slowly, taken with care, carried with a kind of love for the hope and promise it represented, reached out its awareness and found the rest of itself. 'Freedom,' it thought. The box glowed with its new understanding.

The vuim, conscientious as ever, and having no knowledge of the abanaks' actions, had started the long process of unloading the lander below decks, and packing their prize into the holds. They had decided to use the perishable-bulk stasis containers to hold it in absolute immobility, in case it recovered in transit, but they had unloaded only about half of the tonnes they had harvested when it awoke.

It was alive, and it was angry.

It became an army of goblins. It became a group of two-headed lions. It became a giant with a club of stone. It became all of them at once. The vuim screamed and scattered before it.

The Victory of the Youngest Son.

There was a child who was taken from its parents and sold into slavery to a distant kingdom. He was the seventh son of a seventh son, and he knew that if the slavers were pleased with him, if he worked diligently and hard, then they might return to his land and take his six brothers and his seven sisters deeming it a good place to seek captives. So he determined that he would strike against his captors, slaying whom he might, for he thought that if he did so he might teach them that his family were not their prey and his lands were those to be avoided.

And in the lands of his captors he found others like himself and taught them this lesson. So they too rose up to slay their oppressors.

Princess Ebonyblack was stirring in her casket when Fitz and Offram staggered up the last of the stone stairs from the base of the tower. It was the stirring of someone in the grip of a nightmare, not of someone waking. Her hands clawed and skittered on the inside of the crystal coffin and set the iron catafalque on which it lay ringing.

Offram turned to Fitz. 'You are my comrade, my saviour and a good friend. But I'm the Prince.' He winked to show there were no hard feelings, and Fitz guessed that there weren't. What the heck would he do with half a kingdom in this place, anyway?

But before Offram could attempt to open the casket and kiss the Princess, an ogre lumbered in, the body of a woman across its massive outstretched arms. The pose reminded Fitz of Robbie the Robot from *Forbidden Planet*. Then he realised who the woman was. 'Anji!' His hand reached for his sword. 'If you've hurt her –'

'Bricklebrit never hurt Ai. She's to give me a wish,' the ogre said, its homely face split by an expression that was half grin and half simper. Anji patted it firmly on the chest. 'And drop!'

She dusted herself down and met Fitz's gaze defiantly. 'It was better than climbing the stairs. Oh my God,' she said spotting the frantic Princess clawing the glass. 'Get her out of there, she's suffocating!'

Offram pushed Fitz aside. 'I'll do it.' He struggled with the clasp and bent to look closer at it. Ebonyblack's pounding and thrashing became less energetic as the air in the coffin grew stale, the murky dense glass clouded from within now.

Offram spun around with a panicked expression. 'The latch is fused –'

Fitz pulled out his sword and tried to stick the point in between the metal and the glass, but they seemed welded together. 'We'll have to break it.'

'You'll kill her!'

'She'll die otherwise,' Fitz said, and began to search the room for something to use to break the glass. There was a tapestry fluttering on one of the walls and he pulled it back, then immediately reeled away from the sight. The body of a man, not interred in state, but left to freeze or fester, his belly swollen from slow starvation, eyes sunk deep into his face, lay on a truckle bed. 'Jesus,' he said, looking at it again. He covered his mouth. Anji and Offram peered around him. Offram seemed puzzled.

'A retainer probably,' he said. 'Sometimes they are left with a princess to protect her should a marauding beast find its way in.'

'Isn't that what you're supposed to do?' Fitz asked.

'Who cares?' Anji cried. 'She's dying in there!'

Bricklebrit standing at the foot end of the coffin squatted down and without preamble shoved his fist through the glass. He brushed the chunks, shards and slivers on to the floor, reached in, grabbed the girl by her ankles and tugged her out, her bejewelled gown bunching up around her waist as she emerged from her cocoon.

'Haven't invented knickers yet, I see,' Fitz commented. He'd quickly averted his eyes, however, and his face was red. Anji was by her side, tugging and adjusting for the sake of a girl too unconscious to be embarrassed. Offram knelt beside her, looking uncertain as to proper form under the circumstances.

'She needs air,' Anji said. 'Open a window, will you?'

Fitz went over to the big arched window. Leaded panes of pink glass were latched in the centre. He pulled them open and stuck his head out, sucking in great gulps of thin air. 'Where's the Doctor, anyway? I thought he would have beaten us here,' he said. Suddenly he yelped and leapt back. A huge white horse, hooves scrabbling at the ledge, gave a whinny of irritation at him before jumping the hurdle of the casement. It seemed to fill the round tower room for a moment, pawing the floor and snorting triumphantly before its rider exclaimed, 'Now that's a fun-park ride I'd stand in queue for!'

Peeling Janet's arms from the vice grip she had around his waist, the Doctor threw a leg over the horse's back and slid lightly to the floor. He turned and lifted the very pale Janet down, keeping one hand on her for a moment in case she toppled over, before turning to the slack-jawed company. 'So what's the situation? Oh, I see.'

He knelt down and checked the Princess's pulse. 'Still a bit thready, but she should be fine.' He stood up again, and started pushing the glass out of the way with his shoe. 'Help me with this mess, you lot. Push it against the walls. We don't want any nasty accidents, do we?' Typically, he had everyone busy before they could ask any questions. As soon as the four of them were industriously kicking and brushing the glass out of the centre, the Doctor stopped helping. Instead, he stuck his head under the ironwork of the catafalque and came up puzzled. 'Hmm. Nothing here. Belesia was clear the Princess held the answer to the puzzle of the boxes. Perhaps she'll be able to tell us something when she's recovered.' He went to her again and stood looking down on her, as if to speed her recovery by the force of his gaze alone.

'*But I am here, Doctor.*'

It was a voice the Doctor recognised by its kinship to the voice of the box that had tempted him, but this voice came from living lips. Instinctively everyone focused on the Princess. She moaned and her eyelids fluttered, then opened in raw terror. From behind them, something laughed, and on the narrow straw mattress set into the alcove, the body sat up, then stood up and looked at them.

It was the Prince the Doctor had seen long ago when he'd first gazed into the magic crystal, the Prince who had been unable to settle on the colour of the Princess's eyes. His thread-of-gold cloak was tattered. His jerkin was dirty and his trews had been soiled. Without being utterly inhuman, his stance nevertheless suggested something broken.

'*I will take those other seeds now, I've been waiting for them,*' he said, and the hands he held out worked like things mechanical.

'Burn it,' Timtangle screamed, as the stuff, inchoate now, rolling, devouring, forced its way up the levels of the *Bonaventure*, driving his crew back. He had taken command of the vuim, too. There was no time to stop to question his right. They were too busy trying to stay alive.

'I want portable force-field generators set up two floors above. We'll fall back to there, maybe we can halt it.'

Below, someone abandoned in the retreat died noisily.

'Hazel,' the Doctor said. 'Her eyes are hazel. Come and see.'

'*Oh, no. You mistake me. I'm not him. He's – well, at the best, unavailable right now, and you know, the last time I looked for him I didn't find any trace at all, so please, don't try to talk me back to human. I was never human. I am a void waiting to be filled with meaning. And you, Doctor, will supply it.*'

'Me?' The Doctor said. He sounded almost flattered. 'Why on

earth would you want to be filled with me?'

It was a classic straight line, but Fitz couldn't think of a single funny comeback.

The Prince thing circled the Doctor, and the Doctor turned with him. *'I can read the surface of your mind. I have been doing so since you came here. You cannot make me think you a fool; nor can you cheat me of victory. Behold.'*

The stones in the wall groaned as they separated revealing another passageway, secret and dark, and through it two abanak came, blank-eyed, dazed, under the thrall of a master greater than their greed. They carried their trophies aloft like boom-boxes on their shoulders, their forms and their actions like a weird cross between *Fantasia* and *Pulp Fiction*.

'All the boxes, all here, all will be opened – even the dregs of those wasted on fools and petty wishes will be pooled – all will power my apotheosis, my becoming. Not for me this tiny world. I will remake this galaxy. It will become a living thing, a growing mind. It will have every thinking thing for its inhabitants. Come, Doctor, dream me your utopia, and I will write it across the stars for a million years.'

'Oh, my old boxes won't help you,' the Doctor said, tipping out the saddlebag. 'Look, they've turned to stone, see?' Three stones bounced and clattered away into the corner of the room.

'And the one in the other bag, Doctor? I can sense them, you know. You had to bring it. You had no choice. Now, let them be opened. Let it all be opened.'

And the abanak opened their boxes, and the box that Anji had bargained for opened itself, and power poured out until vision and sound alike obscured and blurred with the impacts of other worlds. So it cannot be stated precisely that the Doctor told the Prince where he could stick his utopia (the way Fitz heard it), or whether he reasoned with him for an hour (as Anji heard) arguing that a single world built on dreams might be a refuge for a weary galaxy, and could be kept from danger by the worlds around it. But a *living* galaxy, alone in the great voids, could become the greatest prison conceivable. Besides, he wasn't so vain to think that what attracted him would please everybody, not for a moment.

Either way the Doctor refused.

It made no difference.

The body of the Prince dropped into the thankful dust. His human shade, or the mad gibbering remains of it, flickered for a moment in the afternoon light and vanished. Something else didn't.

The Doctor was on his knees now, and the three boxes, joined and linked, moving like a chain of constellations, orbited him. A ghostly fourth shape – the alien thing from the Prince's mind – joined and fused with them.

Fitz tried to touch the boxes and was flung back into Anji's arms. Offram had eyes only for the Princess. Janet and the ogre had backed against the wall, glass crunching under their feet. The fairy horse leapt out the window as the wave of colour overswept all, pinning them in place. Shadows around the Doctor's light.

In the mind, with no body to judge, who can measure the passage of time? A moment or years passed.

In a mind of doors, something creaks. *Wish!* No. *Wish!* No! A repetition like a drumbeat or a pulse. Bearing down on himself, the Doctor is methodically killing his dreams, before the thing can find them.

It finds him putting romance novels to the sword in an oak-lined library. P.G. Wodehouse is next.

Stop!

'You didn't think I had it in me?' the Doctor asks, referring perhaps to the library of dreams, and perhaps to the rather fine Toledo-bladed rapier. 'What will you retreat to when my mind is grey and absolute and the domain of fact? I'll do it you know. I'll stay here and never wish for a thing until you're dead. Never dream, never imagine, never hope. We'll see who cracks first!'

He raised the sword, whose blade bled words.

Wait! I have read the minds of the traders. Let us bargain.

'I should trust you? A seed must grow. Let's not fool ourselves that I'm talking to anything but a clever mimicry.'

Ourselves, plural?

'Ah, caught me out. Perhaps. It's too easy to decide you don't have thoughts.' The Doctor set down the weapon. 'Tell me why I should bargain.'

The white hole spawned us: you know as much. Each of its kind are different, but this one lives.

It will seed this reality as it has a million others. Only the signal of its progeny spread wide across space and time will cause it to seek fresher breeding grounds. I am, as you say, a seed. I must be the seed that grows. I will give anything for that. I must go on. Bargain with me, then, for if the white hole spawns again it may send many more seeds, more than you could gather or forestall.

'Hmm, and what do you grow into, seed?'

Does the acorn know of oaks? All I can tell you is it will be a billion years before I become what I promise. Until that time, at least, I will be harmless.

'All right, what is the least thing you need to stand a chance, a small one is all I'll give you. You can be a weed growing on the slag heaps of time and hope none of the Gardeners spot you. But I won't give you the galaxy as your flower bed. It's one daisy or nothing. You know I could kill you. Hold you here until you wither in the grey, real, undiverging corridors of the eternal present.'

And yet, you do not wish to, do you, Doctor?

'No, I don't. I don't want to kill a new form of life because I don't understand it. Tell me, what do you need to grow?'

A wish. A wish that changes everything. Make water red,

make humans immune to evil thoughts, bring universal peace. I will grow in the change, in the difference, in the fracture between what was and what is. That is my tiny meadow.'

'And *I* choose the wish, and you will release me and my friends?'

Yes, and here, on this world born from a previous, partly failed seeding, you may trust even the word of a blind process.

'Yes,' the Doctor agreed, 'I rather thought I might.'

The orbiting boxes fell, rolling into one mass.

'The box,' the Doctor screamed, in a tone so horrible, so frantic, so redolent of every *hey-kids-drugs-ain't-cool* film Anji had ever seen that she immediately pushed the glowing mass the boxes had become at him, because either the Doctor was Doctor-like – really unaffected, but just temporarily unable to make his point in a calmer way – or he was really suffering, and she couldn't bear to think that.

'Good.' He closed his hand on it. 'Christina? I know you're here. Come out and bring what you've stolen with you. Christina!' There was a soft mew from the alcove and a white cat squeezed itself out from under the truckle bed. 'Here kitty, kitty,' the Doctor rasped. 'Come on. There's a good kitty.' The cat slunk over to him and he slipped the collar with its three dangling silver bells from around its neck.

They too merged into the flurry of light and motion that had been the other boxes. That ought to be all.

The cat immediately dashed back under the bed leaving the rest of the company gap-mouthed as they watched the tail disappear.

The Doctor craned his head to one side. 'Janet, break out the gnome from the saddlebag, and tell him I'll set him free if he can get me vision.'

'Doctor, ah, Know-All calling the trade ship *Bonaventure,* come in please.'

'You know, I don't think this is working,' Inex said grumpily from inside his glass prison. Static zinged through his head, making the wisps of his beard that survived (despite his warty green 'sprite-o'-the-glass' persona) stand on end and reach out to touch the inner surface of the globular chunk of glass in which he floated.

Then his face wobbled, expanded and reformed – as someone else. The face in the glass now was a hippopotamus – for a moment – and then it was clearly something different, alien, only vaguely like its animal analogue. Its skin was cracked and mended with cosmetics. Its eyes had a conscious alertness that spoke of mind, and it had a gold earring in the curly edge of its left ear.

The Doctor coughed politely. 'Am I addressing the renowned Trader-Captain, Wulfstan Timtangle? Hello, can you hear me? Over.' Inside the glass, at the back of the new image (with an excellent view of the back of Timtangle's head), Inex fumed at fulfilling the function of a mere relay. Furious but trapped, he settled for making the trader's ears flick on and off in green and puce, and for putting the occasional crimp in the vertical hold.

The abanak on the screen had a voice like grit.

'You are. Can you tone down your transmission? The signal is impacting on our navigation systems. What the hell are you using?'

'The miracle of crystalline gnomology, Captain. Listen to me, I've not come to tell you off, or dust you down at high noon, but this must end – I'm empowered to end it for you with a profit. You can take your money and run to the first galactic bank. Provided you leave.'

'What must end? Who are you? Get off this frequency, you are interfering with legitimate space exploration.'

'You are raping this planet, sir, and that's not a precious metaphor, but fact! Your great skimming butchers have ripped away material that formed a vital part of its linked intelligence. You are killing a world, you are killing the colonists and you are killing your own kind.'

'I did not order the landers to bring back so much material, that was the vuim's doing. I bear no responsibility for that. But I claim it nevertheless. This world attacked us, drowned our scout, denied the vuim fair-landing, took and no doubt killed the humans' Captain. It turned on the abanak I sent to look for her – volunteers all. It ran amok on my ship, even now it is penned only by force. It is a wild beast, disguised as a home. All I see it do is kill.'

'It's not like that,' Janet shouted, darting in front of the Doctor. 'There's danger here, and fear at times, but there's joy too, and the unexpected thrill of finding a unicorn in your garden, or tasting honey left by the wee folk in payment for a generous deed. I've seen the sort of world you live in, in the minds of my sisters: greed, and vanity, and petty stupid squabbling over energies flung out freely by the wanton suns. I think you should just go. Leave us alone!'

The Doctor patted her shoulder. 'Well said, but I doubt Timtangle was listening. I think he's making a speech, you see, getting his justifications down on the ship's media so that he can pose as a liberator, wrenching a human colony out of the grip of an alien horror like someone pulling a good tooth out of a rotten mouth.' His eyes hadn't left the image in the glass and he said, 'I doubt the things you've unleashed have been penned quite so thoroughly as you claim. What's happening up there? Is a horrible mimetic alien on the rampage? A thing that can learn to be anything, maddened, torn from its home, living and breeding and growing only to kill, and kill, and kill again!' He waved his fingers in the air like claws.

Timtangle's hippopotamus eyes, wide, unmoved, and no longer funny, stared him down. 'I do not expect you to understand my loyalties, nor do your threats interest me. The outbreak on my ship has been contained. I will have my fellows back, and I will have all the material this planet can provide to fill my holds. It can be packed on planet in stasis containers and shuttled up outside of time – it will never feel loneliness, and I will take it to new worlds. Really it ought to thank me.'

'And if it refuses this kind offer to be transported into slavery, to be torn into fragments of itself muttering on the workbenches and laboratories of eternity,' the Doctor asked, 'what then?'

'Then it will be made to,' Timtangle said. 'It's that simple. You can't harm me, you can't bargain, but I can harm your precious world, and all its human parasites. The *Bonaventure* is not designed to land but it can come close, and its secondary sublight drive is thoroughly nuclear. If you do not provide me with my lost people, and prepare this world for its new function – harvesting – I will be forced to burn it out, island by island, continent by continent, until it learns who is master here.'

The Doctor shook his head. 'You don't even want to hear my counteroffer? I took you for an alien I could do business with.'

'I will give you one minute to make your sales pitch, solely to amuse me. But I doubt there is anything you can offer that we cannot take.'

'Isn't that just the point, Captain? You can't *take* what is offered freely. You want to bear your family's gifts back to your home, be feted, hailed as great among your kind for the wealth you have won your family from other worlds. Do you really want to do that knowing the wealth came from murder, from slavery, from ecological genocide?'

'Thirty seconds, Doctor.'

The Doctor held up the boxes: shapes now linked together in strange topologies; shapes now flowing together like things trying to eat each other very slowly. 'These were seven seeds,' he said. 'I think this whole world grew from one of these, lonely, uneducated, lacking vision – until the colonists came. They made this world what it is. Their human tales, their human foibles. With what I'm offering, you could be hailed as the abanak who made a new world for his people.'

He ran the glowing mother-of-pearl confusion of the linked

boxes over and around his hands like smoke as he talked. 'These are awaiting the wish to let them grow. They have chosen to leave that wish to me. And I – I will trade it to you.'

Janet hissed in the Doctor's ear. 'He'll waste his wishes, he's the kind that does.' The Doctor managed a half-nod to show that, yes, he'd thought as much.

'So. You've made your speech.' Timtangle said, his voice heavy with irony. 'And I am *so* not convinced. However, you have upped my demands. My people, the holds filled, and your pretty baubles. I give you one hour to make this magic world obey me, then it begins to burn.'

'Oh no,' the Doctor said. 'You see, I've decided it isn't a trade. It's a special, free, one-time-only offer.'

He gestured at the boxes with a set of hand movements he'd seen Doc Strange use in a 1970s comic.

They vanished, and in the crystal of the gnome he saw them appear in Timtangle's lap.

In her Castle of Sighs, Belesia held her head in her hands and wept from the pain. In the forest the wodewose howled. In his castle the Giant moaned on his golden bed. *I do not understand. Why should I offer gifts when they have taken so much already?*

Timtangle was turning away from the microphone, raising his hands in triumph, starting to formulate his first demands, when out of nowhere / out of the opening door / from his place at Timtangle's side / in perfect health / in his last breath / in a hovering medical harness / Vuim-Captain launched himself at the spiralling shape that had appeared in front of him.

In the blue-fizzing globe of the communications unit, the face of the human who called himself the Doctor looked on clear-eyed, into and through the maelstrom of might-bes and soon-to-bes. He was shouting something, and somehow Vuim-Captain realised he could understand him. This thing was an engine of miracles, primed for one great wish. It was his hoped-for treasure trove.

So he wished.

There was once a man who resembled a great insect so much so that people called him Captain Grasshopper. He would go about the World with a basket on his back scooping up bits of it: a leaf, a bush, a clump of dirt, sometimes a lamb or a pretty girl, whatever struck his fancy. He hoped to make a world of his own one day, a world where nobody ever got sick, and everyone lived happily ever after, for he had seen that on the World this was so and it was not so where he was from. And the World, beset by other problems, could do little to stop him and was sick at heart, for all of its parts were part of the whole and each missing piece, no matter how small or large, was like having a hand or toe cut off. At first the World took other parts of itself and made of them a poultice to patch the wounds where this tree had been taken or that rock picked up. It whimpered a little with the pain but not so loud that the people noticed. But when Captain Grasshopper had gathered enough in his basket and took it far away, the World screamed so loud that the people felt it lurch and rumble beneath their feet and though they ran they found no safe haven on the World. For the World was everywhere, and everything on the World began to change and the people were sore afraid.

So the World said to a wise man, 'What shall we do to sate this Captain of the Grasshoppers who wants naught but a whole world?' And the wise man thought for a time and then he said, 'Give him what is best for him, unstintingly, and he will depart in peace.' Now the World was but poorly minded to follow the advice of the wise man saying in its many hearts, 'But if we do this will not others like to the Grasshopper come and devour us all, World and People, People and World?' But the wise man spoke to the World after his fashion, and the World knew what had to be.

* * *

'A waste,' Timtangle snarled. 'There were more lucrative wishes. Still perhaps it is not without merit; our family company has large investments in medical research to help your race, new drugs swell our portfolios. A cure will be worth billions on the vuim market and the firms that make it will pay dividends to us.' He laughed. 'What an irony that would be, Vuim-Captain, if the discovery you wished into being makes us even richer.'

'I think it will not.' Vuim-Captain stood up straight. He was no longer gasping for breath and his carapace gleamed, the skin that showed beneath the healthy green of spring grass. He had taken no drug.

Timtangle shrugged, an attempt at casual dismissal that was diminished by the nervous edge to his voice. 'No matter. So one wish failed. We still have a world of them to pluck.'

'Maybe not, cousin – er, Captain,' an abanak said, backing away from the console, 'the matter pinned below the decks – it's vanished! And...' He hesitated and uttered his next words haltingly. 'The white hole no longer seems to register on our sensors.'

'What?' Timtangle roared, rushing to the console, fat digits prodding the display while his younger cousin looked on anxiously.

'Indeed,' Vuim-Captain said. He moved in smoothly and plucked the gun from Timtangle's belt. 'Then we have nothing to gain here, and some matters to settle.'

'Vuim-Captain,' the abanak underling said. 'It looks like we're receiving transponder signals from all three scout ships.'

Imagine a disc of white power interpenetrating a galaxy. If it moved, it did so at speeds far in excess of light. Maybe it was just there, suddenly, without progression: a thing felt rather than seen, a sudden stab out of the unknown. All the energies of the boxes, of the Doctor's promised 'universal wish' went into it, guiding the parts of the planet on the ship who gave up their own 'lives' to make it so, and taking from the Doctor certain necessary knowledge.

Later when notes were compared, slowly, at mere starship speeds, it was discovered that on every world where the vuim made their neat and tidy quester's homes, in every distant ship, in every space habitat or hospital ward, the dying vuim had healed between two ticks of an atomic clock, within a single vibration of a caesium atom across a hundred thousand light years. More than remission. Cells renewing, nerves regrowing, a regeneration of their race wherever the illness touched them. As if the power had learned how to rebuild people in an instant.

Of course there were consequences other than the simple miracle. Later, a dozen pharmaceutical companies that had pinned their stock market shares on stabilisation drugs and long-range slim-chance cures sold to a desperate and captive market quietly went belly-up. CEOs and enterprising venture capitalists numbed by the loss occasionally threw themselves from tall buildings or pooled what resources they had left and sneaked out like thieves in the night abandoning both business partners and loving families alike. Some entered monasteries and learned to rake gravel in a Zen-like fashion.

Timtangle would not be among those, though he would find out later he was very, very poor indeed. But before then he would have to face the vuim and the humans, and the courts of his own kind, which did and do not smile on failure or anything that tarnishes the friendly reputation of the abanak short of success. Of all his crimes, the one of insufficiently covering his tracks weighed heaviest with them.

Ebonyblack looked at Offram. 'I suppose you should kiss me now.'

'Yes,' he gulped. 'I suppose I should.'

She arranged her gown and lay back on the floor, folding her hands across her stomach and closing her eyes. Offram knelt beside her, leaned over and kissed her tentatively on the mouth.

She opened her eyes.

'My Prince,' she said.

Chapter Eighteen
Journey's End in White Sand Weddings

The ceremony was held in a gazebo in the breakwater on the beach of the Bay of Moons, below the Castle of Sighs. There was dancing on the sands afterwards, and a finger buffet. There was to be a more formal reception at the castle later that evening.

'Of course,' the Doctor was saying, working on his eighth champagne, 'once it came down to a wish, it had to work out all right. It was bound to end up being taken by the people who most needed it.

At last an uncomplicatedly happy ending!'

'Unless the vuim turn out to be a military super-race in the next two dozen centuries,' Fitz said, cramming another sausage into his mouth. 'They're bouncing with vim now. Vuim, vim,' he added, pleased with his inebriated half-pun.

'True,' the Doctor admitted, 'but all we can do is live in the present after all. Besides. We'd beat 'em.' He clinked his glass to Fitz's and downed the contents in a gulp. The Doctor hadn't quite recovered from the giddy excitement of catching the bouquet, Fitz decided. It was tucked into the pocket of his duster, petals, ivy and ribbons trailing out and spilling over the white sand.

'Where's Anji?' Fitz asked.

'She went back to the castle to get ready for the ball.'

Fitz shaded his eyes. The sun was just past its zenith. The sky above the bay was a glorious blue. 'That's hours from now.'

'Goodness, Fitz, even *I* know women take longer to get ready for these things than men.'

'Well, yeah, but –'

The Doctor grabbed another bottle of champagne from a passing Iron Guard in servant's livery. 'I think she's trying to decide what to do about her lovesick ogre. He's been sitting on the sidelines looking glum. This is the best champagne I've ever tasted. Icicles and moonbeams and just a hint of apples.'

Fitz said, 'Maybe you ought to ease off the champagne a little.'

Bricklebrit sat at the periphery of the festivities looking uncomfortable in his court finery and more uncomfortably at Anji as she danced with other men. The Doctor came over and sat on the bench beside him.

'She looks very pretty in that dress, doesn't she?' he said.

The ogre twitched his shoulder. 'She looks pretty in anything.'

The Doctor laughed softly. 'I've seen her in the morning and know for a fact that's not the case.'

'She's your lady, then.'

'She's her own lady. No wish of yours could change that.'

'Never wanted Ai to change, Doctor. Only me.'

'I see. And how did you hope to change? Handsome as the Duke of Toads once was? Clever? Rich?'

Bricklebrit hung his head, clearly feeling foolish. 'I only wished to be the sort of fellow she *could* love.'

'Ah.'

The roundel ended, music fading into the babble of laughter and thank-yous, silks swishing and heels clattering as the dancers moved away for refreshments or paired up again for the next one. Anji spotted them on the bench, and ran lightly across the floor, her dark eyes shining. 'Dance with me, Doctor?'

'I'm afraid I've promised the next one to Janet.'

She grabbed Brick by his huge hand and tried to tug him to his feet. 'Come on you.'

'What? I don't – I never danced before Ai –'

'It's easy. I'll show you.' With a grunt she pulled him up and, seeing his expression, went up on tiptoes to kiss his cheek. She laughed and rubbed at the smudge of lipstick she'd left on it with her thumb. 'Don't worry. I won't let you step on my feet.' And with that she dragged him into the swirl of music, light and people.

Through an archway, standing near the punch bowl, he could see Fitz trying it on with one of Rozered's daughters while Rozered sat with the other matrons keeping a watchful eye on him. In her lap, a little red fox named Alex lay curled, his tail twitching occasionally as she fed him titbits. Across the hall opposite the musicians' dais, Prince Offram and Princess Ebonyblack sat on thrones, their hands clasped across the space between them. They looked overwhelmed and dumbstruck and a little frightened by the festivities surrounding their recent marriage, two young people who'd awakened to find themselves each committed for life to a complete stranger. But perhaps that was what it felt like to anyone just wed, pauper or prince. They would be good rulers until their times were through and another princess fell under a spell and another prince stormed another tower wrapped in briars. Their new major-domo, Inexplicable Wottlewort, stood nearby, jaunty in his uniform. A serving-maid bustled past, her silver metal hands gleaming.

Janet came over, but instead of claiming her dance she sat beside him. 'You'll be leaving soon,' she said.

'Yes.'

'But for all your help you've not wished for anything and surely you are owed that much.'

'How do you know I haven't got my wish already?' he asked.

'Have you, then? I would feel better at your leaving if you had.'

'Well, I've learned something important. Something wonderful.'

'The secret of the fairies' never-empty cooking pot? What is behind the seventh door? How to shudder?'

He laughed. 'Well, I know how to shudder, believe me. And behind the seventh door is the first step on a journey that leads to wisdom or death. And the reason the fairies' cooking pots are never empty is because they don't need food like you and me. No. What I've discovered is even more wonderful.' Her eyes were wide and she held her breath, waiting. 'It is that I love what I do and I want to go everywhere and see everything and do what I love. That's the gift I take with me. And I thank you for it.' He brought her hand to his lips and kissed it.

They sat happily for a while saying nothing. Then her eyes caught sight of something that made the joy fade a little. 'Oh, heavens. My sisters are here.'

He looked, and standing at the top of the grand staircase waiting to be announced were six young women whose resemblance to Janet was unmistakable. He recognised the eldest as the girl who'd thought he was a highwayman.

'Those are the most bizarre dresses I've ever seen,' he said.

William pushed the control that unclamped his ship from the embrace of the *Bonaventure*. He wasn't a man for crowds, they led to complications, and earning to support a family or an entire race gave birth to too much greed for him. Vuim-Captain had given him a notional share of the *Bonaventure*'s profits for its entire trade journey prior to rescuing him, and he'd bartered it straight for a new drive for his ship, and the additional life support he'd need.

The little white cat had her own suit, cut up and reworked from a child's suit the ship stocked to trade. He didn't know if the little cat was really Christina, but the planet refused to harbour her, and was quite adamant about not changing her back, according to the Doctor, that strange magician figure, whom William had met briefly when he and the other humans had gone down to retrieve the abanak and the scout ships. The Vuim-Captain had wanted to make a ritual apology, but the planet refused that as well. The Doctor explained that it didn't want to be touched by them, and the best way to make amends would be to keep its location a secret. And Vuim-Captain had vowed he would make that so.

William suspected he would enforce it on the other members of the crew, human and abanak as well.

As for Christina, there was no technology in the known trade zones that could do or undo a change at that level. She wasn't talking like the fox – that allegedly was all that was left of Alex Volpe – but that might just be stubbornness. The fox seemed content to stay on the planet, grateful even, but William suspected its mind was either broken or remade somehow, more the planet's creature now than Alex. The woman who'd agreed to care for him seemed genuinely fond of the creature. And so his hope ran deeper, illogical though it seemed. Judging from all he'd learned about that world, there was always the cure wrought by the proximity of love. He lifted the cat and put her in his lap.

'Well, Christina. Shall we see what's out there?'

Epilogue

One by one each wicked sister began to feel the effect of her enchanted ball gown. First the eldest felt hot, then hotter yet as her gown began to flicker and spark. 'Oh, sisters, help me, for I am burning up with fever and feel that I should catch fire.' But the others stepped back, afraid that their own gowns would alight from the flames licking at their sister's feet and moving up. She screamed and beat at the flames but to no avail, until at last even her beautiful hair was aflame, and with a final cry she burst and was nothing left but ash. Each in turn fell under a similar spell, as the gowns became prisons or executioners. This one's gown became a shower of icy water that poured constantly over her naked flesh until she died from pneumonia. And another of the sisters felt something twisting around and growing up her legs until she was encased in a mesh of tightly woven nettles that stung horribly and boiled her flesh. Yet another turned into a pillar of ruby-coloured salt, and another felt the cage of boning squeeze tighter and tighter until she couldn't breathe and fell dead. The last of them was forced to wander the earth dragging a bustle the size of a boulder along the ground behind her until she too died from exhaustion.

Their youngest sister, whom they had greatly wronged, tried to the last to help them, begged the world to show mercy. Alas, to no avail. She wept and prayed for their lost souls, but what more could she do? It was the way of the World.

Anji closed the book with a sigh and put it back in the strange box. Fairy tale endings. Of course she'd got to see close up that real life was never quite that cut and dried. She stuffed the box back on the shelf where she'd found it, and cast a last look around the ramshackle mess that was the Doctor's library. *I wish that, for once, things would stay tidy around here*, she thought with the venom that only a week of unrelenting housework could have explained, and headed towards her own neat bedroom. The room subsided into darkness again behind her – apart from the faint glow of white light that escaped the edges of the wooden box and the frantic scurrying of the books as they dusted themselves down and shuffled into alphabetical and categorical order.

About the Authors

Kelly Hale lives in Portland, Oregon, USA with a teenaged son, Simon, and a cat named Lumpy. She did not graduate from any university, buys Egg McMuffins en route to her job in a health food store, and lives in a seedy little apartment in the barrio. Her previous novel 'Erasing Sherlock Holmes' won a large cash award in a contest, but has yet to see print. She is older than all of you, but not very wise, thus her deceptively youthful appearance.

Simon Bucher-Jones lives in Wallington, Surrey, England, with two young daughters, and a wife called Sarah. He did graduate from university, and also buys muffins on the way to work although he's not supposed to, and lives in a house he couldn't afford to buy now. None of his novels have won any large cash awards – but if someone wants to nominate this one he'll be grateful. He's older than most of you, and only thinks he's incredibly wise, thus his dented appearance from the brickbats of the resentful.

BBC DOCTOR WHO BOOKS
FEATURING THE EIGHTH DOCTOR

DOCTOR WHO: THE NOVEL OF THE FILM by Gary Russell
ISBN 0 563 38000 4
THE EIGHT DOCTORS by Terrance Dicks ISBN 0 563 40563 5
VAMPIRE SCIENCE by Jonathan Blum and Kate Orman
ISBN 0 563 40566 X
THE BODYSNATCHERS by Mark Morris ISBN 0 563 40568 6
GENOCIDE by Paul Leonard ISBN 0 563 40572 4
WAR OF THE DALEKS by John Peel ISBN 0 563 40573 2
ALIEN BODIES by Lawrence Miles ISBN 0 563 40577 5
KURSAAL by Peter Anghelides ISBN 0 563 40578 3
OPTION LOCK by Justin Richards ISBN 0 563 40583 X
LONGEST DAY by Michael Collier ISBN 0 563 40581 3
LEGACY OF THE DALEKS by John Peel ISBN 0 563 40574 0
DREAMSTONE MOON by Paul Leonard ISBN 0 563 40585 6
SEEING I by Jonathan Blum and Kate Orman ISBN 0 563 40586 4
PLACEBO EFFECT by Gary Russell ISBN 0 563 40587 2
VANDERDEKEN'S CHILDREN by Christopher Bulis
ISBN 0 563 40590 2
THE SCARLET EMPRESS by Paul Magrs ISBN 0 563 40595 3
THE JANUS CONJUNCTION by Trevor Baxendale
ISBN 0 563 40599 6
BELTEMPEST by Jim Mortimore ISBN 0 563 40593 7
THE FACE EATER by Simon Messingham ISBN 0 563 55569 6
THE TAINT by Michael Collier ISBN 0 563 55568 8
DEMONTAGE by Justin Richards ISBN 0 563 55572 6
REVOLUTION MAN by Paul Leonard ISBN 0 563 55570 X
DOMINION by Nick Walters ISBN 0 563 55574 2
UNNATURAL HISTORY by Jonathan Blum and Kate Orman
ISBN 0 563 55576 9
AUTUMN MIST by David A. McIntee ISBN 0 563 55583 1
INTERFERENCE: BOOK ONE by Lawrence Miles
ISBN 0 563 55580 7
INTERFERENCE: BOOK TWO by Lawrence Miles
ISBN 0 563 55582 3

THE BLUE ANGEL by Paul Magrs and Jeremy Hoad
ISBN 0 563 55581 5
THE TAKING OF PLANET 5 by Simon Bucher-Jones and
Mark Clapham ISBN 0 563 55585 8
FRONTIER WORLDS by Peter Anghelides ISBN 0 563 55589 0
PARALLEL 59 by Natalie Dallaire and Stephen Cole
ISBN 0 563 555904
THE SHADOWS OF AVALON by Paul Cornell ISBN 0 563 555882
THE FALL OF YQUATINE by Nick Walters ISBN 0 563 55594 7
COLDHEART by Trevor Baxendale ISBN 0 563 55595 5
THE SPACE AGE by Steve Lyons ISBN 0 563 53800 7
THE BANQUO LEGACY by Andy Lane and Justin Richards
ISBN 0 563 53808 2
THE ANCESTOR CELL by Peter Anghelides and Stephen Cole
ISBN 0 563 53809 0
THE BURNING by Justin Richards ISBN 0 563 53812 0
CASUALTIES OF WAR by Steve Emmerson ISBN 0 563 53805 8
THE TURING TEST by Paul Leonard ISBN 0 563 53806 6
ENDGAME by Terrance Dicks ISBN 0 563 53802 3
FATHER TIME by Lance Parkin ISBN 0 563 53810 4
ESCAPE VELOCITY by Colin Brake ISBN 0 563 53825 2
EARTHWORLD by Jacqueline Rayner ISBN 0 563 53827 9
VANISHING POINT by Stephen Cole ISBN 0 563 53829 5
EATER OF WASPS by Trevor Baxendale ISBN 0 563 53832 5
THE YEAR OF INTELLIGENT TIGERS by Kate Orman
ISBN 0 563 53831 7
THE SLOW EMPIRE by Dave Stone
ISBN 0 563 53835 X
DARK PROGENY by Steve Emmerson ISBN 0 563 53837 6
THE CITY OF THE DEAD by Lloyd Rose ISBN 0 563 53839 2

COMING SOON:

THE ADVENTURESS OF HENRIETTA STREET by Lawrence Miles
ISBN 0 563 53842 2 (Nov '01)
MAD DOGS AND ENGLISHMEN by Paul Magrs
ISBN 0 563 53845 7 (Jan '02)

PRESENTING

DOCTOR WHO

AN ALL-NEW AUDIO DRAMA

Big Finish Productions is proud to present brand-new
Doctor Who adventures on double CD!

Available from October 2001

COLDITZ

A four-part story by Steve Lyons.
Starring **Sylvester McCoy** as the Doctor
and **Sophie Aldred** as Ace.

*October 1944: As World War II draws towards its conclusion, a Nazi defeat begins to seem
almost inevitable. But that might be about to change…*

*Two intruders are captured in the grounds of Colditz Castle, the most secure POW camp
in Germany. At first, the guards think they're dealing with British spies. But the strangers
arrived in an advanced travelling machine,
the like of which they've never seen before.*

With this 'TARDIS' in their hands, the Third Reich might triumph after all.

If you wish to order this, please photocopy this form or provide all the details on paper.
Delivery within 28 days of release.
Send to: PO Box 1127, Maidenhead, Berkshire. SL6 3LN.
Big Finish Hotline 01628 828283.

Please send me [   ] **copies of** *Colditz* each @ £13.99 (£15.50 non-UK orders) Prices inclusive of postage and packing. Payment can be accepted by credit card or by personal cheques, payable to Big Finish Productions Ltd. Name... Address.. .... Postcode... VISA/Mastercard number .... Expiry date... Signature...

Other stories featuring the Seventh Doctor still available include:
THE SHADOW OF THE SCOURGE   DUST BREEDING

For more details visit our website at
http://www.doctorwho.co.uk